PRAISE FOR K.D.

"Lady Codebreaker is a refreshing and brilliant standout addition to the library of historical fiction. Based on a true story, K.D. Alden masterfully tells the sweeping story of codebreaker Grace Feldman, a woman ahead of her time whose tireless daring helped defeat the likes of Al Capone and Adolf Hitler, but whose gifts were mostly overlooked due to her gender. This isn't just another war story, but also a tale of love and sacrifice along with fascinating historical anecdotes and characters to add richness to an already compelling narrative. Alden's meticulous research brings Feldman's story to life making this an emotionally gripping and utterly satisfying novel."

—Karen White, *New York Times* bestselling author

"K.D. Alden brings history to life with rich storytelling and deep emotion."

—V. S. Alexander, author of *The Magdalen Girls*

A MOTHER'S PROMISE

"*A Mother's Promise* just became a new classic that all readers should have on their shelves."

—*Urban Book Reviews*

"An extraordinary debut novel...one of those must-read books."

—*Historical Novel Review*

ALSO BY K.D. ALDEN

A Mother's Promise

LADY
CODEBREAKER

K.D. ALDEN

FOREVER

NEW YORK   BOSTON

Forever
Hachette Book Group
1290 Avenue of the Americas, New York, NY 10104
read-forever.com

First Edition: March 2024

Forever is an imprint of Grand Central Publishing. The Forever name and logo are trademarks of Hachette Book Group, Inc.

The publisher is not responsible for websites (or their content) that are not owned by the publisher.

Forever books may be purchased in bulk for business, educational, or promotional use. For information, please contact your local bookseller or the Hachette Book Group Special Markets Department at special.markets@hbgusa.com.

Library of Congress Cataloging-in-Publication Data.

Names: Alden, K. D., author.
Title: Lady codebreaker / K.D. Alden.
Description: First edition. | New York : Forever, 2024.
Identifiers: LCCN 2023041005 | ISBN 9781538723661 (paperback) | ISBN 9781538723678 (e-book)
Subjects: LCSH: Friedman, Elizebeth, 1892–1980—Fiction. | Cryptographers—Fiction. | LCGFT: Thrillers (Fiction) | Romans à clef. | Novels.
Classification: LCC PS3611.E53378 L33 2024 | DDC 813/.6—dc23/eng/20230908
LC record available at https://lccn.loc.gov/2023041005

ISBN: 9781538723661 (trade paperback), 9781538723678 (ebook)

Printed in the United States of America

LSC

Printing 1, 2023

Knowledge is power.

LADY
CODEBREAKER

PROLOGUE

Grace Feldman stood in her bright and airy kitchen, sipping coffee and bracing for the day. Outside the bay window, pink blossoms rioted, exuberant on the branches of the old cherry tree. Unlike her, they took joy in the advent of spring. The warming weather and the sunshine unnerved her, since it would only encourage Robert to take long drives on his own. And what she'd found in the back seat of the old Studebaker last August had made her hands tremble, her heart stutter and her brain freeze.

Robert wasn't up yet. It was only her and Krypto. The German shepherd raised his nose, inhaling the scent of her toast with appreciation.

"I'll give you some scrambled eggs," she promised him.

While Grace didn't expect him to say thank you, she also didn't expect his hackles to rise. His low growl chilled her blood as he loped to the front door.

Outside, two unmarked government vehicles pulled up to the house. It was barely eight o'clock in the morning, and Grace was still in her robe. She'd slept in after a particularly difficult night. It was one of the benefits of working at home.

Five years ago, she would have dashed to her closet and jumped into a girdle and stockings, dress and low heels to greet these unexpected visitors. Not today. Grace was exhausted, hadn't invited them, and was puzzled as to why they were here. They could damn well admire her old blue bathrobe and slippers.

The drivers got out, both clean-cut gentlemen in dark suits, crisp white shirts and unimaginative ties. They were indisputably federal agents of some kind. One wore black-framed glasses, the other a hat reminiscent of the late thirties. It was probably meant to lend him an air of authority, but instead it made him look absurdly young. She knew him. He was a new hire at the NSA.

Krypto growled again and then barked, bellowing his and Grace's displeasure at the presence of the two agents. But they marched up the sidewalk to the front door anyway.

"Hush," Grace said gently to Krypto. His barking subsided, but he emitted another low growl as she opened the door. "Stay," she told him. Then she looked calmly at the two gentlemen. "Good morning. How may I help you?"

They took in her bathrobe, slippers and mussed hair without comment. "Mrs. Robert Feldman?"

"Yes?"

"I'm Agent Bart Sommers of the FBI. And this is Mr. Lawrence Thompson of the—"

"NSA," Grace finished for him.

"Yes. Well." Agent Sommers stood there awkwardly while Thompson's color rose. "Would it be possible for us to come in?"

Krypto voiced his displeasure at this idea, but Grace repressed a sigh and stood aside. "Certainly." She closed the door after them. "It's all right, Krypto."

"Krypto? Interesting name for a dog," Sommers remarked.

Not for a family of codebreakers. "Would you like to sit down?" Grace asked.

"Is your husband home?" Sommers countered.

"He is. He's...indisposed at the moment."

Uncomfortable pause.

Grace folded her arms over her chest. "How can I help you gentlemen?"

They exchanged a glance.

She raised her eyebrows.

"Well, you see..."

I don't.

"We're here for the books, I'm afraid."

"The books?"

"It's come to the notice of both the FBI and NSA that Colonel Feldman has acquired quite a library on cryptanalysis and cryptology. A library that contains top secret materials that should not fall into the wrong hands."

Come to the notice, indeed. What you mean is that it's come to the attention of your boss, J. Edgar Hoover.

"Colonel Feldman and I have jointly assembled the library over the last several decades. And we *wrote* some of the books in it," Grace said tartly. "You needn't fear that they will fall into any hands but our own."

Another awkward pause ensued. She didn't bother to fill it with pleasantries.

At last Sommers asked again, "Ma'am, is Colonel Feldman available?"

"I've told you he is not."

"Then will you show us to the library, please?"

"I will do no such thing. This is our private home, and you're overstepping your bounds. I'd like you both to leave."

"I'm afraid we can't do that, Mrs. Feldman. Because of the...ah... circumstances, leaving the library in Colonel Feldman's possession poses a national-security risk."

Grace felt her blood pressure rising. "To what *circumstances* do you refer?"

The gentlemen exchanged another glance. Thompson answered. "We do understand that this is a matter of some delicacy, but it's our understanding that your husband spent three months at Walter Reed in a state of—"

The acid of pure fury dissolved the toast in Grace's stomach. "Exhaustion? Overwork? *Heroism?* Is that the state to which you refer, Mr. Thompson?"

"Mrs. Feldman, there's no need to become agitated."

"I'm not." She eyed him fiercely.

He tried again. "Your husband was discharged from the Army's Signal Intelligence Service because—"

"He was reinstated at full rank, and you know it."

"He's been in and out of treatment at least three times."

"He's sought help, received it and is fully healed."

"Mrs. Feldman," Sommers broke in, "there is concern that his mental illness makes him a security risk."

She rounded on him. "How dare you? My husband is not *mentally ill*. He is suffering from years of exhaustion. He often worked *twenty-hour days* during the war and sometimes didn't go to bed *at all* for *seventy-two hours* at a stretch. Have you ever in your life, Agent Sommers, worked for seventy-two hours without sleep? What about you, Mr. Thompson?"

Both men looked deeply uncomfortable.

"Have you ever saved thousands of men's lives at a time? Have you ever been almost single-handedly responsible for preventing a foreign invasion of the United States? Have you ever successfully read the minds of multiple enemies and thus won a world war?"

Silence.

Dear Lord, am I talking about Robert, or about myself? And I've said far, far too much.

"I didn't think so," Grace snapped.

"Regardless, ma'am—"

"And now you dare question whether my husband could be a *traitor*?"

"We didn't use that word."

"No, but it's certainly implied, isn't it?" Grace narrowed her eyes upon Thompson. "You have implied that the man who essentially built the NSA from the ground up will now betray its secrets, and you're using as an excuse the lie that he's weak, damaged or feebleminded."

"Again, not language that we employed—"

"Don't insult my intelligence. The very fact that you two are here is an outrage and an utter disgrace. Hoover should be ashamed of himself, and you may tell him that I said so. Now get out of my house."

"Mrs. Feldman, we have a search warrant."

"I don't care if you have a writ from God himself. Get. Out. Of. My. House."

"Ma'am, because you're overwrought, we will do as you ask. But this isn't over."

"*Now!* Or Krypto here is going to ensure that you have a very bad day."

"We will be back, Mrs. Feldman."

Grace slammed the door on them and leaned against it, then slid down to the floor. Krypto whined and licked her face. "Good boy," she said absently. If only she could sit here in her bathrobe all day. But she had a man to raise from the dead.

"Robert, sweetheart?" Grace called as she opened the door to their bedroom. "It's time to get up."

He made no answer; simply stared up at the ceiling without seeing. His hair, once so dark and glossy, lay in gray, unkempt wisps against his pillow. He wore light blue pinstripe pajamas along with the same blank expression she encountered each morning.

"Bobby? Time to rise and shine. Carpe diem and all that."

Nothing.

She braced herself for the struggle. She slipped her arm behind his neck, levered him forward, then slid her own body behind him so that she could push him up and into a sitting position. This was no easy feat since she weighed 112 pounds to his 206. She was five feet, three inches tall; he was six feet two.

Robert didn't resist, as he sometimes did. But he didn't help, either. She was Sisyphus, pushing the boulder up the mountain each morning. "Come on, my love."

Now came the tricky part. Grace managed to keep his torso propped up with her weight while pulling one leg and then the other to the side and out of bed until his feet were on the floor. "Up," she said firmly. "We are getting out of bed, Bobby. *Now.*"

He turned his head and looked at her, finally saw her. "Good morning, my darling," said her husband of almost forty years. And he smiled.

Her relief was sharp and painful, before sheer gratitude washed it away. He was back. In his mind. No longer missing. "Hi, there. Sleep well?"

"I suppose." He yawned. "Did I hear men's voices downstairs, or did I dream that?"

Deep breath. "You did hear voices. We'll talk about it over coffee, once you've had a shave and a bath, all right?"

"All right, my darling. Why are you lurking behind me?" He pulled her into his lap and kissed her.

"Because I'm a spy. And we spies love to lurk." She kissed him back, and then slipped to the ground. "I'll run your bath, sweetheart."

She served him breakfast at the hand-hewn round oak table in the kitchen alcove, complete with flowered place mat and matching napkin. While she'd never been able to cook worth a damn, she could sew— mostly because she'd had to make her own clothes as a child, then had earned money during college working part-time as a seamstress. Dry pork chops, jerky-like bacon and soupy lasagnas tasted much better if presented with lovely, homemade table linens. That's what she told herself, anyhow.

"Eggs, dear?"

Bobby made no reply. He was clean-shaven, hair neatly combed, in a starched shirt and tie. But he was still in his pajama pants, barefoot, as he stared vacantly at the headlines of the day's *Washington Post*.

Horrifying to see him this way, this brilliant man, this beautiful soul.

"Aren't your feet chilly, love?" she asked.

He looked up absently. "Hmm?"

She gestured toward his lower half.

He frowned. "Why, yes, now that I think about it." He looked down at his pajamas and frigid toes. "Ah. We can fix that."

"We certainly can, my darling. Why don't you go back upstairs and put on your trousers and shoes. I'll start your eggs. All right?"

He nodded, got up and headed for the stairs. "I had a breakthrough on the Mayan symbols last night," he called as he went up.

"That's wonderful! Tell me all about it when you come down."

Grace cracked three eggs into a bowl and whisked them, wishing she didn't feel like such a scrambled egg herself. Telltale creaks and the closet door opening and closing upstairs told her that Bobby had found and climbed into his pants and was fetching his socks and shoes. All good.

She heated butter in a pan, then poured in the eggs. Added salt and pepper.

The sounds of movement upstairs had stopped. Grace looked up, willing it to start again. Oh dear. She turned the heat down a bit, wiped her hands on a kitchen towel and went in pursuit.

Now fully clothed, Robert was seated on the bed, staring vacantly out the window.

"Sweetheart?"

No answer.

"Bobby."

"Do you think Shakespeare," he asked slowly, "had any views concerning the ethics of interception—the collection of secret intelligence? What may he have thought about its use in conducting the affairs of a democracy, a supposedly free and open society?"

"Well, Shakespeare was living under a monarchy, so it hardly applied."

"For example, the Babington Plot that cost Mary, Queen of Scots her head. She wrote to her men in code, but the letters were intercepted and decrypted, then resealed and sent on their way."

"She *did* conspire to steal Queen Elizabeth's throne."

Her husband turned to her. "But who was right? Technically, Elizabeth had been declared illegitimate."

The smell of eggs beginning to burn wafted up the stairs. "Bobby, come back downstairs now that you've got pants on. Have some coffee."

He remained seated like Rodin's *Thinker*. "Doesn't it ever bother you, Grace?"

"It was a tragic struggle for power," she said carefully. She took his hand and tugged him to his feet.

"Aren't they all tragic?"

"Depends on whether one is speaking to the victor or the defeated." She half dragged him to the door. "Come on, darling, we're in a hurry."

"We are?"

"Yes." She all but pushed him down the stairs and propelled him back to his chair at the kitchen table. But the process took far too long.

"What is that horrible smell, Grace?"

"My cooking," she said wryly, though she'd gotten better over the years. The eggs were blackened and smoky, the pan probably ruined. She grabbed it, turned off the burner and ran out the back door with it, setting it on the stoop. Then she returned. "How would you like cereal today, Bobby?"

"Oh, that'd be fine. Just fine."

She set a bowl of cereal and a spoon in front of him, then poured more coffee for herself and sat opposite him as he ate. She took a sip. "So do you remember the voices you heard earlier this morning?"

"Hmm?" His face was blank.

"The NSA sent some men to the house." She didn't mention the FBI. "They—" She took a deep breath. "They want to remove our collection."

Robert's hand, the one holding the spoon, began to tremble. Milk sloshed on the edges of the bowl. She guided his hand down, and gently unwrapped his fingers from the handle.

"The books? Why would they take our books, Grace?"

Because J. Edgar Hoover sees a chance to drown your star in a trough. Along with mine. But she couldn't say that. Her battle with the Toad was private. "My darling, they've decided to . . . reclassify . . . some of the materials."

"Why? Our collection exists to educate the next generation. Why would they want to hide any of it?"

"They don't want to hide it, *per se*. They want to limit its circulation." Dear God, but tact was a four-letter word.

"Those are our books. Nobody else's," Robert said. "Tell them to go to hell." His anger sizzled and curled into the air, mingling with the black smoke and rank odor from the eggs.

"I did. But they have a warrant. They're coming back."

"Then perhaps I'll shoot them."

"Bobby!"

"The new top brass has been gunning for me—the general whose specialty is *mules*, for God's sake—*mules*. How many mules does the United States currently have in the Army?"

Grace didn't see the need to reply to this.

"Why would they put an *ass*-man—sorry—in charge of anything to do with *intelligence*? He couldn't decode his way out of a paper bag."

"Agreed." *Which makes him insecure, which makes him more receptive to Hoover's innuendo and gossip...*

"So why on earth—" Robert stopped. Peered at her. "What aren't you telling me?"

Grace cracked her neck. "Nothing."

"I've been married to you for close to forty years, sweetheart. I know damn well when you're lying. So out with it."

Grace's eyes filled with sudden, unwelcome tears. She couldn't formulate the words.

"Ahh." Robert's hands curled into fists. "Damaged goods, am I? Of 'unsound mind' and therefore suspect?"

"Something like that."

"Bastards."

Why, oh, why, had she ever been foolish enough to tangle with J. Edgar Hoover? He was ostensibly America's supreme protector of Truth, Justice and the American way. He was also the pettiest, most vindictive man alive.

Grace gazed down into her coffee, which became a black hole of memory with a handle. And she'd thought that "Colonel" Garrett Farquhar at Riverbank was bad...

PART I

RIVERBANK, 1917

What the hell do you know?

—Garrett Farquhar

That, sir, remains for you to find out.

—Grace Smith

CHAPTER ONE

"Who do you think you *are?*"

The scathing words ricocheted in Grace's skull, dislodging more than a few emotions. Anger, of course. Discomfort. Embarrassment. Frustration with her own honesty. Something close to despair.

It was a question her own father had asked her more than once, and clearly the response expected was *Nobody.* She was supposed to meekly hang her head and allow shame to wash over her, dissolving her opinions and ideas, her hopes, her dreams.

But Grace's neck remained stiff, as did her upper lip. She met the furious gaze of Mrs. Elizabeth Wells Gallup without flinching. "My apologies, ma'am, but I simply don't believe that Sir Francis Bacon is the secret author of William Shakespeare's works."

The formidable Mrs. Gallup almost burst her corset. Her steel-gray head quivered with outrage, her jowls worked and her pale blue eyes darkened in the face of Grace's effrontery. "What do your *beliefs* have to do with anything? There is proof. Proof I've put in front of your willful, silly nose."

"Ma'am, I do not perceive the bilateral alphabet that you . . . seem to see. There are irregularities in the letters, to be sure, but—"

"You are relieved of your duties."

There: the six words Grace had known were coming. They hung leadenly in the air for a moment, then crashed around her. She was fired. This was what honesty got you.

After scouring Chicago far and wide and fruitlessly for weeks, she'd been offered a job that was actually interesting, a job that employed her mind and not just her smile. One she'd been overjoyed to find—only to discover that it was, in reality, a con job.

Mrs. Gallup had a bosom like the prow of a ship, the voice of a grand duchess and a vested interest in her Bacon theory. It intrigued her boss. It kept her housed, clothed and feted. It funded her European lecture tours and fascinated her audiences. Sir Francis Bacon was her bread and butter. Add a cup of tea and he provided a complete breakfast—not to mention lunch and dinner.

"Did you not hear me?" Mrs. Gallup thundered.

Grace sighed. "Yes, ma'am. I heard you."

"Then be off to pack your things."

Grace nodded, turned and left the room. There weren't many things to pack, other than her unruly thoughts, her dismaying integrity and her desperation not to return home to Indiana, where she'd be again under her father's thumb—unless she got married and traded it to live under a husband's. But she owed it to Garrett Farquhar, Riverbank's mad and mercurial owner, to say goodbye. And she actually wanted to say goodbye to Mrs. Farquhar, who'd been nothing but kind. Motherly, even, in her eccentric way.

The thought of leaving made her heart ache. *Why can't you turn a blind eye, Grace?*

The answer lay not only in her own character, but in the teachings of William Penn and the Quaker meeting house in which she'd spent too many Sundays of her life. *Right is right, even if everyone is against it, and wrong is wrong, even if everyone is for it.*

Grace retrieved her coat, hat and pocketbook from the stand near the door. The coat was too big, the hat too small, the pocketbook a castoff of her mother's. She wound a muffler around her throat, slipped on her gloves to ward off the chilly October air and trudged toward the Villa, which was roughly a fifteen-minute walk through the magnificent estate at Riverbank and all of its oddities: the lighthouse on an island in the river, the Dutch windmill, the Japanese gardens, the swimming pool with its crumbling Roman columns, the airplane hangar, the laboratories. Not to mention the exotic animals that Farquhar had brought home with him from his travels. She could still hardly believe this place existed, much less that she'd been working here for three months. But Col. Farquhar had enough money to build a kingdom of his own if that's what he wanted to do.

She ached to stay. Summer had faded into a spectacular autumn, and the leaves on the trees were gilded with gold and copper, rustling in the cool sunset of their lives. What would Riverbank look like in winter, blanketed in white and silver and holiday joy? She wouldn't see it. She'd see the interior of her parents' Indiana farmhouse. She'd see the stove, the laundry tub, the scrub brush, her mother's querulous misery.

Before she'd unexpectedly landed at Riverbank, Grace had resigned her teaching job and run away from home. She'd spent two weeks in Chicago, marching in and out of every employment agency she could locate, waiting in lines, filling out applications and taking typing tests for speed and accuracy. She acquitted herself well in interviews. She kept her hands gloved and demurely folded in her lap; she pressed her knees firmly together and crossed her ankles underneath her chair; she wore her hair coiffed neatly under a sensible hat. Her lipstick was a muted rose and her nose was powdered. She smiled until her face ached.

Why no, none of the agencies knew of any research positions open to women at local colleges or universities. But they did have secretarial jobs. Filing clerk positions. Placement for nannies and housekeepers.

Grace managed to keep her chin up, reminded each little gray man at each little gray agency that she had a college degree in English Literature (she had to repay her father for tuition at 6 percent interest) had studied Latin and spoke fluent German.

She was offered two dead-end jobs answering telephones and replying to mail, but after quick calculation it was apparent that she could not afford rent, groceries, stockings and loan payments to her father on such miserable salaries unless she lived in a dog kennel or sold herself on a street corner at night.

The situation was growing desperate—the horror of taking the train back to Indiana, tail between her legs, didn't bear contemplation. Grace redoubled her efforts, to no avail. Where was the eccentric elderly lady she'd dreamed of finding, the one with a giant Victorian mansion dripping with gingerbread trim, eight empty rooms and a passion for unearthing the secrets of George Sand...or translating T. S. Eliot into German?

She was a fool.

Her last interview was with a kindly, rotund gentleman who steepled his fingers upon his desk and gazed at her myopically through smudged spectacles. She was halfway through her qualifications and feeling a tiny bit optimistic—he nodded at her every word—when he interrupted her to say, "My dear. Whatever is your father thinking, to allow you to stray so far from home—alone and in a big city?"

Grace pressed her lips together. *I didn't ask his permission.* But the words could not be permitted to escape during this meeting.

"The problem is that I will have just gotten you trained to our company's specifications when you'll blow in one morning waving a sparkly gewgaw on the fourth finger of your left hand. After your great song and dance about desiring a career, you'll think nothing of leaving us in the lurch."

Grace opened her mouth to protest, but he cut her off.

"Do spare me the profuse denials, Miss..." he looked down at her application, "Smith. My best advice to you is to try a church social or a harvest dance. You're exactly like all the other girls I've interviewed today."

"I'm not!" Grace flared at him. "But even with spectacles, you can't seem to discern that. I've more or less despised every young man I've ever had the dubious pleasure of meeting, and I have no desire to ever get married, even with the consolation prize of a flashy *gewgaw* on my fourth finger to remind me that I once had my freedom." *Oh dear. Really, Grace?*

"It seems you are indeed different: You're impertinent and you have a strident and unbecoming attitude." He stood, removed his spectacles again and gestured with them toward the door.

Grace wanted to remove her left shoe and throw it at his head, followed by the right one. Instead, she took his cue—what else was there to do? She marched out of his office with her head held high, feeling his gaze searing her bottom as she did so.

Men. Tall, short, lean, round, older, younger...every last one of them was impossible.

Grace's frustration and sense of impending doom impelled her to go and see a few sights in Chicago before she trundled back to Indiana, her childhood bedroom, and her father's stringent rules. To her inevitable fate as a broodmare like her faded, exhausted mother.

She bypassed the Museum of Natural History in favor of the grand Newberry Library, where the collection included an original folio of Shakespeare. The Bard was by far her favorite author—she especially loved his comedies—and the pull to see his words in handwritten script was too strong to resist. The idea that someone had painstakingly copied each letter, each word and line of dialogue so that the plays could be disseminated and shared...it was an awe-inspiring task. One performed by someone far more patient than she could ever hope to be.

The Newberry Library was an imposing Romanesque revival structure, with three massive stone arches at its entrance and three more above those, soaring straight for the sky.

Grace felt dwarfed by the building, puny in the face of its collected knowledge. How many books, folios, scrolls and letters did it contain? How many thoughts, dreams and ideas? But despite her intimidation, she climbed the steps and made her way through the polished brass doors, each of which weighed far more than she did.

The interior took her breath away. A red carpet in the vestibule gave way to marble floors and coffered ceilings that surely only God could be tall enough to construct. Carved wood banisters and library tables warmed the space. The sacred smell of old volumes and human curiosity permeated the air. It was like stepping into a cathedral of intellect.

She made her way to the room where the Folger Collection was housed and stepped up to the tall, polished wood counter where a librarian was making notes on a clipboard, nervously nodding as a pompous, nattily dressed young man gave the woman staccato instructions. He wore a name tag that pronounced him Mr. J. Edgar Hoover, from the Library of Congress.

"It's called the Dewey Decimal System, Miss Langhorne. It's not brain surgery, I assure you. It's simply a method for categorizing and shelving the volumes in the library, all right? Now, once again, it's based on relative *location* and relative *index...*"

The librarian nodded and scribbled down the terms while Grace waited patiently. The young man had broad, blunt features, the coldest and flattest stare she'd ever seen and a rigid, disapproving military bearing that extended even to his ears. Like an annoyed cat's, they jutted toward the back of his neck.

The librarian glanced at Grace, as though she wished to be polite and help her but was afraid to interrupt the gentleman who held her attention.

Grace cleared her throat, raised her eyebrows quizzically, and offered a smile.

The young man turned and eyed her as though she were a dung beetle crawling on the counter.

"May I help you, ma'am?" ventured the librarian.

"Miss Langhorne, my time is valuable," the young man rebuked her.

"I—I—" the librarian stammered. "My apologies..."

He turned back to Grace. "Perhaps you could return at a more opportune time, ma'am?"

Something about his self-importance got her dander up. "I wish I could, sir, but I leave Chicago very shortly, and it's my dearest wish to—"

Mr. Hoity-Toity Hoover curled his lip at her and walked away without allowing her to finish. "Five minutes, Miss Langhorne," he called over his shoulder. "I'll return in five minutes."

Grace blinked. The librarian stuttered an apology.

Without delay, Grace explained what she wanted, and within

moments she was gasping at the sight of one of the First Folios of William Shakespeare.

"Is there a particular play you're interested in?" the librarian asked.

Grace's mouth twisted involuntarily. "Perhaps *The Comedy of Errors*?"

"A very funny one," said the lady.

As long as one's life isn't going that way. But Grace smiled.

"We have a Shakespeare Devotees group," the librarian told her. "Every Wednesday afternoon."

"Oh, I don't live in Chicago," Grace said wistfully. "I wish I did. I've been searching for a job, but nothing's worked out. If only I could spend my life studying Shakespeare!"

A peculiar expression crossed the librarian's face. "Tell me about your background, dear. Oddly enough, I may be able to help..." She checked her watch wryly. "Yes, I just have time to make a quick call before Mr. Library of Congress returns."

And that is how, precisely thirty-three minutes later, Grace found herself nose to sternum with an enormous gentleman who had whiskers like a walrus and a mad gleam in his eye. He surged out of a chauffeured motorcar, up the Newberry's steps and into the grand hall.

"Miss Smith?" he roared, coming at her like an armored tank.

"Y-yes." Grace fought the instinct to step backward.

"How do you do?" He was almost upon her.

"Quite well, thank—*yaaaagh!*"

For Colonel Garrett Farquhar had grabbed her under the armpits and yanked her up a foot off the floor. She hung there, astonished.

He poked his nose toward hers, stopping only a millimeter away from it.

"And what do *you* know, missy?" His voice reverberated around the library walls, his breath hot on her face.

After a lifetime of bullying by her father, after the several weeks of frustration, after the day she'd had, it was too much. Without breaking eye contact, she snapped, "I know that my feet must be planted firmly on the ground before I will agree to an interview."

"Ha!" The colonel barked. With a great guffaw, he put her down. "She's got spirit, I'll give her that," he remarked to no one in particular, while the entire library gaped at them. "Well, come along, then."

"I beg your pardon?" said Grace.

"What, are you hard of hearing? *Come. Along.*" Colonel Farquhar grasped her by the elbow and towed her toward the front entrance of the library.

"Sir, I see no reason why we cannot conduct our conversation right here in the Newberry."

"No, no, impossible—we'll be late for dinner."

"Dinner? I haven't agreed to have a meal with you, sir—"

"Of course you're having a meal with me."

Somehow, they were at the big brass doors of the library, one of which Farquhar flicked open as if it were made of cardboard. "Ladies first."

"No!" Grace said, hanging on to her hat as he ejected her bodily from the building. "No dinner, sir. I barely know your name...I don't feel comfortable going anywhere with you. This is highly irregular!"

"*Regular,*" he snorted, placing a hand on her back and propelling her down the steps. "Regular is overrated. Regular is mediocrity disguised as something benign. Why on God's green acre would anyone wish to be regular? Do try a little harder to make a good impression, Miss Smith."

Grace goggled at him.

"I don't hire mewling namby-pambies, you know."

She thought about calling for help, but the implication that she was mediocre or had ever, at any time during her life, *mewled*...it stuck in her craw. And experience had taught her that the only way to deal with a bully was to stand firm—even if one weighed 112 pounds in the face of a Goliath who must easily weigh three hundred.

Grace straightened her spine and threw back her shoulders in the hopes that she'd appear an inch or so taller. "Before I take one farther step, sir, I need your assurance that the job you've mentioned does in fact involve the analysis of Shakespeare."

The Colonel managed to look amused and exasperated at the same time. "Don't be mutton-headed. Why else would the librarian have called me upon your behalf?"

Grace turned her head and looked back through the glass doors at Miss Langhorne the librarian, who now stood alone—no sign of Mr. Hoover—and raised a hand to say goodbye. The woman didn't seem fazed in the slightest by her predicament. She even looked a bit amused. Surely a respectable employee of the Newberry wouldn't set her up for a kidnapping.

Before she could process anything further, Grace found herself bundled unceremoniously into the large black motorcar purring at the curb, while the human walrus squeezed in beside her.

"Where—" Grace began again.

"Rail station, Digby! At once! At once! Call ahead and have them hold the train."

Rail station? Call to hold the train? Who is this madman?

Farquhar settled back into the cushy leather seat of his motorcar and eyed her balefully. "Now, Miss Smith. I'll ask you again: What the hell do you know?"

Two could play at being irregular. Despite her misgivings, Grace produced an enigmatic smile. "That, sir, remains for you to find out."

CHAPTER TWO

"Now," the colonel said, once he and Grace were ensconced in a plush, private first-class train carriage, "allow me to explain that you may be an aficionado of the so-called William Shakespeare, but this does you no credit at all."

Grace raised her eyebrows. "Oh?"

"None." Farquhar shook his head. "For you, like thousands upon thousands of other sheep, are missing the most critical elements of his texts."

"Whatever do you mean, sir?"

Her kidnapper leaned forward and slammed a hand down on the white-clothed table between them. *"For I have sworn thee fair, and thought thee bright, Who art as black as hell, as dark as night..."*

Grace began to wonder if he was sober, though she hadn't smelled any alcohol on his breath. Best not to argue with either the drunken or the insane. It never led anywhere logical, much less good.

"None of those plays, none of those sonnets, were written by Shakespeare! They were authored by Sir Francis Bacon, and my team at Riverbank is in the process of proving it. The greatest literary scandal in the Western world: we're about to crack it wide open." The colonel sat back in his seat, his breathing labored, his eyes gleaming with an unholy light. Just like that, his demeanor underwent a lightning shift, from outraged to celebratory. He snapped his fingers at a liveried attendant doing his best to disappear into the far corner of the carriage. "Champagne!"

Though she'd never tasted alcohol, she said nothing as the attendant set down a crystal flute of bubbly, pale-gold liquid in front of her so that she could toast the most outrageous lie she'd ever heard.

"Now," Farquhar said, "the First Folio. Do you realize that hidden in the prose is a complex system of codes and symbols? Messages, in fact, from none other than Francis Bacon himself. He was Elizabeth I's printer."

Now he had her attention. "Really?"

"It's an ingenious bilateral cipher—Bacon himself reaching out from the grave to pursue the acclaim that should have been his during his lifetime. Did you know that he was also the rightful heir to the throne? *Son* of Queen Elizabeth?"

Baloney. But Grace cocked her head at him as he kept spewing this outlandish tripe, his eyes alight with an evangelical fervor, the ginger hairs of his tufted eyebrows and walrus mustache bristling and quivering as he proselytized.

"My employee Mrs. Gallup has been breaking the codes embedded in the so-called Bard's prose for a period of years now. She's brilliant, dedicated to her craft—but her eyesight is fading and she needs a team of young people to help her crack the rest of the ciphers and reveal the full extent of Bacon's messages. That, Miss Smith, is where you come in."

Quite unconsciously, Grace picked up the flute of champagne again and brought it to her lips. The liquid tasted quite strange—dry but not bitter, effervescent and rather mercurial. "Tell me more, Colonel Farquhar."

Grace was still trying to decide what ratio of mad to possible genius Farquhar was when the train at last slowed and pulled into the tidy, small-town station of Geneva, Illinois.

"Ah. Here we are," said the colonel, surging up out of his seat and towing Grace toward the exit before they'd even come to a full stop. "Whiskeyville."

She looked at him quizzically.

"Founded by a whiskey distiller; still runs on booze and always will—unless those damned Puritan prohibitionists have their way."

Oh dear. He was now insulting her family... good Quakers and long-standing members of the Anti-Saloon League. Grace opened and then closed her mouth. To be offended by this man was clearly a lost cause.

He propelled her along the length of the platform, through the station and outside to yet another chauffeured limousine.

"Hallo, Jensen," Farquhar said as the liveried driver popped out to open their doors. "Call ahead to Nellie, would you? And tell her we'll be along in a quarter of an hour or thereabouts."

"Yes, sir." Jensen touched the bill of his smart black-and-gold cap, started the engine and followed orders.

"How does it work?" Grace couldn't help asking. "The telephone? Without wiring?"

"Eh? Oh." Farquhar raised a bushy eyebrow. "Works by radio signal. Fascinating stuff."

"Nellie is your wife?"

"That she is," confirmed the colonel. "Pansy is the monkey."

"The—?"

"Chimpanzee. Kleptomaniac. Always running off with something or other. You just missed Teddy Roosevelt, by the by. You'd have met him if you'd gone to the Newberry on Tuesday instead of today."

"Oh my."

"Nellie has invited Mary Pickford for August, and Chaplin should be along for a visit in the next few weeks. We've had Edison, Ford, Einstein..."

Name-dropper. But the list of luminaries who'd visited Farquhar's estate was impressive.

They drove down a paved road, the Lincoln Highway, until they approached a towering stone wall with a pair of giant wrought iron gates set into it. Jensen had just gotten out to open them when the air was rent by a series of explosions.

Jensen hit the ground. Grace shrieked and dove for the floorboards, losing her hat. Farquhar cursed, opened the car door and thundered, "Not so near to dinnertime, boys! And not so damned close to the Lodge!" He slammed the door, then called out to Jensen. "Get up. Get up, man." To her, he explained, "It's a military exercise. Experimenting in the trenches with a new kind of grenade."

Grenade?! Grace, shaking, stayed down.

"Miss Smith, there's absolutely no cause for alarm—here's your hat—oh, bloody hell. The zebras have bolted. Jensen!"

Zebras? Curiosity got the better of her.

Grace cautiously poked her head up and accepted her hat from Farquhar, trying to pin it into place again as Jensen scrambled into the driver's seat. He drove them through the gates, then leapt back out to close them before the panicked black-striped creatures streaking toward them could reach the exit. Wild-eyed, snorting, foam at their mouths, bucking and trembling, they looked like stockier versions of mules with comical broom-like tails.

Grace felt instant sympathy for them. But weren't Zebras from Africa? What were these doing here in the Midwestern United States? "How—"

"Brought them back from a safari. Seemed safer than a lion." Farquhar slid her an amused glance.

Jensen pulled the motorcar up to a two-story farmhouse. "This is the Lodge, miss."

"You'll be staying here overnight," added the colonel. "There's a housekeeper and a few other female guests."

Grace tried not to exhibit her relief. She was still trembling from the unexpected explosions, still off-kilter from the whole "interview" and spontaneous journey and still unsure whether Farquhar was sane.

"So," he said. "We'll give you a brief driving tour of Riverbank before we lose the light. Then Jensen will bring you back here to the Lodge to change for dinner and drive you to the main house."

"Sir, I don't happen to have a dinner dress in my pocketbook."

"I'm aware of that, Miss Smith," Farquhar said dryly. "Mrs. Jensen will show you to your room. Simply look in the wardrobe. You should be able to find something suitable."

So she was not the only woman to be snatched and interviewed at short notice. Grace nodded her thanks, and they began the tour of the estate.

Rolling green hills and a long curving drive stretched before them to the right, culminating in a huge, sprawling modern house with enormous picture windows.

"Designed by none other than Frank Lloyd Wright," Farquhar informed her.

Tucked into a copse, some distance from the house, was a vast swimming pool fed by a nearby spring and surrounded by Roman columns. Grace had never seen anything like it.

They motored past a cluster of boxy buildings that Farquhar referred to as the laboratories. "We invent things—some more useful than others." Then they came to something he called the hangar, which contained not only several airplanes, but also what looked like a prototype of the very first flying machine. Grace marveled at it. "Tried to hire those *other* Wright fellows," the colonel grumbled, "but they refused to relocate."

Last, they purred toward a large barracks full of soldiers with its own mess hall. "Brought 'em from DC," the Colonel said. "Government contract. The estate, all 350 acres, is surrounded by trenches used in military drills. After today's stunt," he mused, "I should force them all to *sleep* in the trenches. It'd serve them right since they also roasted my peacocks."

They drove on to see orchards, barns, paddocks, pastures dotted with cattle and horses and a bunkhouse for the ranch hands.

"We raise most of our own meat, grain, vegetables and fruit," Farquhar informed her.

"Very impressive," murmured Grace.

"All right. That's enough—it's almost fully dark. Let's head back to the Lodge, Jensen."

Grace raised her eyebrows as a windmill came into sight. And a lighthouse in the middle of the river. A series of flashes from it split the darkening sky, two white and then three red.

Farquhar chuckled. "Know what that means?"

Grace shook her head, mystified.

"Twenty-three skiddoo. It's a code."

"Meaning?" she asked.

"KEEP OUT. My guards are apt to shoot first and ask questions later."

Grace swallowed. *Keep out?* Well. It was rather too late for that, wasn't it?

CHAPTER THREE

Dinner at Riverbank was an elegant affair, hosted in a grand dining room at a table that seated no fewer than twenty-eight people. Above the table hung a glittering chandelier, and below it was spread the finest—and largest—Oriental rug Grace had ever beheld. The table was covered by a snow-white cloth and festooned with sterling silver and sparkling crystal goblets. Each place setting sported a dizzying array of flatware and fine porcelain.

Grace, in her borrowed evening dress and plain daytime pumps, was utterly out of her element, and of course the room was filled with people she'd never laid eyes upon. A server was circulating with small glasses of what she presumed to be sherry. When he extended his tray to her, she gratefully took one—to heck with her "damned prohibitionist" heritage. She could use a bit of liquid courage to get through this evening, and when the image of her father's disapproving face came to mind, she determined to positively enjoy it. So Grace held the tiny glass to her lips and sipped.

It was nothing like the champagne she'd had earlier. This was sweet, tawny, and a bit smoky... with a sly burn at the finish. It was delicious. She was examining the florid *F* etched into the delicate crystal when a magnificent, continental female voice said, "How do you do? I am Mrs. Elizabeth Wells Gallup. And you are?"

Grace looked up and into a formidable cleavage, then into a cascade of sapphires, and finally into a haughty countenance topped by a steel-gray chignon. Her pale-blue eyes skimmed discreetly over Grace's inappropriate shoes.

Grace introduced herself, wishing she could hide her footwear under the nearest table. At least it was evening, and in candlelight it was less conspicuous. "Mrs. Gallup?" She didn't *seem* like a crackpot.

"Colonel Farquhar has told me a bit about the work you do here. It sounds fascinating."

"Oh, it is!" The lady launched into a soliloquy about Baconian messages being cleverly concealed in the serifs of the Folio's individual letters, while Grace tried not to be dazzled and distracted by her avalanche of sapphires. Despite looking like a duchess at a ball, Mrs. Gallup was utterly serious and rather convincing. More so than their bombastic host.

In a voice like plum preserves, she relayed that she'd traveled all over Europe, staying as a guest in aristocrats' "old piles" and palazzi, researching and lecturing on her theories.

Grace decided to put her doubts on ice until she could examine the text with her own eyes. "The Colonel brought me here today from Chicago—rather unexpectedly and forcefully—to meet you, I believe. He says you're looking for an assistant?"

"Indeed, I am. Several. There's a clock ticking on our research, and we need someone presentable who can give talks to visiting scholars—drum up national support. You might do—have you any talent for public speaking?"

"Yes," Grace said. "I used to teach school."

"Excellent. We'll talk everything over later...do come and meet some of the other guests."

Mrs. Gallup introduced her to at least ten people in short order. She met an incomprehensible Czech engaged in radio communications and another fellow who did acoustics research. She met Veronica Fuentes, a charming woman from Mexico who studied Mayan symbols. She met Utsidi "Ursula" Nashoba, a Choctaw girl—evidently Farquhar was interested in the language. Elma Fay Trent, unfortunately confined to a wheelchair, had a riot of untamed red curls, a sweet, dreamy smile and didn't look a day over sixteen. Yet she had a degree in astronomy and a love of engineering. Alice Martenz was a tall, stunningly beautiful girl with ice-blue eyes and Teutonic features that might have been chiseled from granite. Alice was pursuing a PhD in mathematics.

At dinner, Grace was seated between a quiet, strikingly well-dressed gentleman and an electrical engineer who wasted no time claiming her attention. He lectured her on theories of electricity, particularly AC circuits (in between audible slurps of his soup) until her eyes glazed over.

When the coq au vin arrived, Grace was glad to turn to the quiet, handsome man on her other side. He was quite a Beau Brummell, impeccably dressed in a crisp white shirt, jacket and bow tie. On his feet were pristine white bucks.

He smiled at her, and her brief impression of him as a dandy vanished. For it was an extraordinary smile, one that offered a wealth of humor, generosity, understanding, empathy and intelligence—all in the simple curves of his mouth. It warmed his expressive hazel eyes, and when her gaze connected with his, Grace experienced a peculiar sense of recognition. As if they'd already met, though she'd never before encountered this man.

"Hello," he said. "I'm Robert Feldman." He had a very slight accent that she couldn't place.

"Grace Smith. Lovely to meet you."

"The pleasure is all mine, Miss Smith." That smile again.

"Grace, please. I loathe my surname—it's so dull and nondescript."

"Why? It indicates that your ancestors may have been highly creative master craftsmen, forging delicate silver chalices or mighty steel swords. How is that dull?"

Grace laughed. "It's far more likely that they pounded out iron skillets and stood cheek to hindquarters with draft horses while they shod them."

He lifted a shoulder. "But you don't know that for sure, Grace..."

She liked the sound of her name on his lips.

"So you may choose how to portray them."

"While I am a lover of fiction, Mr. Feldman, I'm not one to embroider the truth. I have strong suspicions that my family's smithy—if it ever existed—was fairly pedestrian."

"As you wish. But call me Robert, please."

"Thank you. So where are you from, Robert?"

His lips twitched. "Oh, me? I'm from the windmill."

Grace paused. "Indeed? And do you tilt at it, like Don Quixote?"

"Every day," he confirmed. "I only wish I had a Sancho Panza to keep me company."

Grace laughed again. "I think I've been brought here to do the same. Tilt at windmills, that is."

Robert looked amused. "Many of us here are—even Colonel Farquhar himself, on a grander scale than the rest of us. He collects people, scholars, imaginations, knowledge. But that said, Riverbank is a fascinating place to be—rather like a homegrown hodgepodge university campus. And some ingenious inventions have come out of it all."

Grace nodded. "How long have you been here?"

"About a year. The colonel found me at a eugenics convention." A shadow crossed his face. "He hired me on the spot to come here and crossbreed corn, wheat and various other grains."

"So that's what you do in the windmill."

"Yes. Genetic experiments."

"Where did you work before?"

"I had a job that I strongly disliked," Feldman said. "But when one is the son of impoverished Russian immigrants, one cannot always be choosy. So I accepted a position at the Eugenics Record Office in Cold Spring Harbor, New York." His extraordinary smile had vanished.

Grace pushed a couple of green beans around on her plate, poking them into her coq au vin. "I didn't mean to pry. My apologies."

"Not at all." Robert took a sip of his wine and changed the subject. "And how did you come to Riverbank?"

"I'm from a small town in Indiana, where I was unhappily teaching school, but I left to search for a job in Chicago. Our host kidnapped me from the Newberry Library earlier today when he learned that I have an interest in Shakespeare."

"That must have been unnerving."

"Yes. Yes, it was. I feel a bit more at ease now, even in this ill-fitting borrowed evening dress and workaday shoes."

"They're not so bad. But the ensemble doesn't do you justice," Robert said gallantly.

She flushed. "Are you flirting with me?" Grace asked, and then immediately wished the floor would swallow her up. *Hussy!*

Robert cocked his head at her. "Only a little. Do you mind?"

She smiled and didn't answer.

He changed the subject. "The colonel—who isn't really a colonel, by the way; it's an honorific—clearly intends for you to work with Mrs. Gallup. Have you met her? She's the one dripping in sapphires."

"Yes. She seems very nice. Truly enthusiastic about proving that Francis Bacon is the true author of Shakespeare's works."

Robert cleared his throat. "What do you think of the Bacon theory?" he asked.

Grace sighed. "Between the two of us? I think it's extremely unlikely to be true, but I will approach it as objectively as possible."

"And what will you do if you discover it to be false?"

"I'll say so."

Robert toyed with his wineglass. "That probably wouldn't be wise, Grace."

She stared at him. "But I can't participate in some ongoing charade. I'll tell the truth. It's the right thing to do."

"And you always do the right thing, Grace Smith?"

She nodded decisively. "Always."

"I like that about you." Robert straightened his bow tie—unnecessarily—and got to his feet just as the dessert course was brought out. "My apologies, but it's time to get back to my windmill."

She was ridiculously disappointed. "No crème brûlée for you?"

He shook his head. Oh, there was that smile of his again. "I'm off to collect virgins."

Surely Grace hadn't heard him correctly. *"Virgins?"*

He nodded.

She couldn't help herself, though she could feel her color rising. "And do they flock to you?"

Robert threw back his head and laughed. "They do. Dozens and dozens of them."

The sheer impropriety of the conversation had her blood humming. "You Casanova, you. And I thought you were such a lovely man."

Robert chuckled. "Do forgive me for having a little fun at your expense, Miss Smith. My dozens of virgins are merely fruit flies in a genetic experiment. Au revoir." And with that, he left the dining room and disappeared into the night.

Grace woke early, having slept in a pair of men's pajamas provided by Farquhar. She bathed and dressed again in her clothes from the day before, then went downstairs in search of coffee. She found Mrs. Gallup waiting for her. Today she wore a high-necked Victorian blouse and simple pearl earrings. She was all business.

After breakfast, she led Grace to her office in the Lodge, where she handed her a piece of paper covered with an assortment of letters in groups of five.

TheWo   rkeso   fWill   iamSh   akesp   earec   ontai
ninga   llhis   Comed   iesHi   stori   esand   Trage
diesT   rulys   etfor...

"Can you make sense of this?" Mrs. Gallup asked.

Grace stared at the page, then took a pencil and wrote underneath it: *The Works of William Shakespeare containing all his Comedies Histories and Tragedies Truly set for(th).*

Mrs. Gallup nodded approvingly. "Good. You're quick, too. Are you familiar with the Latin phrase 'omnia per omnia?'"

"Anything for anything?"

"Exactly. It was a cipher invented by Francis Bacon himself, demonstrated in his book *De Augmentis Scientiarum*, which came out in the same year that Shakespeare's First Folio was published. A strange coincidence, is it not?"

"Quite strange," Grace agreed.

"So what Bacon meant is that to form a basic code, anything can be substituted for anything: say, an apple for an orange. To use the code, one simply has to know the key. So if I say to you, Miss Smith, that I shall deliver to you fifty apples, you understand that I actually mean I'll send fifty oranges."

"Makes sense."

"It's easy, it's safe and it arouses no suspicion from anyone who's not in on the secret. Those are the principles of a good cipher."

Grace was intrigued.

"Francis Bacon, genius that he was, determined that all the letters of the alphabet can be represented by only two letters, if the letters are rearranged in blocks of five."

"I'm afraid I don't understand," Grace said.

"Let's make those two letters *a* and *b*," Mrs. Gallup continued, "and take into account that during Bacon's lifetime, *i* and *j* were interchangeable, as well as *u* and *v*."

She wrote out some gibberish on another piece of paper, then handed it to Grace.

A	B	C	D	E	F
aaaaa	aaaab	aaaba	aaabb	aabaa	aabab

G	H	I / J	K	L	M
aabba	aabbb	abaaa	abaab	ababa	ababb

N	O	P	Q	R	S
abbaa	abbab	abbba	abbbb	baaaa	baaab

T	U / V	W	X	Y	Z
baaba	baabb	babaa	babab	babba	babbb

It made Grace's brain hurt to look at it, though she had to agree it was logical. Each letter became five letters—and there were only two originals.

"Can you spell your first name using this cipher?" Mrs. Gallup asked.

Grace hesitated. Then she took the pencil and wrote, *"aabba baaaa aaaaa aaaba aabaa."* She looked up at her interviewer. "It looks so complicated, but it's the same concept as Morse code, with its dots and dashes, isn't it?"

Mrs. Gallup smiled. "Something like that. Using a biform alphabet, Bacon left coded messages in the so-called Shakespearean texts to reveal his most explosive secrets: that he was, in fact, the author of them, as well as of Christopher Marlowe's work…"

Marlowe, too? When had Bacon slept?

But Grace didn't dare say it aloud. "Fascinating," she murmured.

Mrs. Gallup looked at her approvingly. "You're hired, Miss Smith. I'll let you work out the details with Colonel Farquhar. He's at the Villa. Jensen will walk you over there."

And just like that, she had a job. Dazed, Grace floated through the grounds by Jensen's side, noting all sorts of peculiar statues: a sphinx, a giant duck, a Mayan warrior. As they got closer to the Mediterranean villa, she glimpsed a large cage with iron bars. A rank odor emanated from a shed at the rear of it.

"What is that for?" Grace wrinkled her nose.

"Tom and Jerry. The bears." Jensen couldn't have been more matter-of-fact. "Grizzlies."

"Bears?" Grace was aghast. "Why…?" Words failed her. "Whatever do they eat?"

Jensen grinned. "Employees who've displeased the colonel."

She choked.

"Pulling your leg, miss. They eat meat. And scraps."

"This is a *most* peculiar place."

"Here we are, Miss." Jensen escorted her inside. "If you'd like to wait in the drawing room, I'll fetch the colonel."

Grace entered a large sunlit room and stopped dead, nonplussed. It was dotted with colorful rugs and paintings, with well-tended plants and neat stacks of books. But every piece of furniture in the salon was suspended from the ceiling by *chains*. Even the tables were legless and swung gently to and fro at the slightest touch. It made her nervous for the Murano glass vase on one of them.

Heavy boot steps approached and Farquhar suddenly filled the doorway, pulling on his ginger mustache. "Hallo there, young lady! So you're hired, are you?"

"I've been told so, sir, but I'll need a few more details before I—"

"No need to worry your head about the details. It's all very simple. Riverbank provides lodging, board, recreation and a small salary. You'll have a cottage of your own and an automobile to drive as necessary."

She couldn't believe her ears. This was too good to be true. A cottage and a motorcar?! "That's very generous of you, sir. All right, then. I'd be pleased to come and work with Mrs. Gallup."

CHAPTER FOUR

And now, only three months later, she was fired. Riverbank had indeed been too good to be true. Grace approached the Villa with her feet dragging.

Jensen opened the door at her knock. "Come in, Miss Smith. What brings you to the Villa?"

"I—I must speak with Colonel Farquhar. Is he available?"

"Where the *bloody hell* have all my neckties gone?" This was bellowed from somewhere on the second floor. Neither Jensen nor Grace had any trouble identifying the voice. It was the colonel's.

"Garrett! Must I remind you again?" called another voice, Mrs. Farquhar's. "Don't use foul language in the house, dear." A plump, pretty blonde, she clumped into the hallway in an orchid silk dress and tall rubber boots, wielding a pair of garden shears. She was trailed by a large black-and-white potbellied pig in a pink floral silk scarf.

"Why, Miss Smith!" she exclaimed, with a sunny smile.

From the second floor: "That damned thief of a chimpanzee! If I catch it, I shall roast it on a spit!"

"You'll do no such thing," shouted Mrs. Farquhar. "You insisted upon bringing her here from her natural habitat! Now you must accept the consequences." She turned to the pig. "Sit, Delphine."

Delphine obediently sat down like a Labrador on the Oriental runner.

"What brings you up for a morning visit, dear?" Nellie Farquhar inquired.

"I...well, I wished to say goodbye."

"Goodbye?" Nellie's eyebrows rose. "But you've only just arrived."

Grace felt her color rising. "I've been relieved of my duties, ma'am."

Nellie eyed her sympathetically. "And why is that?"

"I don't think Mrs. Gallup's Bacon theory is valid—"

"What's that?" thundered Farquhar from the second story.

"It's not polite to eavesdrop, dear," called his wife.

The colonel came lumbering down, red faced and sans necktie, and loomed over them. "Who the devil are *you* to question her research and results?"

Grace sighed. *This again.* "Sir, I am unable to reproduce her results, which seem to be arbitrary. I also must question why, if Bacon were the true author of Shakespeare's works, his so-called hidden messages in the text are written so clumsily, so woodenly?"

"Ah, now you're a literary critic!"

Nellie poked him again. *"Listen* to her, Garrett."

"As for this supposed bilateral alphabet in the text, I find no evidence of it, only the natural variance of handwritten letters."

Farquhar seethed. "Do you know how much time and money we've devoted to this project?"

"I'm sorry, sir. It's truly a fascinating theory, one that deserved attention. But I cannot subscribe to it, and I told Mrs. Gallup so. So she has
relieved me of my duties."

"As well she should," snapped the colonel. "Jensen will drive you to
the train station."

Nellie pursed her lips. "Garrett. She's a bright young thing, she has
convictions and she stands up for them. Why don't you put her on the
new government project?"

"Why don't I boil my head?" Farquhar's eyes had gone stormy.

Nellie's twinkled back at him. "Because it's not a good look, and
you've got to meet with the War Department, dear."

"So I do."

Nellie raised her eyebrows at him. "You'll need staff." She inclined
her head toward Grace, who held her breath.

"Fine," the colonel muttered. "If she can locate and retrieve a single,
solitary necktie from that thieving primate, then she's rehired." So saying, he stomped back up the stairs.

Nellie dimpled at Grace and tucked her arm through hers. "Excellent.
Let's be off on a treasure hunt—I know most of Pansy's hidey-holes."

"But you'll have to see that she's decently dressed for the job!" he
called from the landing. "She looks like a bloody Pilgrim."

Pansy had stashed the colonel's ties in the dumbwaiter, an easy find. So,
true to his word, Farquhar agreed to put Grace on the new and mysterious War Department project. She was to meet him to discuss it this
morning, in a borrowed peach silk dress of Nellie's.

"Ah, there you are." The colonel lurched out of a green leather wing
chair to greet her.

Grace had not set foot in Farquhar's personal library before. It was a
room with a crackling fire and soaring walnut shelves, packed with an
exquisite collection of leather-bound volumes that spanned centuries of
human thought, inquiry and expression: From Aristotle to airplanes,
from Erasmus to electricity, from Cicero to ciphers. Grace wanted to

climb the sliding walnut ladder to one of the higher shelves, crawl into a book and never come down.

She could imagine it: slipping between the pages, deep into a paragraph, reclining on a particularly elegant sentence, caressing its words...holding a single letter in the palm of her hand before carefully, respectfully replacing it exactly as she'd found it.

Grace was rudely jolted out of this fantasy by the appearance of—*ugh*.

"Miss Smith," the colonel said, "may I introduce to you Mr. John Edgar Hoover. Mr. Hoover, Miss Grace Smith."

They each nodded politely.

He had the same cold, soulless black eyes Grace remembered from their encounter at the Newberry in Chicago. The same blunt features and ruthless mouth.

"Hoover's here to catalog my library at Riverbank," explained Farquhar.

"I know you," said Hoover, frowning. "The Newberry. Folger collection."

"Yes." Grace eyed him. He was stiff rumped and decked out in cream linen with a silk pocket square that matched his tie. Something about his clothing put her off. *It* wore *him*. He didn't have the easy elegance of, say, Robert Feldman.

Oh, Grace, really. Who are you to judge, the "bloody Pilgrim" in another borrowed dress?

Farquhar turned at a knock on the library doors. "Come in!"

It was Robert. Grace flushed, since she'd just been thinking of him.

"Ah, there you are, Robert. Our guest is waiting."

Guest?

Farquhar led the way to the reading room doors, which he closed behind them.

Waiting inside was a tall, rugged-looking man in an olive drab Army uniform.

"Miss Grace Smith and Mr. Robert Feldman, meet Colonel Parker Hitt," Farquhar said. "Parker is an infantry commander with a reputation as a bit of a cowboy." Farquhar winked at him. "He learned cryptanalysis by accident in the field while fighting in the Spanish–American War. You'll meet his bride, Genevieve, at dinner. When he's traveling for the Army, she often pinch-hits for him at Fort Sam Houston in San Antonio. The gal knows her way around secret writing."

A female codebreaker? Fascinating.

"Colonel Hitt," Farquhar continued, "is one of our foremost authorities on breaking military ciphers and codes. He's written the go-to manual on that, and he's here to give you two a crash course."

"*Military* ciphers?" Grace wasn't sure she'd heard correctly.

"Yes. There's a war on, as I'm sure you're aware."

She gritted her teeth. Everyone knew there was a war on. The newspapers were full of terrifying updates.

"And, since the sinking of the *Lusitania*, the United States has been on the brink of joining it—"

Robert shook his head. "I don't think President Wilson has any intention of doing that, sir. He's got a hundred thousand troops on the southern Texas border; his hands are full with Carranza in Mexico. He's made it clear—"

"Don't interrupt me, Feldman." Farquhar's ginger mustach quivered with indignation. "I have highly placed friends in Washington. We're going to war against Germany, and soon. I can feel it in my bones."

"It's a pleasure to meet you both," Parker Hitt said diplomatically.

"Likewise," Grace said, producing a demure smile.

Robert nodded, only his eyes giving away his irritation at Farquhar.

"Here's the thing: while there's some Yardley fellow chewing over foreign telegrams at the State Department, the US military currently has no formal codebreaking unit of any kind, and we can hardly rely on State or use decades-old Civil War stuff. It's not secure. So I've offered to set up a unit right here at Riverbank. And, after Colonel Hitt gets you up to speed, you two will train the others and run it."

Robert's face was as blank as her own must be. "I beg your pardon?

Apologies, Colonel Hitt. But sir, may we have a word with you in private?"

"No problem," Hitt drawled. "I'll step outside."

Farquhar glowered at them before turning back to Hitt. "Apologies for the rudeness of my employees, Colonel."

"What the devil?" barked Farquhar, as the door closed behind Hitt's lanky figure.

Robert responded calmly. "I cannot have understood you correctly, sir. I'm a geneticist—"

"Not significant. You have a first-rate mind. Set your bloody fruit flies free to frolic. This is far more important than sowing oats by moonlight."

"Sir," Grace said, trying to tamp down desperation, "how does examining Shakespearean texts qualify me as a cryptanalyst? And for the US military during a war?"

The idea of the United States entering the war terrified her. So did the idea of the government relying on a twenty-three-year-old girl and...and...the Ringmaster of the Fruit Fly Circus...to solve crucial coded messages when there might be thousands of lives at stake.

"I've already made the pitch to the Army, and they've accepted," their irascible boss said. "They need our assistance. It's a patriotic duty."

"But—"

"Miss Smith, that's quite enough. What do we do here? We chase knowledge. Knowledge is power. Never forget that."

She tried again to reason with his insanity. "My point, sir, is that neither Mr. Feldman nor I have *any* knowledge of cryptanalysis."

"So acquire it! We've kept Colonel Hitt waiting far too long because of your recalcitrance. Learn what you can from him while he's here for the next few days. After this evening, you're excused from dinner for the week so that you can get to work right away, educating yourselves. Read my collection of volumes in here on the history of cryptography and cryptanalysis." He pointed. "That shelf over there, second from the bottom. Make yourselves at home. This isn't a request. It's an order."

Colonel Hitt aimed a genial smile at them as he came back into the library. "Y'all ready to start smashin' some codes?"

Grace frowned at him. "Hardly."

He grinned at her. "Sure, I felt the same way when I looked at my first set of jumbled letters. Didn't know whether to sh—uh, crap or go blind, if you'll excuse the sayin'. But there are different ciphers and codes, and different methods of breaking 'em. From what I hear, y'all have been analyzin' a bilateral cipher, right? Alternatin' alphabets, skinny letters versus wide ones."

Robert nodded. "Well, Grace has," he amended. "I only enlarged the letters with a camera so they were easier to examine."

"All right. So you've been strainin' your eyes to differentiate between letters. From here on out, we're gonna be lookin' in a whole other way. You know the sayin' that you get judged by the company you keep?"

"Yes."

"Well, words are the same way. Letters in words are the same way." Both Grace and Robert stared at him blankly.

"It's like this: What are the most common letters in the alphabet?"

"*I?*" guessed Robert.

"Good. Others?" Hitt glanced at Grace.

"*A? E?*" she supplied.

"Bingo. Now, think on what the most common word is in the alphabet?"

"The?" asked Grace.

"And," said Robert.

"Exactly. What letters can you string after *the?*"

"There, then, theory, thesis..."

Hitt nodded, his eyes sparking. "How 'bout before—and let's try after—*and?*"

"Band, candy, dandy, gander, hand."

"Now we're cookin'! So my point is, let's say you solve correctly for the three letters that make up *the* in a cipher. You now have a piece of the puzzle, right? Then you can start plugging in guesses—some more educated than others—for other letters."

Grace and Robert nodded.

"But it may be helpful for me to start with a little history of cryptography—the science of secret writing—first. When do you think it originated?"

"With the Greeks?" Robert ventured.

"Good guess. The Romans and Persians also used codes; the Chinese wrote messages on silk in invisible ink...Julius Caesar used a shift cipher. But hell, secret writing has existed since writing itself. It probably dates all the way back to Adam and Eve in the Garden of Eden. So let's run with that. Let's say Eve wants to tell Adam to eat the apple. Eve, bein' a resourceful lady, thinks up a cipher. Like ole Julius, she shifts the alphabet over a smidge. Just by one letter."

"Ah..." Robert frowned. "You mean, beginning the code alphabet with *b* and not *a*?

"Exactly." Colonel Hitt looked around until he spotted some of Farquhar's stationery and helped himself to a piece of it, along with a pen. He wrote out all twenty-six letters in order, and then shifted the alphabet beneath:

A B C D E F G H I J K L M N O P Q R S T U V W X Y Z
B C D E F G H I J K L M N O P Q R S T U V W X Y Z A

"See that? The first version of the alphabet is in regular order. But with the shift, it starts with *B* and ends with *A*." His pupils nodded. "So Eve's gonna tell Adam to chomp down on that forbidden fruit. How's she gonna code that message?"

He handed the pen to Grace, who wrote:

CJUF UIF BQQMF.
BITE THE APPLE.

"Beautiful!" Hitt crowed. "Well done, Miss Smith."

"It's fun!" Grace said. *A lot more fun than staring at those fake Bacon ciphers.*

"It can be a *lot* of fun. It can also be frustrating and mind-bending and crazy making. Eve, in our example, only shifted her alphabet by one letter, and kept the following letters in order. But if you scramble the cipher alphabet randomly, you can get 400,000,000,000,000,000,000, 000,000 different ciphers."

Grace stared at Colonel Hitt with horror.

Robert's face had fallen, too. "How is it remotely possible to solve such a problem? The odds against it are astronomical."

"You're going to have to guess, intuit or steal the key word used to encipher the message . . . or, like the ancient Arabs, you devise methods of codebreaking by other means. Now, I won't get into a whole lot of detail here, because this is all new to y'all. But what we were doin' earlier in the lesson is what we call 'frequency analysis.'"

Hitt explained further. "There's a study, just came out. A scholar analyzed a hundred thousand words of English text, and found that there were only ten thousand individual words outta all of them. Imagine! That cuts your possibilities down to roughly ten percent. Lot less intimidatin', right?"

Grace felt faint with relief.

"Then outta those hundred thousand words, only *eleven* words made up about a quarter of the total! Know what those words were?"

"*I* and *a*," Robert said. "*The . . .*"

"*An, and, in, to,*" Grace added.

"*Of, that, it* and *is,*" Hitt finished. "Anyway. When you have a page of gibberish in front of you, and you're tryin' to solve what it says in plain English, look for those combinations of letters. Plug in guesses and see if they work. It isn't possible to write a coherent message in English without them. And from there, you riddle out the rest. What's likely to be a verb? A noun? What's the context?"

Grace and Robert looked at each other doubtfully.

"You'll get the hang of it in no time," Colonel Hitt said cheerfully. He checked his pocket watch. "Now I'll need to change for dinner. Here's some homework for y'all to look at later." He handed them each a copy of a different scrambled message.

"Enjoy. Be here tomorrow at 0800 hours. We'll talk about Edgar Allan Poe's *The Gold-Bug* and Sir Arthur Conan Doyle's *The Adventure of the Dancing Men*. Sherlock Holmes will have nothin' on you after you read 'em! Followin' day will be Vigenére squares and some military lingo, and then you'll be on your own. Read up. Your boss has some great books on that shelf. You'll need 'em."

CHAPTER FIVE

Washington, DC, 1958

Krypto was even less pleased than Grace when Sommers and Thompson inevitably returned. The fur on his neck stood up, and his bark held not only hostility but all the profanity of a platoon sergeant. At least this time the agents had the decency to call first, so Grace could prepare.

"Oh, are you here for the furniture, too?" she asked when she opened the door and saw the rented truck they'd brought.

Thompson's face reddened.

Tight-lipped, she led them down the hall to the library, where after a mighty struggle earlier that morning she'd deposited Robert at his desk, seething but fully dressed. He did not get up to greet the invaders. Courteous to a fault, this was for him the height of hostility.

"Colonel Feldman." Thompson shifted his weight from one foot to the other, hat in hand. Grace hadn't offered to take it. "How are you, sir?"

Robert glowered at him. "Do what it is that you're tasked with doing. Then please leave."

"Yes, sir."

"You're not to touch the Voynich manuscript, nor the della Porta."

"Sir?"

"*De Furtivis Literarum Notis.* Burgundy binding, first volume on the second shelf. Dates from 1591. Touch it and I will shoot you."

"I, ah—" Thompson looked at Sommers.

Robert opened a drawer of his desk and removed a revolver, which he placed precisely on the upper right-hand corner of his blotter.

Grace knew it wasn't loaded, because she'd hidden all the ammunition.

But Thompson didn't. He swallowed.

"See here, Colonel, we understand that you're upset," Sommers said. "But there's no need for—"

"You understand nothing," Robert said. "You also will not remove the book about the Beale Treasure, nor any of the Union Army cipher volumes, nor the ones with Mayan pictographs."

"With all due respect, sir, we will make that call—"

"*Respect?*" Robert repeated in scathing tones. "Do you dare speak to me of *respect*, when you've stormed our home and are removing our belongings, after my wife and I have spent our entire lives in service to the US government?"

"We've hardly stormed—"

"Do not address me again. Nor my wife. Now get on with it."

Sommers and Thompson shut their mouths and began to inspect books on the shelves.

Robert's hands tightened and shook on his desk, his face white as they worked.

Grace was both distressed by and glad of his anger, since it would likely keep him focused and in the present. She walked to her own desk, standing guard by his side.

They could take the books. They could take anything they

wanted—except Robert's reputation and his dignity. She simply would not allow them to walk out the door with those.

As for his mind...they couldn't take that, either. She would fight to her dying breath to hang on to it, for his sake and her own. Battle the black fog of his despair, drag him back again and again from the darkness that threatened to consume his brilliance, his talent, his faith, hope and character. Not to mention his love for her and the children.

They took forty-eight volumes in all, hardly enough to fill the trunk of a car, much less the superfluous truck. They removed books and papers dating to World War I, and even Robert's own published paper on the Zimmerman Telegram, which had catapulted the US into World War II.

"What nitwit has decreed that you take my own work? Published work?"

"We have our orders, sir."

"Ah yes," Robert muttered, "from the mule specialist, no doubt?"

Grace shot her husband a warning glance. *Robert, don't get yourself fired for gross insubordination.* Though officially retired, he was still an NSA consultant and still drew an income—which they needed.

Luckily, Sommers and Thompson didn't appear to have heard him.

They made a list of all the materials they were taking, dated it, and asked politely for Robert's signature at the bottom of it. They, too, signed it.

"We'd like a notarized copy of that list, please," Grace said.

"Yes, ma'am. We will make one and send it to you." Then the two agents picked up the boxes of books and departed.

Grace followed them down the sidewalk, where she collared Thompson and took him aside. "If you have any decency or respect for the man who made your agency possible, you'll forget what my husband said to you. He was quite upset. He hired you personally. And you should know that he has heart issues."

Thompson swallowed, shifted his weight from foot to foot, and nodded. But then he side-eyed Sommers. "Unfortunately, there's a witness."

"Is there? To something that didn't occur?"

Grace turned on her heel, marched back to the house and shut the door on them as Krypto growled by her side. She returned to the library to find Robert slumped over his desk, unresponsive to her questions. She rolled him in his office chair to the living room sofa and got him to lie down on it. She covered him with a blanket.

Then she went out to the back stoop, sat down and wept.

CHAPTER SIX

Riverbank, 1917

Grace stared at Robert. "We're in no way equipped to do this."

Robert looked back at her, one eyebrow raised and that mouth of his playing silent music that reflected whimsy, amusement and the willingness to take on any challenge. "We can run away," he said slowly. "Or we can learn. I somehow earned a PhD—it's got to count for something. You graduated Phi Beta Kappa. Come now, we've had a thorough lesson. Let's solve these ciphers."

One was a relatively short message, only a three-line paragraph. Following Colonel Hitt's process, they isolated the one, two and three-letter words and began guessing at them, then plugging in the solved letters into longer words. They found repeating letters and guessed at those. And before long, as a knock came at the door and Jensen delivered them a sandwich tray, Grace exclaimed, "Got it! It's a five-letter-shift cipher! Look, it all works." She quickly wrote down the original alphabet, then the shifted one underneath.

The message spelled out:

I HAVE GREAT FAITH IN THE NEW CODE BREAKERS AT
RIVERBANK.

THEY ARE GREEN AS A SALAD BUT DEDICATED AND BRIGHT
ENOUGH

TO CRACK THIS CIPHER BEFORE DAWN BREAKS OR
DERANGEMENT SETS IN.

Robert chortled and grabbed her in a bear hug. Colonel Parker Hitt
had a sense of humor.

Grace hugged him back and then froze awkwardly in his arms. One
didn't hug colleagues, especially not those of the opposite sex. Robert
smelled of a cologne that had hints of rosemary, mint and cedarwood.
He smelled of starch and wool and a scent that was all his own, one that
she couldn't define.

She broke free, her gaze roaming to the bookshelves because it felt
uncomfortable to meet his eyes.

"We did it," he said in a low voice. "We did it."

"Yes. Now's a good time for a sandwich and some tea."

From the dining room of the Villa, they could hear the clink of crystal, the clatter of silverware on china, the buzz of conversation occa-
sionally punctuated by laughter. While a part of Grace felt isolated and
left out, another part of her thrummed with excitement. She wasn't
sure she could even describe the thrill of solving the code, but every
fiber of her being hummed with it. Neurons ricocheted through her
brain, her sight had somehow sharpened, her blood rushed through her
veins...and yet she didn't feel anchored to the earth. Her mind was
an eagle, soaring over mountains of possibilities, clues, frequencies,
secrets.

While they ate, she looked at the second sheet Hitt had left with
them. It filled the entire page, comprising rows and rows of numbers
separated by commas. There were thirty lines in all. It was intimidating, to say the least.

"They don't make any sense," Grace said, barely tasting the cold chicken, butter or freshly baked bread. "They don't seem to correlate to words."

Robert took a big bite of his sandwich and chewed while trying to analyze the sheet. "There are single digits, like three, four, one and two...but there are only two words in the English language that are one-letter words: *I* and *a*."

"They can't all be page numbers in a book," Grace took a sip of tea, "because there are quite a few repetitions."

They puzzled over it as they finished their picnic dinner in the library, down to the last crumb. They counted how many times the numbers recurred. They threw oddball theories and guesses at each other. Nothing worked. They couldn't find a chink in the armor of the code.

After their previous success, it was demoralizing. Perhaps Colonel Hitt's faith in them was misplaced. And if they couldn't even solve the second puzzle he'd given them, then how on earth were they going to break coded messages for the US military? Crucial messages that might affect the outcome of the Great War?

They'd long ago turned on the lamps in the library, and the fire made both of them drowsy, despite the occasional crackle or pop from the burning logs. Grace rubbed at her eyes, which now felt more like a mole's than an eagle's.

Robert smothered a yawn. "We can't expect to be masters of the craft after a few hours. Let's call it a night."

"We'll each borrow a book to take to bed," Grace decided. She seized Hitt's *Manual for the Solution of Military Ciphers* and tucked it under her arm.

Robert chose a tome on the history of cryptology. "Allow me to walk you back to Engledew Cottage?" he asked. "It's dark."

Grace nodded. When Robert looped his arm through hers, she felt torn between discomfort at the contact and pleasure in the simple companionship of the gesture. There was nothing improper about it—a gentleman escorting a lady to her quarters—but a physical awareness of him as a man hummed through her.

He walked her to the cottage's porch and gazed down at her fondly while she disentangled her arm with churlish haste. "We'll make a great team, Grace. I can feel it."

She smiled politely. "Yes, indeed. Thank you for the escort, Robert."

At 0800 hours, Colonel Hitt ambled back into the library, where Grace and Robert met him with hangdog faces, frustrated and exhausted. Each of them had read until the wee hours of the morning, and each had tried yet again to solve the full-page cipher.

Hitt sat on a table, dangling his long legs, crossed his arms over his chest and grinned at them.

Grace eyed him with resentment. What was he so cheerful about?

Robert yawned and rubbed at his eyes.

"Well?" Colonel Hitt prompted.

"We solved the first message," Grace said. "Thank you for the encouragement. But I'm afraid your faith in us may be misplaced."

"The second cipher? It's diabolical," Robert said.

"That it is." Hitt swung his legs. "Beale cipher. Never been solved. Been around since 1820, published in a bunch of newspapers and then a pamphlet in 1885—and may be an actual treasure map. It's ruined more than one man's life. Don't get hung up on it. I can't solve the dang thing, either. But I thought I'd see what you two could do with it."

"A treasure map? What do you mean?" Grace couldn't help but be intrigued.

"It's a real interestin' story. Man named Thomas Beale shows up in Lynchburg, Virginia, in 1820. Unbeknownst to a soul, he buries a few thousand pounds of gold, silver and jewels. He's worried, though, that somethin' might happen to him. Men have been killed for a lot less than that.

"So he finds himself a citizen in town with a stellar reputation.

Honest Innkeeper. And he gives this man a box to safeguard, which he ain't to open unless he receives a letter with specific instructions to do that. Long story short, no letter shows up.

"After twenty years, Honest Innkeeper opens the box to find three long ciphers and a plaintext letter, explaining what the visitor had done. The second cipher turned out to use the Declaration of Independence as a key text, but the other two have never been solved—despite an awful lot of tryin' by a good number of folks."

"I don't feel quite as stupid now," Grace said.

Robert looked thoughtful. *"How* many pounds of gold?"

"Several thousand," Hitt said. "Buried in iron pots six feet underground."

"I say we crack this thing, Grace." Robert waggled his eyebrows at her. "Live like kings for the rest of our lives."

"Good luck with that." Hitt ran a hand through his silvering hair. "Don't get obsessed. There are tales of treasure hunters goin' blind tryin' to break the cipher. Blowin' huge holes in the earth with dynamite to no avail. Losin' their own minds and fortunes on account of not bein' able to leave it alone."

"Some clever, lucky person will solve it one day," Grace said.

"Sure he'd be lucky?" Colonel Hitt shrugged. "Dig it up, and then *his* life's in danger—have to bury it all over again."

Grace couldn't help herself. "Perhaps the person will be a woman."

Hitt flashed his white grin at her again. "Maybe it will be. I'm hopin' it's my Genevieve. She's got a real talent for solving ciphers. Now. Back to work. Let's talk about the pigpen cipher. Used by Freemasons in the 1700s..."

Grace and Robert lived in Farquhar's library for the next week. They shared the long walnut study table, each seated at one end. And they educated themselves, reading every book in the collection, taking notes and quizzing each other on codebreaking history, techniques and terms.

"Steganography!" Grace called out to Robert.

He quirked an eyebrow. "The life and times of a stegosaurus."

"Wrong. Stop joking around."

"You're no fun. Fine. Steganography: From the Greek *steganos* meaning covered, and *graphein* meaning to write. Secret writing. Runs the gamut from invisible ink to writing on a fellow's shaved head, then waiting for his hair to grow and sending him off to deliver the message by shaving his head again."

"Correct."

"Cryptography," he flung at her.

Grace couldn't help herself. "Biography of the dead."

"Thought we had no sense of humor, here? Guess again."

"From the Greek *kryptos*, meaning hidden. The encrypting of plaintext."

"What are the two branches of cryptography?"

"Transposition and substitution. In transposition, the letters of the message are scrambled. In substitution, each letter in the plaintext is swapped for an alternate letter to create the cipher, or encoded text."

"What's an algorithm?"

"I don't know, and I hate it already."

"A basic system of encryption. Both sender and receiver must know the key."

"What's cryptanalysis?"

"Breaking a coded message without benefit of the key."

"And what's the difference between a code and a cipher?"

"A code works by substituting entire words or phrases. A cipher substitutes single letters."

"Splendid. Now—"

A knock came at the library door.

"Yes?" Grace called.

Jensen entered. "Letter arrived for you, miss."

"Thank you." He retreated, and she turned to Robert. "Do you mind if I read this quickly? It's from my mother."

"Not at all."

Grace scanned it and laughed.

"Amusing, is it?"

"I'll read it to you," Grace said, a little surprised at herself. Somehow over the past week, she and Robert had gone from being colleagues to friends. "You may find it entertaining."

"Dearest Grace,

I beg you yet again to return home. The reputation of That Place is scandalous, and I fear your good name will be ruined if you remain there at Riverbank. Rumor has it that Garrett Farquhar is unstable and unhinged—"

"True," Robert said.

"—that he's quite depraved and dozens of harlots romp freely on the grass! That zoo animals roam the premises. That war games take place on a daily basis—"

"Zoo animals? Yes. War games? Correct. Dozens of harlots? Alas, no."

Grace swatted him on the arm.

"Only joking," Robert said.

"Your father and I insist that you come home..." Grace sighed. "That's where it gets less entertaining."

"Alarming, in fact." Robert frowned. "And will you be an obedient daughter?"

"I've never been obedient. Much to my parents' chagrin. But my mother says she's ill."

"Oh dear. Should you go and visit?"

Grace folded the letter and avoided his gaze. "She's always ill. She's in a permanent state of exhaustion, melancholy or despair. Which makes my father even more impatient with her, when all she longs for is a kind word or a gesture of affection... even the fantasy of a holiday."

She sighed. "Should I go and visit? Yes, a dutiful daughter would. But if I do, I'll never escape again."

Oh, Grace, my head throbs so. Grace, I feel faint... would you mind sweeping/dusting/collecting the eggs/polishing the silver/scrubbing the clothes on the washboard/hanging them to dry? Grace, will you wash my hair, dear? Grace, let us pray for your father's soul... I'm too tired to go to Meeting, Grace. Will you accompany your father in my stead?

Robert remained quiet, giving her room and space to talk.

"She'll take to her bed, you see. And I'll have to step into her shoes. She'll chain me there out of guilt, because I'm the last remaining unmarried daughter."

"Surely you'll get married one day, Grace."

She seared him with a glance that would have turned a lesser man to stone. "I *won't*," she said fiercely. "I won't become a martyr, a slave, a broodmare to a bully."

"But—"

"Robert, I love my mother. I truly do. If I thought that a visit from me would help her in the slightest, I would go. Please understand that. But I can't help her. The only thing that would set my mother free from her misery, her *illness*, is a concept that she will never, ever entertain: a divorce."

His eyebrows shot up.

"Yes. I do mean that. They are impossibly ill-suited, my parents. She's his doormat and he wipes his feet upon her. Always has, always will."

"I don't know what to say, except that I'm sorry."

"But she'll never leave him. The scandal and the ostracism would kill her. So there's nothing to be done."

"Nobody she might go and live with? Other daughters?"

"Yes, three. All of whom live fairly close by. But she's too proud. So she turns to me, and asks me to give up my freedom to share her prison. I can't. I simply can't."

He nodded. He reached for her hand and gave it a warm, empathetic squeeze.

Taken aback, Grace immediately pulled her fingers from his.

"I have no idea what we're actually doing here, Robert," she said. "Or if we can pull it off, but I'm *learning*. I'm being paid to use my brain. To help our country in a time of need. To *matter*, just a little bit—in a way that I'm driven to matter. If I leave Riverbank, that all goes up in smoke. So, despite my guilt about my mother, despite Farquhar's dubious character, despite the oddities and the zoo animals, despite being asked to do the utterly impossible—I will remain here."

Robert slowly began to clap.

Startled, her gaze flew to his.

"Brava," he said. "Brava, Grace."

CHAPTER SEVEN

Two weeks later, Army Colonel Joseph Mauborgne paid a visit to Riverbank.

Grace was on hand to greet him along with Robert and Farquhar. She wore another hastily altered silk dress of Nellie's.

Mauborgne was a big, muscular man, almost as large as Farquhar. The difference between them was that he channeled calm and competence, not mania. His eyes were shrewd and sharp behind round spectacles, and he seemed to pick up on the awkward currents between Grace, Robert and his host instantaneously. As if he had a radar for them.

"Meet the man who sent the first radio signal from a plane to the ground," her boss announced. "And broke the British Playfair cipher. He knows his antennas, and he knows his codes."

"Call me Joe," said Mauborgne, extending his hand for a firm shake. Grace took it.

"Joe," Farquhar said, "meet Mr. Robert Feldman and Miss Grace Smith, our resident cipher experts."

Grace forced a smile, though inwardly she was appalled. *Experts?*

"Hello," said Robert.

"Lovely to meet you, sir," she said.

"Likewise."

Farquhar escorted them all into a laboratory building that Grace and Robert had never set foot in before.

"Welcome to the Riverbank Department of Ciphers!"

Twelve souls, half of whom they'd never met, were busy typing, filing, translating, radioing, telegraphing and telephoning...in English, German and Spanish.

Grace exchanged a glance with Robert. Beaming, Farquhar clapped them both on the shoulders and shoved them forward a few inches toward Mauborgne. "These two young people run the place."

We do? Grace's stomach roiled. Who was she to give anyone orders? And on codebreaking, for God's sake?

"They both have extensive experience with cryptanalysis..."

Horsefeathers! Grace wanted to crawl under the nearest desk but kept her expression impassive and her most pleasant smile pinned in place.

Mauborgne nodded as Farquhar made his pitch, but was that a hint of humor lurking in the enigmatic dark eyes behind his spectacles? He turned to Grace. "In your opinion, what are the two most crucial traits of a good codebreaker?"

"Patriotic duty!" supplied Farquhar, without invitation.

"Patience," she said. "And intuition."

"Do you agree?" Mauborgne asked Robert.

"Yes. But if you'd like a few more, I'll add curiosity and playfulness. A fascination with puzzles."

"A love of language," Grace put in.

"An eye for patterns," Robert said.

Mauborgne turned to Farquhar. "They've got the right instincts."

We do? Grace hid her shock.

"They're the best!" the boss man said.

Mauborgne adjusted his glasses without comment. "Let's discuss security."

"Riverbank has three miles of trenches and my own private militia, the Fox Valley Guards. It's in the sticks, so to speak. And we can monitor all comers from the lighthouse. There are also loudspeakers all over the estate that play music and can be used to make announcements or give orders."

Ah, yes, the loudspeakers. Grace had begun to wonder if they worked both ways, transmitting the conversations of anyone nearby. Farquhar often seemed to know things that he couldn't—or shouldn't—know. There'd been his odd comment after she told Robert she wasn't going to visit her mother... "So glad you'll remain at Riverbank despite my dubious character," he'd said acidly the next day.

It gave her the willies.

"All right, Colonel," Mauborgne said. "I've seen enough to make my report to the Army and the War Department. Miss Smith, Mr. Feldman, I look forward to working with you in the very near future."

Grace was petrified. But she was also exhilarated.

"No one here is to speak to *anyone*—not spouse, family member, friend nor priest—about the work that you do. If asked, you do something boring and clerical. You're a typist, a filing clerk, a proofreader. Anyone caught betraying the new Espionage Act could face criminal prosecution, a ten thousand–dollar fine, twenty years in prison—or even the death sentence. Understood?"

This sounded quite ominous, but a chorus of yeses followed Mauborgne's question.

"All messages delivered here by courier are to be stored in the vault," Mauborgne ordered. "Work on one at a time. You will never, ever take a message back to your living quarters with you. You will never copy such a message to take out of this building. You will never share the contents with any other soul, whether it's still in garbled form or not—though it's perfectly fine to collaborate here in the office with another colleague or translator. Is this clear?"

"Yes, sir," everyone replied simultaneously.

When the two colonels had departed—one fake and one all too real—Grace looked at the group before them and took the initiative. "Well, good afternoon, everyone. Since we've just represented to the US Army that we're a cohesive codebreaking unit, why don't we learn each other's names, to start...for those who don't know me, I'm Grace Smith, background in English literature and German, Hillsdale College."

Robert cleared his throat. "Robert Feldman, originally a geneticist. Cornell."

Grace's eyes were drawn to a dark-haired man whose pale-blue eyes were alight with intelligence and humor. "Joe Rochefort," he said. Nothing further.

"Any specialty?"

"Card sharp, puzzle ace. Before you ask if I have a college degree—I don't. Joined the Navy right out of high school, and the Navy'd like me to learn something about signals intelligence, so here I am."

Next to Joe was Elma Fay Trent in her wheelchair, with her mass of barely restrained copper curls and cerebral blue eyes. If not for the clear brilliance in those eyes, she could have passed as a life-sized china doll. "Call me Fay." She gestured down at the wheelchair. "Polio at an early age," she said. "Degree in astronomy. Audited as many engineering courses as I could. The colonel brought me to Riverbank to work on a machine that defies gravity, but he's decided I'm to be a codebreaker."

The striking Latina next to Fay cackled. She wore a starched white blouse and red lipstick that no other woman in the room would have dared to wear. "I tell you, half the...how you say?...contraptions aqui are useless. But Riverbank is never boring."

"Tell the group your name?" Robert asked politely.

"Veronica Fuentes. I am from Mexico, and I study Mayan symbols. The colonel, he wish to possess knowledge of ancient civilizations."

"And...Utsidi, isn't it?" Grace's gaze rested upon another woman she'd met at her first Riverbank dinner, who was clearly of Native American ancestry. Her long black hair was braided tightly and pinned at the neck. She wore a simple, well-tailored gray skirt and blouse and a man's pocket watch around her neck. For some reason she blushed when she answered. "Yes. My English name is Ursula, but I prefer my Choctaw name, please: Utsidi Nashoba. I came to Riverbank because Colonel Farquhar wished to learn my language."

"I hope you'll give lessons to the rest of us," Grace said.

Utsidi lifted a shoulder. "It's a bit difficult to teach because it's oral. We didn't even have a dictionary until about five years ago."

Alice Martenz was next: tall and golden haired with cold blue eyes, chiseled lips—stunning. "Mathematics and physics," she said. "Wellesley. I then pursued a PhD in math at MIT."

There was a tall, fair, wispy-haired gent in a tweed jacket who had a degree in classics from Yale and knew both Latin and Greek. A physics major from Vanderbilt with a minor in German. And a self-taught chess champion, a high school dropout, from Brooklyn.

These were to be some of Grace's and Robert's strange bedfellows in the new Riverbank Cipher Department. Over the next week, the offices filled up with stenographers, typists and translators, too, until the place became a bulging bedlam of activity.

The large central room contained two long, massive tables that seated eight people on either side, with a mess of worksheets, pencil stubs, frequency tables and dictionaries in front of each. Cabinets full of messages, telegrams and transcripts flanked the walls behind them.

Alice Martenz seated herself at the head of one of the tables. While the gents from Yale and Vanderbilt instantly became flustered in her presence, the boy from Brooklyn addressed her as, "Oh, Goddess," making her laugh.

The Yale man then took up the challenge for her attention. "But *which* goddess? Athena? Artemis? Aphrodite?"

Brooklyn rolled his eyes.

"Don't be a bore," Alice said. "I'm Bellona, Roman Goddess of War. Will that do?"

Brooklyn snickered as Yale turned scarlet, then slunk away with his tail between his legs. Vanderbilt wisely said nothing at all—but did position himself just to the right of Alice.

"Don't bother," she said. "I'm not here to flirt. I'm here to run circles around all of you."

An awkward silence followed, which didn't seem to bother Alice in the slightest. And, while taken aback, Grace had to admire her confidence—though she suspected that perhaps something painful lurked in her past, something that had created her tough shell.

"All right," called Robert. "We'll get to know each other over the next few days. For now, am I to understand that everyone here in a cryptanalyst position has read Parker Hitt's *Manual for the Solution of Military Ciphers?*"

A chorus of yeses followed.

"Excellent. Then I suggest we get to work," Robert said.

And they did.

That evening, the new unit gathered at the same table for dinner, which began with vichyssoise, continued to venison with a port-wine sauce and roasted veggies and finished with an applesauce cake dusted with cinnamon.

"I don't think I've ever eaten so well," Grace said.

"This does outstrip a New England boiled dinner," Alice admitted.

All the Yankees agreed, with the exception of Brooklyn, who longed for manicotti and spaghetti Bolognese.

"You've never had my mother's brisket." Robert forked a bit of venison into his mouth. "Or her apple kugel." A dreamy expression drifted over his face.

"Oye!" Veronica sniffed. "One day you will eat a homemade tortilla, an enchilada, some ceviche—and never look back." She poked at the venison.

"I miss my mama's fry bread," said Utsidi. "And wild onions with eggs."

"I can't cook," Grace mourned.

"Que?" Veronica was amused. "Surely you can follow a recipe?"

Grace shrugged. "I don't have a feel for the ingredients."

"Say, this is some interesting work we've got, eh?" Vanderbilt sawed into his venison with renewed vigor.

"Interesting? I'd call it mind-numbing. But I'll be enlisting soon, anyway." Yale inhaled a baby carrot. "Coming here was always just a lark for me, and we'll be needed at the front."

Vanderbilt nodded reluctantly. "Riverbank sure beats slogging it out at my old man's law firm, but I'll never be able to hold up my head at the club again if I don't join up."

"Army or Navy?" Brooklyn asked.

"Navy," both of them said.

Grace's heart sank. They were already losing team members? She looked at Robert.

"What's wrong with serving your country as codebreakers?" he asked.

The two men exchanged looks. "Nothing, old sport," Vanderbilt said. "Nothing at all."

"Perfectly respectable," Yale chimed in.

But clearly, they thought otherwise. *Real* men of their age were heading off to war.

Robert, flushing slightly, took a sip of his wine.

"The Navy sent *me* right here to Riverbank," Joe Rochefort told them.

Grace felt a subject change was in order. "Utsidi, what do you think of our new task? Codebreaking, I mean."

Utsidi took a sip of wine, grimaced and put down the glass. She shifted it over and pulled her water forward, then froze for a moment before putting everything exactly back in place the way it was. "The letters are disguised, like masked performers in a ceremony."

"Yes!" Fay agreed.

"And we must dance with them, converse with them, in order to peer under those masks." Utsidi's high forehead hinted of her wisdom, her thin upper lip of strength, her plush lower lip of tenderness. What did the rearranging of her place setting signify?

"*Dance* with them?" Yale scoffed at her.

"It *is* a dance," Robert said.

Vanderbilt raised an eyebrow. "More of a wrestling match, if you ask me."

"What utter claptrap," Alice said. "It's mathematics, plain and simple."

Fay came to the rescue. "To me, codebreaking's more of a puzzle."

"It's a challenge, a mind game," Joe put in.

Grace nodded. "All valid. I do wish that there weren't thousands of messages to crack open, and only a dozen of us. We have to get faster at it."

"We will." Alice lifted her chin. "I'm going to get so good at it that the Navy will *beg* me to accept a job. So take that, gentlemen. Perhaps you'll work for me in the future."

Yale chuckled. "You're wasted on the Navy, Alice. Marry me instead."

"Not that fellow!" Vanderbilt objected. "Me. You want to marry *me*."

Alice yawned at them, then turned to her applesauce cake with far more interest.

Fay stared off into the distance, her mouth quivering with some unnamed emotion.

Joe Rochefort's concerned gaze fixed on Fay's profile.

The next day, Grace and Robert stood side by side, eyeing three bulging mail sacks with despair. They overflowed with intercepted encoded messages that seemed to mock them in their cumulative yards of gibberish. Which ones were more important than others? Where should they start? What if they weren't up to the job? It seemed all too likely that they weren't.

Grace reminded herself that the English language was gibberish, too, if one didn't already understand how its alphabet worked to create words with meanings and nuances. Just as the Cyrillic alphabet was incomprehensible to her. But it was possible to learn it, if she were to set her mind to it.

The bald fact was that the US government needed them. There were perhaps four other people in America who knew anything more than they did about cryptanalysis. She was not going to let her country down. Neither was Robert. She might not be a genius, but she was stubborn and more than willing to learn.

"All right," Grace said briskly. "Let's begin by sorting them into piles. Some are telegrams from embassies. Some are military communications, intercepted radio transmissions or telegrams. Some are actual letters..."

"That should help us prioritize," Robert agreed.

"Then we'll each take a sack."

They'd just moved toward them when a flash of bright green silk appeared in the doorway, along with Nellie Farquhar's rubber boots, a straw garden hat adorned with silk leaves and porcelain limes and Delphine snuffling in a sky-blue scarf spotted with daisies.

"Hello, my dears!" Nellie called. "I've come as a reinforcement."

Robert blinked.

"What? Can't you use me? Either put me to work or I shall murder Garrett—he's installed a quite tasteless granite replica of Manet's *Olympia* in my rose garden. It's horrid." A force of nature, Nellie surged toward the sacks, Delphine following and peering at them as if hoping they contained food.

"So, what've we got here?"

"We're trying to make sense of it all," Grace said, ruefully.

"I'm afraid I'm useless at breaking codes, but I can certainly organize this mess for you..."

And so she did. Nellie created files for the cables and radio inter-cepts by country: Germany, Austria, Mexico, Italy, Spain and so on. Telegrams and seized letters she efficiently sorted the same way. She then managed to separate Navy radio intercepts from Army and Coast Guard ones, God bless her.

A tornado of swirling green silk, pearls and porcelain limes, she was done in under ninety minutes, leaving the unit with their work cut out for them. "Voilà!" she exclaimed. "Anything else I can help with before I commence Garrett's bloody murder? Though I still haven't decided how to pull it off." She frowned.

Grace's lips twitched. "Perhaps you could avoid prison and arrange for one of the new grenades the boys are testing to find its way into *Olympia's* lap, instead."

Nellie dimpled and clapped her hands. "Brilliant! Though I would pin the crime on someone else, of course."

"Of course," Grace agreed.

"Now, my dear... I must admit that I'm here for another purpose as well." Nellie leaned toward Grace and whispered in her ear. "Especially since you're running the show, Garrett does insist that you be... how shall I say this tactfully? Outfitted properly."

Grace cast a glance down at her customary gray dress and white collar. She couldn't really argue with the colonel's assessment, however rude it was.

"Have you got an hour or so to spare," Nellie asked, "now that we've got your communiqués sorted properly?"

Grace glanced guiltily at the boxes and piles.

"Come on, now—it won't take long." Nellie took her hand and tugged her in the direction of the Villa. "This will be great fun, decking you out to represent Riverbank! Let's go and raid my wardrobe, dear."

"But you've already given me two dresses—"

"Tut-tut. Come along..."

Three days later, Grace was the reluctant new owner of *ten* of Nel-lie's freshly altered ensembles, as well as a crocodile handbag, a cloche hat with a matching crocodile band, a heavy woolen coat, a fox stole, a pair of kid gloves, two slips, and three pairs of silk stockings. A package arrived from Marshall Field's, containing two pairs of size seven Italian leather pumps and silk unmentionables.

"But I can't accept all of this—" Grace protested.

"Nonsense."

"At least allow me to purchase it? I can't all at once, but in installments?"

"What does my husband pay you, dear?"

"I, ah…" Grace trailed off, embarrassed. "Thirty dollars a month."

Nellie gaped. "My dear girl, whatever were you thinking to accept such a pittance?"

"I—well, the room and board, you know, and the motorcar…"

"Garrett's taking advantage of you," Nellie said flatly. "So you're not to say another word about reimbursing me. All right?"

Grace hesitated, then reluctantly nodded.

"Let's go and show him the new you, shall we?" Nellie flashed her a smile and took her by the hand, again. "Come along, Delphine. We're having a fashion show."

Farquhar looked Grace up and down, making a noise of approval. "Nice work, Nellie. But we must have some pearls, old girl. Have you got some to spare?"

Horror. He wanted to strip his own wife of her pearls and bestow them upon Grace? Grace thought about hurling herself out the window. Running for the swimming pool with its Roman columns and drowning herself in it. Or painting herself with pâté and jumping into the bear cage.

"Of course, Garrett," Nellie said, unperturbed. "Drawers full." She turned to Grace with a yawn. "Back up the stairs, my dear. Does she need earrings, too?" Nellie asked her impossible husband.

"Yes. And a brooch."

"Oh no, that won't be necess—"

"Come along, now," Nellie said, towing her out of the room.

"B-but—" Grace buried her face in her hands. "This is...I've asked far too much of you already, Mrs. Farquhar."

Nellie chuckled. "It's easier to give in and go along with it, really. He's like an alligator with a toothache until he gets his way—and who wants to listen to him?"

"I heard that!" shouted the colonel.

"Did you, love?" Nellie called back. "Keep listening, and you'll get quite a burning earful. Now, let's go back upstairs, Grace, and select some appropriate pieces."

Back on the second story, Nellie began pulling open blue velvet–lined drawers. "Where is the Spanish strand? Where's it hiding, hmm? Has Pansy been in here, again? That incorrigible, kleptomaniac monkey. He gets into my closet, too—not just Garrett's—and things go missing, especially jewelry. Though he likes fish forks and sugar tongs from the dining room silver chest, too. Dratted animal."

"Aha. Here they are." Nellie slid out a strand of perfectly graduated pearls with a box clasp, adorned with an emerald flanked by two diamonds. "These will suit you beautifully. And here are the earrings..." She handed them all to Grace.

"Mrs. Farquhar, I cannot—"

"Of course you can, dear. I'll still have the French pearls, the antique English ones and the Tahitian set—as well as my opera-length strand. How many similar necklaces does one woman need? My roses make me far happier than my jewelry, anyhow. So do my pig and steers."

Grace stared down at the necklace and earrings. Nellie made this madness sound perfectly reasonable.

"Now, a brooch, he said? Let's see...not the spider. It's off-putting. The rose? No, I'm fond of that one. How about this gold key? That seems appropriate, since you'll be trying to unlock secrets for the government all day long." Nellie closed up her jewelry box, then pinned the key to Grace's dress.

Grace awkwardly clasped the pearls around her neck, screwed on the earrings, and stared at a new, much more sophisticated version of herself in the mirror. The pearls lent her graciousness and authority.

Nellie clapped her hands. "Divine."

"I don't feel right about taking these from you."

"I'm *giving* them to you, which is a far different thing entirely. Enjoy them, Grace. I like you, and they look lovely on you."

"I cannot thank you enough."

Nellie waved away her gratitude, as though it made her uncomfortable.

"Garrett and I weren't able to conceive," Nellie said, staring blankly at a stack of hatboxes. "So I have nobody to inherit my jewelry, anyhow."

Farquhar was paging through a dog-eared, yellowed treatise of some kind when they reentered the drawing room. "Ah. There you are at last. Pearls. Splendid." He eyed her with satisfaction and then turned back to his treatise. "You'll do," he muttered, utterly ignoring his wife. "You'll do very well."

Would she? Grace hoped so.

"You're welcome, Garrett," Nellie said, a trace of acid in her tone.

"What's that? Oh yes, yes. Thank you, my dear. Back to your roses, are you?" He didn't wait for a response, just lumbered over to a chair and settled into it with a creak.

"Steers, dear."

Grace cast an apologetic glance over her shoulder at Nellie, who bared her teeth and brandished her garden shears, as if tempted to use them on something far different from roses.

CHAPTER EIGHT

Sun warmed the offices that Grace and Robert shared with the rest of the unit, illuminating the dust motes stirred up by a faint breeze.

They circled, floated and sank to various surfaces like hundreds of ideas searching for purchase in a human mind.

Outside the open window, a bumblebee buzzed as it tried to penetrate the glass, then the screen, its tiny motor gunning. Again and again, it tried to nudge its way in. Stubborn little creature.

Inside, typewriters clattered and voices volleyed questions in English, Spanish and German. Heels tapped on the wooden floors, telephones rang and radio communications crackled.

The most prevalent smell in the office was that of paper and musty books, but the acrid aroma of burnt coffee mingled with a tinge of motor oil that seeped in from the parking area. More than one perfume warred against clouds of cigarette and pipe smoke.

Grace sat staring at a sequence of digits grouped into blocks. Each one formed a tiny chorus line of hostile code.

This telegram had been intercepted a month prior by the British, from the German embassy en route to India. It was then sent to Scotland Yard, who, unable to solve it, brought it to Riverbank. Considering that there was a war on, anything from the Germans was a top priority—and Grace was the unit member who was fluent in German.

She took another glance at the numbers. The only thing she knew about them was that Scotland Yard suspected Germany was trying to stir up a revolution in India by Hindu separatists.

Robert sat opposite her, looking at the same grouping of numbers. He'd become adept—something of a showman, actually—at twirling a regulation black pencil like a small baton between the thumb and fingers of his right hand. He had sensual fingers and neat, square nails.

She tried not to pay attention to them, or to the flurries of pencil spinning. She herself had a habit of drumming on her own nose with the white eraser at the tip of her own pencil. It probably wasn't dignified, but it satisfied something deep within her that longed for a beat, a rhythm to which her brain could march on the journey to making sense of a given code.

"I'll hazard a guess," said Robert, "that the first groupings of five are from a simple rectangular grid."

"All right. Let's try that." Grace wrote out the alphabet accordingly on a grid sheet, assigning numbers to the letters both across and down.

"So, let's see...38425, according to this chart, would be: BSIAJ."

"Of course. Clear as mud." Grace tapped on her nose with the pencil again.

"We've got to make a guess as to the key word for this jumble."

"But how? Any way we turn it, it's not a word. SIJAB? JIBAS? SABIJ? ABJIS?"

"Let's figure out what letters the other blocks stand for. Then run them back and forth and rejumble them. And remember that the message is in German, not English."

Learning rudimentary German (for Robert) and Spanish (for Grace) was a necessity; a task they tackled at night. Guten Morgen! Ich bin Robert. Ich spreche kein Deutsch. Buenos Días. Cómo está? Mi español es terrible.

They worked on and on. Grace's neck ached. Her brain ached, too. She ignored the discomfort.

Outside the window, the bumblebee's tiny motor kept buzzing as it tapped methodically on a new section of the screen. A blue jay cawed, pressuring them to hurry. And a swatch of scarlet flashed by—one of Farquhar's monkeys in a red diaper.

Grace envied its freedom to roam.

"Could it be double encrypted?" Robert asked, after two hours of trial and error. "This being a second alphabet that stands in for a first?"

Grace groaned. "It's a possibility."

Robert spun his pencil, chin propped on his left hand. "We're looking at it as work, again. We've got to *play*. Like the monkeys."

"Make it a game," Grace agreed. "Make it *fun*, somehow."

"Don't erase your nose to spite your face," Robert teased her, and she realized she was tapping again with the eraser. She stopped, self-conscious. "It's far too pretty a nose to be rubbed out." Robert leaned back in his chair.

Grace felt herself blushing. "If you want to flirt with a woman, you don't talk about her proboscis. You bring her flowers, or quote poetry to her—but don't you dare compare me to a summer's day, or I'll toss something at your head."

"Yes, ma'am. No, ma'am," Robert murmured. "Quite bossy, aren't you?"

Grace ignored this. "Let's look at the second set of numbers. Could they refer to pages, lines and words in a book?"

"Let's take a look..."

"The first two could apply to a book with two columns in it. Page ninety-seven, column two, line fourteen. Page thirty-five, column one, line seventeen."

"But look at the last two. The theory doesn't work. I can't think of a single book that has five columns, or four."

Robert spun his pencil. Grace tapped her nose with hers.

"What if there are three different codes going on here? What if the last two sequences refer to a different book? So page seventy-three, line five, letter three? And page eighty-two, line four, letter three?"

"All right, what if? Let's go with it."

"Books with columns...got to be a Bible or a dictionary."

"Dictionary," Grace said decisively. "The Germans wouldn't communicate with Hindus using a Bible."

"All right, dictionary. Which publisher, and which edition?"

She shrugged. "It's hopeless."

"No, no. We'll simply try a few of the more common German language ones. But first, some wild guesses and some reverse engineering."

They each got a cup of bitter, burnt coffee and kept working.

"Solve for SIJAB, or I'll compare thee to a summer's day," Robert said.

Grace scowled at him. "Don't you dare. I'm a frozen, wintry Monday morning. I'll drop icicles down your collar."

"Then I'll shiver with delight."

She groaned again. "Guessing time. Why are the Germans communicating with the Hindus? We've been told they want to foment a revolt. So let's say I'm...Fritz Schoen...and I need to send this military cable. What sort of language am I using?"

"Formal. Clipped to the bare basics."

"Right. So perhaps I begin with Attention: Someone. Then get straight to the point."

"True. The telegram would read something along the lines of, "Attention: German Ambassador, India. We know of separatist troubles and wish to send money or supplies in exchange for...something else that will give Germany a tactical advantage in this war."

Grace nodded. "What are the most common ways of boiling that down to phrases in basic German military-speak?"

They rifled through other, translated German military telegrams and borrowed a couple of dictionaries from the translators.

It was fifty-seven wild guesses, untold erasures, three dictionaries and two days later, as they sat together on a blanket outside on the grass, that they solved it. Perhaps the sunshine and the fresh air, untainted by smoke and stale coffee, helped. What also helped was their two brains, sparking off one another—without distractions or chatter from other members of the unit.

"Sure enough!" Grace exclaimed. "Hindu activists in New York and their coconspirators in San Francisco want to ship weapons and bombs to India—"

"As part of a wider plot to wage a rebellion against Great Britain," Robert finished.

"The Germans offer funding and tactical help, in order to weaken the British by distraction on another front." Grace put down her pencil and rubbed at her eyes.

"It's quite a brilliant strategy," Robert mused. "Say what you like about them, but they aren't stupid, the Huns."

Grace read the translated messages again and again, unable to believe what they'd done.

"We've just produced crucial intelligence for an ally of the United States!"

Elated, Robert sprang to his feet, ran a lap around the blanket, then danced a jig. His normally neatly combed hair was mussed, his bow tie askew, a coffee stain in the middle of his snow-white shirt. He danced his way over to Grace, grasped her hand, and pulled her to her feet to join him. He spun her out onto the grass, then twirled her and reeled her back in; they both laughed until they were breathless, Robert holding her close, gazing down at her from his far superior height.

Grace couldn't look away from his clever mouth, that smile of his that curved in ways that made her ache, made her long to plug into the vast complexity and curiosity of his mind, but also to be held dear to his heart. It bordered on intoxicating. And that was dangerous.

She had no desire to fall for a man—any man—now that she was out from under her father's thumb. Dealing with Farquhar was quite bad enough.

Yet here she was, looking up into Robert's hazel eyes, mesmerized by the tiny flecks of green and gold in them. Here she was, breathing in his scents of wool and starch and shaving cream. Here she was, her body pressed up against his as his mouth lowered toward hers, his lips seeking her own. They were warm and gentle and spoke without words of his desire for her.

A shock spiraled through her entire system at the contact, an odd electricity.

Grace broke away from him and stepped back, averting her gaze, her face suffusing with heat and her pulse pounding.

"I apologize," Robert said quickly, analyzing her face and body language. "I shouldn't have done that."

"It's all right," Grace said automatically. But it wasn't. Because in a split second, they'd gone from being colleagues and friends to something more complicated. Something she didn't want because it threatened her newly found freedom and independence.

Robert jammed his hands into his pockets.

"Well. We should cable this to Scotland Yard right away." Grace picked up her things from the blanket—books, worksheets, pencils. She could feel Robert's gaze on her, warm and wistful. Full of promise and possibility.

She shook it off and headed for the Lodge. Her father had once gazed at her mother that way…and look how *her* life had turned out. Nine children, most of whom had flown the coop. Incessant physical labor. Exhaustion. Illness. A husband who'd fallen out of love with her before their second child was out of diapers, and who disrespected her daily.

No thank you. I'll take codebreaking over heartbreaking any day.

CHAPTER NINE

Despite the teamwork that had gone into solving the Scotland Yard messages, despite the fact that Grace, too, had poked and pried at, dug into and hammered at them to crack open their contents, it was Robert whom the prosecutors wanted to testify at the Hindu separatists' trial in San Francisco. After all, the jury would trust more in the authority of a man. Who could trust a mere slip of a girl—even one in good pearls—on such a weighty and complex topic as cryptanalysis?

Robert smiled apologetically at her as Jensen loaded his suitcase into the motorcar. "I'll return soon. And I'll be sure to photograph the trolleys and the sights for you."

"Don't forget the sea lions," Grace said gaily, trying to mask her disappointment. Why did the world belong to men? Couldn't women have a small slice of it, now and again?

But she had little time to indulge these thoughts. Over the next few days, while Robert was away, she and the team at Riverbank worked at all hours to decipher countless messages from Mexico and Germany for the US government.

Grace found herself missing Robert more than she cared to admit. And when Farquhar summoned her from Engledew Cottage after hours one night, saying it was important news about Robert, she ran.

Farquhar was ensconced in what everyone at Riverbank dubbed the "Hell Chair," which hung on chains outside near a fireplace where Farquhar liked to gather residents and guests to lecture them on various topics. He also liked to call hapless employees there to bark at them, bully them and in short, "give them hell."

As Grace came sprinting across the lawn, he raised a glass of Scotch to her, a double. Then he invited her to sit next to him. "Like one?"

"No, no thank you. What is it? What's the news from San Francisco? Did they win the trial?"

"Shots were fired today in the courtroom. It'll be in all the papers tomorrow."

"*Shots?* Is Robert all right?"

"He's fine. Won't need to testify to the jury, though. The defendant is dead."

She covered her mouth with her hands.

"Someone burst into the courtroom with a pistol, yelled, 'Traitor!' and fired at point-blank range."

Thank the Lord it isn't Robert who's dead. The very thought had her trembling.

"There, there, my girl." Farquhar swung closer to her in the Hell Chair. He put a great, heavy paw on her shoulder and squeezed. Then he slid it farther down her arm, his fingers straying perilously close to her breast.

Grace froze.

"It's all right, my dear. Robert is perfectly safe. But you must have been lonely without him these past few days."

"Robert and I are friends and colleagues."

"I see the way he looks at you, Miss Smith. Can't say I blame him."

"You're mistaken, sir."

"Am I?"

She could smell the alcohol on the colonel's breath, see its influence in the ruddiness of his face and the bleariness of his eyes. A droplet of whiskey clung to his ferocious beard. She'd gathered her skirts up to bolt when he tightened his grip on her upper arm and tugged her onto his lap.

"Wh-what are you doing?!" Grace braced herself on the arms of the Hell Chair and struggled to get off him. The chair swung and rocked wildly.

Where is Nellie?!

"Calm yourself, Grace," the colonel said. "Just give us a cuddle, won't you, dear?" He put an arm around her waist, which sent a shudder through her.

"I'm really not the cuddling kind, sir—"

"You realize that we'll be famous now, eh? 'Defendant Shot As Riverbank Cryptanalyst Prepares to Testify.' Can't wait to see the newspaper headlines tomorrow."

"And that's to be applauded, sir. But your wife would *not* applaud, were she to see this spectacle."

"Nellie? Oh, don't worry about her. She's off in the gardens somewhere, or in the barns." He couldn't have sounded more unconcerned.

Grace gave up trying to push or pry his massive, meaty arm off her waist. Instead, she ducked under it, knew a moment's terror when she dangled by her neck, and then wrenched out of his grasp and ran several steps away. "I do not sit in gentlemen's laps, Colonel!"

"Well, what a pity. You're a fetching little thing. Can't fault a man for trying."

Grace's heart plummeted with the sudden knowledge that, fascinating work or not, she needed to leave Riverbank—and soon. Her boss had just made that abundantly clear.

But where would she go? What would she do?

Robert was to return within a few days, days during which Grace skipped the formal dinners at the Villa, choosing to pack a sandwich begged from the kitchen each day and work until late at night. She had no way of knowing if Farquhar even remembered the incident in the Hell Chair, and she wouldn't be able to look Nellie in the face without feeling guilty and dirty, even though the "cuddle" had been against her will.

After a particularly trying day of codebreaking, Grace was tucked into her twin bed at Engledew Cottage and fast asleep (though not peacefully) when a thunderous hammering on the front door began.

What on God's good earth would bring someone to the door at— she checked the clock—1:40 a.m.? Grace stumbled out of bed and stuffed her arms into her dressing gown. Then the door to her own room flew open, and Alice held up a lantern, half blinding her. "Jensen's here. You're needed up at the Villa."

"What?" Grace asked groggily. "Why?"

"There's a courier, just arrived, with an urgent message that needs to be decoded. For some reason, Farquhar thinks *you're* the one to do it." Resentment rolled off Alice in waves.

Grace did her best to ignore it. "Then I suppose I'd better get dressed."

Alice raised her eyebrows. "You don't want the colonel to see you en déshabillé? Surely, he has already, judging by your fancy new wardrobe."

Grace goggled at her.

"Alice, that is utterly untrue and unfair," she snapped. "Has he seen *you* that way? Because frankly, you're far more beautiful than I am, and we both know it."

Alice blinked at this unexpected compliment.

"He just sees me as easier prey," Grace added.

"Then where did all your fine new frocks come from?" Alice folded her arms. "Your new pearls?"

"From his *wife*, because he wanted me to look more like the head of a codebreaking unit. It was mortifying. Now, will you stop with the waspish innuendos and be useful? Hand me my dress and slip while I roll on my stockings."

To Grace's surprise, Alice did so without comment, retrieving the items from the hook where they hung on the wall. She stood there in a sky-blue silk negligee, her long blond hair plaited into a braid that hung over her shoulder. "Perhaps I've misjudged you."

"Perhaps you have," Grace agreed, cursing the awkward stockings and wishing that women could simply jump into a pair of trousers like a man. "Why he didn't choose to fixate on you, I don't know."

"I do."

Grace looked up, surprised.

"I'm not nice," Alice said with a shrug, followed by a bitter twist of her mouth. "I don't smile at people or offer pleasantries—nor am I in the least tactful. I can't be bothered."

This was all true, but Grace could hardly say so.

"Look at you," Alice said, irony now playing around her lips. "You can't even agree with me, because you have such good manners, Miss Smith."

Grace opened and then closed her mouth. She dropped the slip and then the dress over her head. Found her shoes.

"Learn to be rude," Alice advised. "Not only is it necessary at times, but it's *delicious*."

Grace couldn't help but chuckle as she wrestled her coat off its hanger in the armoire. "I'll take that under advisement."

"Good. Beauty's not the blessing you think it is, by the way. Now hurry up—Jensen is waiting on you in the motorcar."

A skinny young private with protuberant pink ears awaited her in the colonel's library.

"Good evening," Grace said. "What is it that you've got for me?"

He looked her up and down and gaped. "I, er. Miss, I was told to entrust this message to a codebreaker. The head of the unit."

"Yes," Grace said briskly. "That's me. Now what is it you've got that's so urgent?"

His ears got even pinker in the light of the wall-mounted sconces. "You cannot be Mr. Robert Feldman."

"Of course I'm not Robert Feldman. He's away at the moment, testifying in court. I am just as competent; I can assure you." She reached out her hand, palm up.

"But—"

"Give the lady the message, Private," snapped Farquhar, surging into the library in his dressing gown and striped pajamas.

Grace froze at the sight of him.

His eyes were glassy; she judged he'd been into the whiskey again. He gave her a quite improper once-over.

Her pulse kicked up, and her heart clogged her throat.

"Give her the message, then get yourself to the kitchen, man," he rumbled. "Cook will arrange some coffee for you and a snack." The young officer, ears now flaming, reluctantly relinquished the paper to Grace.

No, no, no . . . he cannot leave me alone with the colonel.

"They found this sewn into the jacket of a suspected German spy, Miss," the courier said. "Caught at the US–Mexico border carrying a Russian passport in the name of Pablo Waberski."

Grace frowned at it. "Why is it so urgent?"

"On account of they think he's dangerous, and they can only hold him for seventy-two hours without further cause."

"Well, let's get to work, then, young lady," the colonel ordered.

The paper trembled in Grace's hand. She could either fight or flee. Meeting Farquhar's gaze with a fierce one of her own, she mouthed, "NELLIE."

"Er, which way is the kitchen, sir?" The boy didn't seem to pick up on the tension, thank God.

Farquhar's eyes narrowed. His mustache quivered.

"NELLIE," Grace mouthed again. "I WILL TELL HER."

The colonel's eyebrows snapped together as his color heightened. "I could use some coffee myself, come to think of it. I'll never get back to sleep now...Come along with me, young man."

To her profound relief, Farquhar turned tail and lumbered off with their unexpected guest.

Grace released a breath she'd been unaware of holding and took a fresh gulp of air. She unfolded the message and examined it. The letter consisted of three columns of nonsense.

A German spy. *No pressure, then. Of all the times for Robert to be gone.*

She rolled up her sleeves and got to work. It stood to reason that the cipher text was written in English, German or Spanish. After some preliminary steps, she determined that there were twelve *k*s.

*K*s were numerous in German, but practically nonexistent in Spanish. Spanish was full of *q*s, and there were no *q*s at all.

So it was a good bet the language was German.

The message contained seven *z*s in addition to the twelve *k*s.

Z and *k* were very common in German.

Hmm...*h* and *k* were often preceded by *c* in German. So how to bring those combinations of letters back together?

Grace counted the total number of letters in the cipher message: 424.

It was time for some figuring. There was probably a mathematical formula that had been used to rearrange the plaintext.

She applied a statistical frequency analysis to the jumble of letters.

She worked without stopping, hunting for patterns.

When Grace was able to isolate the words *peso* and *Nacional* in the cipher, she gave a whoop.

Republik and *Mexiko* were next. Slowly, bit by bit, she was prying meaning out of the code.

"*Agent!*" yelled Grace at an unladylike decibel, just as Alice and Fay joined her in the library at 4:00 a.m.

"Can we help?" Alice handed Grace a steaming mug of coffee.

"Oh! I could *kiss* you for this."

"Please don't," Alice said. "Success, I take it?" Her tone was sour.

"Close."

By four fifteen, the three of them had banged out the rest. It was a German transposition cipher of a difficulty that surpassed any example or exercise in Parker Hitt's manual.

Breathless, Grace rapidly typed it into English.

> *To The Imperial Consular Authorities in the Republic of Mexico. Strictly Secret!*
>
> *The bearer of this is a subject of the Empire, Otto Schroeder, who travels as a Russian under the name of Pablo Waberski. He is a German secret agent.*
>
> *Please furnish him protection and assistance, also advance him up to one thousand pesos of Mexican gold and send his code telegrams to this embassy as official consular dispatches.*
>
> *Von Eckhardt*

"We've got him! We've got him!" Grace crowed.

Alice gave a rare smile, which she swallowed again immediately.

"*Bing! Bang! Bing 'em on the Rhine*," sang Fay.

"Got whom?" Robert's voice inquired behind them. "Hello, Fay. Hello, Alice."

Grace spun around, giddy with their success. "Robert! You're back! And unhurt, thank God." She fought the urge to hug him. It wouldn't be professional, much less proper.

His smile made her knees wobble. "Yes. So? Got whom?"

"The faux-Russian Pablo Waberski," Alice said. "German spy and saboteur, picked up on the US–Mexico border. We just deciphered a message found on him."

He smiled. "Congratulations, Alice—"

"Grace worked on it all night," Fay said, with a challenging glance at Alice. "We only helped her at the tail end."

Alice's nostrils flared.

"Congratulations to all of you," Robert said tactfully. "Well done. What's the spy's real name?"

"Otto Schroeder," Alice said.

"Schroeder?" Robert repeated, his eyebrows flying up. "As in, the fellow behind the Black Tom explosion last July?"

Grace stilled.

Windows all over lower Manhattan had shattered; the Statue of Liberty itself was pitted by shrapnel. Two million *pounds* of munitions meant for Great Britain had exploded in the Black Tom railroad depot in Jersey City. Deliberate sabotage by German spies.

"With this evidence, they're sure to hang him," Alice said.

Grace sobered, the adrenaline fading from her bloodstream. It was one thing to be excited about cracking a very difficult cipher. It was another thing to feel responsible for a man's death.

Robert seemed to read her mind. "You're not the spy, Grace."

"In a way, I am. Spying on secret correspondence."

"Correspondence meant to harm the United States."

"Twenty million dollars of US military supplies went up in smoke, thanks to this man," Alice reminded them all. "Three people died. And a *baby*. Hanging's too good for him."

Grace nodded, exhaustion enveloping her after so many hours of work and so little sleep. She changed the subject, uncomfortable. "Robert, I'm so glad you weren't hurt. How did a man bring a gun into the courtroom?"

"Smuggled it in under his jacket." He, too, looked bushed from the ordeal and his journey.

"Must have been truly awful." Grace tried to read his expression, but it was carefully blank.

"I've never seen a man shot in front of me," he said. "Never seen anyone die violently. I hope I never do again. It's not pretty."

Unspoken in the room was that millions of British and French soldiers were dying violently on the battlefields of Europe in the most gruesome trench warfare. And if the US were to be drawn into this dreadful war, American soldiers would die, too.

"Well," Grace said. "I've got to get this to the courier who's waiting to take it back to Mauborgne."

"I'll wait for you, and then walk you to Engledew Cottage." Robert put on his hat again.

Grace nodded, then turned to Alice and Fay. "I cannot thank you both enough for your help."

Alice yawned. "Of course. It's why we're all here." She headed for the door. "I need more coffee."

Fay smiled at Grace after she left.

"Thank you," Grace said. "For setting the record straight."

"Thank you for allowing me to help." She gestured down at her wheelchair. "It gets old, you know, being discounted as an invalid. Perhaps my legs don't work, but there's nothing wrong with my brain."

"You're brilliant. A goddess in a chariot." Grace leaned down and kissed her cheek.

Fay looked stunned. "I love this work," she said, simply. "It gives meaning to my life. Meaning that never existed before."

Grace nodded. "I feel the same way."

Riverbank, with all its eccentricities, exotic animals and celebrity visitors, had changed her, made it impossible to go back to who she used to be. It had opened not just doors but entire vistas of possibility for who she could become.

Dread draped itself around her shoulders like a heavy fur in summer. If she had to leave Riverbank because of Farquhar, what would become of her? She had discovered that her mind was a potent weapon. She refused to fire it into a washtub or a stove.

CHAPTER TEN

Robert, ever the gentleman, was true to his offer of an escort in the darkness before dawn.

Grace usually didn't enjoy being dwarfed by tall men, since they used their height to dominate or patronize her. Tonight, though, with her hand tucked into the crook of Robert's arm, she felt comfortable, safe and protected. And he was a buffer in case she should bump into Farquhar and his whiskey again. She rather resented needing male protection, but it was reassuring to have it, all the same.

If Riverbank was lovely during the day, it was magical by moonlight. Hundreds of stars glittered in the midnight-blue expanse of sky overhead. Crickets played their night music, the wind rustled the trees, the Fox River spilled along sleepily, a silver ribbon tied around the gift of the landscape.

"I could have used your help," Grace said to Robert. "It was a monster of a cipher."

"Seems to me that you gals did fine without me. Better than fine. Waberski's no minnow. He's a whale—and you reeled him in: an active saboteur of US and British interests. A very dangerous one."

Grace took a moment to absorb this. She had, hadn't she? Grace Smith, runt of the litter off a farm in Huntington, Indiana. With a pencil, a worksheet and sheer stubbornness, she'd caught a murderous Hun—perhaps had an impact on the Great War.

Imagine that.

"Well. I missed you," she admitted. Immediately she felt awkward. "Your mind," she amended. Then she felt even more awkward for qualifying what she'd missed about him.

He slid her an amused side-eye, then they walked along in silence for a bit.

"What's wrong, Grace? You should be on top of the world, riding the crest of a triumph. Farquhar will shower you with champagne."

"Horrid man," Grace said. "I haven't been to the Villa for dinner in days. I don't wish to see him."

Robert stopped. "He's certainly irascible, unpredictable and eccentric, but horrid? Why do you say so?"

"No reason," she muttered.

Robert peered down at her.

She fixed her gaze on the lighthouse, with its odd flashes of light: *twenty-three skiddoo!*

He slid his index finger under her chin and gently raised it so that she had to meet his eyes. The gesture was too intimate between colleagues, but she didn't smack his hand away. "There's something you're not telling me."

"I'm... I'm going to have to leave Riverbank, Robert."

Shock slackened his features. "But *why?*"

"It's awful, because despite the sheer oddity of this place, I love it. And the work—where will I ever, *ever* be able to find work this exciting again? I want a life that's outside of the ordinary! And I'd found it here... it all feels so cruel and unfair..."

"Grace, what happened?" Robert's voice was gentle but also firm.

Reluctantly she told him, though the whole incident made her feel dirty and somehow at fault—ridiculous. She'd done nothing to encourage Farquhar.

Anger and disgust flashed across Robert's face, as well as something more primitive.

"Bastard," he said, quietly but with heat. "He's an overgrown, spoiled child. A dangerously intelligent, filthy-rich child. And we are his toys. His chess pieces to move around the board as he pleases."

It was true. Farquhar was a collector: of land, of property, of exotic animals; of books and ideas, knowledge and inventions. He was also a collector of people... people he treated as puppets. People who would put up with his erratic behavior to live and work in this paradise, and not in a box in some big city.

"He's gone too far."

"Yes, indeed he has. And part of the reason I've been avoiding the dinners is that I adore Nellie. She's been nothing but good to me, and I'm riddled with guilt."

"You didn't make the advances, Grace. He did."

"It's still beyond awkward. How can I dissemble and make small talk in this situation?"

Robert thought for a moment, then took off his hat and brushed the hair back from his forehead. "Grace. I care for you. I want to solve this."

"It's not a code or a cipher, Robert."

"No, but I want to protect you."

"You're sweet, but it's not so easy. I hardly think you should punch the colonel in the nose."

"Oh, how I'd like to," he said, his jaw clenched.

Grace was taken aback. Robert was a big man, physically imposing, but a gentle, thoughtful one. He wasn't the barroom brawl type.

"Thank you for the sentiment," she said. "*I'd* like to hang him from a treetop by his mustache. But it's not your problem to take on."

"Grace, let's get engaged," Robert said, without any preamble.

"What?"

"If my ring is on your finger, Farquhar won't bother you."

Grace gaped at him. "Robert, that's . . . very kind of you. Thank you. But the incident with the colonel isn't a reason to . . . get married."

"I'm making a hash out of this," he said, flushing. "We don't actually have to go through with a wedding, not if you don't want to. But . . . I'd like to. I've never met anyone quite like you before."

His eyes were so kind, his words so earnest and generous. She was briefly tempted by his offer, until she came to her senses again. "It's impossible. I'm a Quaker and you're a Jew. Religion is an issue, and you know it."

"My mother will have strong hysterics and need smelling salts. But you said you didn't care about my religion," he said quietly, searching her face to see if it was true.

"I don't give a damn about your being Jewish, Robert! It's a heritage, a faith. Not some sort of disgrace or taint! But others might..."

"Your parents?" His gaze intensified.

"They're Quakers. They wouldn't be delighted, but Quakers teach tolerance for others."

"Who else might care?"

"Your family would be greatly upset."

"I'll tell them to go to hell." He smiled.

"Neither kind nor diplomatic."

"All right. I'll use a different tactic. So is that a yes, then?"

"No."

"Why not?"

Grace threw up her hands.

"Is it a perhaps? Will you think about it quite seriously?"

Grace simply stared at him. The dear, sweet, lovely, chivalrous man. Which was better than the alternative sort of man, the one who tossed back whiskey while swinging in a chair on chains.

"You wouldn't be the *worst* husband in the world," she mused.

"Thank you." He grinned.

"But here's the thing, Robert. And I'm serious. I don't want to marry *anyone*. It's not personal. I just don't think I'm good wife material."

"Why not?"

"I've watched my father boss and bully my mother for over two decades."

"I'm no bully. Besides, we're only talking about an engagement, not an actual marriage. Remember?"

She sighed. "I'm stubborn, I'm cheeky, I have a bad temper, I loathe ironing and am hopeless at cooking. As for cleaning..." she trailed off, shaking her head.

"All qualities I desire most in a wife. Or at least in a fiancée. I have a list, you see."

"A list?" Grace asked, perplexed.

He nodded. "At the top, it says: Must Burn Holes in Shirts. Second on the list is: Must Toss Pots at My Head When Unhappy."

"Stop it, Robert." But she couldn't help laughing.

"Third on the list? Tongue Like a Viper."

She punched him lightly on the arm.

"We could send my shirts out to a laundry, you know. Even hire a housekeeper."

Grace stared at him. He looked absolutely serious. *I think I just fell a little bit in love with you. But only a little.* The words "hire a housekeeper" tripping off a man's lips...combined with a smile like Robert's...they were enough to make a gal swoon.

"Ah, I'm getting somewhere," he crowed.

They'd arrived at her cottage. The front windows glowed with lamplight that spilled out onto the porch. Stepping into a puddle of it, Grace said, "Robert Feldman, I suppose there's no other man to whom I'd rather be faux engaged. I accept."

It's not as though it's real. Grace, her stomach quivering and her chest tight, changed back into her nightgown for a few hours of much needed sleep. She rubbed at the bare fourth finger of her left hand as she rested her head on her pillow. *Nothing there, see? No tiny manacle. It's all just words. Words of friendship, not love.* Robert hadn't tried to touch her or kiss her. He'd teased her, affectionately. He'd reassured her. He wanted to protect her from Farquhar. He was such a kind and decent man.

Grace eventually sank into sleep for a couple of hours, but woke again in a cold sweat—haunted by the image of a boy swinging from a noose, clawing futilely at the rope around his neck.

She sat up gasping for air and feeling nauseous, trying and failing to shake off the nightmare. *He's a saboteur, Grace. A murderer. A spy.*

She slid out of bed, washed and dressed quickly. The best antidote to this—what was it? Farquhar would call it mawkishness—was to get back to work so that her brain would swirl with tornadoes of letters and numbers, not guilt.

Useless emotion, guilt. Especially under these circumstances. She went downstairs, tossed back some coffee and took a slice of toast with her on her walk back to the codebreaking unit's offices.

Once there, she hunkered down over yet another transposition cipher, the text of which had been transmitted via a mysterious but strong signal from a wireless station that had been overheard just as clearly in Dallas, Texas, as in San Antonio, near Fort Sam Houston.

Though Grace verified that the message was in German, radio operators had also picked it up clearly in Laredo and Del Rio.

"Dios mio," Veronica said, blinking rapidly. "They use, how you say? Goniometer along border. They triangulate the signal. Is coming from Chapultepec! In Mexico."

"What?" Grace stared at her.

"Si. Says so, aquí." She brandished the familiar yellow paper of a telegram. "Chapultepec, it is—"

"The official Mexican Government wireless station." Grace moistened her dry lips. "Good heavens. Our supposedly neutral neighbors to the south—"

"Don't seem to be so neutral," Alice cut in.

"The same message is repeated often at regular intervals. The station call changes each time. The operator never signs the message."

"Estraño, muy estraño." Veronica drummed her nails on the oak table.

"Hidden, and therefore almost certainly—"

"Importante."

"All right. Let me think. Let me continue to crack this beast…" Grace bent to her task again. Her coworkers disappeared from her consciousness, replaced by sequences of numbers diving, swimming, ducking and kicking through her eyes into some odd corner of her brain that analyzed them, noted repetitions, categorized them and ultimately pried meaning out of them.

A packet of cigarettes materialized in front of her at some point during the day, and Grace murmured a thank you without recognizing who'd put it there. She raided, lighted and smoked them one by one until the packet was empty and her throat stung.

A sandwich and a glass of water magically appeared at another point. Grace ate and drank unconsciously after another murmured thank you, not tasting a thing.

Hours went by; she didn't notice how many. She cajoled, guessed, wrangled and wrestled the plaintext letters from the belly of the German cipher beast, one and sometimes two at a time. She forced the monster to regurgitate a vowel here and there. She pried open its jaws and flossed its fangs for clues. At last, without mercy, she slew it.

Grace swam, dazed, back into consciousness and broke the surface of reality again. Smells registered first: the acrid black coffee in front of her, the whisper of stale bread crust, the toxic corpses of sucked-dry cigarettes littering her ashtray.

Then sounds returned: clattering typewriters, chattering telexes, ringing telephones, clicking heels, frustrated mutters.

Finally her colleagues rematerialized as she returned to earth from her travels inside the strange galaxy of her own brain.

Upon landing in the here and now again, Grace felt like a wet, muddy sock—if a sock could have strained eyeballs and a neck and shoulders that shrieked in agony.

"Oho, she's back with us!" Robert exclaimed.

She registered his smile, answered it automatically with her own, and then blanched when the word *fiancé* popped into her mind. Fiancé. She, Grace Smith, was engaged to be married to him. Had he really offered? Had she really accepted? Or was it all a dream?

Avoiding the topic, she looked back at the message she'd cracked, which at the moment was far more important than anything personal— this was about national security. She swallowed hard. "We've got to cable Washington right away. Germany is trying to set up direct wireless communication with Mexico, and to bribe Carranza to set fire to the oil fields in Tampico—"

"Qué?!" Veronica's black eyebrows shot up.

"—just as Berlin engineers a series of strikes, civil unrest and attacks on America's war-related industries. It's quite a diabolical plan—a plan that, if executed, will force us to join the war."

CHAPTER ELEVEN

The entire unit gathered around Grace and her plaintext, exclaiming and murmuring. "Are you quite sure?" Utsidi asked. "Why would Mexico agree to burn their own oil fields?"

"You mean Standard Oil's. It would hurt Mexican interests, but it would hurt American interests even more," Joe Rochefort pointed out. "John D. Rockefeller won't like this one bit."

"No, I daresay he won't," Fay said.

"What are the Germans offering in return?" Robert mused. "What might President Carranza want?"

Their answer came not via eavesdropping on the stations at Nauen or Chapultepec. It came in the form of the Zimmerman Telegram and was followed by none other than Colonel Mauborgne himself.

On March 1, 1917, Grace ran with the morning's newspaper to the codebreaking unit offices. She arrived breathless and burst through the door, waving it. "Robert! Fay! Alice! Veronica! Utsidi...have you seen this? The Zimmerman Telegram?" She slapped the *Washington Post* down on the long, ink-stained oak table. The headline blared: **GERMAN PLOT TO CONQUER US WITH AID OF JAPAN AND MEXICO REVEALED**.

"British intelligence intercepted a coded Western Union telegram from Berlin—before it could reach the German ambassador in Mexico City. They cracked it and handed it over to US intelligence—now we know what Mexico negotiated for. Look at the actual text of the telegram."

"Good Lord," Alice said. "The Germans offer to return Texas, New Mexico and Arizona to Mexico! In exchange for money, cooperation and diplomacy in recruiting Japan to their side."

Robert nodded gravely. "This will mean war."

"Of course." But Grace felt sick. "How else can President Wilson respond? He's turned somersaults to stay neutral, but this—he cannot ignore this."

"And they plan to bring England to its knees via submarine warfare. What utter bastards," Joe said. "Pardon the colorful language, ladies."

Grace shrugged. "Wilson's already furious that their U-boats destroyed four American ships just last month."

"Offering up territory to Mexico is a nice touch, isn't it?" Fay said dryly. "Keeps our troops occupied at home instead of being sent to Europe. It's similar to the Hindu separatist gambit."

"Those states did originally belong to Mexico," Veronica pointed out. But she subsided under their collective withering glare.

"And the US once belonged to Britain," Grace said tartly.

Utsidi raised her eyebrows but remained silent. Nobody ever acknowledged that the entire country had been stolen from the Native Americans, their cultures and tribes and languages virtually wiped out.

Robert cleared his throat as if thinking exactly that, then patted his pockets for cigarettes. Alice produced her own pack. They handed the smokes around, everyone lighting up with trembling fingers.

War.

Thousands—tens of thousands—of American boys would die. It went without saying. Sons, grandsons, nephews, brothers, cousins... every family in the United States would be affected. Every US citizen would become a prisoner of constant, gnawing fear, starved for any scrap of information available, praying every waking moment that loved ones were safe.

Colonel Mauborgne arrived at Riverbank the next week to speak to Farquhar and the unit. His eyes no longer twinkled behind the round spectacles he wore, fleshy pouches had formed underneath the wire rims and his complexion had gone as green as his uniform.

Farquhar strutted at his side, clad in a fine three-piece suit that somehow made him look like a caricature of a statesman. He'd even waxed his mustache for the occasion.

"Good afternoon, ladies and gentlemen," said Mauborgne. "First, allow me to thank you most sincerely for your stellar cryptanalytic work over the past eight months. Your progress here at Riverbank has been truly remarkable, and the United States is in your—and Colonel Farquhar's—debt. As you well know, we began this century at a cryptological disadvantage, relying upon outdated Civil War codes and ciphers while other nations surged ahead. We were too busy with Reconstruction in the South and healing the collective wounds of the country.

"It's with deepest appreciation to you brave and committed souls that we are now catching up in terms of codebreaking. Your work is also leading to the development of more secure cryptological systems and devices—systems and devices that we will need to rely upon as we move inevitably toward the Great War in Europe."

"What did I tell you?" Farquhar said aloud, to no one in particular. "War."

Mauborgne sighed and rubbed at his chin. "Once Congress declares war on Germany—and for that matter, Japan—Uncle Sam will still need each and every one of you. But protocols on the handling of sensitive materials will change, effective immediately. We can no longer send large batches of coded transmissions via courier, train or even telegram. It's too risky—"

"What's this?!" Farquhar looked as though Mauborgne had thrown a combat boot at his head.

"So I've come personally to invite you all to take up similar jobs in Washington, DC, for a new unit called MI-8 at the Army War College…"

"The hell you say!" Farquhar's blood was up. "My unit stays right here, on *my* property. How dare you, sir?"

Grace exchanged an uneasy glance with Robert.

Alice looked amused.

Most of the other codebreakers kept their expressions carefully blank.

Mauborgne turned to face Farquhar. "I suggest we speak about this privately."

"I suggest that you not be a bloody ungrateful stinking poacher!"

"Colonel," said the real one to the pretender, "as I've said, the Army *is* most grateful for your aid and your patriotism. But this decision comes down from the highest levels, with the knowledge and approval of General Pershing himself. It's out of my hands."

"Banana oil. These are MY people. They'll go to Washington, DC, over my dead body. I'm of a mind to paste you!"

Mauborgne stayed deadly calm. "Do so, *sir*, and you'll leave here in a meat wagon."

The two men were both of the same height, but whereas Mauborgne was trim and fit, Farquhar was bloated. Yet Grace didn't like the mad gleam in his eyes.

Robert, sitting beside her, stood up.

Oh dear. Grace wanted to tug him back down to his chair. *He's going to try to redirect the tension.*

"Colonel Farquhar, it seems to me a question of simple patriotism— and duty—for the unit to relocate to the capitol."

"Did I ask for your opinion, Feldman?" Riverbank's owner roared. "Sit down before I knock your teeth down your throat."

Robert didn't say another word, but he didn't sit, either.

One by one, the other men in the unit stood up: Joe Rochefort, the Yale man, Vanderbilt, Brooklyn and all. Grace climbed to her feet, too, followed by Alice, Utsidi and Veronica. Grace took Fay's hand.

Joe Mauborgne assessed them all with his cool gray eyes and nodded his thanks for their unspoken support.

"Not one of you is welcome at my table tonight!" shouted Farquhar.

He was sending them, like naughty children, to bed without supper.

"And I'll bloody well have any deserters shot at the gates..." He subsided into bluster and muttered curses, then marched out of the room.

PART II

WORLD WAR I

[Codebreaking], particularly in the early stages of a diffi-cult cryptanalysis, is perhaps the most excruciating, exas-perating, agonizing mental process known to man.
                                        —David Kahn, *The Codebreakers*

CHAPTER TWELVE

On April 6, 1918, the *Washington Post* headlines were brutal: **HOUSE, IN ALL-NIGHT DEBATE...VOTES FOR WAR**. And the next day it was official. The *Chicago Daily Tribune* blared: **US AT WAR**.

"I want to go and work in Washington, DC," Robert told Grace. "But I don't want to leave without you. Marry me?"

She dropped her pencil and stared at him. "Robert...I want to leave, too. I want to do this work. I want to help my country. But I'm not ready to be a wife."

He cocked his head. "You say *wife* as if it's a curse."

She locked eyes with him. "It is. We've had this talk. And Robert," she hesitated. "I adore you as my friend. You know that. But I'm not madly in love with you."

He blinked. "You realize that I'm working to change that."

Grace flushed.

"I *will* change that." His tone was decisive.

"Is that some kind of challenge?"

"No. It's a fact." He smiled at her.

Grace's lips parted. *Is there anything more attractive in a man than confidence?* "I see."

"No, I don't think you do. Being of the inferior sex, you wouldn't understand the subtleties of my plot."

"*Oh!*"

He grinned. "If you don't marry me, your father will fly into a rage and say it's not proper for you to go unchaperoned to the nation's capital."

Grace couldn't deny it.

His eyes twinkled.

You devious man, you.

"How about it?" Robert stood up and stretched his arms behind his back. He rolled his head back and forth, trying to ease the tension that built there after hours of codebreaking work.

"Colonel Farquhar would fly into a rage, too."

Robert's mouth flattened into a thin line. "And?"

"The kind of rage we've never seen."

"Farquhar doesn't own us. We are not his property. He cannot dictate our lives."

"He's certainly doing his best. Do you really think he'd shoot us?"

"I won't let him, Grace." So saying, he caught her in his arms.

She froze, gazing up into his hazel eyes. A lock of his hair had fallen over his forehead, and his expression was so tender that it made her heart ache. His smile played the *Wedding March*, and it was coming for her.

What is he doing to me? Why is he so magnetic, this man?

And then Robert kissed her, deeply. It was a knee-weakening kiss, unlike any of the previous ones. This was a kiss that altered her perception of him forever.

It wasn't polite. It wasn't scholarly. It wasn't elegant...and he didn't apologize.

It left her breathless, and he knew it. The knowledge shone from his eyes, tilting the axis of power between them.

Grace liked it. But she didn't *like* that she liked it.

She pulled out of his arms and ran from the room.

The idea of leaving the cocoon of Riverbank to work for the War Department in the nation's capital was both exhilarating and intimidating, not to mention forbidden—as expected.

Grace,

Enough is enough, wrote her father.

You are to return home at once. You are doing grave, if not irreparable, damage to your reputation and good name—which, may I remind you, is my own good name...

Your mother is beyond upset at your behavior and continued will-fulness. She's weak and ill. Your recalcitrance and callousness for her feelings will no doubt contribute to her demise, and that will always stain your conscience.

We have need of you, Grace. I will forgive your college debt if you return home; I never had a prayer of you repaying me anyhow.

Your silly fascination with a long-dead playwright is bad enough. I will not tolerate a daughter of mine living unsupervised in a big city. To that end, I enclose the funds for your train ticket back to Indiana, where you belong.

Your loving father,

J-S

Grace crumpled the letter and threw it across the room.

Robert looked up from the message he was poring over and lifted an eyebrow.

"Your father?" Robert queried.

"Yes. Orders me to return home." Grace buried her face in her hands.

"Then ignore his edict. Marry me. Marry me and let's go to Washington."

She stared at him. *This, again...this impossible dilemma.* What was wrong with her? Wasn't marriage what every girl dreamed of?

Robert crossed the room and went down on one knee. He took her hand. "Do me the honor. It's the only way you'll be free."

Her heart turned over.

It was true—and yet it wasn't.

I'll be exchanging one cage for another. Grace, feeling helpless, put her other hand up to his cheek, sandpapery with stubble. She traced his angular jaw. He closed his eyes and leaned into her touch, revealing a naked yearning for her.

It caused her shame, made her feel cruel. She didn't want this peculiar power over him. It unnerved her. What was she to do with it, when she didn't reciprocate his desire? His...passion.

Even the concept made her uncomfortable. *What an overblown, fevered word for an ephemeral emotion vomited up by a thousand long-dead poets.*

Passion…merely a euphemism for an undignified animal urge. One that she didn't feel in the slightest. And if she married Robert, she'd have to…submit…to him.

She could imagine hugging him, kissing him. But her mind shut down at the thought of anything more. He was her friend, her colleague, her puzzling partner.

All Grace wanted was to be independent, to live a life outside the mundane.

And marriage: Could anything more truly embody the mundane? It meant sharing walls, sharing meals, sharing thoughts and soap and tooth powder and…a toilet. Sharing her body, which would no longer be her own. *Nothing* would be her own.

"You're such a good man, Robert," Grace managed.

His eyes flew open, more green than hazel at this moment. "I don't want to be a good man." His voice had gone gravelly. His fingers tightened around hers. "I want to do wicked things—" His gaze fell to her bosom.

Her mind froze; her body tensed.

"I love you, Grace." He said it roughly, threw it at her as if he hoped it would knock down her resistance.

She untangled her fingers from his and would have stood up if he hadn't blocked her way, being almost in her lap.

"I'm sorry. I'm scaring you." Robert stood up and ran a hand roughly through his impeccably combed hair, mussing it. "I'm a brute."

"No," Grace said. "That's the last thing you are. You're brilliant and honest and kind and thoughtful and funny. But…I don't…I can't… love you. I'm not sure why. I wish I could."

Robert's face fell. Then he brought his chin up. "Do you like me?"

"Of course."

"Trust me?"

She hesitated, then nodded.

"Then the rest will come. I promise you. It will." He stood tall, sure of himself, sure of her—which both touched her and annoyed her. He displayed not a trace of wounded ego or anger. Only simple, dogged determination.

How can a man be so confident in the face of rejection?

"Marry me, Grace. You'll learn to love me, I swear."

Her mouth had gone dry. He was a good man. She wouldn't find better, and she knew it. She wanted to go to work in Washington.

Grace nodded.

"I'm afraid Farquhar will have our throats cut," Grace said to Robert while packing up the day before they left.

"He's a bully, not a murderer."

"The one doesn't preclude the other, does it? Besides, I can't leave without saying goodbye to Nellie."

"Do you think that's wise?"

"I don't care if it's wise or not...she's been good to me."

Grace found Nellie in the rose garden, plucking aphids off the American Beauties and dropping them into a mason jar. The aphids looked disgruntled, and Grace supposed she couldn't blame them.

"Nellie?"

"Hmm?" Mrs. Farquhar turned. "Hello, Grace." She screwed the lid onto the jar, then gave the creatures a shake while they scrambled for purchase on the slick glass. "Little beasts. How are you?"

"Very well, thank you. So...there's no easy way to say this. And I must ask you to keep mum. Robert and I—we're going to...elope."

Nellie's face lit up and she seized Grace's left hand, looking puzzled when she found no ring.

Grace felt herself flush.

"Congratulations, my dear."

"We'll be working in Washington, DC, for the War Department. I wanted to say goodbye. And I can't ever thank you enough for giving me a second chance here."

"A chance you richly deserved, my dear."

"The colonel won't be happy. Will he set the dogs on us?"

Nellie laughed. "Of course not." Then she looked speculative. "Perhaps the bears."

Grace's mouth dropped open.

Nellie chortled and slapped her lightly on the arm with her gardening gloves. "That was a joke, dear. Garrett's bark is much worse than his bite. He's a bully and a show-off and his need to control everything is quite tiresome, but deep inside he's simply a ten-year-old boy who could never please his father."

Grace tried to digest this. Reconcile it with the tyrant she knew.

"When are you leaving, dear? Can I give you two a lift to the railway station?"

"The colonel won't like that," said Grace.

Nellie cast her an amused glance. "No, he won't. That's part of the fun."

Fun?

Grace reached into her pocket and pulled out Nellie's pearls and pin. She held them out. "I can't take these with me—really, I can't."

Nellie closed Grace's fingers around them. "You can and you will. I gave them to you, and I haven't changed my mind."

"Thank you." Grace swallowed. "You were forced to, though. And I...that is to say...I...want you to know that there has never been anything...untoward...with your—"

"My dear," Nellie interrupted. "I know that. Garrett gets intermittently smitten. I can't be bothered about it—keeps him out from under my feet. Now, when shall I fetch you two from Engledew Cottage? Tomorrow morning?"

Grace nodded, thanked her profusely and went back to the unit's offices in a daze. The Farquhars' marriage was even odder than her own promised to be. She wasn't sure how she felt about that. Nellie seemed contented enough, even knowing that her husband strayed.

What if Robert looked elsewhere? Something hot and sharp flashed through her. She hated the idea.

Nellie showed up the next morning as promised. She was resplendent in a yellow silk dress dotted with white daisies, rubber rain boots and a rope of opera-length pearls that she'd triple-draped around her neck. She wore a hat adorned with artificial lemons, a scarf holding it in place and tied under her chin. But her most striking accessory was the pair of zebras in harness pulling the buggy she drove.

Nellie waved gaily. "Climb in, my dears!"

Grace hadn't seen the zebras since the day Farquhar had kidnapped her and they'd bolted due to the grenades going off in the trenches. "They're tame?"

"Heavens, yes." Nellie held the reins with authority. "They're a pair of glorified mules—eat their heads off. Sorely in need of exercise, so the trip to the station will do them good. Now, hop in!"

Robert and Grace exchanged a glance. His shoulders shook. But he kept his head down and loaded their trunks and suitcases into the back of the buggy. It was shiny black with the wheels painted yellow.

Robert then helped Grace up and into the back seat before he joined her. With a snap of the reins, they were off. The buggy lurched forward, swaying behind the rhythmic clop-clop of the zebras.

Nellie kept up a steady stream of chatter along the way, calling over her shoulder to them. "Now, Grace, promise me that you'll write. I shall enjoy hearing all about your adventures in the capital."

"Of course," Grace said.

"I have something for you two—actually, let's give it to Robert— and a letter of introduction that may prove useful." Reins in her right hand, she patted around for her pocketbook with her left.

Grace eyed the zebras nervously, but they didn't seem interested in bolting.

"Aha. Here they are." Nellie handed back a sealed letter and a small, lumpy brown package tied with string. "Don't open the package until later, Robert, dear."

"All right," Robert said. "Thank you." He slipped it into his pocket.

The letter was to... Grace's eyes widened. *To Mrs. Franklin D. Roosevelt?*

"Eleanor is an absolute love," Nellie called. "And she knows everyone in Washington. Please do call on her and send my regards. Her husband is assistant secretary of the Navy, you know."

"I—I'll do that. Thank you." Grace hung on to her hat as the buggy veered to dodge a tree limb in the road.

"You know the Hitts, of course?"

"Yes, met them here at Riverbank."

"Genevieve is a darling, isn't she? Also in your field, though she's in San Antonio. Cultivate her," Nellie ordered, making her sound rather like a rare herb or flower. "And meet Katherine Mauborgne."

Grace had no idea how to accomplish this, but she nodded.

"Throw a dinner party," suggested Nellie, beaming.

Oh, of course. Under my supervision, toast burns, eggs congeal, cakes collapse and soufflés fall... but most assuredly, I should throw a dinner party. Not that they even had a house to call their own yet.

Nellie, the buggy and the zebras attracted quite a bit of attention as they neatly swerved around a milk truck and a taxi and pulled up to the front entrance of the railway station. The drivers of both vehicles gaped. Children pointed and wanted to pet the strange "horses." Mothers held them back. Nellie seemed not to notice.

"Here we are! Now, Robert, you find a porter while I say my good-byes to Grace." She waved him off and helped Grace down herself. "Well. You're off on a brand-new adventure, aren't you? An important one. Our country needs you far more than Garrett does, so don't fret."

Grace nodded.

"And don't be afraid of marriage, dear." Nellie patted her cheek. "Mine may be odd, but it works, for better or for worse."

Startled, Grace asked, "How did you...?"

"It's written all over your face. He's a good man and he loves you, my dear. Allow yourself to love him back."

"I—"

"You can love someone without him swallowing you whole. You can still have a mind of your own—ambitions of your own."

"That isn't how things work in my family," Grace said. "My father's still demanding that I come home. I know obeying him would have been the right thing to do—he's my father—and I *always* do the right thing…but in this case, I couldn't. I'd shrivel up and die there. Disintegrate into dust."

Nellie nodded, compassion and understanding in her eyes. "Well," her tone was brisk. "Now the right thing to do is to stay with your husband. Your papa can't argue with that."

Grace twisted her fingers and examined the daisies dotting Nellie's dress.

"Ah. You haven't told them yet? Your families?"

Grace shook her head. "We were waiting to get to Washington first."

"Ooh. So it's a properly scandalous elopement." Nellie's eyes sparkled. "Excellent."

Robert reappeared with a porter, who dealt efficiently with their luggage.

Nellie seized Grace by the shoulders and kissed her on both cheeks. "It will all be perfectly fine, dear." She held out her hand to Robert and shook his. "Bon voyage! Do come back to visit. Don't be afraid of Garrett—in a few days, he'll be distracted by something else and forget all about the unpleasantness."

CHAPTER THIRTEEN

They were married at the Chicago courthouse, the plan being to continue on to Washington the day after. Robert sported an elegant gray morning suit and bow tie.

Grace purchased her white lace dress and a veiled fascinator at Marshall Field's on credit, with a down payment of money she usually sent to her father each month. She wore the silk unmentionables and stockings Nellie had supplied, which whispered decadently over her skin. She slipped her feet into white satin slippers that were so pristine and elegant they surely belonged to someone else—someone less complicated than she, someone normal and full of joy on her wedding day. A girl who'd ask her father to give her away, who'd treasure the moment—not a daughter so jaded and shameful that she hadn't even told him of her wedding.

Who do you think you are? His words—and Mrs. Gallup's—echoed through her mind. The unspoken words of all the little gray men at the employment agencies.

Who do you think you are?

I'm Grace Smith, soon to be Grace Smith Feldman. I am a woman and yet a codebreaker for the United States Army. I am a soldier with a pencil instead of a rifle. A soldier in a corset and garters. And . . . I'm proud of myself.

Grace also wore Nellie's pearls and a frown—which Robert turned upside down with both index fingers and a chaste kiss to her forehead.

He'd brought her a bouquet of white roses, and she was absurdly touched. He'd also brought Nellie's lumpy package, without the string.

"What is it?" Grace asked, as he slipped it into an inner breast pocket of his suit.

"Something useful," he said, his mouth curving mysteriously as he echoed Nellie's words.

And he'd brought along his grandmother's wedding ring, given to him on her deathbed.

Robert took her small hand in his large one and squeezed. She swallowed a lump in her throat. His confidence reassured her. She sent up a message to his grandmother.

I want to love him. I truly do. I'll try. And I'll be the best wife to him that I'm capable of being. I promise.

The judge looked impatiently at his pocket watch, as if he had better things to do than entertain the nerves of a silly, recalcitrant bride. "Shall we get on with things?"

"We're waiting for the witnesses, Your Honor," Robert said. "Apologies. They should be here any moment."

Witnesses? Grace hadn't even thought to ask any. She turned as a polite hubbub erupted in the hallway outside the judge's chambers and gasped.

The entire codebreaking unit had arrived, spit shined and polished, dressed in their very best. Joe Rochefort pushed Fay's wheelchair in first. He was followed by Utsidi, Veronica and their plus ones. Yale man, Vanderbilt and Brooklyn came in next, and of course Alice, who radiated ennui and had brought along a date of her own. The entire party was ushered in by none other than a sunny, mischievous Nellie, towing a glowering Farquhar.

While she could have done without *him*, Grace was so touched by the presence of the others that her eyes filled. And she quite respected Nellie for putting her husband's randy ambitions to bed with such utter aplomb.

Nellie winked at her. *Winked.*

Grace bit back a grin and glanced up at Robert. "Bobby, you absolute *sneak.*"

He gazed down at her tenderly. Oh, that musical smile . . . as if it were playing *Pachelbel's Canon*. It plucked at her heartstrings.

Then it occurred to Grace that witnesses were the last thing she wanted at her faux wedding. They made it all too real, these people she'd worked with so closely and come to care about.

The judge cleared his throat and looked again at his pocket watch. He was of course clad in black robes. Suitable for the funeral of her freedom.

Grace swallowed panic and lost time for a bit as he began the timeworn nuptial vows, until his words brought the occasion sharply back into focus.

"Do you, Robert Feldman, take this woman, Grace Smith, as your lawfully wedded wife?"

"I do," Robert said, imbuing the words with male pride and a dreadful enthusiasm.

The image of Rascal moving against Dolly's hind end on the Smith family farm flashed into her mind. Heaving and straining, scrabbling for purchase as his hooves slipped off the mare's hindquarters.

Robert fished into his pocket for Nellie's lumpy package. He opened it to reveal a note, which was wrapped around a handkerchief, which was wrapped around an enormous cushion-cut diamond ring.

"Wh—what is *that*?" Grace whispered.

Bobby flashed the note at her.

From my first husband, Nellie had scrawled. *Wear it proudly, darling. Lord knows I don't need it any longer...xo.*

"Is there a problem?" the judge asked.

"Yes," Grace said. *This was Nellie's* second *marriage?*

"Not at all," Bobby said, overriding her. He slipped the monster diamond ring, along with his grandmother's wedding ring, onto a bemused Grace's fourth finger. The diamond flashed at her like Farquhar's lighthouse. *Twenty-three skiddoo! Keep out.*

The colonel's face purpled, and he cast an outraged glance at his wife, who simply patted his beefy arm while Grace fought an utterly inappropriate urge to laugh—and simultaneously weep.

"Do you, Grace Smith," the judge intoned, "take this man, Robert Feldman, as your lawfully wedded husband?"

She blinked again in shock at the ring. *No. Why can't a woman go off to a new city and take a job just like a man, without aspersions being cast upon her character? Why must she marry first? And how can I possibly accept this...this...boulder from Nellie? It's much, much too much!*

At least the vows didn't involve protestations of love.

Robert waited, a muscle twitching at his jawline. The poor man. Patient and sweet, even as the tension in the chamber mounted and the risk of his utter humiliation grew.

"Miss Smith?" prompted the judge, eyeing the gargantuan gewgaw and raising splendid white eyebrows, as if to question her sanity as a female if she didn't accept it.

Nellie nodded so enthusiastically that the tulips around the crown of her hat danced and jiggled. She flapped her hands at Grace.

The entire room held its collective breath.

At last Grace said grudgingly, "I do." *Oh dear. This is a promise, same as you made to the US government when you agreed to adhere to the Espionage Act. One you must not break.*

Robert squeezed her fingers. His joy and relief were palpable.

The impromptu peanut gallery cheered.

"I now pronounce you man and wife," stated the judge. He shot Robert an indulgent smile and leaned back in his chair. "You may kiss the bride."

Robert turned to her with a fond expression and took her face between his big, warm hands. "May I?" Was that a trace of humor in his voice?

She glowered at him. "Yes."

"You won't bite?" His eyes danced as he leaned toward her, brushing his lips against hers, soft as a feather.

She'd steeled herself against the kiss, and so she felt nothing.

Then he whispered into her ear: "Is it so miserable to have acquired a husband this afternoon?"

"Quite." But his whisper sent a shiver through her, even if the kiss had not.

"You can try me on at different angles and for different occasions, Grace. Rather like a new hat," he teased.

"Sign here," the judge ordered, waving the marriage certificate at them, along with a pen.

Grace took the pen reluctantly and scribbled her name through the smear of moisture that had gathered in her eyes. She was no longer self-possessed.

She was possessed by Robert Feldman.

Which, she supposed, was better than being possessed by the devil.

*   *   *

Nellie had arranged a surprise reception at the glorious Palmer House hotel to celebrate Grace and Robert's wedding before they traveled on to Washington, DC, the next day. "Such a pity that you can't honeymoon in Italy, my dears, what with this wretched war going on...but look! The champagne's arrived, and the cake awaits." She clapped her hands. "Come, let's have ourselves a lovely toast to our newlyweds!"

Everyone had a champagne coupe in hand and turned as one to raise them. "To Mr. and Mrs. Robert Feldman! To your happiness!"

The closer they got to retiring for the evening, the more nervous Grace was about doing her "duty." She'd purchased a negligee and peignoir at Marshall Field's, with matching slippers. But what was a girl to do after donning them?

Robert will know...

The whole idea of it horrified her. The act she'd seen horses engage in on the farm was so crass and undignified. Worse, she no longer had a choice. A wife must submit to her husband.

Grace felt sick as they arrived at the door to their room.

Robert gazed down at her tenderly as he opened it, then swept her up and carried her over the threshold. She thought of the rotating arms of the windmill back at Riverbank, and wanted to flail her own.

Her new husband carried her all the way to the bed while she did her best to combat a cold sweat. A silver bucket containing ice and a bottle of champagne rested on the nightstand.

Robert set her down and kissed her lightly on the lips. "For my new bride."

He poured the fizzy liquid gold into two crystal flutes, waited patiently for the foam to subside then topped them up. He handed her one.

"To our mutual happiness," he said, and clinked his glass against hers.

Grace drank hers straight down as his eyebrows lifted. Then she sneezed because the bubbles had somehow convened in her nose.

Robert gave her a quicksilver smile and his beautifully folded handkerchief, then excused himself to the bathroom.

Grace looked around the room—anywhere but at the dreaded bed. She drifted to the balcony doors—they were on the third floor—and peered out at the thousands of tiny lights in the distance, beckoning her into a new life.

"More champagne?" Robert asked from behind her.

"Yes, please." She might require an entire bottle to get through the coming ordeal.

Hooves slipping on hindquarters...pants...grunts. Grace closed her eyes.

Robert observed her as she tossed back half of her second flute. "You might wish to drink that a little more slowly."

Grace froze, then set the flute down. She took a deep breath and then went to her traveling case.

"What's wrong, darling?"

"Nothing at all." She extracted the package that contained the nightgown, robe and slippers and went into the bathroom with it.

When she came out, she avoided Robert's gaze and hung up her wedding gown.

"Grace," he said, his voice husky.

She steeled herself and turned to face him.

"You're..." He seemed barely able to speak. "You're so lovely. So beautiful."

She stood there awkwardly.

"I can't believe you're mine." He leaned his palms on his knees and shook his head.

Despite the compliments—and what girl didn't want to hear a man say those things?—anger flashed through her. *I'm no longer me. I'm your wife. An accessory, not a person in my own right.*

Robert got up and moved toward her, his eyes full of stars.

She had to blink sudden tears away because those stars hurt her. He was in love, and she didn't know what that meant. He was in love with *her,* and that was terrifying. Right here and right now, she was already letting him down. *Oh, Robert...I'm an awful person. Why did I allow you to talk me into this?*

He gathered her into his arms, snugging her head under his chin. His body was warm against hers, his heartbeat a little fast, and something hard nudged against her abdomen. Something she refused to picture. "I love you," he said.

Say it back. Say it, Grace. It's now your job. But she couldn't. She'd choke on the words if she tried to say them. "You're the best man in the world, Robert." She pulled away and smiled. "And so very handsome."

All right. Let's get this over with. Grace shimmied out of the peignoir, hung it on the coatrack by the door and took another slug of her champagne. Then she sat on the bed, waiting for him to join her. Do the Thing that had to be done.

Robert contemplated her. Unknotted his tie. Took a sip of his own champagne. He removed his shoes and socks. He slipped out of his jacket and vest. Unbuttoned the top two buttons on his shirt. Had another sip of champagne. Unbuttoned his trousers and slid them off, revealing well-formed, muscular legs.

He hung every item up at leisure, in a corner wardrobe she'd barely noticed.

Grace could no longer stand the suspense. "Shall we...that is to say...get on with it?"

Robert turned to face her in his shirt and undershorts. His mouth quivered almost imperceptibly. "It?"

Her face burned. "You know."

As he crossed the room, her heart almost galloped out of her chest. Her pulse thudded in her ears. *What will he look like without the shirt?*

Robert sat down next to her on the bed. He pulled her into his lap and kissed her, gently exploring her mouth, letting her explore his. Then he got to his feet, still holding her, flipped back the eiderdown and sheet and snuggled them both into the bed, spooning against her.

He pulled the covers back over them, tucking them under her body to ward off the chill.

He didn't undress her. He didn't poke at her. He didn't pry or prod.

Grace lay against him, internalizing the rhythm of his heartbeat, growing more and more confused. Didn't he *want* to do the Thing? Was something wrong?

"Good night, my love," Robert said.

And then the dratted man fell asleep.

Grace lay there, mystified. She wasn't sure whether she was relieved or disappointed.

She decided upon relieved as she, too, drifted off to sleep.

She woke to Robert's lips on the nape of her neck, an unexpected pleasure that sent eddies of sunshine down her spine. She was deliciously warm, his arms still around her. She felt…safe, not trapped. Protected, not pinned down.

Then the realization that she was now a *wife* washed over her again. As a wife, she should get up instantly to anticipate his needs. Put on water to boil for coffee. Make toast.

She wriggled free of his arms, ignoring his mumbled protest, and slipped out of their warm nest only to remember that they were in a hotel. Of course there was no kettle. Nor was there any bread, or even an icebox.

"Why are you prowling, woman?" Robert asked sleepily.

"I was going to make breakfast—I forgot where we were."

"Come back to bed." He smiled, his hair mussed from the pillow.

She eyed him warily. Did he want to do the Thing? And with no champagne to make it easier?

Robert sighed. "I'm not a monster, Grace. I'll never force myself on you. Ever. Even if we both die celibate—"

For some reason, that struck her as hilarious: two wrinkled old virgins being tipped into their coffins, her heroic husband instantly acquiring a halo before arriving at the pearly gates.

"—perish the thought," he finished on a glum note. "What are you laughing at?"

She clamped a hand over her mouth and bent double, her shoulders shaking.

Robert sat up. "You find it *amusing*, do you?"

"S-sorry," she gasped.

"You were quite entertaining yourself last night. What were you going to do—lie back like a Victorian maiden and do your duty?"

Ouch. Grace bit her lip.

"I thought so," Robert said wryly. He threw off the bedclothes and got up.

So this is marriage. What an interesting start.

CHAPTER FOURTEEN

They found a starter apartment in Washington, DC, which was, in reality, a large piano-and-ballet studio during the day, with a sleeper sofa and a kitchenette. They kept away during business hours, when the owners gave music and dance lessons to retirees, bored housewives and students. But the price was right, and in the evenings, it was all theirs. Below it was a bakery, which made breakfast simple.

Grace had put off writing to her parents to tell them the big news, but her sister Evie threatened to tell them herself if she didn't.

1918, Washington, DC

Dear Mother and Papa,

I have some news that you may find a bit startling, but there's no gentle way to break it: My friend and colleague Robert Feldman and I have gotten married! Bobby is a wonderful soul, and before you ask, Papa: yes, he's a man of good "prospects."

In fact, we have both accepted positions with the Army Signal Corps. Bobby has been commissioned a first lieutenant. I will carry on support duties as a clerk—They wanted Bobby so badly that they accepted me, too. It is very kind of the Corps to allow me to aid in the war effort, and I feel that I'm doing my part.

The Munitions Building, where we will work with fourteen thousand(!) other employees, is on the National Mall. Trolleys and motorcars create a bedlam in the city, and often there are armies of suffragettes marching on the Capitol and the White House with signs, urging President Wilson to address the voting rights of women. Of course, he's got much on his mind these days—the Great War—so crowds of hostile men remind the marchers of this and tell them to go home.

We've rented a darling apartment and plan to enjoy the theater and symphony as much as possible. I've not gotten much better at cooking, sad to say.

At any rate, you'll be relieved that I've left That Place and salvaged my reputation . . . though reports of harlots performing vaudeville in the vegetable gardens were greatly exaggerated.

> *Your loving daughter,*
> *Grace*

While Grace felt it was perfectly reasonable to announce their news to her parents in writing, Robert said the same could not be done with his parents. He was the eldest child, and they had to tell them in person. So she and Robert boarded a train bound for Pittsburgh.

The Feldmans lived in a second-floor walk-up apartment in a shabby-chic neighborhood. Robert held Grace's hand as they approached their door, which faced them at the end of a hall with peeling flowered wallpaper that someone had tried to glue back down, with limited success.

Grace felt her new wedding ring digging into her finger as Robert rapped. "My mother will love you," he said reassuringly.

The door opened to reveal a tidy, plump woman in a starched apron, her hair scraped back in a severe bun. Her hazel eyes, so much like Robert's, lit up at the sight of him. "My darling boy! My boy!"

Grace stood awkwardly to the side as she hugged him, kissed him, hugged him again and then pinched his cheeks. Meanwhile, a tall, gaunt man with a neatly trimmed beard came to greet them, clapping Robert on the shoulder. "Well, then," he said gruffly. "Well, then. Good to see you, son."

The couple's eyes then turned to her. "And who is this, my dear?" asked Robert's mother.

"Mama, Papa." Robert beamed. "This is my wife, Grace."

"Your...?"

Grace produced her most charming smile and held out her hand. "How do you do, Mr. and Mrs. Feldman?"

Robert's mother fainted dead away.

Mr. Feldman caught her before she hit the floor. He and Robert made the poor woman comfortable on the couch, while Grace rushed into the unfamiliar kitchen, searching for a kettle and some tea. It was full of unfamiliar aromas and foods: a platter of eggs and salted fish, a great pot of thick, crimson soup that smelled of beets, a pan full of yellow dumplings, a loaf of black bread. If she wasn't mistaken, there was brisket in the oven.

There simply wasn't room for a kettle on the stove. Grace moved the pan of dumplings onto the kitchen table, lit the burner they were on and put the water to boil.

She searched the cupboards and located mugs and a canister that held strong loose-leaf black tea. She spooned some into a mug—no sign of a strainer anywhere.

She peeked into the parlor, where the men held smelling salts under Mrs. Feldman's nose.

She revived, batted them away, sat up and moaned, "*Wife?* Oh, my boy—what have you *done?*"

Grace retreated, mortified. Robert murmured something to his mother that she couldn't quite overhear. Then came several strings of words in a language she couldn't understand, punctuated by the word *shiksa*. Wailing followed.

To Grace's relief, the kettle soon screamed, since she couldn't. She plucked it off the stove and filled the mug with boiling water, doing her best to tamp down the tea leaves with a spoon.

The wailing in the living room did not abate, even though the men did their best to soothe Mrs. Feldman.

After a minute or two, Grace chased the tea leaves around with the spoon, fishing them out as best she could. Some had already sunk to the bottom of the cup, and evaded capture. There was no sugar to be found. Perhaps it was kept in the dining room.

She carried the steaming mug out to her new mother-in-law, whose face was mottled and blotched with tears. "Ma'am?"

Mrs. Feldman pressed her lips together but accepted the mug.

The frozen, polite silence that ensued was somehow worse than the wailing.

Grace looked in mute appeal at Robert, who crossed the room and slid his arm around her. "Mama, perhaps we should give you some time to absorb the news," he said.

Mr. Feldman walked them to the door. "Come back for dinner," he said. "Everything will be all right by then." He leaned down and pecked Grace on the cheek. "Welcome to the family, my dear."

Grace smiled gratefully, and they made their exit.

Mrs. Feldman's brisket was as hot and tender as the woman herself was cold and forbidding. Her borscht—though Grace disliked beets—was wonderful, as were the dumplings and everything else she set on the table. The apple kugel was particularly divine.

Grace kept up a steady stream of polite conversation, to which Robert's mother replied in monosyllables, punctuated by more bouts of weeping. She did apologize.

"Forgive me, yes? It is a shock. He is my malysh, my firstborn..."

"Of course," Grace said in soothing tones.

Mrs. Feldman sobbed into the eggs and pickled fish. She blubbered into the borscht. She deluged the dumplings. She bawled into the brisket. And she cried into the kugel, especially when Grace pronounced it delicious and asked for the recipe.

Grace's nerves were shredded by the end of the meal. When she tried to help with the dishes, her new mother-in-law flapped her hands and shook her head.

"Oh, but please," Grace persisted. "You must have been cooking all day…"

The woman shook her head. "You are guest."

Grace gave up and sat down at the dining table again, feeling useless as her new mother-in-law cleared the table. She asked Mrs. Feldman for the kugel recipe again when she rejoined them, her eyes now blessedly dry.

"Yes, please, Mama," Robert beseeched. He produced his best little-boy grin.

His mother disappeared into the kitchen and returned with a recipe card, which she handed to Grace.

The following Monday, Grace and Robert reported to the Munitions Building, an ugly concrete eyesore sprawled on the National Mall. Inside it, fourteen thousand Army and Navy employees clicked, clacked, buzzed, rang, greeted and gossiped. Their Army Signal Corps unit was only a tiny cog in the giant wheel, responsible for intercepting and disseminating communications and encrypting or decrypting them as necessary.

They were shown by Joe Mauborgne to a cramped, windowless office with a couple of regulation desks and chairs. Otherwise it was accessorized with only a telephone, a typewriter, a few reams of onion-skin paper and a package of pencils. No view, no artwork, no hot meals served on premises, no Bacon ciphers or zoo animals.

"It's paradise," Robert said, spinning around.

Mauborgne lifted an eyebrow, but Grace nodded. "Perfect. We can work together?"

They could. Grace could hardly believe it. She was employed as an official cryptologist for the US Army. No more amateur hour—she wasn't just a petticoat pressed into emergency prewar preparation. She'd now be helping to build Army Signal Corps from the ground up.

She and Robert would be designing an entire system of codes and ciphers for the Army—the first official one in American history. Their task was by no means simple: the speed of wireless/radio communication far outstripped the scratchings of mere mortals with pencils. How could the human mind travel faster than electricity?

CHAPTER FIFTEEN

War brought more frightening things than a mother-in-law.

"What do you mean, you're being deployed to France?" Grace clutched at her stomach, pressing down on a rising wave of terror that masqueraded as nausea. "No—we've only just arrived in Washington. We're barely settled. They can't do this."

"They can," Robert said gently.

"No," Grace repeated. "They *can't* deploy you."

Robert crossed the kitchen and took her face between his big, warm hands. "They can, Grace. The Army decides where I'm needed, then acts accordingly. They require people on the front lines to create secure codes for military communications. People like me."

"Then they can use me, too."

He shook his head. "I'm sorry, my love. But no. Women on the battlefield? Never."

"Nurses are allowed. The Hello Girls are allowed. Women drive ambulances. Why not a female cryptologist?"

Robert kissed her, trying to soothe her. "You're needed here."

"They only hired me, Robert, because they got an extension of you for half the price," Grace said bitterly. "And we work on the same encrypting project...we're most effective together, as a team. Two heads better than one and all that."

"Agreed."

"Then can't you explain to them? That they need to send me with you?"

Robert sighed and shook his head. "The very last place they want an officer's wife is in a sodden, stinking trench somewhere in war-torn France." He tried a smile. "Lipstick and shampoo are in short supply, you know, and your heels would get stuck in the mud."

"It's not funny, Robert."

He pulled her back into his arms.

"I know. But I don't make the rules," he murmured against her lips.

"Blithering idiots make the rules."

"Perhaps. But I have to say, I'd be one of them in this case. I'd be so worried for my girl that I wouldn't be able to get a thing accomplished."

Grace harrumphed.

"I'll miss you very much, my darling."

"And I, you. Robert, you're my best friend. I can't imagine how I'll pass the days and nights while you're gone."

"You'll spend them attacking and shredding codes and ciphers for the war effort."

What if you don't return?

Grace tamped down her panic. She'd boil her own head before she said such a thing aloud. Not exactly good for a man's morale. *And we haven't even—*

She was damned if she'd become a widow without truly knowing what it meant to be a wife. Regardless of her reluctance to experience the intimacies of marriage, poor Robert didn't deserve to go off to war without...*having* her. Which made her sound like a cup of coffee, or a bowl of cereal.

She changed the subject. "I've made dinner. A roast with potatoes and turnips. And your mother's apple kugel."

Robert whistled. "What have I done to deserve such lavish treatment? Our first home-cooked meal as a married couple."

Grace proudly set out plates and utensils while Robert uncorked a bottle of wine and poured two glasses for them. She transferred the potatoes and turnips to a serving bowl, then stood by while he carved the roast. It smelled delicious.

His grateful smile became fixed as he began to saw at the big lump of beef. It had the consistency of a log, and it eventually split, the edges shredded.

Grace's own proud smile fled in dismay. This tough brown thing in the pan did not resemble her mother's roast in any way. Surrounding it was a puddle of grease, and underneath it had turned black. She vaguely recalled that she should have elevated it on a rack. Not that she had one.

The potatoes were raw in the middle, the turnips limp and oily. As if that weren't bad enough, she'd oversalted everything.

Robert ate like a warrior and staunchly complimented it all. "What a scrumptious feast you've made, my darling," he lied. "I'm a lucky, lucky man."

"It's *disgusting*," she said.

"No, no—not at all. I'll have seconds," he said, looking queasy. Sweat beaded on his brow as he reached for the platter of splintered log swimming in lumpy, viscous gravy.

Was there anyone on the planet more chivalrous than this mendacious man? More dear? Grace felt herself falling even more for him.

"Robert, I think I might love you," she blurted.

He set down his fork and knife. "You know I—"

She barreled right over him. His own protestations of love made her uncomfortable. "At any rate, whatever it is I feel for you, it's too strong to allow you to eat that. I'll give it to the neighbor's dog."

Robert struggled mightily not to laugh and fell into a coughing fit.

"There's kugel, remember? So you won't go hungry. But for now, perhaps you should...take me to bed."

He went utterly still. Then he turned questioning eyes on her.

Grace stared back at him with a half smile. Then, to show him she was serious, she undid one button on her blouse, then two. And a third. She didn't know the first thing about seduction, but surely that was a good start.

He stopped breathing.

She turned and made her way toward the stairs.

Robert got to his feet. He caught her halfway there and swung her up into his arms.

"Oh," Grace said afterward, flushed and dazed. "*Oh*. I had no idea..."

Robert stroked her hair, smiling at her.

"Can we do that again?"

"Oh, hell yes. Just give me a moment."

"I thought it would be like the horses..." she mused.

"You *what*?" He buried his face in her pillow, shoulders shaking.

"Horrible and undignified and slapping and grunting."

He collapsed laughing again.

"Why is that so funny? It's the only time I've seen it, you know. On the farm."

"Allow me to recover my equine-imity," he gasped. "And then I'll neigh-say you..."

Grace's own lips twitched. "Well, I'm sorry. But it didn't look like very much fun for the mare. Do you suppose that's where the word *nightmare* comes from?"

"Stop," begged Robert.

Grace poked him in the ribs. "You're the one who started it, mister."

"Not true." He scooped her up and pulled her on top of him. "You want to do it again? I'll show you a different way."

"There's another way?"

"Several."

"How did you learn all of this?"

"From a manual. Now pay attention, *wife…*"

Grace decided that in this context, the four-letter word wasn't so bad. In fact, marriage itself didn't seem quite as awful as she'd thought it would be, even if she had a few things to learn about cooking. At least there was the apple kugel.

Wearing nothing but Robert's shirt and a shocking amount of beard-burn, she lovingly served him a huge portion and herself a smaller one. The poor man hadn't had much dinner.

"Thank you, sweetheart." He spooned a big bite into his mouth. "Mmm." He sat motionless for a long moment, a peculiar expression on his face.

"Everything all right?" Grace asked. "Is it good?"

He nodded. Began to chew. Turned greenish. Chewed some more. Swallowed. *"So* good."

Grace frowned at him. "Then why are your eyes watering?"

"Sentiment," he said thickly. "Makes me homesick."

Suspicious, she took a bite of her own kugel and went hurtling to the sink to spit it out. It was bitter, overly spiced, dense and just plain god-awful. "I don't understand," she wailed. "I followed the recipe to the letter. Measured everything twice."

She turned as Robert, with the air of a martyr doomed, reached his trembling spoon for another bite. *"Don't,"* she said. "For the love of God. You must think I'm trying to poison you."

"Not at all." But he set down his spoon and exhaled with audible relief. "Perhaps a second glass of wine, my dear?"

Robert deployed a week later. Grace went with him to the train that would take him to New York, where he'd ship out to join the AEF in Chaumont, France. Gone was his trademark bow tie, his starched white shirt, the lock of hair that often fell over his forehead as he worked on a particularly challenging decrypt.

He was tall and commanding in his olive drab uniform, looking as serious as she'd ever seen him. His musical smile was nowhere in evidence. Her husband was an officer in the US Army, going off to war. To battle.

Grace felt simultaneous pride and terror that she'd never see him again. She'd wasted so much precious time evading him, mistrusting and avoiding intimacy. *Can I have it back, God? I've been a fool. Such a fool.*

The train rumbled and chuffed into the station, bringing acrid fumes that enveloped them. This was it. As soon as it disgorged the previous passengers, it would devour Robert and all of the other soldiers waiting with them on the platform.

Grace launched herself into his arms, holding on for dear life. She inhaled the clean wool of his uniform, the scent of his shaving cream, the dearness of him. She held it in her lungs, wishing she could bottle it for the lonely nights ahead.

"You're getting rid of the husband you didn't want," Robert murmured against her hair.

"I do want him. I just didn't know..."

"Getting sentimental in your old age?"

"Yes." She tightened her arms around him. "I'll learn to cook," she said brokenly. "I promise."

Laughter vibrated in his chest, so tight against hers. "Why not focus on becoming the best damn codebreaker America has ever seen?"

"America will never see me, Robert. I'm just a girl."

"You're *my* girl." He reluctantly disentangled from her as the train whistled, signaling its imminent departure.

"Please don't go." Grace wiped at her streaming eyes. "I love you so much."

Around them, a sea of olive drab surged for the open doors of the train.

"It snuck up on you, did it?" Robert kissed her, hard. Possessively. And she didn't mind at all.

She nodded.

He wiped away her tears with his thumbs, then kissed her again. "Good. I love you beyond reason. Now you go sneak up on those German bastards. Read every word you can get your hands on. I'll be doing the same. Let's blow them to hell and beyond."

Then Robert turned and disappeared into the waves of soldiers surging onto the train. Would she ever see him again, this man who'd restored her faith in men? Invited and coaxed and encouraged her to love?

Dear God, please keep him safe. Just keep him safe, I beg you.

CHAPTER SIXTEEN

Grace settled into her new job at the War Department, buoyed by the presence of Utsidi, Fay and Veronica. At her request, they joined her in the stuffy little Munitions Building office, pooling money for cigarettes, sharing concerns about their husbands and brothers overseas and helping each other solve particularly intransigent ciphers.

They were proud to be working in a codebreaking capacity for the War Department. They decrypted and translated messages by the metric ton: diplomatic cables, private letters forwarded by post office censors, strange coded radio transmissions broadcast from far-flung outposts.

Most of them were unexciting but could be useful in the context of an information stockpile on each country engaged in the war. Ostensible friends could always be operating as collaborators or traitors.

Yet a month or so into her new employment, the daily dispatch brought a letter packaged inside of a fresh envelope, upon which someone had typed: *ATTN: Mrs. Feldman, Top Priority.*

She slit it open to find a letter addressed to Señor K. Tausch, Calle Tacuba 81, Mexico, DF. A note was attached: *Intercepted letter smuggled out by prisoner O. Schroeder, Fort Sam Houston. Decryption needed ASAP.*

His angelic face had been in all the newspapers, and it swam before her now: the youthful skin; wide-set pale eyes; chiseled lips; mussed, carefree hair swept to one side. A very slight dent in his chin added character to his beauty. *Just a boy.*

She pictured him locked away in a cell, desperate for help, clinging to hope. Pity again stirred a guilt deep inside her. *Stop it. Black Tom explosion. Murder. Sabotage. Enemy combatant.*

Grace opened the letter, smoothing and spreading out the coded words on the onionskin, exposing them to the harsh utilitarian light. Though it had been some time since she'd cracked the message sewn into Otto Schroeder's jacket, some sort of periscope in the recesses of her brain emerged from the depths to peer at the target... which, now that she considered it, represented a battleship of sorts. One that she could easily torpedo.

Schroeder couldn't be the only spy using this particular German code. It was undoubtedly the Huns' code for all of Mexico—and surely the US could use that to its advantage in this time of war.

Grace dug through her files for the worksheets she'd compiled to break the code at Riverbank just a few months ago. She wasn't sure why, but she'd saved them from the burn bag.

Aha! There they were, at the very back: the papers bearing untold scratches and marks and erasures, creased and limp in places where she'd quite literally sweated into them in her battle with the code.

She compared the worksheets with the smuggled letter. Sure enough, Schroeder/Waberski had used the same encryption process. She cracked it with ease this time. The plaintext read:

Need money and my notebook from Mr. Paglasch's safe—critical to securing my release. The address, Señor Jesus Andrada, Box 681,

San Antonio, is absolutely confidential, ensuring that notebook will be
delivered to me in secret.

Otto Schroeder made no mention of needing hope, prayer or solace.
The text struck Grace as confident, even cocky. Perhaps this, too, was
a sign of his youth.

She took the message immediately to Herbert Yardley, the man in
charge of MI-8.

Yardley was a smooth customer, a player, intelligent, but a bit too
impressed with himself. He had blunt features that seemed to have
oozed down a couple of inches too far, set under a very high forehead.
He put down his pipe and winked at her, not rising to his feet. "What
can I do for you, Mrs. Feldman?"

"Good morning, sir. I've decoded and translated the plaintext of the
Schroeder letter, the one smuggled out of Fort Sam Houston."

"*Have* you?"

She handed him the typed plaintext, along with the original letter,
over his desk.

Yardley scanned the few lines. "Attagirl." He picked up his pipe
again, sticking it between his teeth.

Grace did her best not to bristle. "Thank you. So of course, we
should interview the gentleman in San Antonio and explore the contents of his safe."

"Yes, indeed," he said blandly.

"However, it occurred to me that all the German spies posted to
Mexico are likely using the same encryption process. Which perhaps
gives us the opportunity to run a few spies of our own?"

Yardley's eyebrows snapped together.

Grace supposed she *was* venturing outside the scope of her duties,
but she pressed on. "Masquerading as German spies themselves and
using the same code."

Yardley put down his pipe again. He cocked his head at her, running his tongue over his teeth. "What an interesting idea. I commend you, Mrs. Feldman. And thank you for the quick work."

Grace flushed and looked down at her shoes. She couldn't help being gratified.

"Tell you what, doll—you are some lady codebreaker."

At times, it was beyond awkward to be female in such an environment. One morning, their daily batch of puzzles to solve included an interception from a wireless station in Mexico, addressed to an officer at Piedras Negras from a general soon to arrive.

Grace and Veronica pored over it using the official cipher disk of the Mexican Army, a wheel with the alphabet on its outer diameter, corresponding numbers laid out in five rows of concentric circles that narrowed to the center and included four nulls.

"Que bestia," Veronica muttered after they'd gone after it systematically for some time, the pile of cigarette corpses in the ashtray a testament to the hours.

Grace agreed that yes, it was a beast.

They at last pried out the words *pariente, hembras* and *mejores.*

Sirvase decire al pariente alistar dos de las hembras mejores.

"Oh dear," Grace said, heat suffusing her neck and face.

Veronica began to cackle madly.

Grace pressed her lips together. "I'm not delivering this translation in person."

"What've you got there?" Fay called from her desk.

"I'd rather not say." But Grace's shoulders shook involuntarily. "We've just devoted two hours of precious time to a matter that certainly does *not* involve national security."

Veronica dabbed at her eyes with her handkerchief.

"Well?" Utsidi prompted. "Don't keep us in suspense."

"It's highly improper..." Grace shook her head.

"A Mexican general is traveling from HQ to Piedras Negras," Veronica said in her husky voice, still gurgling with amusement. "He requests that his 'auntie' have *two* of the best women ready for him upon arrival."

They all dissolved into shameful giggles.

"So much for war rationing," Fay quipped.

Apart from work, Grace lived for Robert's letters.

June 4, 1918

Grace, my darling,

First chance I've had to write to you in too long. The rest of the boys off duty are playing poker and getting cross-eyed on firewater . . . which I've never found to be helpful in our line of work—especially not the next morning. To each his own, however.

Wish I could tell you where I am or what we are tasked with doing, but the censors would not appreciate that, eh?

I miss you desperately. Your head under my chin, your body curled into mine, your lips parted and our breath mingling as we sleep. Oh, and those tiny, effervescent snores . . . deny all you like, but it's true! I am an affectionate witness.

Here, when I sleep, it's not long enough or deep enough—but I dreamed, the other night, that we had a baby, a little girl who looks just like you, my love. Dark curls, large, sleepy chocolate eyes, a button of a nose and a rosebud mouth. Imagine: she had not a teddy bear in her cradle, but a pencil and a crib sheet (pun not intended! No, really). Any chance you're expecting? I can only hope.

Well, I must close and get to my cot if I'm to function properly tomorrow—the fellows at poker will barely know their own names.

> *All my love and more,*
> *Your Bobby*

Grace read and reread the letter, kissed it and then tucked it into her brassiere. Robert was safe! Or at least he had been at the time he wrote. She sent up a prayer of thanks.

Not expecting, my love...and with apologies, I am glad. I'm only just getting used to being a wife. I can't even imagine being a mother.

July 1, 1918

Dearest Robert,

I'm writing this by lamplight and entertaining homicidal fantasies, having just discovered that Farquhar published the index of coincidence we developed—in France, if you please, so we wouldn't notice—and without even your name upon it! The pleasant image of him boiling alive in oil serves to distract me from worrying about you, my darling.

I can only imagine the conditions you are living under. Are you in a tent, or do you have a proper roof over your head? Please God you're not hunkered down in a waterlogged trench or sleeping in a filthy convoy truck...selfishly, I wish this in spite of the fact that many thousands of other husbands, no doubt, are dozing in those very conditions. I feel guilty every night for a warm and comfortable bed, even if you are not here to share it with me.

The team here is doing well. We continue to analyze and solve messages, though we greatly miss your keen insight, and the guessing games aren't as spirited without you.

Sending sixty trillion kisses to you...

ETORONRI

JADEMMA!

p.s. Censor, unknot your unmentionables. In plaintext: J'e t'adore mon mari!

July 22, 1918

Dearest Grace,

Of course I cannot tell you exactly where I am, but I can reassure you that I'm not sleeping in either a trench or a convoy truck. I'm billeted quite comfortably, even if the lady of the house is a touch

*miserly with the jam. Considering the war rationing, who can
blame her?*

*I miss you beyond reason at night and during the days I miss you
even more, since we have always solved codes and ciphers together, you
and I, with a ping and then a pong of wild guesses, jokes and intuition.
Here, every man works alone, and the circumstances are not conducive
to hilarity.*

*The damned Germans seem to be breaking our codes as fast as we
break theirs . . . we've been tasked with—oh, hell, I can't write that or
some censor will have a litter of kittens and report me straight away.
I'd rather avoid a court-martial.*

IEROU!
LVYHL!
OUMSDO
VOUISS
EYCHAY

Bobby

*P.S. Censor, I take pity upon you. Before you poke your eyes out:
read it down the first column, up the second, and so forth.*

It worried Grace as much as Bobby that the Germans were easily busting the US trench codes in France. After a sleepless night, she arrived an
hour early at the Munitions Building to find Utsidi already at her desk,
smoking a cigarette and downing black coffee.

Utsidi's high cheekbones jutted in sharp relief to the sunken dark
circles under her eyes. She inhaled her Chesterfield as though she could
pull a solution to the war's problems through its filter.

"Utsidi?"

"Hello, Grace." Her colleague exhaled a cloud of smoke and gave
her a tired smile. "Have I ever told you how happy it makes me that
you—and the others—don't insist on calling me Ursula?"

"No, why?" Grace asked, puzzled. "Utsidi is a beautiful name."

"When any of us slipped up at the boarding school the government forced us to go to and we used our Indian names, we were beaten."

Grace sucked in a horrified breath. "They *beat* you?"

"Oh yes. If any of us forgot and spoke a word of Choctaw—or Cherokee, Lakota, Creek, Navajo, whatever we spoke at home—it was beaten out of us. We were to forget our language and customs."

"That's horrid."

"We thought so. We only whispered in Choctaw at night when it was safe."

"But...you're here. Working for the United States in a time of war."

"Yes, I am."

"Why? After being treated that way by the government? Torn away from your family?"

Utsidi's black eyebrows snapped together. "Why? *Because this is my country*, even if I disagree with some policies. Our people were here centuries before anyone else."

Grace felt sheepish for asking the question. "I'm sorry," she said.

The words hung awkwardly in the air between them.

"How old were you when you were sent away?"

"Twelve."

Grace shook her head. So young, to be on her own. "Were you at least able to write to your parents, your family, from the boarding school?"

Utsidi sighed. "As I've told you, Choctaw is an oral language. Even if I'd been able to write it back then, my family wouldn't have been able to read the letters."

Choctaw is an oral language. The words echoed inside Grace's brain.

Problems with the trench codes...codes relayed orally by field telephone.

Grace stared at Utsidi, thinking rapidly.

"Are you all right?" the girl asked.

Grace nodded. "I apologize for changing the subject, but something just occurred to me. The Germans are breaking our trench codes in France as fast as our boys can generate them. Did you know?"

Utsidi shook her head.

"So a language, a language that can be *used as a code*, that the Germans haven't an inkling of…"

Excitement dawned in Utsidi's eyes. "Choctaw!"

"*Yes.*"

Utsidi grinned, then began to laugh. "That's brilliant. And a lovely, subversive revenge."

"Isn't it?! What if I write to Robert and you write to your fiancé, Daniel, and they put their heads together? What if the Choctaw units become code talkers for the US Army?"

"Anumpa warriors," Utsidi said. "Language soldiers. It's brilliant."

Grace's blood hummed with purpose, with excitement. "Let's do it! Let's post the letters today." She pulled a fresh piece of air mail paper out of a desk drawer and rolled the sheet into her typewriter.

Utsidi hesitated. "Shouldn't we take this up the ladder?"

"No," Grace said. "Let's keep the idea to as small a circle as we can."

August 17, 1918

My Dear Bobby,

*How I wish the mail could be sent and arrive instantaneously! Wouldn't that be a marvel, if by some miracle that could be managed one day in the future? Of course, it might be disagreeable if all sorts of people one did **not** wish to hear from could also drop letters into one's postbox. Farquhar, for example. He's predictably incensed that I've objected to his theft and publication of our work.*

In reference to your last letter, Utsidi and I had a most interesting conversation. Remember what she said about her native language: that it's taught orally, and has, for the most part, not been written down?

Let your imagination take flight, my love: could it not be useful in the relay of information via field telephones?

Utsidi has written to her fiancé, Daniel Munn. Remember, you met him at our wedding reception. We believe he will be of great help to you.

All my love and more,

Grace

p.s. NDPDO DFKHU RNHH!

p.s.s. Oh, Censor: All I've said is that I love him—hardly a matter of national security, is it?

September 9, 1918

My darling Grace,

All your letters are precious to me, but your last one—truly marvelous. You have handed to me the most ingenious solution to the ongoing problem we have at the front. I got up and danced a jig, to the surprise and consternation of my superiors, who thought I'd quite lost my mind. Perhaps I may have, if not for your brilliant idea. We are lucky to have over thirty men like Daniel serving at the front. I send fondest greetings to Utsidi and our former team, by the way.

I'd write more, my love, but duty calls. Know that your photograph is my greatest treasure, and think of me often.

Xoxo,

Bobby

CHAPTER SEVENTEEN

Grace was ordered to Fort Sam Houston to testify about her code-breaking in the Pablo Waberski/Otto Schroeder trial. She traveled long hours by train, from Washington, DC, to New Orleans to Galveston to San Antonio.

The Wild West wasn't nearly so wild as she'd imagined. An Army major collected her at the rail station and drove her in an open vehicle to the Crockett Hotel, where she would spend the night, just steps away from the Alamo.

Fort Sam Houston itself was like any other sprawling military installation: utilitarian buildings and barracks, dusty unpaved roads leading in and out, companies of soldiers executing various drills. The courtroom—though she'd never actually set foot in one—was unsurprising. Lined with polished, dark-stained oak, presided over by a judge in an olive drab uniform, two sets of lawyers at tables on either side of a long, formal aisle.

What discomfited Grace was the angelic face of Otto Schroeder, aka Pablo Waberski. As she'd seen from the black-and-white newspaper photographs, he was only a boy. A boy with short blond curls, enormous blue-green eyes, and a polite demeanor. A boy any girl could fall in love with, and one for whom any mother would set a place at her table.

Grace sat down, knees together, ankles crossed slightly to the side, and clutched Nellie's alligator pocketbook with her gloved fingers to stop them from trembling. Her mouth went dry. Based on her testimony today in this courtroom, Otto Schroeder could, and most likely would, be put to death.

The judge and the two Army judge advocates went through a few formalities before Grace was called to the witness stand. She stood, knees shaking, and made her way to the front of the courtroom. With her hand on a Bible, she promised to tell the truth, the whole truth, and nothing but the truth, so help her God.

The judge asked her to please be seated, and she sank gratefully into the hard wooden chair behind her. She stole a glance at Schroeder, whose mouth had dropped open a bit. A fleeting expression of shock—perhaps it was scorn—passed over his face. Why? Because the codebreaker who'd exposed his secret message was a woman?

"Please state your name and occupation," directed the prosecuting attorney.

"Grace Smith Feldman, cryptanalyst, United States Army."

"And how long have you held this position, Mrs. Feldman?"

She hesitated. "For almost three months."

An audible snort came from the defense table.

"And where were you employed before you came to work for the Army?"

"At Riverbank Laboratories, Geneva, Illinois."

"And what was your job there?"

"I ran a codebreaking unit along with my husband, Lt. Colonel Robert Feldman."

No snort this time.

"Would you explain who trained you and your husband, please?"

"We were trained by Colonel Parker Hitt, United States Army."

"And is it your understanding that Colonel Hitt is an expert codebreaker?"

"Yes, sir. He and my husband are both currently serving the country overseas in France."

The prosecutor produced a piece of paper and called it into exhibit. "Do you recognize this code, Mrs. Feldman?"

"I do. It is the same code given to me to solve at Riverbank a few months ago."

"Let it be known to the court," said the lawyer, "that this code was found sewn into the jacket of the defendant, Mr. Otto Schroeder, traveling under the Russian alias of Pablo Waberski."

He held up two documents next. "And these?"

"The first is the plaintext of the code, in German. The second is my translation of those German words into English."

"Are you fluent in German?"

"I am."

"And would any other codebreaker have come to a different conclusion than you did, Mrs. Feldman?"

"No, sir."

"How can you be certain?"

"Any cryptanalyst would follow the same basic methods."

"Will you explain those methods to the court, please?"

Grace gave a summary of basic codebreaking and then the more specific methodology by which she'd broken the German/Mexican code.

"So it's a long, painstaking process," the prosecutor noted.

"Very much so, sir. But not impossible." Grace took a sip of water from a glass that had been provided for her. She stole another glance at the defendant's face, which had hardened, his eyes chilly and fixed implacably upon hers. Otto Schroeder was certainly not delighted by her presence or her codebreaking skills.

The defense, predictably, cross-examined her. She only had a few months of experience, did she not? Was it possible that she'd made a misstep, misinterpreted, misspoken?

Grace held steadfast. She'd been trained by the best. She'd broken hundreds of coded messages correctly and would continue to do so. She was employed by none other than the United States Army, and the defense was welcome to bring in any other cryptanalyst to challenge her work.

At last, she was dismissed from the witness box and driven back to the Crockett Hotel. She took a side excursion to the Alamo, for how could she not? Two hundred men had died there after a thirteen-day standoff, defending the fort from Mexican forces in the Texas Revolution—including the legendary Davy Crockett, for whom her hotel was named. Not even a hundred years had passed since those brave men had given up their lives.

Grace stood alone in the fort, imagining the blood and stench and chaos of battle, the crack of musket balls, the clang of blades on blades, the warning shouts, the screams of the injured, the moans of the dying.

And now, eighty-odd years later, it was all happening again in the stinking, gore-splattered, muddy trenches of Europe—with the man she loved in the middle of it all.

Grace said a brief prayer and left the ghosts of the Alamo behind. She walked slowly back to the Crockett Hotel and drank a toast to the man in the coonskin cap, to Jim Bowie, the man for whom the Bowie knife had been named, to Lt. Colonel William B. Travis and all their companions.

She'd cabled Genevieve Hitt, who met her at the Crockett that evening. Genevieve caused a stir when she strolled in, cloche hat set at a rakish angle over her dark hair, skirt swirling around her excellent legs, waving to any number of diners. She was a handsome, friendly woman who seemed to know everyone at the hotel, from the barkeep to the maître d' to the servers.

"Miss Genevieve!" the maître d' exclaimed. "Welcome, as always."

"Alonzo, I've been married eight years now. I'm a missus," she said, with her wide, warm smile. Her Texas drawl was part of her charm.

"You'll always be Miss Genevieve to me," he said.

"I know. As you'll always be Señor Alonzo to me. I'm meeting Mrs. Feldman, Sugar. Right over there, at the corner table."

"Of course." Alonzo led her over immediately, waited as she kissed Grace's cheek, then pulled out her chair and settled a snow-white napkin over her lap. "I will bring chilled wine, compliments of the house."

"The dear man. He used to bring me lemonade as a little girl, over at the Menger Hotel. My father would take us as a treat. Now he brings me wine."

Alonzo placed some in front of Grace as well, along with a menu that held a bewildering number of items in Spanish.

"You like spicy food?" Genevieve asked.

"Not really," Grace admitted.

"Good to be truthful, otherwise you'll drink an entire bottle of wine to put out the five-alarm fire on your tongue."

They settled on a supper of salad, roast quail, corn bread and peach cobbler.

"How is Robert?" Genevieve asked.

"How is Parker?" Grace asked at the same moment. Both of them laughed. "Bobby's in good spirits," Grace said. *Thanks to Utsidi and me.*

"Parker's frustrated—I can tell by the tone of his letters. But thank the good Lord they're alive. And I'm also thankful that I can help out here at Fort Sam in his absence. As I said to his mother, codebreaking's a man-sized job, but I seem to do just fine at it."

"You're the very first female codebreaker," Grace said. "I wasn't at all sure I could do it until I met you at Riverbank. But I told myself, *If she can—*"

"Then you can," Genevieve finished for her. Another wide smile. "And you sure have. How'd the trial go? Did you hold your own?"

"I did. Part of my credibility came from being trained by Parker."

"Mine, too, of course. Parker," Genevieve repeated softly. "I miss him so. When he told the top brass at Fort Sam that I could crack most anything he could, they didn't believe him. So he laid 'em a bet. He told me to put on my best dress and hat, towed me in there like a show pony and told 'em to try me. I could have shot the man." She smiled fondly.

"And what happened?"

"They put me through my paces. I cracked all but one of the messages—and the solution to that one hit me overnight. So Parker drove me back over next day, trotted me in again, put his hand on a Bible and swore he hadn't helped me."

"So they gave you a job?"

Genevieve snorted. "No, dear. They asked for my *assistance* once he got shipped overseas. Wasn't until this spring that they deigned to pay me a salary."

Grace rotated her wineglass. "May I ask a question?"

"You may ask several." Genevieve shrugged out of her fox stole.

"How do you . . . that is to say . . ."

Amusement washed over Genevieve's features—not at Grace's expense. "Put up with the male egos and their nonsense?"

Grace poked at a slice of orange in her drink. "Something like that."

"Be smart, but be quiet about it," Genevieve advised. "Always be a lady. Don't challenge a man directly, especially not in front of other men—even if you win the skirmish, they'll never forgive you and they *will* get revenge. Come at them sideways instead, with a pretty smile. Supply them with answers that make them look good. Don't get upset about who gets the credit—you know they'll claim it, dear. You just do your bit for the country.

"I repeat: don't get mad. Though it's perfectly fine to get even, just as long's they don't realize it. Document your work, dear, and keep it in more than one place. The truth about what you do may not come out anytime soon, but eventually, it will find the light of day."

Grace nodded. "Thank you. You're very wise."

Genevieve laughed. "Oh, honey. This isn't wisdom. It's pure Southern-gal pragmatism. We are taught it from the cradle. Squall all you like if you want to get handed to the nursemaid and banished from the room. Coo sweetly, and Daddy will pick you up himself to hold you in his big, strong arms."

Grace struggled to keep her expression carefully blank, but she must have failed miserably, because Genevieve shot her a knowing glance from under her lashes.

"Now Parker, he always saw through my—pardon the expression, but Texas gals are a bit more plainspoken than Deep South gals— Parker always saw through my bullcrap. Not that he didn't appreciate the pure art of it, mind you. He used to say that I spun dung into gold."

Grace grinned. "Something tells me that he didn't use the term *dung.*"

"Something told you right, honey." Genevieve grinned right back. Then her expression sobered. "Now, about your German spy."

"He's hardly *mine.* And he's just a kid." Guilt tugged at Grace again.

"Listen up, doll: Don't let his looks fool you. Schroeder's no innocent kid. He's been operating for the German secret service down in Mexico for years, pitting Huerta and Villa against each other. Also has some family ties in Cuba and South America. He's not a nice customer, and he's as slippery as they come."

"They're going to sentence him tomorrow," said Grace. "I doubt he'll slip out of a noose."

"I wouldn't put anything past him."

The peach cobbler, topped with vanilla ice cream, was the best Grace had ever had. She wanted to lick the bowl, but restrained herself.

They had a brief tussle over the check, which Genevieve won, citing Grace's status as a guest in her hometown of San Antonio. And when they stood up to say farewell, she found a package being thrust into her arms.

"For the train ride home," Genevieve said cheerfully. "You can't get cowboy cookies in Washington, DC."

The next morning's *San Antonio Express* headline announced that Pablo Waberski, aka German spy Otto Schroeder, had been convicted and sentenced to death.

Grace bought the paper at the train station and stared at his photo again: tousled blond hair, cerulean-blue eyes, impish quirk playing around his lips. *You did this, Grace. You.*

This boy would die because of her testimony.

Would they execute him by firing squad? Hang him? She didn't know. Nice customer or not, she couldn't help but send up a silent prayer for his mother, his family at home somewhere in Germany, loyal to their kaiser.

She stopped short of an apology, though. German secret service?

Boys like Otto Schroeder were committing acts of sabotage and violence. Boys like Otto were roaming in wolf packs of submarines, sinking Allied ships with thousands of men on them. Boys like Otto could very well be shooting at Bobby this very moment, while she took the train home to Washington, DC, and their piano-studio apartment, so empty without him.

Genevieve's cowboy cookies were exquisite. As best Grace could tell, they contained chocolate chunks, rolled oats, pecans and loads of decadent sugar.

She conserved them as long as she could, but otherwise lived on sandwiches. She played the piano in the evenings, long mournful pieces like Mozart's *Requiem* or Albinoni's Adagio in G Minor—or when she got too blue, spirited ones—Schubert's *Wanderer Fantasy* or Stravinsky's *The Rite of Spring*. She wrote letters to Robert, to her sister Evie, her parents and a thank you note to Genevieve.

And when she thought she might go quite mad from the loneliness of her own company, she cut patterns for dresses out of newspaper, spread the pieces out on the closed grand piano and pinned them to fabric that she scraped together pennies to buy. She sat at the old Singer machine in the corner and sewed three new frocks.

The steady staccato stitching drove her a bit mad, reminding her of machine-gun fire. When she could stand it no longer, she did her part by knitting socks for soldiers. She gazed into the fireplace, her hands on autopilot, and ran code sequences through her mind.

She wrote letters to Nellie Farquhar—who easily saw her loneliness between the lines and demanded to know if she'd looked up her dear friend Eleanor.

CHAPTER EIGHTEEN

Grace perched gingerly on a blue damask settee in Mrs. Franklin Delano Roosevelt's front parlor. She'd been a bit reluctant to call on her, afraid to be seen as some sort of social climber. But Nellie's letter of introduction had produced an instant invitation, so here she was, admiring silver-framed photographs of the Roosevelts and their children lined up on a baby grand piano.

Within a couple of minutes, Eleanor bustled in. She had a wide, warm smile, seeming not at all self-conscious about her rather protuberant teeth. Intelligence crackled from her blue eyes. She wasn't naturally elegant, but she was well-groomed and held herself with pride. The only things that gave away her privileged background were her cultured, continental voice and the three strands of lustrous, perfectly matched pearls around her throat.

"Hel-*lo!*" she said, bubbling with enthusiasm and offering her hand to Grace. "Delighted to meet you. Nellie's got such lovely things to say about you."

"Thank you, Mrs. Roosevelt. Likewise."

"Do call me Eleanor. I feel sure we'll become friends."

Grace nodded, a bit taken aback by this statement, since Eleanor was close to American royalty—President Theodore Roosevelt had attended her wedding to Franklin.

"And you work for the Army in signals intelligence alongside your husband? How interesting!"

"Well, not really," Grace demurred. "He's in France. I file, answer the phones, make coffee."

Eleanor cocked her head and raised an eyebrow, evaluating her. "Mmm. Just as Alice Martenz does for the Navy, I understand. I hear she makes *stellar* coffee." She offered that wide smile again.

"I'm sure she does," Grace managed. But she adhered to her training and kept her mouth shut. "So how is it that you and Mrs. Farquhar know each other?"

"We went to school together ages ago. Both of us a bit too mischievous for our own good. Kept in touch. Her first husband was a friend of Franklin's. Poor man."

The engagement ring on Grace's fourth finger chafed under her glove. "What…that is to say…I don't like to pry, but—"

"What happened to him? He fell off his horse. Skull fracture. Such a pity—he was a good man. A far better man than that loathsome— Oh dear. Things I shouldn't say." Eleanor smiled a bit too brightly and nodded her thanks as a uniformed maid in a white apron and cap entered, set down silver service on the walnut coffee table between them, then retired from the room.

"Tea?" she asked.

"Please."

"Sugar? Milk? Lemon?"

"A bit of sugar." Grace accepted the proffered cup and saucer with thanks. She was rather afraid it was Sèvres porcelain and prayed that she wouldn't drop it.

"Well." Eleanor poured a cup of tea for herself and settled more comfortably on the settee. Her wide smile radiated kindness and comfort. "How may I ease your way into Washington, my dear? You'll come to my ladies' teas, of course. And once Lieutenant Feldman returns—as he shall safely, never fear—Nellie thinks our husbands will get along famously."

This seemed far-fetched, since in addition to being assistant secretary of the Navy, there was talk of "Franklin" becoming a candidate for vice president of the United States. "Thank you, ma'am."

"Eleanor, please. So what are your causes, Grace?"

"Causes?"

"What charities do you support?"

"I—"

"There's the Red Cross, the College Settlement, the Junior League, St. Elizabeth—"

"I'm not quite sure," Grace said honestly. "I knit socks?" She worked so many hours codebreaking that volunteering hadn't crossed her mind.

"Socks. How lovely."

Grace searched her tone for sarcasm but found none.

"Well, all of those organizations do wonderful things for the community, and you'll meet people through them."

"Yes, I'm sure. I've had my hands full with my job, though, you see—"

"To be sure." But Eleanor galloped on.

"Then there's women's suffrage. Have you looked into NAWSA? We've come a long way, though the treatment of Alice Paul has been dreadful. What with President Wilson changing course and endorsing voting rights for women, I can't help but think we're close to victory! It will be such a thrill to vote for the very first time. Can you imagine?" She flashed her exuberant smile again. It was infectious.

Though very few women of her acquaintance followed, much less discussed, politics, Grace found herself smiling right along with her. "I do hope the Susan B. Anthony Amendment will eventually pass."

"Yes! I must admit, I was hesitant at first. We, as women, have been fed such nonsense. 'Politics is dirty; why sully yourself?' 'Nice women don't actually want the vote—only a few radicals do.' 'Women won't vote anyway—they're too busy with domestic duties.'"

"My favorite," said Grace dryly, "is that thinking is dangerous for the ovaries. I just read an article devoted to the subject."

Eleanor chortled. "Of course it is! My ovaries are just fine, thank you; I've somehow managed to produce five healthy children. And yet I think the most wonderfully dangerous thoughts over breakfast every day. Do *you* think, Grace, while you're *making coffee*? Do you dare?"

"No, never." Grace eyed her, deadpan.

Eleanor's chortle revved into a cackle. "Well. When it passes, as it will, I shall be at the polls with bells on. We'll get some ladies together and throw a party to celebrate. Mind you: you're under no obligation to vote my preference just for a cup of tea, or if my husband should be on the ticket."

Grace was impressed by her hostess's honesty and forthrightness.

"And what do you think of this Volstead fellow from Minnesota?" Eleanor asked.

"I beg your pardon?" Grace asked.

"The House representative pushing for national temperance measures?"

Bloody lost cause; pissing into the wind. Garrett Farquhar flashed into Grace's mind, swinging in his Hell Chair, splashing back Scotch whisky.

"Oh." She hesitated. "Well, truth to tell, I can't say I've been following the topic."

"They want to outlaw the consumption of alcohol, dear. I think it's rather a good idea, what with the damage it's causing to so many American families. Though I'd perhaps miss an occasional glass of sherry or champagne..."

She chatted in this vein with Grace for almost an hour. She was so engaging and kind that it was almost impossible not to like her.

At last Grace rose to take her leave, pulling on her gloves. "Thank you, ma—Eleanor. I've so enjoyed meeting you."

"And I you, dear. It's been lovely, and I shall tell Nellie so."

It was easy to see why Nellie and Eleanor had been drawn to each other at school, even though Nellie was apolitical as far as Grace knew. She was a force of nature, didn't take no for an answer and handled Farquhar admirably, but Grace couldn't imagine her marching on the White House with signs as the suffragettes did daily, or getting arrested for it.

Eleanor, on the other hand...Eleanor Roosevelt seemed fully capable.

Grace took a detour from her walk to the Munitions Building one morning and watched as the protesters stood silently, wielding their signs.

Votes for Women!
Mr. President, How Long Must We Wait for Freedom?
Give Us the Vote, Now!

They were protesting peacefully. Why had two hundred of them been rounded up, imprisoned and treated so abominably? Beaten, assaulted, force-fed? It was shameful.

As the day wore on, these ladies, too, would probably be rounded up and removed for being a public nuisance.

Jeannette Rankin, recently elected House representative from

Montana, had been dubbed a "crying schoolgirl" and a "dupe of the kaiser" for voting against the war.

"Hello, there!" called one of the women. "Come and join us!"

It took Grace a moment to realize that the suffragette was addressing her. "Oh," she said, her color rising. "No, thank you."

They didn't look like radicals with pitchforks. They were dressed respectably, conservatively, very much like she was. Hats covering coiffed hair, lace collars, brooches, skirts to their ankles. Several were fanning themselves in the morning heat and humidity.

They looked like women she could easily be friends with—if she did the simplest of all things: cross the street. Stand with them.

But who would bail her out of jail? Bobby was somewhere in France. She could hardly call a work colleague, or her new acquaintance Eleanor Roosevelt.

Grace stayed right where she was, until a trickle of shame masquerading as perspiration skittered down her spine. "I've got to get to work," she called, a perfectly plausible and effective excuse. But was she making it to them, or to herself?

In mid-October a telegram came from Grace's father with bad news: Regret to inform you that Mother has passed STOP Funeral services to be held in two days STOP Come at once STOP.

The yellow paper shook in Grace's hands. Her mother was gone. Just like that. She hadn't had a chance to say goodbye, or even to introduce her to Robert.

She hadn't seen her at all since she'd left home for Chicago a year and a half ago. Guilt almost paralyzed her.

Grace sat down on the piano bench facing the wrong way, still holding the telegram. She read it and reread it until the letters swam in front of her eyes, blurry from unshed tears. The only ones she could still make out were STOP STOP STOP.

But nothing did. It seemed so odd that she could still hear traffic outside and the wind in the branches of trees. Footsteps echoed in the bakery below, and the aroma of fresh baked goods seeped through the building as usual.

Her mother was gone...but the rest of the world went on about its business. Didn't notice, didn't care, wasn't affected in any way. It felt surreal.

Grace stared down at the telegram again, remembered thinking and speaking of her mother in less than complimentary terms to Robert while at Riverbank, and felt shame engulf her.

She hadn't been at home to help. She'd wanted a different life—a life out of the ordinary. And she'd gotten it, all right. She'd made her escape, chosen her own future. But in the process, she'd been a rotten daughter. She'd abandoned her mother.

And now it was too late to change that.

Mother was gone.

Grace went home to Indiana by train for the service. She stood next to her sisters and father, looking at the closed pine box that held her mother's body. None of it seemed real, least of all that she'd never again see her mother or feel her touch—the affectionate brush of Mother's fingers against her cheek, a kiss good night. She'd never hear the sound of her voice again, or inhale the aromas of a meal she'd cooked for them all.

She held hands with her sister Evie. Evie was a taller, stouter version of Grace, with the same intelligent gray eyes and no-nonsense attitude. The similarities ended there. Evie was a country gal with a plain gold wedding band who wore her long hair wound up in a bun. Grace had become a city girl, had cropped her hair and now had a diamond on her left hand. It looked ludicrous in this bucolic setting.

After the simple graveside service, they hugged each other, Evie the first to pull away. She palmed Grace's cheeks and said firmly, "It was a release for her. She was unhappy and ill."

Grace nodded. "I know. But I—"

"Hush," Evie said. "No guilt. Papa will provide plenty of that."

They shared a rueful smile and a look of understanding that only siblings can exchange.

Papa did try to get Grace to stay longer. "I can't," she said. "I have a job to go back to."

"Your job is family," he said. "Not secretarial work. Why I sent you to college, I'll never know."

"About that," Grace said. She opened her pocketbook and took out an envelope, which she handed to him.

"What's this?"

"The rest of the money I owe you for the tuition. I told you I'd pay it back."

He opened and then closed his mouth. Then he nodded. "All right, then." He stood there awkwardly with the envelope, looking lost.

Grace's heart squeezed.

"Papa, I love you. But I can't stay. I know you don't think much of my work, but... well, somebody's got to do it."

He didn't answer, just tugged at his mustache, his eyes vacant. Grace's guilt gnawed at her. *He'll be so lonely. Who will cook and keep house for him? You're a bad daughter.*

He sighed and surprised her by setting a hand on her shoulder and kissing the top of her head. "Y'always were a little different, Grace."

She couldn't argue that.

"I'll write," she said. "Every week. I promise."

CHAPTER NINETEEN

Grace expected Monday, November 11, 1918, to dawn just like any other Monday in a Washington, DC, autumn, though one hoped... one hoped... that the Armistice would at last be signed. It was dark and chilly when at 4:00 a.m. she was awoken by cheers, whistles and gun-shots fired into the air. People poured out of their apartments in their dressing gowns to hug neighbors, friends and perfect strangers. With a few strokes of a pen in a railroad car in France, the Germans had sur-rendered to Marshal Foch. The Great War was over at last!

Grace climbed out of bed, slid her feet into her slippers and wrapped a warm dressing gown over her nightclothes before throwing open the drapes and leaning out the living room window of the piano studio to witness it all, laughing as people across the street banged on pots and danced jigs and hooted and hollered. The notoriously grumpy super of the building opposite twirled an octogenarian tenant (head covered in curling papers and hairpins) under his arm and then swung her back out again. Was this really staid, straitlaced Washington, DC?

She went to work in the Munitions Building as usual, where the mood was just as celebratory. Fay wheeled herself into the office with a bottle of champagne in her lap, Veronica brought a flan and Utsidi a bouquet of hothouse flowers. They drank the champagne from cof-fee cups and gobbled down the flan for breakfast, dipping their spoons straight into the pan.

In the days and weeks to come, they'd consume dark and startling statistics instead: twenty million dead and twenty-one million more injured. Endless grief, horror and trauma endured by the survivors, many of whom envied the escape of the dead. Women left alone, hav-ing lost not only their husbands but their sons to the war.

Grace, Utsidi, Fay, Katherine Mauborgne and Genevieve Hitt knew how lucky they were that their men had been somewhat protected and were returning safely because of their peculiar specialty in cryptanalysis.

November 11, 1918

Dear, dear, dear Robert!

Can it be true?!? It's all over the radio and the newspapers that the kaiser has abdicated and an armistice is signed! God has answered our prayers... I am overjoyed and cannot wait to have you safe at home.

In anticipation, I have checked out three cookbooks from the library and will do my utmost to learn from them before your arrival. I gave myself a stern lecture, you see. I said to myself, "Grace, surely someone who can crack German codes and ciphers—someone who can expose a spy and make him pay for his dastardly deeds—surely that same individual, namely YOU, can learn to decrypt a recipe?"

Yes, Robert, I did. If the Allies can beat the kaiser, I told myself, then I can beat the kugel. (Though I'd swear on a Bible that your mother altered the recipe, and I shall get to the bottom of that one day.)

It seems a stretch to have you back before Thanksgiving, but perhaps for Christmas? Oh, I hope so—what a poignant gift it would be to have you back in my arms.

Unless you've forgotten me and become entranced by some sleek, overseas sheba?

All my love,
Grace

December 3, 1918
Dearest, most gorgeous girl,

You're the only sleek sheba for me, and if you don't know it by now, then I shall have to teach you the ins and outs of that particular lesson (over and over and over, in many different ways) immediately upon my arrival. What do you think about that? Are you blushing? You should be... (wicked chuckle enclosed).

I'll be home for Christmas, and I don't give a tinker's damn whether you can cook or not. You know that. However, I must defend my mother's honor—she's a woman of upright character, and I'm sure she gave you the correct recipe for the kugel. You will conquer it one day soon.

I do dream of a turkey dinner, since stale biscuits and tinned creamed beef grow old. A roast turkey... with stuffing and potatoes and gravy and cranberry sauce... my mouth waters and my head

swims with the vision. If I close my eyes, I can smell it, and not the
rank odor of armpit and foot fungus from the next bunk over.

So, my Queen of Shebas—I'll cable you when I know which
ship I leave on, and then which train I'll take from New York to
Washington, DC.

I cannot wait to see you, my darling wife, after all these months.

Love upon love upon love,
Bobby

Two weeks later, Grace stood on tiptoe on the crowded platform, fingers frozen inside her gloves, craning her neck for a sight of Robert through the smudged, dirty windows of the train that was pulling into the station. She was another sardine in a tin full of eager wives, girlfriends and families, trapped in a fog of wet wool, Cara Nome perfume and Pall Malls.

Her toes had been trodden on and her ribs had been elbowed more than once. It wasn't that people were rude; there just wasn't enough space. Grace was amazed that the whiskers and hats of those at the front hadn't been sheared off by the incoming train.

Then she saw him: tall, dashing, handsome and weary, standing patiently behind a squealing family whose children were climbing their father like a tree. He saluted her.

Grace's breath caught in her throat and her heart rolled over. *Robert.*

At last, the officer with the children dangling off him like monkeys managed to step out of the way with a murmured apology. Robert laughed indulgently, then strode toward her, his hazel eyes alight with joy. He picked her up and swung her around. She wound her arms around his neck and covered his face with kisses as he walked with her toward the exit. "I can't put you down, darling, or you'll be lost in this crazy sea of welcome."

Grace burst into unexpected tears. "I-love-you-I-love-you-I-love-you-I-love-you," she blurted. "I've never been so glad or relieved to see someone in my entire life."

Robert cradled her tenderly. "So you're trying to tell me, subtly of course, that you don't *entirely* regret marrying me?"

Grace nodded and smiled through her tears. "Not entirely."

"And that you've become, in my absence, a fabulous chef and peerless laundress?"

She grimaced. "No."

That musical smile of his played around his mouth. "I'm devastated."

"But I did go to Fort Sam Houston and seal the fate of a diabolical German spy. Does that count for something?"

Robert pretended to think about it. "Perhaps I won't divorce you until *next* year."

"*Oh!* Put me down this instant."

"Nope. Don't think I will." He continued to walk with her until they squeezed through the exit doors and into the frozen air outside, where he did put her down but tucked her against himself with his left arm while hailing a cab with his right.

"Where are you taking me?"

"Anywhere you'll allow me to take you. More than once, and preferably more than twice. Does the Willard suit you, darling?"

"Slumming, I see. But if we must..."

"We must."

Robert ordered a bottle of champagne to celebrate. "May as well enjoy it while we can. I hear they've got the votes to pass the Volstead Act and will do so any day now."

Once they were alone, Robert threw his cap and jacket on a chair, ripped off his tie and yanked his shirt tails out of his trousers. He undid his top two buttons. Then, as Grace stood a little shyly at the end of the bed, he went to his rucksack and extracted a package from it, one with a fancy Parisian label. "For you," he said, with a mischievous grin.

"What is it? And how did you bring it from a *battlefield*?"

"Open it."

Grace did. She parted the delicate tissue and simply stared. Robert had brought her a French silk teddy of blush pink trimmed with black lace. "How..."

He threw back his head and laughed. "Mauborgne knew a fellow who knew a fellow. We ordered them custom for you girls, and they were delivered to us when the crates of vegetables and tinned meat arrived for the mess hall. Of course, that part of the story is less glamorous." He winked.

"How did you guess my measurements?"

"Guess?" Robert looked offended. "I know them by heart."

Grace took it into the sumptuous marble bathroom, undressed and shimmied into the teddy. It was a perfect fit. And it transformed her into a downright sultry, slinky sheba. She ran her fingers through her short curls, bit her lips and undulated back out to her husband.

"Dear God in Heaven," Robert breathed. "Just let me look at you..."

Grace smiled. "See something you like, Lieutenant?"

"Yes," he said hoarsely. "C'mere, wife."

After that, words fell by the wayside.

Grace was so happy to have Robert home safely that she almost failed to recognize that they were living through further extraordinary developments in history. On January 16, 1919, the Eighteenth Amendment was ratified. The sale, transport and distribution of intoxicating liquors would be outlawed in order to save America's families from destruction and the devil: strong spirits.

Anxious arguments from bean counters at the Department of the Treasury about loss of tax revenue were waved aside in favor of moral rectitude. Head shaking by officials about how to effectively enforce the new law was also summarily dismissed. Progressives believed that government could and should protect American citizens from social ills.

Grace had her doubts, but who was she to voice them?

CHAPTER TWENTY

"Drink up, my dear—we must hide the evidence." On New Year's Eve of 1919, Robert handed a flute of bubbly to Katherine Mauborgne with a wink. Her husband, Joe, was at the baby grand near the window, banging out popular tunes with gusto. Parker and Genevieve Hitt were in Washington for a brief sojourn, and Joe Rochefort had brought Fay. Everyone had invited not only friends but also friends of friends.

Invitations went out in code, naturally, because the crowd was full of cryptologists.

It seemed especially urgent to celebrate this New Year's Eve because of the new ban on alcohol. The Eighteenth Amendment had passed. Oddly, it wasn't illegal to *drink* it—just to manufacture, transport or sell it. So everyone had been squirreling away bottles of booze ever since. And technically, the law didn't go into effect until January 17, 1920.

Grace welcomed another couple of guests and thanked them for the champagne. *New Year's without champagne? Impossible.* She added the newly arrived bottles to the stash on ice in the bathtub.

That evening, the place was jammed with Army Signal Corps friends and their wives, the cohorts they'd brought from Riverbank and Navy cryptanalysts, too. Utsidi and Daniel were there, as were Fay and Joe, as well as Veronica and her handsome, attentive date from the Mexican embassy.

Gorgeous Alice Martenz, the Navy's secret weapon, had draped herself over the piano. Tonight, starlight and streetlamps glittered madly on her sequined gown. She'd dropped a shoe, and held her champagne glass at a provocative tilt while her date Ed Heburn sang "Oh, by Jingo."

"He's a convicted *horse thief*," whispered Genevieve to Katherine.

"How many horses did he steal?" Katherine asked.

"It don't matter," Parker Hitt said. "In Texas, that's a hangin' offense.

Though he don't look well hung to me," he added, with an irrepressible smile.

Robert choked on his champagne, spraying some out of his mouth. Parker handed him a cocktail napkin. "I beg your pardon, ladies."

But they, too, were chortling.

Heburn had to wrap up his throaty tribute to Alice quickly, since Joe Mauborgne, after a mischievous glance at Grace, launched into Isabella Patricola's "All the Quakers Are Shoulder Shakers Down in Quaker Town."

Robert grabbed Grace's hand and tugged her onto the dance floor.

"I can't," she said. "My mother will spin in her grave."

But he would not be denied. "Gives the poor woman something to do, God rest her soul."

"Robert!" But the tune was hard to resist. And the Great War wasn't long in the past—even Mama wouldn't grudge them a little celebration. Grace let her limbs relax and liquify as they poured themselves into the music.

All the Quakers are shoulder shakers
Down in Quaker town, things are upside-down
The jazz bug bit 'em, how it hit 'em . . .

Her husband, eyes sparkling wickedly, twirled her until she was breathless, then reeled her back in.

Alice raised her already lofty eyebrows at the sight of Grace and Robert shimmying to such irreverent lyrics. Parker Hitt threw back his head and laughed. Genevieve tugged him, too, onto the floor.

Oh! The home of William Penn, won't be quite the same again,
'Cause all the Quakers are shoulder shakers, Down in Quaker
* Town . . .*
It's a most peculiar sight, and it doesn't seem quite right,
To see all the Quakers dancing, way into the night . . .

Mauborgne finished up the number with a flourish and then segued into "Baby Won't You Please Come Home," which every woman in the room had played on the Victrola over and over again during the long months of 1918.

Genevieve, Katherine and Grace swallowed the lumps in their throats, toasted their husbands and tipped back more champagne in sheer gratitude that their men had returned.

Joe's finale, though, "The Boys Who Won't Come Home," had them all weeping into their flutes. So many *millions* had been lost to the bloody, stinking war, mothers and fathers, sisters and brothers, children... even babies that their fathers, the brave men in uniform, never got to meet.

Parker and Robert met Joe's eyes on the last chord, and the three men silently filed out onto the little balcony to smoke. To Grace's surprise, a crowd of people had gathered below to listen to the music and they sent up a cheer. Joe took a bow.

Some other fellow took over the piano to lighten things up. He decided on Irving Berlin's "You Cannot Make Your Shimmy Shake on Tea," which brought Alice slithering off the piano and onto the dance floor.

"She *is* stunning," Grace had to admit. The sequins spotlighted simply unfair curves. Her pale hair was a cloud of champagne, her eyes blazed bluer than Mrs. Gallup's sapphires, and that *mouth*—it should be outlawed.

"She's a cobra." Genevieve turned on her heel and walked toward the kitchen.

But to her chagrin, Grace stood there mesmerized. So did every man in the room.

As Alice undulated on the floor, she caught Grace staring. The woman shot her a defiant glance and raised her chin as some hard-to-read emotion slid over and then off her face.

What is it?

A peculiar mélange of pride, shame and frustration?

Alice was in the spotlight and yet she looked...lonely. Fractious, forbidden and...forlorn. As if she hadn't one friend in all the world.

It dawned on Grace and she felt an unwelcome twinge of empathy.

Women hate her. Men desire her, but they don't respect her. She's utterly brilliant—she has it all—and yet she cannot win. She may be a cobra, but she wants to shed her skin.

As she stood there watching Alice, Alice watched *her*. She saw Grace's realization, her sudden pity, and loathed her for it.

Grace, accidental voyeur, flinched at the naked hatred on the woman's face.

While Grace herself longed to be spectacular, to be known and given proper credit, Alice the Extraordinary wanted to be *normal*. Wanted the one thing that, because of her face and figure, she'd never be able to have: the ability to blend in.

The countdown to the new year began, and everyone rushed to refill their champagne glasses. *Ten, nine, eight...*

"Haaaaapy New Year!" It was officially 1920.

In August 1920, the Nineteenth Amendment was also ratified. Women had won the right to vote.

That November 1920, Mrs. Roosevelt was true to her word. Grace received an invitation to line up at a polling station with what must have been a hundred women of Eleanor's acquaintance. They braved the crowds and queued up, waiting to approach the bunting-covered tables and the large wooden ballot boxes for the first time in United States history.

The atmosphere thrummed with excitement, women of all classes and ages filling the streets. A parade of disapproving men booed, hissed and mocked them. And a large contingent of anti-progressive women marched with signs—one of which featured a large cartoon of a woman exiting her home while her hapless husband in a business suit clutched two small children in his lap. A baby wailed from a nearby cradle.

Someone in the crowd threw an overripe, moldy tomato, which

splatted all over the fur collar of a lady in Eleanor's group. Without any outward reaction, she produced a handkerchief from her pocketbook and wiped it off.

Grace took it all in, fascinated and swept up in the historical significance of the moment. Warren G. Harding and Calvin Coolidge headlined the Republican ticket, James M. Cox and Franklin Delano Roosevelt on the Democratic ticket.

She filled out her ballot in a state of suspended wonder that she *could*. She cast it into the box and received a nod of approval from the fiercely proud old lady manning the polling station, an ostrich plume flying from her hat like a pennant.

Grace nodded back and then went to Eleanor's for tea. Life would never be the same. Women now had the ability to vote on issues that shaped their lives and futures.

Though Roosevelt lost the election, Eleanor's spirits weren't visibly dampened. "If I know Franklin, he'll run again," she said, and promptly threw several dinner parties. To Grace's surprise, she and Robert were invited to one.

She was delighted to see Joe and Katherine Mauborgne at the party, and Joe Rochefort with Fay.

"Is that…?" Grace gleefully snared Fay's left hand, where a diamond sparkled.

Her friend nodded, glowing. "I never thought…" She gestured down at herself, the wheelchair. "I—"

"Oh, Fay." Grace kissed her cheek. "He's a very lucky man."

"Yes, I am!" Joe said, grinning.

"Congratulations to you both."

They introduced Grace and Robert to another young naval officer, Eddie Layton. Layton had an interest in codebreaking, was being trained by none other than Alice Martenz and had actually heard of their work. As usual, Grace demurred and deflected questions about her role.

Shortly afterward, Alice Martenz herself swanned in on the arm of a young lieutenant commander. He was trying to disguise his dazzlement by appearing artificially suave; she was coolly assessing the sensation her looks caused the moment she entered the room.

Among many others, Franklin Delano Roosevelt noticed her. A handsome, patrician and charismatic man, he smoothly disentangled himself from the couple he'd been speaking with and came ostensibly to greet the lieutenant, his eye on Alice. "Ah, there you are, Charles. Just back from overseas, are you? And who is this lovely lady?"

Across the room, a shadow passed over Eleanor's face, but she laughed merrily at some anecdote and helped herself to a canapé from a roving waiter's silver tray.

"This lovely lady," the lieutenant said, "happens to be the Navy's secret asset. She's a whip-smart codebreaker, and she runs circles around most of the men in her unit."

"Ah," Franklin said, his eyes roving over her appreciatively, "so *you're* the famous Alice Martenz."

"Yes," Alice said.

Her date suddenly looked uncomfortable at her lack of expected modesty. Roosevelt's eyebrows shot up, which Grace noted wryly.

And just like that, their host's interest in her vanished. The warmth seeped out of his expression. "Pleasure to meet you, Miss Martenz. Good to see you, Charles." He moved on.

Women may have won the right to vote, but they were still expected to fade into the woodwork unless their beauty won them notice.

The circulating waiter approached, and Grace accepted a petite beef Wellington off his tray. She'd just popped it into her mouth when the sight of another familiar figure almost had her choking on it.

J. Edgar Hoover stood deep in conversation with another gentleman near the cavernous fireplace. She wanted to look away, to turn back and join the conversation with Robert, Rochefort and Mauborgne, but something wouldn't let her.

As if he felt her scrutiny, Hoover paused in his conversation and stared right back at her. Flustered, Grace forced herself to nod, then managed to find something inane to say about the tiny beef Wellington to Katherine Mauborgne.

It wasn't long before Hoover appeared at Grace's elbow. "Miss Smith, isn't it?"

"It's actually Mrs. Feldman now, Mr. Hoover." She poured honey into her voice to disguise her dislike of him. "How nice to see you again."

He lifted an eyebrow. "My felicitations."

"How are you?" Grace felt compelled to ask. "Back at the Library of Congress?"

"No, no. I'm at the Department of Justice since graduating law school. I head up the Radicals Division."

"Good gracious—that's quite a change."

Hoover nodded. "With Communists and anarchists everywhere, I felt compelled to serve my country. We cannot allow people such as Alexander Berkman and Emma Goldman to threaten our way of life. We cannot have bombs exploding outside Attorney General Daugherty's home. It's my duty to ensure that these... undesirables... are rounded up and deported or imprisoned."

"Well," said Grace. "That's quite a big job, I'm sure."

"Yes, it is." Hoover's impenetrable black stare turned from her to Robert, assessing him openly and not with admiration. "Your husband has a trace of an accent."

"Does he?" she asked, as if she'd never noticed.

"Russian, perhaps?"

Oh dear. The last thing we need is the head of the Radicals Division at DOJ suspecting that Robert's a Bolshevik.

Grace produced the most charming smile she could dredge up from her repertoire. "Mr. Hoover, it's lovely to see you again, but I'm afraid Mrs. Roosevelt's just waved me over. Please excuse me."

The outright lie sat bitterly on her lips.

She wove through the crowd until she reached Eleanor's side and complimented her on the hors d'oeuvres.

Eleanor shot her a quizzical glance. "Escaping from someone? You crossed the room to my side in quite a hurry to comment on the food."

Grace couldn't help but laugh. "Yes."

"Let me guess: the insufferable Radical Hunter."

Grace pressed her lips together and didn't answer.

"Dreadful toad. Gives me the willies. Watch out for that one. He's connected. I hear that his mother sees Madam Marcia, the same astrologer that Florence Harding does. Isn't that amusing? He got the DOJ job through his uncle, a federal judge. I'm rattling on, but my point, you understand, is this: don't make an enemy out of him."

Some weeks later, Heburn the Horse Thief from the New Year's party made a second appearance in Grace and Robert's lives. He'd invented an unusual coding contraption that appeared on Robert's desk to be tested.

Joe Mauborgne stepped into the office to explain. "The Navy's all agog and wants to order some of these. Nobody over there's been able to break it, but top brass wants to be sure it's secure before they finalize things."

A throaty chuckle came from the open doorway. "I see you got Ed Heburn's machine." None other than Alice Martenz stood there, smiling like the proverbial cat with cream.

"Alice. How are you?" Grace asked.

"Having a lovely morning, thank you," Alice replied.

"What brings you this way?" Mauborgne asked.

"I came to see Grace, actually. I wanted to let her know that I've agreed to go into business with Ed. I just gave my notice to the Navy—which, by the way, is considering a preliminary order of four thousand machines. And I recommended Grace as my replacement."

And then she walked out of the room, leaving them all stunned.

Mauborgne called Grace into his office two weeks later and politely asked her to sit down. "Grace, I'll just cut to the chase. Commander

William Halsey of Naval Intelligence has formally requested your services to replace Alice Martenz."

She blinked at him. "I suppose that's quite flattering, Colonel. But I don't wish to work for the Navy. I'd rather stay here and work in conjunction with my husband."

Mauborgne steepled his hands on his desk. "Grace, it's not really a request. It's more of a requisition. He wanted Robert."

Of course he did.

"We had a bit of a tussle, if you must know. We don't have to give them Robert, since he's a commissioned officer in the Army. But we don't have as much of a claim on you since you're a civilian."

You mean since I'm a woman.

"And we're no longer at war..."

Meaning the boys are home and females really should be back in the kitchen and the nursery. Meaning I'm taking up a man's job here.

"And we feel the need to compromise, try to honor the Navy's request in some way."

"I'm sorry, but Robert and I have always worked together. We're better that way—we spark ideas off each other—"

Mauborgne sighed. "Yes, about that. Unfortunately, top brass is uncomfortable with Lt. Colonel Feldman continuing to work with his wife. He's going to be brought into some higher echelon projects, Grace."

She straightened her spine. "Meaning I'm not trusted enough to work on them, too?"

"Nothing of the kind. It's just...I'm sorry to say...but it looks odd."

"To whom?"

"I'm really not at liberty to...Does it matter, Grace? You're being offered an excellent job, working with highly qualified, highly intelligent officers and gentlemen in the Navy. It's a compliment that they want you." Mauborgne's eyes held empathy, but they also held steel. "We've arranged for you to start work next Monday. Will that be satisfactory?"

No! Nothing about this is satisfactory. You're pawning me off as a compromise, a token female to replace their missing token female.

Quiet, Grace. Say any of that aloud and you'll be packed off home, staring at your bitter enemy, the stove. Shrieking at the walls of the apartment as they close in upon you.

"Well, this comes as a surprise, of course. But yes. I'll report to Navy headquarters at Constitution Avenue on Monday."

"Excellent. You'll be at the research desk in room 1645."

CHAPTER TWENTY-ONE

Grace reported for duty as instructed. Room 1645, Naval Intelligence's "research desk," was in a low-ceilinged wooden building, where she sat with a crew of disgruntled officers who didn't want to be there, since shore duty as a desk jockey was not the way to advance their careers. They wanted sea duty and command.

Most of them all but rolled their eyes when Grace joined them, though they weren't outwardly disrespectful. And the mitigating feature was that Joe Rochefort himself headed up the unit.

She was given a desk of her own and handed a Japanese naval codebook from 1918, surreptitiously discovered in a steamer trunk during a highly clandestine raid of the Japanese consul general's office. Every page had been photographed before it was replaced, and it was now Grace's job to make use of it to aid in the study of developing Japanese naval fleet communications.

Alice had left notes: the Japanese used *superencipherment* for their fleet code, meaning that they used both a code and then a cipher to disguise their messages.

Grace's new job involved staring for hours and looking for patterns in the gibberish on her carefully transcribed worksheets until her eyeballs bled.

It used to be just her and Robert smoking in a room, but now she could barely see through the toxic fog of twenty men puffing away alongside her. Ash particles littered every surface.

Rochefort himself was unfailingly polite and solicitous, but she simply wasn't one of the boys who went to bars together, belonged to the same clubs and told filthy jokes that she pretended not to hear—or failing that, not to understand.

She fielded the occasional come-on with a raised eyebrow and a nod at her wedding ring.

On the day some idiot left a dead rat in her chair, she simply extracted a handkerchief from her purse, picked it up by the tail and held it aloft. "Does this belong to any of you gentlemen?" she asked, unruffled.

"Rochefort's fiancée sent it for his lunch!" someone called.

"I don't think so. I know Fay. She's a fine cook, and she'd have poached it in tawny port first."

This reply was met with amusement, and one of the officers relieved her of the creature to dispose of it.

Grace began to feel peculiar—nauseated at unexpected times, her blood humming with unexplainable joy at others. She had odd cravings for things like pickled beets—why? And she developed unexplainable dislikes for some of her favorite foods. She'd always loved a toasted bagel with a little cream cheese and salmon, but now the salmon caused a gagging reflex.

She was a terrible cook, but now she didn't even try, because she was afraid she'd be sick on the stove.

"You're pregnant," Robert told her, his eyes alight with joy.

"What?" Grace waved away the notion. "Nonsense."

"Go and see a doctor."

"But—" Grace sat down with an unladylike plop. "No." *I can't be...*

Yes, I can. Obviously, we know what causes the condition. But I'm not ready! I don't even know what to do with a baby. I don't want to become my mother...

After a thoroughly humiliating examination, a doctor that Eleanor recommended confirmed it: Grace was indeed pregnant. She felt a reluctant joy—how could she not be happy to have Robert's child? But her overriding emotion was anxiety.

At least she had a few months to finish her projects at work before she was confined alone in the apartment.

She continued to go to work, though one day—in the absence of Rochefort—she got a dreadful jolt after opening what looked like an official Navy binder that had been left on her desk. It was full of pictures.

Grace's brain could barely process what she was looking at: naked women, bound and blindfolded; women, their skirts raised and panties down, being whipped. Women kneeling, engaged in sexual acts. Close-ups of female genitalia.

She knew all eyes were upon her, that this had been placed deliberately for her to find. She slammed the notebook closed and walked with it to the wastebasket. She turned to face the avid expressions of the men in the unit. "Really, boys? Are you so threatened by women that you have to reduce them to *that*? Grow up."

Snickers ensued, while Grace displayed not one iota of emotion. "Are you quite finished?"

No answer.

"By the way, *gentlemen*, if you're wondering why you haven't been able to make much headway with these new fleet codes, it's because after the Japanese encode them, they're using columnar transposition. They're transmitting them *vertically*, boys, even if they're writing them out horizontally. And while you're at it—be on the lookout for false noncarrying addition."

She took an early lunch, too angry to sit in the fog of their smoke and sheepish resentment.

In the meantime, Robert had brought the Heburn contraption home with him. He stared at the small box, picked it up and examined it, put it back down again. It was based on alphabet wheels, three "rotors," which revolved separately when zapped with an electrical current. This meant that they produced thousands of possible letter combinations that could encipher a message. The wheels could also be removed and changed out for others—making it even more difficult to crack.

Robert contemplated the box for weeks in every spare moment he had. He set it in the middle of the dining table and puzzled over it some more. He placed it on his bedside table at night and rolled over to moon at it when he couldn't sleep.

"It's indecipherable," he concluded to Grace.

"I doubt it. If a human being engineered it, then another human being, such as your brilliant self, can reverse engineer it. I know you can, Bobby."

"Thank you for your faith in me, my darling."

They were getting dressed for a dinner party at the Mauborgnes' when an odd expression settled on Robert's face.

"Are you all right, my love?" He looked rather like an owl having an epiphany—and since she was no ornithologist, she wasn't sure that was possible.

Robert gave a long, slow blink, and then sheer exultance lit up his face. "I've got it! I've got it, Grace—I've solved the damned thing!"

"And... which thing would that be?"

"I've busted Heburn's unbustable box!" And he proceeded to explain how.

Grace was excited for him. She truly was. But, oh dear: Alice had left the Navy to go into business with its inventor. She wasn't going to be at all happy.

Alice was, in fact, furious. Grace became personally aware of this when she showed up in room 1645 one morning. "Get away from my desk," she snapped. "*I* sit here."

Grace goggled at her. "Hello, Alice. How nice to see you again. This has been my desk for six months."

"I don't care," Alice said implacably. "I'm back. Thanks to your husband."

Oh my. "I think we should talk about this privately, don't you?"

"I have nothing to say to you."

Grace's temper awoke, though she did her best not to display it. "Alice, my husband simply did his job. Would it have been better for the Navy to have ordered and distributed thousands of the Heburn machines, only to have a foreign enemy crack one and read every coded message the United States sent upon it?"

Alice all but growled at her. "I recommended you for this job. But I did not authorize you to take my desk. Out of my chair, if you please."

Part of Grace wanted to smack the woman for her rudeness. The other part understood that she was angry, disappointed that she hadn't made a fortune with Heburn and territorial. Did it really make sense to go to battle over a silly desk?

Grace got to her feet. "It's all yours, Alice." She stacked up her worksheets, commandeered a couple of extra pencils and moved to a different desk.

"I wouldn't get too settled in at another, if I were you," Alice said cryptically.

"What does that mean?"

Grace discovered what it meant in short order. Her ecstatic husband, Robert, had shared the good news that she was "in the family way" with Mauborgne and Rochefort at a lunch. These three men, charged with some of the most secretive work done in Washington, had gossiped about her like old biddies, and even worse, had decided her fate among themselves, without consulting her.

She was pregnant, which in their minds was a handicap. And Alice was back at Naval Intelligence. Rochefort, seeing the enmity between the two women, wanted to avoid any "catfights" in the building on Constitution Avenue. And Mauborgne wouldn't take Grace back at the Munitions Building in her delicate condition.

So the band of merry men had decreed that she'd retire, effective immediately. It was for the best. Robert announced this tenderly over a dinner of sliced roast beef and salads from the local deli.

"I beg your pardon?" Grace asked, stunned.

"Sweetheart, you must rest and gather your strength for the baby. A stressful job outside the home isn't good for either of you..."

She put down her fork and knife, even though she had a savage urge to stab her husband through the eyeball with the latter. "Bobby, did it even occur to any of you—but you, especially—to ask *my* opinion?"

"Now, Grace. Don't get crotchety—"

"I'm not crotchety, Robert. I'm *furious*."

He had the nerve to be surprised. "Why, my love? Be reasonable. You have a nursery to prepare, and—"

"Why? Because this is *my* job you gentlemen did away with. *Mine!* Without any consideration for my feelings on the subject. Without treating me as an adult, a human being! And the insinuation that I'd ever engage in a *catfight*—oh! That's unjust and simply humiliating."

"Grace, you're emotional, which is understandable in your condition—"

"My condition has nothing to do with my emotions!" she shouted.

Robert stared at her as though she'd sprouted horns.

"When I married you, it was on the understanding that I was—*am*— not your subordinate. I'm your equal."

"Yes, of course."

"Equals consult one another before making decisions that affect each other's lives!"

"Well, but—"

"You didn't say a word to me about this." Grace got up from the table and slammed her plate of uneaten food down on the kitchen counter.

"Rochefort said that Alice was quite rude to you, and that the situation, going forward, was likely to get even more uncomfortable. You will have to retire soon anyhow because of the baby...I was simply solving a problem for you, my darling."

"Oh, so you did me a favor!" Grace flared at him.

Robert blinked. "Well, yes. I thought so."

"You thought wrong, Bobby. Don't think for me. Don't dictate to me. Don't treat me like a child."

"I didn't mean…that is to say…you're my *wife*, Grace. It's my job to look out for you. I'm sorry if that makes you angry." He looked truly bewildered. "I'm sorry if I did the wrong thing. Truly, I am."

His apology, clearly heartfelt, took the wind out of her sails. And there was truth in what he said: she would have had to retire in a matter of months. The whole situation galled her.

But Grace, knowing Robert's true character—and indeed, that of all the men involved—and seeing as there was absolutely nothing to be done about it now, stalked off; she eventually conceded the battle.

She accepted her new lot and wrote to her sister, her father and Nellie of the good news: she was to be a mother. She left it to Robert to inform his parents.

Grace rented a small house for them. She found a secondhand crib. She sewed sheets and pillowcases for it. She turned the spare room into a nursery. Nellie sent a hand-knit baby blanket and a quilt she'd made herself. Her sister Evie sent a heartfelt letter, telling Grace that she'd be a wonderful mother and that she'd come to help her when her time came.

Grace followed the doctor's orders and rested. She read novels she'd been meaning to read. She discovered a hilarious, witty new author named Dorothy Parker, née Rothschild, who wrote pieces for *Vanity Fair* magazine and others. She glared at Heburn's machine, which Robert had brought home again and set like a trophy on his desk. She invited Fay, Veronica and Utsidi to a potluck supper, which they turned into an impromptu baby shower.

Otherwise, she was lonely. So lonely and bored that she took Heburn's machine apart bit by bit, key by key, screw by screw. She studied how it worked, how the wheels of the alphabets stepped and adjusted. And she, too, came to understand its weaknesses.

I can break you, too, you clever little device. She allowed herself a smidgeon of pride.

It was either a blessing or a curse that Robert was away on business when she awoke in the middle of the night with agonizing cramps, the sheets soaked with blood. Her shock overrode the pain; mortification and shame led her to clean up what resembled a murder scene before she called for help. Grace bundled the sheets into the garbage—a shocking waste—because she couldn't bear to wash them. She used two sanitary towels and pulled on five pairs of drawers for the taxi to the hospital, praying that it would all be adequate.

When Robert rushed to her side, she could barely look at him. "I'm sorry," she whispered. "I'm sorry..."

"It's not your fault." He took her in his arms while they both wept.

Isn't it? I admitted to God that I wasn't ready for this baby. I resented it. I wanted to work—even under less-than-pleasant circumstances. What if He took the baby away because of that?

To her shock and eternal gratitude, Nellie Farquhar arrived shortly after Grace returned home. She bustled in wearing an orchid silk dress, a strand of perfectly matched pearls the size of marbles, and a hat festooned with silk hummingbirds. She wore sensible pumps and stockings—Grace found that she missed the crusty old rubber boots—and brandished a box of fancy chocolates instead of her customary garden shears.

"Hello, dear!" she said, clacking right into Grace and Robert's bedroom. "I won't ask how you are, because I know you're perfectly miserable, in a deep-blue funk. Perhaps even a bruised-plum funk. Aren't you?"

"I—" Words failed Grace. Two tears plopped out of her eyes instead and rolled down to her chin. She dashed them away with the sleeve of her bed jacket.

Her visitor surged forward, sank down onto the mattress beside her and took her hands. She squeezed them. "It's going to be all right, love. I promise."

Grace's mouth trembled. Far from comforting her, the words made her almost angry. "How do you know that?"

Nellie gave a long sigh and then unpinned her hat, tossing it over one of the bedposts. "Oh, my dear. How do you *think* I know it?"

Grace shook her head wordlessly.

"Hmm? How is it that I can say such a thing with such confidence?"

Grace had an unwelcome flash of memory, of sitting on the tufted stool in Nellie's closet back at Riverbank. *Garrett and I weren't able to conceive...*

"I'm sorry," she whispered.

"Thank you. So am I."

The words sat with them in the room like unwelcome visitors before Nellie shooed them out. "But one gets on with life. As you will. And I suspect that you'll be just fine."

Grace closed her eyes and shuddered, trying to block the image of the bloody sheets. "Nellie, it's so lovely of you to come all this way, but we haven't even got a guest bed—"

"Don't trouble your head about it, love. I'm staying at Eleanor's, of course. Though she drew the line at Delphine." Nellie chuckled, then remembered the fancy box of chocolates she'd brought. "Here, dear. These are for you." Her color heightened a bit. "My most fervent apologies, but I was famished on the train, the dining car had closed and so I... well, that is to say..."

Grace laughed. "Nellie, thank you. And I'm glad you sampled them."

"Well." Nellie dimpled. "I did have to make sure they were top-notch."

"So you did."

Nellie stayed for almost two weeks, bringing covered dishes from the Roosevelts' kitchen, and even Eleanor herself, who clucked and fussed and made tea while a mortified Grace wondered if she'd ever set foot in such a down-at-heel abode as the small rented Feldman house, barely a step up from the piano studio. Eleanor herself showed not the least sign that it was anything less than perfect. Her manners were flawless and her heart was pure gold.

The two ladies, along with Robert and her friends from the code-breaking world, helped Grace recover, put her mourning aside and embrace life again. But what would it hold for her?

Washington, DC, 1958

"What's wrong with Dad?" Grace's son Christopher, home on a visit, was as tall as his father now and a lieutenant in the air force. His slightly curly dark hair was razed short, and Grace's own level gray eyes stared back at her from his face. His father's musical smile was nowhere in evidence at the moment, and his chin jutted out, meeting his concern head-on.

"Why, nothing at all, dear," Grace said. She continued beating egg whites with a hand mixer, urging them into a froth that would eventually form peaks for the lemon-meringue pie her son loved. Krypto observed with interest.

"Mom. He's building…I don't know…castles or something. With the books in the library."

"Yes?"

"Yes, Mom. It's very strange."

"Why?" Grace asked serenely. She urged the insubstantial egg whites on, daring them to climb to heights they'd never dreamed of when locked inside their shells.

"What do you mean, *why*?" Christopher asked, exasperated. "Books are meant to be read. They're not meant to be used as building blocks."

"Well, dear, that's certainly the conventional thinking. But your father has never been a conventional thinker, now, has he? Besides, when you were a boy, you tried making houses out of playing cards."

"That's different."

"Is it?" Grace frowned at the egg whites, which were turning bubbly and opaque but not climbing the sides of the bowl yet. She sped up the mixer.

"Mom, he's a grown man. And he's just sitting there in his pajamas, balancing books on top of each other like some kind of fool."

"Your father is a genius, not a fool," Grace said sharply. "As you well know."

"Well, he's not behaving like one! And when I speak to him, ask him what he's doing, he doesn't answer me."

"He doesn't answer me, either." Grace's hand was tired, so tired, but she kept cranking the mixer anyway. *Froth, froth, froth.*

"Does that not worry you, Mom?" Christopher's voice had risen.

Oh, sweetheart. If you only knew what worries me. All the time, at every minute of every hour of every day. "Not particularly," Grace said aloud.

"Mother. Can you *stop* that and look at me, please?" Her son's voice rose another decibel.

"Not for long, dear, or it will be ruined." But Grace paused, flexing her sore hand, and gazed into his accusing eyes, meeting them as placidly as possible in hopes that she'd reassure and not infuriate him.

"There's something wrong with Dad. You know it. I know it."

"Oh, is that the elephant in the room?"

"*Yes.* Why can't we talk about it?"

How do you eat an elephant? One bite at a time.

"Perhaps because it's too big, Christopher. And it takes up all the available oxygen."

Her son stared at her. "What does that mean?"

She shrugged.

"How can you be so callous?"

Grace's mouth tightened and she turned back to the egg whites, now doing their best to collapse in the bowl. "You think I'm callous, Christopher? What would you rather I do? Go into the library and screech at him like a fishwife? Ridicule him? Take away his books and put them back on the shelves and shake my finger at him and order him not to touch them?"

"I—I—" He looked nonplussed.

"He's grieving, darling. Men from the FBI and NSA came to ransack the library, did you know? They carted off about fifty books that he'll never see again in his lifetime. His *treasures*."

"Why?"

"Ask the bureaucrats."

"What right did they have to confiscate his own property?"

"An excellent question."

"It makes no sense."

"Mmm. And yet, you're asking your father to behave sensibly in the wake of this slap in the face? After all he's done for this country. After everything he's given...they continue to take. And take away." Grace stopped the eggbeater again and made an attempt to soothe the pain in her right hand, massaging it with her left.

"Let me help, Mom." Her son took a step toward her.

You can't help, my dear. Nobody can. There's no treatment or doctor or pill that can help. All I can do is love your father, make sure he's safe. Feed, groom, clean up after the elephant of depression. It is quite large, isn't it? And dark gray, wrinkled with exhaustion, ashamed of its yawning, lugubrious, never-ending need.

"Oh! No, darling." Grace dredged a smile out of the sugar canister. "I'm fine. But thank you. Just a touch of arthritis, that's all. You go off and see your friends while you have the chance. Come back in time for supper, all right?"

Christopher side-eyed her, then shook his head. "Okay. See you later, Mom." He kissed her cheek, leaving her to her baking. Leaving her alone, as always, with the elephant.

Grace needed the large oval serving platter, the Meissen one, from the top of the china cabinet. It didn't quite fit inside with the jumble of other good porcelain, so she'd propped it up in a decorative stand. It was the only thing to carve the roast on for this evening's supper, but she wasn't tall enough to reach it.

She wiped her hands on her apron and went into the garage for the stepladder. Ah, there it was. As she retrieved it, a flash of yellow on Robert's workbench caught her eye. A premonition slithered down her spine as she turned to examine the item more carefully.

Grace's hands, the right one still aching from her bout with the mixer, tightened involuntarily on the top rail of the two-step ladder. The breath that she sucked in petrified in her lungs and then dropped into her stomach like a brick.

Rat poison. Three boxes, stacked neatly on top of each other next to Robert's toolbox. Rat poison...though the Feldmans had no rodent problem.

The stepladder fell to the floor.

Grace's mind felt like a wind sock in a hurricane, whipping back and forth. She trembled as she took in, then rejected, then took in yet again what this meant.

Then she launched herself at the boxes, snatched them and bundled them in her apron, having no idea what to do with them. She simply stood there like the village idiot, clutching enough rat poison to kill the entire neighborhood.

What-to-do-what-to-do-what-to-do-what-to-do-what-to-do? Her brain was frozen.

She couldn't simply toss it in the garbage. Robert took out the garbage. He'd see it. And even if he didn't, surely it was unsafe to dump poison into a landfill. It would seep into the ground, get into the water... same thing would happen if she buried it, or tossed it into the river.

Grace's eyes alighted on an old, desiccated, rusty bucket of paint. It surely hadn't been opened since they bought the house decades ago. Still clutching her apron full of poison, she rushed to Robert's tool kit, opened it and removed a flathead screwdriver.

She unsealed the paint bucket, wincing at the smell. Then she opened the contents of the boxes in her apron and dumped them into the ancient paint. She hammered the lid back onto the can. She ripped the boxes into tiny shreds and dumped those into a paper lunch bag. She tossed that into the garbage can.

Then Grace took the paint bucket and set it on the floorboards of the passenger seat in her car. She'd take it to the city dump the next day and nobody would be the wiser. She took several deep breaths, retrieved the stepladder once again, marched back into the kitchen with it, and washed her hands three times with soap.

That evening, her special dinner glowed in a candlelight that Grace found macabre. Christopher had brought home a charming girl for the meal, and she made light chitchat with her hostess as Robert, now bathed and dressed, gallantly complimented and carved the roast while Krypto looked on, licking his chops but behaving himself. It was the Feldman dog and pony show, put on for the benefit of their son and his guest.

Grace murmured something inane while she fixated upon Robert with the carving knife. *Should he be trusted with that?*

What would happen when he found his stash of rat poison gone? Grace put both hands on her wineglass to disguise the fact that they were trembling again. A wave of exhaustion washed over her.

Perhaps, if it's truly what he wants, I should let him do it.

But that thought was followed with a wave of anger that crested into fury.

No! It's not what he wants. It's what the elephant wants: the massive, dark, stinking melancholy that sits on his chest, making it impossible for him to move, to laugh, to create, to breathe. And I won't let it win. I won't.

PART III

PROHIBITION

Prohibition has made nothing but trouble.

—Al Capone

CHAPTER TWENTY-TWO

Washington, DC, 1926

"I'm here to see Captain Charles Root," Grace said with a polite smile. She stood in the reception area of the Treasury Building, the operations center for the US Coast Guard.

Outside the building, an enormous bronze statue of Alexander Hamilton stood guard: the man who'd not only created America's monetary system but also the fleet responsible for the capture of pirates—thieves and tax dodgers who cost hundreds of thousands of dollars to the US Customs Service.

"Do you have an appointment, madam?" asked the clerk behind an imposing walnut desk.

Grace hesitated. "I'm here to offer my services."

The clerk's eyebrows rose. He scanned all five feet, three inches of her from head to toe as Grace's irritation rose. "Your services? Captain Root already has a secretary."

Her gloved fingers tightened on her pocketbook. "I'm not a secretary. I'm a cryptanalyst."

It wasn't possible for the clerk's eyebrows to climb any higher—they'd have fallen over the back of his head. "A *what*?"

"A codebreaker," Grace said, with as much patience as she could muster.

"Madam, this is the United States Coast Guard. We deal in maritime issues. Boats, you understand? Ships."

"Yes," she said. "And you police five thousand miles of coastline against smugglers, correct? You have a paltry number of patrol boats—two hundred and three, I believe?—to track untold numbers of rumrunners coming and going in every direction. And lately, the bootleggers have taken to communicating in code. You have a backlog of thousands of messages that you have no ability or staff to solve. I can help."

"Madam, I can neither confirm nor deny—"

Grace closed her eyes. *I had a feeling it might come to this.* "Will you please inform Captain Root that my husband, Colonel Robert Feldman, sent me?"

The clerk's eyes rounded and he jumped to his feet. "Oh. Colonel Feldman. Yes, of course, ma'am. Why didn't you say so?"

Perhaps because I'd rather get the job on my own merits.

The man discovered a sudden solicitude. "Care to have a seat?"

"Yes, thank you." Grace sat on her resentment—and pride—that Robert's reputation opened doors that would otherwise be slammed in her face. She waited less than two minutes before Captain Root himself emerged from an office and greeted her warmly.

"Mrs. Feldman, how kind of you to offer your aid."

Aid? Does he think I'm here to volunteer for free?

He had ginger hair, boyish good looks and oversize ears that somehow added to his appeal. She smiled. "I'd like to apply for a job, Captain. My husband thought perhaps—"

"You may be the answer to our prayers. How much has Bobby taught you about codebreaking?"

Before she could tamp down her irritation and muster an answer, he asked, "Is it true that he broke the Kryha machine in three hours, including a forty-minute break for dinner?"

As usual, Grace's indignation warred with her pride in her husband. "Yes, it's true. He said that though the pork chop and greens were delicious, it was the custard that provided the solution."

Root laughed. "His Riverbank publications on codebreaking are the new standard."

"Actually," Grace hesitated. "Robert and I cowrote most of the Riverbank booklets on cryptanalysis. We worked out those concepts together."

"Did you?" Root leaned back in his chair, evaluating her for...what? Deception? Egomania?

Grace folded her hands over her pocketbook and let him make up his mind.

"Pretty as a picture, and smart, too."

He wasn't trying to be patronizing. It came out as a genuine compliment. But still. It made her blood boil. Again came an unexpected flash of sympathy for beautiful, waspish Alice. How much worse was it for her?

"So what kinds of codes can you decrypt?" Root asked.

"Anything Robert can."

"Really?" Captain Root leaned forward, clasping his hands on his desk.

"Really." Grace smiled at him, radiating competence from every pore.

"And you can work full-time? That is to say, you have no, er, obligations at home?"

Grace shook her head and resolutely blocked all memories of her pregnancy and miscarriage. The lack of fertility since then. "No children."

"When could you start?" Root asked.

Grace shrugged. "Right away, if you'd like. But let's talk salary, shall we?" She'd learned a thing or two since accepting a job from Farquhar. "And I do have a couple of requirements."

He steepled his hands on his desk. "Yes?"

"First, I'd like to work from home." *No filthy jokes, no dead rats, no pornography.*

He hesitated, then nodded. "You'll need a safe installed."

"Done." *Well, that was easy. Perhaps we can replace the stove with it, and I'll never have to cook again.*

"And?"

"I don't like flying blind, so to speak. So you'll have to get me on board a ship so that I can see for myself what's going on."

He balked, as she knew he would. "That would be highly irregular, ma'am. A ship is no place for a lady."

"Well. You see, Captain Root, the field of cryptanalysis is no place for a lady, either—and yet, you're offering me a job. Codebreaking is 'highly irregular' in itself, and requires wild guesses, odd insights, facility with language, luck and often a bit of magic. That's the polite word for it. The more accurate term is 'insanity.'"

Captain Root chuckled.

She aimed a level stare at him. "I'm not joking, sir. So, if you please, let's agree upon a salary. I'd also like to bring my own assistants on board if possible: a Miss Fay Trent, a Miss Veronica Fuentes and a Miss Utsidi Nashoba."

"I'm afraid we don't have the budget for three assistants. I may be able to grant you one who is already employed here."

Well, that was disappointing. "I understand. But please do get me on a Coast Guard vessel, sir. It will help me to understand the scope of my job."

"You're not going aboard a Coast Guard cutter, or any other kind of ship," Robert said, filling the doorway of their small bathroom with his broad shoulders. He looked as severe as she'd ever seen him.

Grace, who stood in her nightgown in front of the sink, finished wiping the cold cream off her face. "Why not? It's for research."

"You don't need to research for this position. You simply break codes."

"Robert, I need a feel for the atmosphere, the challenges the Coast Guard is facing from the rumrunners, the language used—"

"It's salty."

"I'm sure it is. I doubt I'll faint," she said dryly.

"My dear, I don't worry about you fainting. I worry about—" Robert broke off, his mouth grim, his brow furrowed.

"I can handle myself. I did with Farquhar."

"That *bastard*." Her husband's hands curled into fists.

"Yes—that bastard with whom *you are exchanging letters*." Grace glared at him from the mirror. "How can you? It's outrageous."

When all else fails, pick a fight. Successful diversion from the sticky topic at hand.

"I've told you why, Grace. I want to retain access to his cryptology collection. One day, someone is going to write a history of codes, ciphers and cryptanalysis, and I'd like that someone to be me..."

"You? Or us?"

"Us, of course," Robert hastened to say.

"And this really justifies maintaining a friendship with the man who made advances toward me? Who *laid hands on* me?"

"Grace, if I'd been there at the time, I would have torn him limb from limb."

"But you weren't—"

"I was testifying in court for the Allies!"

"Yes—which makes it even more despicable that he'd try to seduce me. You were helping to make a name for him."

"So you'd like me to go and take a swing at him now? What is the point of this argument, Grace?" Then it dawned on him. "Damn it all, I know the point: you're distracting me. I *forbid* you to go aboard a ship full of randy, uncouth sailors—"

"Oh, you forbid it, do you?" Grace bared her teeth at him, which was easy to do since she was brushing them. "We had an agreement before we married: that you'd never boss me."

"I'm not bossing you. I'm protecting you."

"You're bossing me in order to protect me, and I don't want your protection in this case. I want to do my job."

Robert sighed. "I make a decent living. You don't *need* a job, Grace."

"Yes, I do. Our country is at war with the smugglers, and it's getting uglier and uglier. It's not just people thumbing their noses at an unpopular law. The 'gentlemen's game' has been replaced by violent crime syndicates. The 'rumrunners' have become opium smugglers and human traffickers and murderers. So our country needs me, too. And I want to help."

"Grace, I know you're my equal—in fact, you're probably even smarter than I am. I've never questioned that. But understand that your working makes me look as though I cannot provide for you. Makes me less of a man in the eyes of others."

"Why do you give a fig?"

"That's easy for you to say."

"Bobby, I cannot be a wife who does nothing but go to teas and luncheons for worthy causes. Not that there's anything wrong with it—but it's not who I am. It bores me silly."

"It will be easier for you to conceive if you're not driving yourself mad cracking codes."

This again. "I need something to do, and the idea of being a mother has always terrified me, anyway."

"And drunken sailors don't? Violent smugglers?"

Grace sighed. "I'm not ready to be a parent."

"When will you *be* ready? Neither of us is getting any younger."

Grace took refuge in humor. "Yes, yes, Robert. I'm an old crone. Now please, help me get my wrinkled, arthritic body into bed…"

CHAPTER TWENTY-THREE

The ship was called *Hogan's Goat*, according to Grace's escort. It was an ancient, foul, dilapidated rust bucket that looked as if it had been christened before the Civil War, and it listed to one side like the victim of a stroke.

"That's a *Coast Guard* vessel?" She eyed it with trepidation. She tugged down her cloche hat, which was being challenged by a stiff breeze, and clutched her overnight bag.

"Yah, Madam. This way." Her escort was an enormous, bronzed, burly Norwegian with a permanent squint from peering into the sun. He gestured toward the gangway. "Your valise, may I take?"

"That's kind of you." She relinquished it, and he escorted her toward the ship. The water was choppy and gray; it smelled of brine and mildew and a tinge of something rotten—dead fish?

Sailors began to sprout along the rails as they approached, pointing, hooting and catcalling in all sorts of languages she'd never heard before. "These are *American* sailors?"

"Yah. We haf many immigrants: Danes, Norwegians, Finns, Swedes, even Australians."

"What are they saying?"

Her escort flushed and chewed on his lip. "Some of them...ah, find you attractive, Madam."

Oh dear. "Tell them I'm married."

"Yah. Not so sure they mind, Madam. They not, ah, looking to marry you."

That's horrid. "Well, tell them that they'd best behave themselves," she said crisply. "I am here in a *professional* capacity."

The giant Norwegian fell into a coughing fit. "Yah, Madam."

Too late, she realized how that sounded.

Up the gangplank they went, Grace picking her way carefully in her low heels, but trying to keep her chin up and her shoulders back.

Her welcoming committee got louder and more enthusiastic, adding jeers and slurs to their whistles. "Ahoy! Skirt to starboard! *Whoo-ee* hotsy-totsy Jane! How much to come skate with me, sister?"

Grace's mouth dropped open.

"Shut your yaps!" roared her escort. He added something incomprehensible in Norwegian.

They laughed and ignored him. "Cha cha, chippy! Nice pins, angel face!"

As she stepped aboard, a strong gust of wind blew the cloche right off her head and sent it spinning into the rough sea. "Oh dear—"

"I love you! I get for you! I *love* you! I get..." A sailor on the lower deck hurtled over the rail and dove into the bay, where he floundered, spat up water and failed miserably to retrieve her hat. Chivalry might not be dead, but it did appear to be drowning—the sailor was somehow impaired.

"Blimey, Kaczka's gotten into the hooch again. Someone fish him out…" A tall, redheaded ensign appeared on the bridge and tossed down a life preserver. He nodded to her.

She nodded back as the floundering sailor worked his arms and head through the floating ring.

The wind chose this moment to gust again, tearing her skirt up to thigh level, exposing her garter straps and sending her hair to hell.

The men went wild as she fought the fabric down.

Grace's cheeks flamed. *She is clothed with strength and dignity…*

It was a Bible verse often quoted by her dearly departed Mama, who'd been drained of both.

"Oy!" The redhead was Australian. "Shut your filthy mouths, you animals! This lady is a special agent with the Coast Guard, and you'll treat her with respect, or I'll toss you overboard."

"We're like to sink anyway, Cox—women are bad luck aboard a ship," one sailor called.

"We're not going to sink, you arsehole," Cox called back. "She's only with us a couple of days. Oh, *shite*. Pardon, Madam, pardon my French."

Grace dimpled. "Ce n'était pas Français."

He looked mock pained. "Merde. Just my luck you speak actual French. Je suis désolé. Ensign Wimberly Cox, at your service. Call me Kangaroo."

Grace extended her hand. "How do you do, Mr. Kangaroo?"

The sailors within earshot fell about laughing.

"Bugger off, you louts!" But Cox himself grinned. "It's not Mister or Ensign Kangaroo. It's just Kangaroo. Let me show you to your cabin. Don't be alarmed by these hooligans—I assure you there's a lock on the door and the ability to bar it from inside."

"That's a relief," Grace admitted.

"I've been assigned by Captain Egan—and Captain Root—to be your minder. Seems Root got quite an earful from your husband, ma'am."

Grace gritted her teeth. "Is that so?" No wonder Robert had relented. He'd once again plotted behind her back.

Cox gave her another grin along with a wink. "Can you blame him, then? If you were mine, I'd want to keep you safe from this lot, too."

Annoyed, Grace still warmed to the compliment. It was hard not to. Kangaroo had charm to spare, with those guileless blue eyes and the auburn hair. And how was it that a redhead could tan?

Her Norwegian escort handed her bag to her new friend Kangaroo. They crossed the deck, wound their way around massive coils of rope and all sorts of odd equipment and went down a set of winding metal stairs.

A couple of narrow, stifling corridors later, they arrived at her cabin. It held a set of bunks bolted to the wall and floor and a metal desk, also bolted down, with a porthole window above it. "We gave you a room with a view," he said, setting down her bag. "There's a head two doors down."

A head?

Seeing her confusion, he explained. "A loo. We've marked it with a pink envelope so you'll have it to yourself. The men have been told to use another."

"Very kind," Grace said, realizing too late that her demand to go aboard a ship had caused some logistical problems she had not anticipated.

"So I'll leave you to freshen up. Please join us at Captain Egan's table for dinner at 1900 hours. That's seven o'clock to you," he added.

"And where..."

"I'll come to fetch you." And Kangaroo disappeared, leaving her to wonder if Robert had been right about this, her maiden voyage, but determined to prove him wrong.

Captain Egan had a weathered face, shrewd and piercing gray eyes and a neatly trimmed beard. He stood when Grace entered, as did all the other officers, and welcomed her with cool, disapproving courtesy.

"Mrs. Feldman. A pleasure to have you aboard." He pulled out her chair.

"Thank you." Grace took a seat, conscious of being a curiosity in the room.

The other officers sat, too, and Kangaroo made introductions all around. "Mrs. Feldman's husband is Army Colonel Robert Feldman of the Signal Intelligence Service. Perhaps you've heard of him?"

"Feldman! Yes, of course. Isn't he the fellow behind that ingenious plan to use the Choctaw telephone squad in the Meuse-Argonne offensive?"

Actually, that was Utsidi. And me. But Grace nodded and kept her mouth closed.

"Didn't he break the Plett's cryptograph within a couple of hours?"

"Yes." Grace smiled. *After I came up with the second correct keyword.*

"You know the Brits had already manufactured *eleven thousand* of them? Left egg all over their faces."

"He did feel awful about that," Grace said. "But they asked him to break it. So he did. It was supposed to be impossible."

"The King Midas of cryptanalysis," mused Captain Egan. "Everything he touches turns to plaintext."

"Oh my." Grace placed her napkin into her lap. "Robert will be so pleased at his renown. So what, er, type of ship is *Hogan's Goat*?"

Captain Egan scowled. "Please don't call her that."

"I beg your pardon," Grace said, feeling a flush rise up her neck and across her face. "I was told—"

"I know what you were told." The scowl did not abate. "She's a '78 Higgins motor torpedo boat."

Grace was thankful when they were interrupted by the delivery of the first course, a crab soup. An awkward silence ensued, broken only by the clinking of spoons against bowls. "Delicious," she ventured.

Egan grunted.

"So," Kangaroo came to her rescue. "You'll be doing codebreaking work for us, Mrs. Feldman? And you wanted to see what you're up against."

"Yes," Grace said. "I know it may seem odd to you—as it did to my husband—but breaking a code is a combination of something called frequency analysis, with which I won't bore you, and the recognition of patterns. But intuition and guessing and language are quite important, too. So I thought it would be helpful to get a feel for exactly what occurs on a ship like this one, as you battle the smugglers."

As she spoke, a string of lights appeared in the twilight some distance away, visible through the open portholes in the cabin.

"Well, you're about to witness a typical evening," Egan said in a disgusted tone. He pointed. "Those lights out there? That's Rum Row."

"Boats loaded with cases and barrels of illegal liquor," another officer explained.

And they were just watching them? "Forgive me, but why can't you go out and—"

"They're exactly three miles offshore," Cox said. "In international waters. So we can't touch them, and they know it."

"And they bloody well enjoy the knowledge," growled Captain Egan.

As the soup bowls were removed and the second course came in, even more lights came on and the breeze brought the sound of fiddles playing a merry Highland reel.

Grace peered through the portholes as best she could. "Are they . . . are they *dancing*?"

"Yes," growled the captain. "And drinking rum or whiskey, great quantities of it. Right under our noses." He pushed back his chair and stood up. "Do forgive my rudeness, Mrs. Feldman, but I have no appetite. I'm not going to watch this farce this evening." Egan gave a sharp glance to Cox. "See to it that she's kept safe. Post a guard outside her cabin."

Cox nodded. "Aye, Captain."

"A pleasure to meet you, Mrs. Feldman. And now, please excuse me. Good night."

Grace wondered if she, too, should excuse herself. The officers had fallen silent, in contrast to the escalating merriment on Rum Row.

Scottish reels, Irish jigs, sea shanties and the laughter of both men and women traveled through the portholes. She found herself wishing to join the fun. But she was stuck here at this awkward dinner.

"I—I didn't mean to offend Captain Egan," she said at last.

One of the officers whose name she'd already forgotten spoke up. "He spends every moment of every day offended, ma'am. Hates the rummies with a passion—they've made a fool of him too many times."

"That's why he's been demoted to command of this old tub," Cox said cheerfully. "And saddled with the likes of us."

"So why is it nicknamed *Hogan's Goat?*"

The entire table snickered. "Comes from an old comic column called Hogan's Alley, ma'am. Refers to anything that's messed up or stinks."

"No wonder he hates it to be called that."

"Truth is, this ship's a floating penal colony for scoundrels. We'd be dismissed, but they need us too badly."

Mystified, Grace picked at her salad. "What have you done to deserve..."

The other officers glanced at each other.

Cox merely shrugged. "Shall I tell her, mates? Eh, why not. I was a misbegotten lad—"

"Still are!" chimed in another officer.

"—a bit of a disciplinary problem. I ran off at fifteen, landed in America at sixteen. Lied about my age and joined up with the puddle pirates, here." He grinned at the abuse hurled at him from the table.

"So I'm all of sixteen, and it's plain daft to me to pour perfectly good firewater into the mouths of fish and squid, eh?"

"Still is," muttered a stocky officer down the table.

Grace, no idiot, had begun to understand within a few days on the job that Prohibition was the single most unpopular law ever passed in America. In defiance of it, customs officers took bribes to look the other way; uniformed police officers, on the take, made deliveries of liquor to speakeasies in broad daylight. Confiscated spirits were not only routinely "misplaced," but one jury in San Francisco was even in farcical hot legal water for actually *drinking* all the evidence brought in by the prosecution.

But she remained silent as the officers of *Hogan's Goat* relayed their experiences.

"On one excursion," Cox continued, "we approach Saint Pierre near Newfoundland, where there are millions of cases of liquor stored in old fish shacks on the wharves. They're selling gin for six dollars per case, bourbon for seven, whiskey for eight! But our captain, he says we're not allowed shore leave; we're not to fraternize with the rummies.

"We're only at Saint Pierre to gather *information*, if you please. Radio our observations to Coast Guard Intel in Washington, DC, where, as I understand it, you now work, ma'am." Cox flashed his grin. "Well, my apologies, but back then, at least on this particular ship—the *Tampa*— we enlisted men didn't share the ideals of our officers."

Grace repressed a smile.

"So, as we're peering through binoculars and telescopes, as we're noting down the details of each smuggling vessel—home port, flag, name, dimensions, rig, estimated tonnage and speed—we're also slavering for a taste of what's on board. We decide that nothing will stop us.

"We had three things in our favor. First, our captain wished to be rowed ashore to Miquelon to pay his respects to the governor. Second, a lovely Grand Banks fog rolled in to give us cover. And third, the coxswain who rowed in the captain was thirsty, himself.

"He takes the captain ashore and goes off to accomplish our goal. But then, a stroke of bad luck: the customs house had closed for the day. The liquor warehouse wouldn't accept the taxes on their behalf. We were turned away," Cox said mournfully. "It was tragic. So there was nothing to do but pull off a heist."

Grace's eyes widened. "You *stole* liquor?"

The other officers eyed him uneasily, and then her.

"We were that thirsty, ma'am." Kangaroo managed to look as innocent as a choirboy. "Desperate times call for desperate measures. And remember, I was but a lad. A scamp."

"A creative one," said an officer at the end of the table.

"Anyhow, to cut a long yarn short, we rowed out fifty or so hams—"

"Hams?" Grace asked.

"Sorry. Cases of hooch."

"—and the entire crew proceeds to get kippered to the edge of annihilation. The captain arrives back at the ship and goes straight to sleep, but next morn, he can tell what's amiss. Half the crew can't even be roused from their bunks.

"The hands who do make it to their feet are lurching and staggering to their positions. The sailors manning the chain locker are drooling and snoring on the cable itself, and there's not a prayer of waking them, short of setting them on fire. Crikey, the helmsman himself doubles over the wheel and is sick all over the deck."

Grace wrinkled her nose. "The captain must've been thrilled."

"The captain threatens us all with court martial if we don't produce the contraband. Since we're all still half in the bag, we think this is quite funny and hoot at him. We taunt him to find the liquor himself."

Grace gasped. "You didn't!"

"We did," said another officer, ruefully.

"So the skipper and the exec and three junior officers, they all search the ship high and low, every locker and bunk, every nook and cranny. Nothing. They're furious, of course, but they can't do anything."

Grace chuckled. "That's quite a story."

"Oh, he's not done yet," another man said.

"So next morning: exact same thing. Men sleepwalking, tripping over things, passing out cold on deck. Entire ship smells like a distillery. The captain's enraged, purple in the face, apoplectic. Orders yet another search of the ship. This time they check every seabag, boot, pillow... they check the iceboxes, sacks of vegetables—they even look inside the carcasses of beef, pork and turkey! But we've been rather devious, you see." Cox flashed his white teeth again. "Not a single bottle turned up."

Grace found herself rooting for Cox despite herself. "And?"

"Night three, it all happens again. The morning is a soup of soused seamen, and the captain's white with rage. He and the exec and the officers rip apart the ship. They descend into her very bowels. They slosh into the bilges, they inspect the gun magazines, they lower grappling hooks into the fuel tanks. They open the paint buckets. They go down into the chain locker and examine every coil of dirty, reeking cable. Nothing.

"They emerge looking and smelling like a load of rotten fish, the captain screaming and cursing. We almost got away with it, but this, dear lady, is when our luck runs out."

Grace was on the edge of her seat. "What happened?"

"Captain goes to the scuttlebutt for a drink of water. He's hot, sweaty, parched...he turns the tap on the barrel, fills a tin mug, tosses it back..."

"Yes? And?"

"He rears up, paws at his throat, snorts like a wild mustang, jumps a foot into the air. Shrieks incoherently. We fall about laughing, but we know we're in deep sh—"

"Trouble," supplied another officer.

"Right, trouble. Because Captain's found the source of the liquor, all right. Cases of gin, bourbon, Scotch, rye all poured—every last bottle—into the ship's main drinking-water tank."

Grace covered her mouth with her hands.

"So that was the end of our three-day party out of Saint Pierre, ma'am. And the reason why we're all stuck aboard *Hogan's Goat.*"

"Good grief. All of you?"

Cox nodded. His eyes sparkled with mischief. "No single sailor would fess up. So he sacked the lot of us, the entire crew."

Grace evaluated him. He still seemed quite proud of their actions, not abashed at all. *Interesting.* "I must agree that it was an ingenious hiding place."

"Yes, ma'am. Thank you, ma'am." The choirboy smile again. Apple cheeks. Butter wouldn't melt in his mouth. Kangaroo Cox was a little too charming, in her book.

They regaled her with a few more stories, and then Grace turned in early. Sleeping in a bunk on a rolling ship was odd, but she found it enjoyable, rocking to and fro. She fell asleep easily, but woke early to some commotion and cursing. She dressed hurriedly, thanked her guard and went up on deck.

"Buggers," muttered a nearby sailor.

"The cheek!"

"Belling the cat, boys, and you know it."

"Doesn't matter. Captain's orders."

Creaks, clanking, shouts, roars and rumbles ensued, and *Hogan's Goat* surged forward.

"What's happening?" Grace asked a passing seaman.

"We're in pursuit. Contact boat stole over to Rum Row before dawn, loaded up cargo. Didn't think we'd notice."

The old *Goat* picked up speed, its whistle blasting a warning to the fleeing vessel. The rumrunner blithely ignored it. The whistle sounded again, and yet again.

Grace clung to the railing, peering into the distance from the port side of the ship. There was the smuggler, dead ahead, about five hundred meters away. It was small and a much faster craft than *Hogan's Goat*; it clearly had the advantage.

That is, until the ship's guns began to fire warning shots.

A screech escaped Grace at the unexpected fire, but it was lost to the wind. Would the rumrunner fire back?

It did not. Just upped its speed.

So did *Hogan's Goat*. Grace clung to the railing for dear life, getting spattered with salt spray. If she were smart, she'd flee back to her cabin. But then she'd miss all the action.

Bigger guns fired from the *Goat*, now—deeper, throatier, more menacing. A ball of lead narrowly missed the stern of the rummy, but some shrapnel landed on the aft deck. Suddenly the skipper appeared, waving his arms in surrender. His craft slowed, came about and dropped anchor.

Hogan's Goat surged alongside and dropped anchor as well.

A dory rowed over a few men while Captain Egan looked on from the bridge.

A few minutes passed while the Coast Guard boarded and descended below deck to check for contraband. The skipper stayed on deck, whistling and looking unconcerned.

"G'day," Kangaroo said, startling Grace. "Sleep well?"

"Yes, to my surprise. What's going on?"

Cox rolled his eyes. "You'll see soon enough. We're being snookered."

Grace pushed her hair out of her eyes and turned a questioning gaze on him.

"Right. I'll explain. We just gave chase to this fellow, who's waiting amused while our boarding party turns up nothing but empty casks and cases below deck. Meanwhile, back at Rum Row, several other contact boats will be roaring up to load the real McCoy while we're distracted. Captain never stops falling for it. The rummies refer to it as "belling the Coast Guard cat.""

"Oh dear." Grace didn't know what else to say.

"These bootleggers pull all sorts of shenanigans. You know they actually disguise their boats? They'll add fake smokestacks, repaint, register in a foreign country under a different name. They hide cargo under mountains of fish and the like. Very creative fellows."

Sure enough, cursing and screaming came shortly from the bridge, as the lookout communicated to the captain what was happening back on Rum Row. The boarding party came up empty-handed, was told to have a nice day by the sardonic, smirking skipper and rowed back over to *Hogan's Goat*.

They came about and headed back toward the row as fast as the ship would take them. They were greeted by jeers and waving whiskey bottles.

Captain Egan, raging, pulled out the ship's megaphone and addressed them. "Come an inch farther Stateside, you yellow-bellied rascals! One *inch*, and you're mine."

"Oy, Capitan! Only one inch?" one rummy shouted back. "Can't take more than an inch up that tight culo? We can help with that..."

"What's a culo?" Grace asked Cox.

He fought to suppress a grin. "Never mind. It's not for a lady to know."

Then the rummies caught sight of Grace. "Skirt! *Skirt!* Ya through with her, then? Can we borrow 'er for a spell?"

"Oye, neña! Muéstrame tus tetas!"

"What does *that* mean?" Grace asked Cox.

He shook his head. "Nothing."

Apparently it was quite disrespectful, because Captain Egan went purple in the face and raised his megaphone again. "You will not insult a lady on my ship! Apologize to my guest at once. At once, I tell you!"

The smugglers fell over themselves laughing.

"Qué te jodan, old man!"

"Ach, Pops, coom aboard for a wee dram, why don'tcha?"

Spitting with rage, cheeks puffed like a bulldog's, Egan stomped off and issued an order that Grace couldn't quite hear.

The officer who received the order blinked, his mouth dropping open.

"Go!" bellowed Egan.

The man ran.

Shortly afterward, to the collective shock of Grace and the entire crew, the guns of *Hogan's Goat* spat out a barrage of...*potatoes*...onto the decks of the three closest rumrunners.

Cox doubled over laughing, and when he straightened, he had tears in his eyes. "He's defending your honor, Mrs. Feldman." His shoulders shook. "With ruddy *spuds!*"

"*What?*" Grace's jaw slackened.

"He can't fire on them with real ammunition while they're in international waters."

"Cowards and scoundrels and reprobates, all of you!" shouted Egan, shaking his fist.

The smugglers, astonished, dodged the storm of potatoes that rained down upon them as best they could. Then they collected them into buckets.

"Thank ye kindly, Captain!" called one. "I don't suppose ye could spare us some onions as well?"

Grace broke down into shameless laughter herself and had to hide her face, faking a coughing fit.

"Got carrots?" called another.

Egan trembled with rage. "I'll take down you blackguards if it's the last thing I do!"

Cox tapped Grace on the shoulder. "It's probably best that I get you back to your cabin, Mrs. Feldman. There's no telling what will happen next..."

CHAPTER TWENTY-FOUR

"And how was your trip, my dear?" Robert asked, as he collected her from the train station.

"Oh, lovely. I had a sumptuous stateroom on the most magnificent old schooner."

"Did you, now?"

"I sunbathed up on deck while drinking cocktails."

"Mmm."

"And enjoyed delicious five-course meals while I learned all sorts of interesting terms. *Starboard* is right, and *port* is left. *Stern* is the back of the ship. *Bow* is the front. The captain directs things from the *bridge*, and—"

"Grace, my darling, you're a terrible liar."

"And you, Robert, are a wicked schemer."

"Not so. I'm an adoring husband."

"You humiliated me by going behind my back to my new boss."

"I did my best to protect my wife."

Grace scoffed. "How would *you* have felt, Robert, if I'd gone to Black Jack Pershing and asked him for a nanny to protect you while you were stationed in Chaumont?"

"That's different."

"Why? Because you're a man?"

"Frankly, yes." Robert's gaze was steely and uncompromising. "And I was a uniformed officer in the United States Army."

"Well, I'm a special agent of Coast Guard Intelligence. And I find it mortifying that my husband conspired with my superior to treat me like a china doll."

Robert folded his arms. "And I find it quite embarrassing that I had to do so to guarantee your safety, because I cannot control my own wife."

"Oh, it's about control, is it?" Grace poked him in the chest.

"It's not, and you know it. We've always operated as equals, and so you ultimately made your own—stupid, I might add—decision."

"Stupid?!"

"Yes. And pigheaded. You put Root in an awkward position, you embarrassed me, you inconvenienced the ship's captain and you endangered yourself—all in the name of research you didn't need to conduct."

"You, Root and the captain will all recover. Perhaps it's good for men to be knocked off-kilter once in a blue moon."

"Grace, you knocked me off-kilter from the moment we met."

She ignored this. "And I *did* need to research. Smuggling is an entire world outside of letters and books, with a scope and vocabulary that I need to have a sense of."

"Is that so? Please educate me."

"Fine. For example, scuttlebutt—"

"Gossip?"

"No, a water tank. And poop deck—no, nobody poops there. And futtock, which looks vaguely obscene but has nothing to do with a buttock, or anything near one. Then there's escutcheon, bilge and my favorite: baggywrinkle. Those are just for starters…"

"Captain Root will award you a maritime diploma, I'm sure." Robert's voice was dry.

"Don't patronize me, Bobby. It was eye-opening. And these are all sorts of possible key words for ciphers—can you imagine?"

"I can."

"Amazing. Because if you'd had your way, I wouldn't have gone at all."

"Grace, if you cannot understand that I feared for your safety and that my love for you is all-encompassing, then so be it. I won't apologize and I'd do it again."

She glared at him.

He glared back. Then he moved in and snatched a kiss before she could swat him.

Despite her anger, she softened.

"Now tell me how it really was. I know full well you weren't on the White Star's *Majestic*."

Three days later, Grace took the trolley to the Treasury Building to pick up her first thick envelope of unsolved messages from Root's secretary, which she tucked into a shopping bag along with her purchases from the local deli: a head of lettuce, two tomatoes, a cucumber and a cold chicken, which she had hopes of successfully reheating. A loaf of French bread poked out of the bag like an accusatory index finger: *bad wife, can't cook…*

Grace flew into the house, so eager to get to work that she almost forgot to unload the groceries. She'd spread several messages out on the dining room table, getting lost in the clumps of letters and searching for frequencies and patterns, before she remembered and shoved the chicken and salad veggies into the icebox.

Then she settled down with pencil and blank paper and warmed to the challenge. These were telegraph ciphers intercepted by the Coast Guard's radio stations. She went to work on one in particular:

JDSLE 2221 1612 WJJE....DEMPY.

Three *Js*, three *Es*, two *Ds*, four twos, three ones. Letters mixed with numbers. Probably double-encrypted, involving a cipher and some sort of commercial codebook.

Grace began with some educated guesses, trial and error. She was deep down the rabbit hole of the mystery, swinging her pencil at it like a saber and had forgotten to eat lunch. She ignored the rumbling of her stomach. Then the doorbell rang, startling her. She fell back to earth.

She'd entered a trance. She'd gone outside her body and left it sitting at the table, her hand scratching madly away at the puzzle as her brain processed possibilities. As the bell rang again, she realized that she'd kicked off her shoes somewhere. She scrambled under the table for them.

"Yes! One moment!" Grace shoved her feet into the low-heeled pumps and stumbled to the door. She opened it to find a smiling neighbor with a coffee cake in hand. "Oh. Hello."

"I'm Dorothy—Dot—from next door. Dot Brawley." She proffered the coffee cake, which smelled heavenly. "We just moved in. Thought I'd introduce myself."

Oh dear. It was Grace who should have welcomed Dot to the neighborhood with something. But Grace took the pan from her. It was still warm, apparently just out of the oven. "Why, thank you! I'm..." for a moment she struggled to remember her own name. It wasn't JDSLE 2221. "I'm Grace Feldman. Lovely to meet you." *And now I've got to invite you in, you inconvenient woman. I can hardly snatch your cake and shut the door in your face.*

A woman like Dot Brawley would never stop in at a deli to pay extra for a chicken someone else had roasted. She was one of those ladies who made things from scratch, who filled her home with wonderful and inviting aromas and probably even dusted every other day. The horror.

Dot eyed her expectantly, almost avidly. Hungry for a new friend.

"Won't you come in?" Grace stepped aside and held open the door.

"Why, I'd love to, thank you." And she clip-clopped over the threshold, further derailing any trains of thought that might have led Grace to a complete solution of the encrypted message.

"Coffee?" Grace asked.

"Lovely!" She eyed the avalanche of papers on the dining room table.

"Please, have a seat." Grace gestured toward the camel-backed settee in the front parlor. *1612 WJJE . . . DEMPY.* She walked toward the kitchen, put the kettle on the stove and put some beans into the hand grinder. *Crank, crank, crank.* The beans groaned, splintered and reluctantly gave way—much more easily than the encrypted messages did.

Grace spooned the ground coffee into the percolator, then located sugar, cream, plates, forks, spoons, a knife and a cake server. She piled everything onto a tray once the coffee was done and trundled it into the parlor, noting a roving dust bunny under the settee. She prayed that Dot wouldn't locate any others while on the premises.

Grace served the coffee and cut the cake, keeping a pleasant smile on her face as Dot exclaimed over the nice weather they were having, how lovely it was to see the cherry blossoms beginning to bloom and how much she looked forward to planting tomatoes this summer.

Oh dear. Another thing a good wife should do. Grow vegetables and make preserves. "So delicious, this coffee cake!"

"Why, thank you. It's my grandmother's recipe. I'm happy to share it."

Don't. I'll burn it. Or forget to turn on the oven altogether and then wonder why it hasn't baked at all. But she said, "Yes, I'd love to have it."

"So what does your husband do?" Dot enquired.

"Army. Lieutenant. And yours?"

"He works for the Justice Department."

Grace filed this away in her brain. "How interesting. Do you have children?"

"Two boys, and now I'm hoping for a little girl...you?"

Grace shook her head. "Not yet." The innocuous words were surprisingly painful to say.

The conversation went on. And on. Dot was a very nice woman. But Dot was a very talkative woman.

At last, feeling guilty and rude, Grace looked at the clock. "It's been so nice, this visit. And again, thank you for the cake. But I'm afraid I've got to get back to work now."

"Work?" Her neighbor blinked.

"Ah yes—the mess on the dining table."

"Oh."

Silence.

"What is it that you *do*?"

"Just a bit of...translation." Grace smiled. "For a boring old, ah... law office." Not a total lie. Technically, the Treasury was an office, attempting to enforce the law.

"Well. I apologize for the intrusion," said Dot.

"No, no, not at all."

"I was rather hoping you'd join a quilting circle. We're going to meet every Tuesday at two."

My, Dot did move fast to establish herself socially.

"But if you have a *job*, that won't be possible, will it?"

"Thank you for the very kind invitation, but no." Grace injected regret into her tone. "I'm afraid not."

"Such a shame." Dot stood and put on her gloves. "I beg your pardon for asking this, but how are you able to get all the housekeeping and chores done if you *work*? You must have help."

Grace chuckled lightly. "Oh no. It just somehow all comes together." *Or not.*

"Does it?" Dot shot her an odd look. An almost pitying one. "I suppose I'm lucky."

It doesn't occur to her that I want to work. She thinks I have to because of finances.

"Oh, you *are* lucky!" Grace ushered her to the door.

Dot left the house, and before long, Grace had left her own body again, turning inward and tunneling through her brain. By the end of the day, when Robert came whistling through the door to a cold chicken still in the icebox, she'd solved the message:

Heave your anchor immediately and get underway. Stand up the river toward Albany.

The smugglers were boldly chugging up the Hudson River in New York. But which vessel had they loaded with illicit booze?

Before long, thanks to Dot, *all* the neighbor ladies were eyeing her with pity, with a faint air of superiority. But because they were, at heart, very nice people, this resulted in an unexpected benefit: casseroles and pies and loaves of bread came calling, along with their creators. Grace got to know everyone because she was such an oddity—a working wife—that they were curious. And, once she'd solved enough coded messages for the morning or afternoon, she returned their social calls bearing fruit, or jars of jam or pastries from the deli so that they wouldn't see her as taking advantage of them.

"So what languages do you translate?" Mrs. Johnson from across the street asked her, as she handed over a beef stroganoff.

"Oh, a bit of this and a bit of that. Boring legal documents, you know... Doesn't this smell enticing! I can't thank you enough."

"It was my mother's recipe. I'm happy to give it to you..."

Robert was amused. "Your cooking skills have vastly improved, my dear," he said that evening, enjoying the stroganoff a little too much, in her view.

Grace gave him a bland smile. "Yes, haven't they? I'm finally getting the hang of it."

"So what are the ingredients in this dish?"

Uh . . . "Oh, you know. Beef. Noodles."

He looked down at his food, struggling to suppress a smile. "Is that right?"

"That's right."

"Mmm. There's a similar delicious aroma wafting from the Johnsons' kitchen window. I appreciated it on my way home."

"What a coincidence. More bread, Bobby, dear?"

CHAPTER TWENTY-FIVE

"I'm here to see Captain Root please," Grace told the reception clerk at Treasury a day later.

"Do you have an appointment, Madam?"

Oh, not this again. "It's most urgent that I see him."

The clerk eyed her. "I'd be happy to give Captain Root a message on your behalf."

And I'd be happy to give you a wallop in the face with a wet trout, you insufferable little bureaucrat. "I'll wait," said Grace. And she sat down without invitation.

"Very well, Madam," he said woodenly.

It was perhaps thirty minutes or so when Captain Root emerged and escorted a gentleman in dress whites with several gold bars on his epaulets to the reception area.

"Mrs. Feldman, what a surprise," Root said. "I do hope you haven't been waiting long. Rear Admiral Frederick C. Billard, may I present to you, special agent and cryptanalyst Mrs. Robert F. Feldman. Mrs. Feldman, Rear Admiral Billard is—"

"Commandant of the Coast Guard," she said faintly, extending her gloved hand. "Goodness. A pleasure to meet you, sir."

"So, Mrs. Feldman," asked Root. "What brings you to my office?"

She took a deep breath. "It's the *Holmwood*, sir. I cracked the encrypted messages between it and an illicit shore station. It's carrying *twenty thousand cases* of liquor right up the Hudson River and is due to dock at Albany in less than two hours. But if you radio orders—"

"We can divert it and board it before it arrives." Root turned to the clerk. "Ambrose, get me New York CG Intel on the line."

"Yes, sir."

"There's something else, Captain," Grace broke in.

"Yes?"

"The *Holmwood*'s disguised as an oil tanker—fake smokestack and all. Called the *Texas Ranger*."

"Got to give them points for creativity," Root said ruefully.

Rear Admiral Billard began to clap, slowly. "Well done, Mrs. Feldman. Well done!"

"Thank you, sir."

"So you're Bobby Feldman's wife, are you?"

"I am."

"I see he's taught you a thing or two," Billard said.

Grace gave him a tight smile.

"Or did he give you a little help over the dinner table?" Billard chuckled.

"No, Admiral," she said demurely. "He's got projects of his own."

"So I hear. I'd dearly like to recruit him, but General Nolan would have my ass on a platter—begging your pardon, Mrs. Feldman."

"We tried to get him," Root said. "Well. Will there be anything else, ma'am?"

"Yes, actually. At your convenience, would you forward me any information Treasury has on a company called Consolidated Exporters Corporation? Conexco?"

"Certainly."

Ambrose the erstwhile clerk raised his head and clapped a palm over the telephone receiver. "Got New York Intel on the line, sir."

"Excellent."

"I'll see you out, Mrs. Feldman," said Rear Admiral Billard, taking her arm.

"Thank you." Grace collected another thick envelope of coded messages from Ambrose's desk.

"Very nice work, I must say." Billard smiled down at her. Then he cast a glance back at Root. "Charles, make sure that New York Intel doesn't try to claim credit for our lady codebreaker's coup."

A wave of gratitude threatened to undo Grace. She, a girl off an Indiana farm, had just impressed the boss of the entire Coast Guard.

A week or so later, Grace received orders to attend a mysterious meeting at Treasury. She put on one of Nellie's dresses and her pearls and made sure to be five minutes early. Root's secretary rose to his feet when she arrived. "Good morning, Mrs. Feldman. Come right this way."

He escorted Grace deeper into the bowels of the building, to a far grander office with its own reception area, complete with secretary. An older lady with a silvered chignon, she picked up her telephone handset and murmured into it.

Root's assistant left, and the lady led Grace to a set of large mahogany doors. Inside, she found a number of people, including her boss Charles Root, who nodded to her.

Rear Admiral Billard was also there. "Welcome, Mrs. Feldman. Of course you know Captain Root."

Grace nodded politely, wondering why she'd been invited.

"For anyone who does not, Root is the chief intelligence officer of the Coast Guard."

Billard next introduced Grace to the big boss: Secretary of the Treasury Andrew Mellon, who greeted her from behind a gargantuan carved mahogany desk. Evidently, this was his office.

Mellon was a distinguished fellow with a narrow face bordering on gaunt. He had a full head of beautifully barbered white hair, complemented by bushy white eyebrows that mimicked his luxurious white mustache. He wore the finest, most beautifully cut three-piece suit Grace had ever seen.

Billard then introduced Grace to US Assistant Attorney General Mabel Walker Willebrandt, aka the First Lady of Law. She had a pleasant, broad face, wide-set eyes that held both intelligence and humor and a low-key demeanor that gave not one hint of her legal battles with some of the country's most notorious gangsters. Grace was a bit starstruck.

She next met Elmer Irey, the chief of the IRS Intelligence Unit. Irey was clean-shaven, square-jawed and wore round, steel-rimmed spectacles. Grace intuited that his geniality hid a dogged streak.

Prohibition Agent Eliot Ness shook her hand. He wore his dark hair parted in the middle and swept back with hair pomade to either side. His even, regular features looked carved from granite; his demeanor was quietly intimidating, as if something dangerous was coiled inside and ready to strike.

Treasury Agent Frank Wilson looked like a walking stereotype of an accountant: broad, smooth sweep of forehead, balding, spectacles slipping down his nose, thin lips. But the slight dent in his chin hinted at an unexpected toughness, a stubborn bent.

Grace murmured that she was delighted to meet everyone, and they echoed her.

"Please, everyone, be seated," said Mellon.

Grace's eyes were drawn to the wall behind his desk, which was covered with a giant map of North America that extended down over the border of Mexico. Pins wrapped with red yarn depicted shipping routes over land and sea. White labels held various names, and next to them were photographs.

At Vancouver, one of them said, "Conexco/Reifels."

At San Francisco, the label read, "Hobbs Bros/Lim."

At Chicago, it was "Torrio/Capone."

At New Orleans, the label said, "Morrison/Conexco."

Between Miami, Key West, the Bahamas, Cuba and Belize, the red yarn spun into an elaborate web. This area was marked as Russell/Vasquez/Waite/Lythgoe/Various."

Other labels defined smuggling enterprises headquartered at Mobile, Houston, New York, Boston, Cape Cod and the Canadian coast—there were too many to count, and the great lengths of red yarn that stretched over land from city to city got so snarled that they resembled streaks of blood.

"Like my art?" Mellon asked, with a crusty laugh that held no humor. "We had to take down my favorite landscapes—a Thomas Cole and an Albert Bierstadt—to accommodate it." He gestured to a far corner where the two large, upended paintings languished.

Grace raised her eyebrows.

"You don't want to know what I paid for either of those paintings," Mellon continued. "But this—this abomination before you—is worth far more, to my chagrin. Over the last few years, the US Treasury has lost *billions* in tax revenue to smugglers." Mellon paused to level a fierce look at them all from under his intimidating eyebrows. "May I repeat that figure: *billions.*"

Tension rose like a cloud of noxious cigar smoke in the room. It was clear that while everyone knew this information, nobody knew how to respond.

"And we are spending *millions* of dollars to combat them on land and at sea and where the two meet in coves and on beaches—but we may as well try to empty the Gulf of Mexico with a teaspoon. The Volstead Act, while well-intentioned, is an unmitigated disaster. Not only is the public not behind it, but it's spawned more crime in this country than Satan himself. Organized, slick racketeering operations run by men who aren't afraid to get their hands dirty—or bloody."

Mellon was preaching to the choir, but they all knew better than to respond.

"These crooks rake in so much kale that they can bribe our agents double or triple their paychecks to look the other way; they hire uniformed cops to deliver cases of booze to speakeasies in broad daylight! They aren't afraid to blackmail, intimidate, injure or kill anyone unwise enough to tangle with them. Frankly, we don't have the manpower to fight them by force. And we don't have the money to fight the whales like Capone with their obscene profits. We have to get them some other way.

"That's why I've called you all in here. We have to be smarter than these crooks. We have to crack their coded radio transmissions, track their shipments, keep eyes on their people. We have to connect the dots and bust them, ladies and gentlemen.

"They are making fools of us here at Treasury, and I'll not have it!" Mellon snapped. "The president is breathing down my neck. We are sorely in need of a victory or two, and what I want most is Al Capone's head on a platter."

"Take a good look at this SOB." Mellon pointed to an enlarged photo of Capone on the crime board. He was burly, with a receding hairline, black brows, pouches under his eyes, fleshy jowls and lips stretched into a smug smile. "Doesn't he look pleased with himself? I want that expression wiped off his face, do you understand me?"

Nods all around.

"Mr. Wilson," Mellon rose and pointed at him. "You and your boys follow the money." He pivoted. "Mr. Ness, get together a special team of Prohi agents and start shadowing the Capone operation in Chicago. But keep it quiet. You're gathering intel and documenting right now, not busting anyone. Is that clear?"

"Yes, sir."

Mellon peered out from under his bushy eyebrows at the next in line. "Mr. Irey, you'll round up your best people and work with Wilson on building a tax evasion case, understood? That dirty dog is pulling in a hundred million per annum on beer alone, damn him."

Mellon squinted at the Assistant AG. "Mrs. Willebrandt, you're to personally dot the i's and cross the t's on any and all legal matters pertaining to Torrio, Capone and the Chicago Outfit. No mistakes, no irregularities, no loopholes."

"Understood, sir."

Finally, he turned to Billard, Root and Grace. "You all have a different task, but one that's no less important. The Outfit moves most of its booze by way of land, via trucks, but they're expanding their reach, since bootlegging is," Mellon coughed bitterly, "a growth industry.

"Obviously, we've brought you in, Mrs. Feldman, to break the coded transmissions from ship to shore and vice versa. There are a lot of smugglers out there—little fish—that we'd like to round up, but focus on the bigger operations. And what we need you to keep an eye out for *specifically* is anything—anything at all—that might tie a maritime bootlegging fleet to Capone."

"Yes, sir," Grace said. As he issued instructions to Billard and Root, she took a few steps closer to the enormous map behind Mellon, scanning the pictures of the bootleggers. They weren't all as mafioso in appearance as Capone. The Reifels of Vancouver looked like what they were: wealthy hotel magnates. Many of the others were so average in appearance that they could have been her office mates or neighbors. One photograph was of a smiling couple who might very well have been on vacation. Pinned between the Bahamas and Miami, it beckoned to her, and she took another step forward to peer at it. She blinked, not trusting her own eyes, and then took another look.

It can't be. It simply cannot be.

But Otto Schroeder's limpid blue eyes stared back at her from the picture. He had his arm slung around the waist of a tall, stunning, black-haired beauty: none other than the notorious female smuggler "Spanish Marie" Waite.

But Schroeder was serving life in prison—wasn't he?

Robert forked some of Mrs. Hastings's liver and onions into his mouth while Grace tried not to gag at the smell. She nibbled a cheese-and-tomato sandwich instead.

"How can it be?" Grace queried. "The last I heard of Otto Schroeder, he was locked up for life at Leavenworth! How is it possible that he's now not only free but also engaged in *smuggling*?"

Robert swallowed his bite of her least favorite dish with relish. "Well, my dear, Coolidge pardoned him in 1923. For some sort of heroic act—I seem to remember an explosion in a boiler room at the prison? And at great personal risk, Schroeder went in and prevented it from taking out half the premises. At any rate, he was thanked kindly and deported to Berlin."

"*Thanked*?" Grace repeated scathingly. "Did Coolidge not remember that he was a murderer, a saboteur, a spy operating in Mexico against the US?"

"Who knows? Well, Schroeder seems to have liked Mexico," mused Bobby. "And now he's back down south in—where did you say?"

"He was in Belize for a bit. Now Havana, where Spanish Marie runs her operation. It's an outrage," said Grace.

"Well, darling, how else would a murderer, saboteur and spy improve his curriculum vitae? Add smuggler to his list of accomplishments."

"It's not funny, Bobby."

"He probably makes a lot of lettuce. Piles more than yours truly. There's an interesting spice to this dish, darling...is it paprika?"

"What?"

"Paprika, dear?"

Grace stared blankly at his plate of food. "Oh. Yes. Yes, it is."

"I thought so."

"Enjoy. So I'd like to go to San Francisco to consult with a few field offices in the Ezra brothers case. I rather thought I'd fly—so much faster than taking the train."

Her husband set down his fork. "Grace. You're not flying to California in a tin can with wings. It's too dangerous."

She mustered a sweet smile. "You really should compliment my cooking—butter me up, you know—before you order me not to do something."

"I'd gladly give you a compliment if it *were* your cooking, my dear, but I have a strong suspicion that this dish came from either Mrs. Hastings or Mrs. Mauborgne. These are Spanish yellow onions and they're sliced finely, so my money's on Mrs. H."

"What a dastardly accusation." Grace took a bite of her sandwich, clamping down on the bread to keep the tomato slices from escaping. They were as slippery as her white lies.

"Indeed. You'll have to excuse my paranoia. It comes with the government job. But isn't that her blue-flowered casserole dish hidden behind the toaster? And as much as I love and admire you, my dear, you don't know paprika from papyrus."

Grace frowned as she chewed. "You have all the makings of a great spy yourself, Bobby." What she didn't tell him was that she'd started *paying* the good ladies of the neighborhood to cook for them. Besides the obvious benefit to her, it was a way to save face on her husband's behalf—making the point that he *could* support her, and that her job was a choice.

Over obligatory coffee, pie, tea and pastries with the other wives, Grace embellished her tales of losing battles with her stove, and confided fictional suspicions that it was possessed by evil spirits conjured by her mother-in-law. This made the women giggle, and nobody minded a little extra pin money.

Robert finished his liver and onions with relish. "I'm not the only spy, my special agent wife. You unravel the secrets of smugglers all day."

"I do. Which is exactly why I need to fly to San Francisco. Apart from the Ezras, there's an entire fleet operating on the West Coast, run by two brothers named Hobbs. Canadians. And does the name Tony "the Hat" Cornero mean anything to you? He's in Los Angeles and owns a go-fast boat called the *Yurinohana* that can outpace any vessel of the Coast Guard's."

"Oh dear. My wife is getting entangled with a sunny California gangster?"

"Not entangled, exactly. Intrigued by. These messages are like clues in a detective novel, Bobby. One that's full of shell corporations, shady connections, underworld figures...it's fascinating to track the connections and rivalries. For example, the brothers Hobbs loathe and despise a certain Vancouver syndicate called Consolidated Exporters, or Conexco. These people are their competition, and the Hobbses are annoyed that they're stealing away business. Conexco is funded by a family of hotel magnates, the Reifels, and also has a high-rolling American investor out of Boston..."

"That's all very interesting," Robert said as he mopped up the sauce on his plate with a bit of rye bread from the deli. "But have you called for an exorcism of the oven, yet?" His eyes twinkled.

Grace was momentarily nonplussed. "How can you possibly have heard about—"

"My darling. *You* may be the very soul of discretion, but some of the neighbor ladies are not. They gossip to their husbands. And Joe Mauborgne regaled me with the latest."

"Rats."

"Surely not in the oven?"

"Stop it, Bobby."

"So is it to be a priest, a pastor or a rabbi for the exorcism?"

Grace's mouth worked despite herself.

"A domestic sorceress, burning sage?"

"All right, all right, you've caught me."

"And to cast aspersions upon my mother like that...how could you?" He grinned.

"Your mother still cries every time she hears my name."

"Can you blame the poor woman?"

Grace glared at him.

"You know I'm only joking, my beautiful wife..."

To her surprise, the word had lost almost all its negative connotations for her. *Wife.* She might not be a conventional one, but Robert truly didn't seem to mind.

She'd never be obedient. She was getting on that airplane to San

Francisco. She refused to be grounded by her husband—even if she knew his misgivings came from love.

CHAPTER TWENTY-SIX

Grace was the only woman on board the flight, which was packed with businessmen in dark suits, snow-white shirts and sober ties. She ignored the raised eyebrows, the glances exchanged and the disapproving rustle of their newspapers. Men.

So you own the skies, too? As well as the earth?

She shook hands with the captain, who flirted openly with her. She admired the smart uniforms and pert little caps of the stewardesses. She loved the roar of the engine and the sensation of being airborne, flying inside a giant metal eagle with windows into the heavens.

But what impressed her most of all was the sight of America stretched out like a glorious patchwork quilt far below.

"It's not even a bird's-eye view," she wrote to Robert. "It's God's view of the country: the blue expanses of lakes and snow-tipped mountains... the silvery ribbons of rivers, intertwined with furrowed fields and green crops, neatly laid-out towns connected by roads...it's marvelous, truly it is! Pure magic."

San Francisco was another revelation: the steep hills, the trolley cars, the bay. The elegant hotels and high-end shops and cosmopolitan restaurants that she only wished she had the budget to experience. But her five-dollar-per-day stipend didn't allow for five-star accommodations or dining, so she made do with sightseeing and one splurge on a silk shawl and a fan in Chinatown. She found some very fine tobacco for Robert's pipe.

And over the next few weeks, she solved hundreds of messages in three different field offices. She met the Coast Guard Intelligence officers as well as the radio interceptors themselves. They put their heads together and began to triangulate traffic patterns of specific vessels and trace their labyrinthine layers of ownership and partnership.

Grace, feeling pleased and grateful for her new contacts and cohorts, put a bow on the case of the Ezra brothers. Once they were in custody, their opiate-importing empire would crumble, saving perhaps thousands of American lives. But as she flew home to DC, trouble erupted behind her.

Ezra Gang Falls in Trap of Woman Expert at Puzzles blared the *San Francisco Examiner*, in the first of many distressing articles to come. The gist of the piece was that mysterious secret codes used by the drug kingpins to communicate with their transport vessels had been solved by a pretty—but brainy—little lady who'd determined somehow that *wyssa* stood for morphine, *wysiv* indicated heroin and *wyset* meant cocaine.

Not a word was mentioned about cooperation between different Coast Guard units; no credit was given to any of her colleagues on the West Coast. Grace was horrified.

Dear Captain Root, she wrote.

What can I say? I am mortified at the article in the San Francisco Examiner. I assure you that I have given no interviews and I was not in contact with any journalist upon the topic of the Ezra brothers take-down. I wish to make it crystal clear that a great number of my Coast Guard colleagues—whether in local offices, on cutters at sea or in radio analysis—were instrumental in the process of locating, boarding and seizing the ships ... the reporter simply chose to focus on the angle that I'm female and therefore a rarity in the profession of cryptanalysis.

She wrote similar letters to the people with whom she'd worked in the Bay Area, hoping that they would soothe understandably ruffled feathers. She wasn't sure they helped much.

A few days after her return, Grace munched a cold chicken sandwich at her desk, her gaze fixed upon an old newspaper clipping she'd saved from the military trial of Otto Schroeder. *So you're a smuggler now, are you? In cahoots with a notorious—and glamorous—female rumrunner.*

Ignore the little fish, Mellon had ordered. Focus on the whales.

But you're not exactly a minnow. You're a spy, a saboteur, a murderer.

Grace washed down the last of the sandwich with a gulp of tepid coffee, then tapped her index finger on Otto's criminally handsome face. *I was a fool to feel any guilt for your fate, Schroeder. I caught you once, and I will catch you again.*

She refilled her coffee, set it back on her desk and went looking for Captain Root. For once, the dogged Ambrose was not at his desk, to her relief. Root's door was open, and she stuck her head in. "Captain? May I trouble you for a moment?"

He looked up from some paperwork and smiled. "Of course, Mrs. Feldman. That is, it's no trouble."

"Thank you. I have a slightly odd request. I met a gentleman aboard *Hogan's Goat*—"

Root's face flushed, as well it should for conspiring with her husband and placing her aboard that stinkpot. He looked back down at his papers.

"—and this man seemed wired in, so to speak, on a lot of issues. I'd like to consult with him about a smuggler out of Havana."

"Of course, of course. Go right ahead."

"Well, the thing is, I've forgotten his given name and only know his surname: Cox. He's Australian by birth and went by the moniker 'Kangaroo.'"

Root leaned back in his chair and aimed a wry smile at her. "I'm quite familiar with Wimberly Cox. He's gregarious and entertaining, has a knack for meeting all the right people, and was paroled from *Hogan's Goat* not long ago. He's finagled himself a promotion to lieutenant junior grade and is assigned to the *Beale*, which, as it happens, is patrolling the waters along Florida's Atlantic coast."

Grace couldn't believe her luck. "I can contact him?"

"I'll do you one better. I'll radio him and get you an in-person meeting the next time he has shore leave, if you like. Given the *Beale*'s trajectory, it'll be somewhere in south Florida."

"G'day, pretty lady!" Kangaroo Cox called as he strode into the Coral Gables Biltmore Hotel. Grace couldn't quite believe her luck in traveling to Miami for work. The Biltmore was a lushly landscaped palace full of balmy breezes, views of the sparkling pool and fashionable people. Sunbathers reclined under brightly colored beach umbrellas, and a guest's every whim was anticipated and graciously supplied.

"What a pleasure to see you again." Cox was still tall, broad shouldered, redheaded. His eyes still twinkled with mischief.

Grace smiled. "How are you, Mr. Kangaroo?" She deliberately repeated her blunder at their first meeting. She extended her gloved hand; he laughed and bowed over it before seating himself opposite her.

"Thank you for taking the trouble to meet with me on your shore leave."

"Not at all," he said easily. Then he grinned. "Besides which, Captain Root's wish is my command. Good for my career, and all that."

"I see you're still shameless," she teased.

"Would you rather I be any other way?"

Grace raised an eyebrow but didn't answer that.

A waiter came to take their drink orders.

"I suppose you'd frown upon a rum punch," mused Cox provocatively. "Two iced teas?"

Graced nodded, and the waiter disappeared.

Cox leaned back in his chair. "I'm still in touch with some of the fellows from the old *Goat*, you know."

"And how are they?"

"I'll have you know that none of us will ever consume a potato again without fondly thinking of you."

She couldn't help but laugh.

They chitchatted about this and that until their food orders came—roast beef for him and a salad for her.

"So if I may clumsily and perhaps rudely get to the point, Mrs. Feldman, why are we here at the request of Coast Guard Intelligence?"

Grace set down her fork and dabbed at her mouth with her napkin. "What can you tell me about 'Spanish Marie' Waite?"

Cox looked at her for a beat too long and then whistled. "Permission to use a bit of salty language?"

"I'm sure I heard worse aboard *Hogan's Goat*."

He nodded. "Spanish Marie is known as one bad bitch."

"Oh my."

"You don't want to tangle with her—her husband, Charlie Waite, was gunned down by the Coast Guard in Biscayne Bay on board one of his vessels a few years ago. Marie despises us because of it. She took over the business—and by all accounts, she's improved it. She's got a flair for rum-running and for drama. Lands cargo—thousands of cases of rum and other liquor—from Cuba and Mexico to Key West, Miami, the Bahamas and so forth." He stopped and rotated his sweating iced-tea glass.

"What aren't you telling me?"

Cox's mouth quirked. "Let's just say she doesn't appear to have any plans to marry again."

"What does that mean?"

"It's rather unsavory," he warned her.

Grace shrugged.

"Spanish Marie has a reputation for bumping off her lovers once she tires of them."

"How bloodcurdling."

"Well, the woman can gaff and gut a fish, fire a flare and hit her mark with a pistol. With fifteen boats and thousands of miles of ocean, opportunities are rife for disposal of the displeasing or untalented men in her life."

Grace had to smile. *Oh my, Otto. What have you gotten yourself into?*

"If you don't mind my asking, why all the curiosity about Marie?

She's intriguing, but does she really move enough cargo to pique top brass's interest?"

"Let's just say that we're looking into her connections," Grace improvised, thinking she was being discreet.

"Ah. The German spy, then." Cox *tsk*ed. "Careful with that one. All sorts of nasty habits and vicious vices. Might even survive Marie."

"How do you know—" Grace stopped, nonplussed.

"I hear things. He's fluent in Spanish so has no problem living in Havana. Operated out of Mexico during the Great War, making mischief for the US. Caught, tried, sentenced to death—got life instead, and was then inexplicably pardoned by President Coolidge."

She stared at him. "*Where* exactly do you hear these things, Lieutenant Cox?"

He displayed his teeth. "Oh, here and there, darlin'—may I call you darlin'?"

Grace, who had picked up her glass of iced tea, set it down with a snap. "You may *not*."

"Now that," he said almost seriously, "is a tragedy."

"I'll ask you to forward all transmissions you happen across from Mrs. Waite's Havana radio station or any of her vessels to me."

"Yes, ma'am. Her flagship—the one she habitually captains—is called the *Kid Boots*."

"Interesting." Grace reached for her pocketbook and extracted a card, which she handed to him. "Thank you. I believe we've concluded our business, Lieutenant Cox."

He tucked the card into his breast pocket. "Surely not all business, pretty lady? And I believe I prefer Mr. Kangaroo."

Her lips twitched in spite of her best intentions. "You're incorrigible."

He nodded. "That I am. May I pick up the check by way of apology?"

"You may," said Grace.

Other than his clearly flexible morals, there was something highly irregular about Lieutenant Wimberly Cox. She just couldn't pinpoint exactly what it was.

*   *   *

Grace flew back to Washington, wishing she could bottle the sunshine, the balmy, sea-scented air and the utter relaxation of sitting under a beach umbrella with a book in her hand. But part of the magic of Miami was that it didn't exist anywhere else. There was no way to set it atop a dresser or swish it into a hot bath. She'd simply have to go back.

In the meantime, she gazed out the window of the airplane and reflected upon the vastness of the country below—a vastness that, somehow, highly organized networks of smugglers were chopping into territories of crime. The Great Depression only urged them on, since so many men were unable to find work and provide for their families.

The well-intentioned law to dry out the United States had made it wetter than ever, and the thirst for strong spirits had spawned increasingly evil ones.

It was on a chilly, wet Wednesday in the Treasury Building when Grace, after deciphering another 459 garbled coded radio transmissions, put it together. "Good Lord. They're not rivals any longer," she said aloud to her coffee. "The brothers Hobbs and Conexco—they've *merged*. Or rather, the Hobbses have sold their interests to Consolidated Exporters. Truly consolidated now, the network extends on both coasts…from Northern California and Vancouver all the way south to Mexico…and they're operating in the Gulf of Mexico, too."

Her coffee was unimpressed.

"Texas," she mused. "Houston. Louisiana—New Orleans. And who owns the *I'm Alone*? What an unusual name for a ship."

Fortunately, Captain Root was more enthusiastic about these discoveries than her coffee had been. "That's a huge amount of territory for one company," he said, drumming his fingertips on his desk. "Enormous. Definitely smells of racketeering."

"After decoding another few dozen messages, I think it may very well smell of Capone himself."

Root went very still. "Conexco's in league with Capone? What indicates that?"

"There's a gentleman—I use the word loosely, of course—in New Orleans by the name of Bert Morrison. He seems to be a land agent for Conexco, with direct communications not only to and from Vancouver, but also to members of the Chicago Outfit. It seems that cargo is transported over land to certain New Orleans warehouses. Mr. Morrison then arranges transport of the same cargo by boat to inlets on the Texas, Alabama, Georgia and Florida coastlines. Liquor is also smuggled in, as you know, from Mexico, Havana and Nassau. Some of those vessels are owned outright by Conexco, but others are independent contractors."

"So you're saying…"

"I'm not saying that Capone owns stock in Conexco. But I'm pretty darn sure that he's an excellent customer of theirs—that Morrison provides the Outfit regular, dependable distribution by sea."

Root nodded. "For a healthy fee. But Conexco and their agents are playing with fire if Capone's cargo gets seized."

"Yes, indeed they are. I'm afraid I myself may end up in a concrete overcoat," Grace said cheerfully.

The captain eyed her. "Those fears aren't unreasonable."

"I'm just a nosy housewife to these men. I work in the background. They don't even know my name."

"Let's keep it that way, Mrs. Feldman. No more feature articles in major newspapers, that's for damn sure."

"Believe me, I agree."

"All right. Now, on to other things. The Houston office is asking for your help with over six hundred intercepted messages."

"How exciting—I've never been to Houston, though I enjoyed San Antonio."

"Is your husband comfortable with you flying again?"

"Of course," Grace fibbed.

"All right. Ambrose will be happy to assist you with booking flights and hotels. Enjoy your trip, ma'am. My warmest regards to Robert."

CHAPTER TWENTY-SEVEN

Robert was not in the least comfortable with Grace flying again. "Haven't you got that out of your system?" he asked, over Mrs. Mariotti's spaghetti Bolognese.

It smelled delicious, so why was her stomach roiling with nausea? Why did the very thought of taking a bite make her want to...

Oh dear. Oh no. Oh, Lord. But Grace kept her sudden insight to herself. It wasn't fair to raise Bobby's hopes. Was it? And she could be wrong.

"Do you really need to fly again?"

Grace hid her trembling hands under her apron and produced her most winning smile. "How can I resist investigating a one-legged cab driver named Frenchy Armatou? He's somehow connected to this entire network of smugglers that reaches from Canada all the way down the Atlantic seaboard to Mexico."

"What if he objects?"

"He'll never know. By the way, I've sent out your shirts to the laundry and will pick them up before I leave. Mrs. Sokolow, Mrs. Sharp, Mrs. Johnson, Mrs. Holland and Mrs. Tesky will be supplying you with dinners. Now that the cat is out of the bag—or should I say oven?—they'll just deliver them to you personally each day after work. I am the scandal of the neighborhood, but for some reason they all like me anyway."

"If my mother only knew..." Robert said, mock mournfully.

"If you ever breathe one word about our domestic arrangements to your mother, I'll poison you, Bobby."

"She warned me that I'd be ill-treated by a shiksa. That I'd regret my marriage to the end of my days."

"You didn't seem regretful last night, darling." Grace shot him an arch look.

"Well, no," he admitted, his ears flushing pink.

"If I excel in Houston, perhaps I'll be awarded a pay raise and we can exchange the dust balls for a dog and a housekeeper. Wouldn't that be the bee's knees?"

"Your heart's desire: a housekeeper."

"Yes," she said dreamily. And quite possibly a nanny in eight months or so. She was an unnatural woman. Her father would say so.

"I'll miss you." Bobby swallowed a giant forkful of spaghetti. "Don't run off with the one-legged cab driver."

"I can't promise that, Bobby. The name 'Frenchy' is quite alluring, he could show me all the sights...and your mother would be over the moon!"

Houston was miserably hot and oppressively humid. As she fought down nausea, Grace spoke with everyone in the office who could possibly give her insight into Gulf smuggling operations. She examined reams of raw intercepts from the radio posts monitoring the traffic. A junior officer brought her a codebook they'd been fortunate enough to capture. It was illuminating and gave her some insight into the messages she needed to decrypt.

CABZA was *account*, CADIR morphed into *afternoon*, CAGJE became *bring*. MOBAT was *engine oil*, OGVAB indicated *patrol boat following me*, and OGWAC meant *turn off running lights*.

Grace got to work, plowing through more than 650 encrypted messages that used twenty-four different code systems. Frenchy Armatou sure knew the smuggling business, and driving a cab provided excellent cover and opportunity.

She splurged on a few nights at the grand Warwick Hotel, but Grace was confined to a hot, stuffy, borrowed government office during the day. This was fitted with three fans that necessitated makeshift paperweights to keep her papers from blowing to Belize and back.

Meanwhile, Elmer Irey's boys shadowed Frenchy and discovered he had beaten more than one hapless subordinate to death with his own prosthetic limb, which was often carried by his girlfriend Gladys when it got unwieldy or uncomfortable. She had a special cross-body sling for it and was said to wear it with a certain flair.

Dearest Bobby, she wrote.

Alas, though Frenchy Armatou is really quite dashing, he possesses a few off-putting quirks. Despite the euphoria it would cause your mother, I find myself unable to run away with a sociopath who murders underlings with his artificial leg. Perhaps I should feel empathy for what a psychiatrist would diagnose as Frenchy's misplaced rage at the loss of his limb. Unfortunately, I am, it seems, a coldhearted woman—besides which, he is spoken for.

When Grace was done decrypting the messages, she'd proven that their target was not only engaged in bootlegging via his cab network, but also supplied a large vessel, the *I'm Alone,* with cargo. This was owned by a Mr. Dan Hogan—known as the Capone of the Bayous—and his partner "Big Jim" Clark. The Coast Guard impounded Frenchy's taxi cabs and put him in jail to await trial. Frenchy was not pleased with his new circumstances and was quite vocal about it.

Grace, who knew nobody in Houston except for the Coast Guard staff with whom she'd sweltered in the local office, treated herself to a quiet dinner—eaten gingerly so as not to upset her stomach—in a corner of the Warwick's very fine restaurant and then went to get the oversize brass key to her room.

Her neck and shoulders ached, her eyes were blurry from peering at commercial codebooks and frequency tables, her hands were cramped from the constant hours of filling in guesses on worksheets. She was fairly sure she felt a migraine coming on, too.

Grace nodded politely at the elevator attendant and rode up the three floors to her room. She walked—exhausted, no doubt from dehydration—to the door, and then stopped cold. It was open six inches.

Perhaps a maid was inside, doing turndown service? Placing a mint on her pillow?

But something told her this wasn't the case.

Grace used the edge of her pocketbook to push the door open farther and peered inside.

Nobody was in the room. But in the center of the dressing table was a note that didn't need decryption, and it wasn't friendly:

BACK OFF, LADY—OR YOU'LL REGRET IT.
KEEP BREAKING OUR CODES, AND WE'LL BREAK
YOUR KNEECAPS.

Grace stood there in disbelief. The note was written by hand in all capital letters on a piece of plain stationery. Black ink. And someone had either used a key to get into her room or picked the lock. But how had this person known she was staying at the Warwick? And discovered her room number?

Why hadn't the warning been slipped under the door? It was a power play, a deliberate move to let her know that she wasn't safe, even in a big hotel in a big, anonymous city far from home.

Grace's hands had gone cold and clammy; her stomach roiled and her knees trembled. She forced herself forward the requisite number of steps to snatch the note off the dressing table and then backed out the door, closing and locking it behind her.

The hotel manager professed deep shock and alarm as well as a profuse apology. No, to his knowledge, nobody had taken her key from its hook behind the desk while she was gone. No person in the hotel's employ would do such a thing—all hires were carefully screened. Of course, none of them would give out her room number to any unknown person.

Grace hadn't expected different answers than those he gave. She did ask that her things be moved to a different room immediately, and he obliged, telling her that both rooms would be complimentary to make up for her very unfortunate experience.

Even in the new room, with a fruit basket and fresh-cut flowers in a crystal vase, Grace didn't sleep a wink. She assumed that Frenchy Armatou and his prosthetic limb would not be leaving lockup anytime soon, and certainly not before her flight home tomorrow. But what about Mr. Hogan and Mr. Clark? They would not be happy about their business partner being in the clink. She wasn't taking any chances with her life—or with the possible new life growing inside her.

The room was furnished elaborately in Louis-Something-or-Other. Hoping that it was a reproduction, Grace dragged a fussy, carved gilt chair over to the door and shoved it unceremoniously under the knob.

She'd carried with her on her travels the tranche of messages concerning the *I'm Alone*, since the ship's name had intrigued her. They were still in her pocketbook on the flight home when the news broke the next day: the one-hundred-foot US Coast Guard cutter *Dexter* had fired upon, and subsequently sunk, the *I'm Alone*—which, curiously, was registered as a Canadian ship—though Grace knew now from her decrypting that the owners were American.

The Wolcott, another cutter, had spotted a suspicious schooner at about a four-league distance off the coast of Louisiana. *The Wolcott* approached *I'm Alone*, giving four blasts of the whistle and demanding to board, but the schooner quickly headed out to open sea, toward international waters. The Coast Guard gave chase.

Coast Guard brass sent out the *Dexter* from Pascagoula to join in the capture of the rumrunner. The cat-and-mouse game went on for two days—until the *Dexter* opened fire, hitting the vessel below the waterline and ripping a large hole in her side. *I'm Alone* sank five minutes later, though all the crew members except for one were rescued.

Though she was a known smuggling vessel, the incident created an international scandal overnight, with the British ambassador in Washington calling for the State Department to look into the matter and the

Canadian government filing a formal protest and calling for $400,000 in compensation.

"But Bobby," Grace said over toast and tea next morning, since she could no longer stomach coffee, "they have no case."

"And why is that, my dear?" Her husband stood at the much-maligned stove, scrambling eggs for the two of them. She could barely stand the smell.

"Because the *I'm Alone* is actually owned by Americans."

"And you know this how...?"

"Hazard a guess, darling."

"Then I expect Captain Root would be glad to hear from you, as would Rear Admiral Billard."

"I expect they would."

Grace gazed at her husband's dear, sweet face and thought of the threatening note still folded in her suitcase. Should she mention it?

He wouldn't react well. Especially if he suspected that she was in a delicate condition. Which she might not be. He'd want her to stop working immediately. She couldn't bear the thought.

Grace forced down the eggs he served her, ignoring her gag reflex. Other than that, she kept her mouth shut.

Captain Root was slumped in his chair, looking as though he'd slept in his office the night before. He was pale, and dark circles hung in half-moons below his eyes. But he got courteously to his feet when Grace came in. "You have information pertaining to the *I'm Alone* scandal?"

"I do." Grace laid out several messages on his desk. One read:

MOCANA = NEWYORK (NY) = UGUCKMIOSD EPUJSAFAGS PEJYTUSENZ MITEPLPUJS RECKRONY AZ POUDYYIOVB.

Another read:

MOCANA = NEW YORK (NY) = WYBABUCEGZ WYELMUCEFY LEVIRYIBUH LEVIRYICFE LOHOPWYDOH AKBUZWYERS WYEMN.

"Please, Mrs. Feldman. What is this nonsense? My head already hurts. Rear Admiral Billard is furious about this mess."

"Well, I believe the decryptions of these messages may soothe your headache. The first one translates to: 'To Mocana, New York. Referring to telegram of twenty-ninth, eight thousand dollars additional required. Total amount twelve thousand dollars. Shall we pack in sacks (YIOVB).'"

"New York?"

Grace nodded. "The plaintext of the second message is this: "MOCANA, New York. WYBAB. Cannot supply. WYELM. Can supply fifty. YIBUH, fifty YICFE, five hundred WYDOH, also WYERFS, WYEMN." She paused.

"I think you'll find that the still-coded clumps of letters refer to brands of liquors. And just as important, MOCANA in New York is the cable address for a Mr. Joseph H. Foran, Hotel McAlpin, New York City."

Captain Root furrowed his brow. "Never heard of him."

"No, but perhaps you've heard of Dan Hogan, aka Daniel Halpern, known as the Capone of the Bayous. They're one and the same. His partner is Big Jim Clark. Both are Americans."

Root sat down. "*Americans.* Not Canadians."

Grace nodded. "So there's still a convoluted trail of shell companies that 'own' the vessel, but we'll get to the bottom of it. I'm sure Mr. Wilson and Mr. Irey are experts at that sort of thing. At any rate, you'll save not only face for the United States, but—"

"Four hundred thousand dollars in compensation and a truckload of legal fees." Her boss exhaled. "Grace Feldman, I do believe you're a national treasure."

She felt herself blushing. "That's too kind of you, Captain."

"You deserve a medal."

"No, no . . . I prefer to work behind the scenes. It's rather a necessity."

"True. Well, not only will I put in for a raise on your behalf—and a promotion—but I'll also send my wife over with a month's worth of dinners."

Grace choked.

"Oh yes, word is out—far beyond the radius of your neighborhood." Captain Root grinned. "It's all right. Everyone understands."

CHAPTER TWENTY-EIGHT

But it wasn't all right. Not at all.

Key Woman of the T-Men! blared the title of the *Reader's Digest* story, mailed to over a million subscribers. Grace, who already felt light-headed and queasy, was almost sick on it. She'd just celebrated her promotion to cryptanalyst-in-charge at the US Coast Guard, but she hated the attention. Not only were most of the articles insulting, but her work was supposed to be *secret*.

Another article in the *Evening Post* was just as bad:

Grace Smith Feldman may appear to be an unassuming house-wife in low heels and a pink peacoat. But in fact, she's the Treasury Department's secret weapon in the battle against smugglers in vio-lation of Prohibition. The fetching Mrs. Feldman is, in fact, chief codebreaker for the Coast Guard...and just saved face for the US government, in addition to hundreds of thousands of dollars—by proving that the *I'm Alone* was, in fact, American owned.

Fetching? And how often were men's shoes described? Worst of all, it called attention to her work.

The nausea in her stomach roiled into anger and insisted upon an unwelcome purge. Grace dashed for the ladies' room.

"First and only woman breaking codes for the US government, are you?" Alice Martenz jibed, when she came out of an adjoining stall.

Of course. The woman who always turns up when she's most unwelcome.

"Look at you, the celebrated Lady Manhunter of *Detective Fiction Weekly*. But somehow you forgot a few of us other ladies."

"Hello, Alice," Grace said weakly, and hurtled into a stall, slamming the door behind her. She retched helplessly.

"Dear me. Need a tissue or five?"

"Alice, I had nothing"—Grace heaved—"to do with that article—" She heaved again.

"No? What about yesterday's *Evening Post*? Leak it yourself?"

"No!" Grace emerged, rinsed her mouth and washed her hands. Then she powdered her nose with too much force. "How can you think that? I'm mortified."

"Are you? Well, you're also *famous*, dear. *Look Magazine*. The *Observer*. You're quite the heroine of the high seas, lamb chop. You, and you alone, are credited with the takedown of both the Marabella pirate ship and Gordon Lim, the opium and arms smuggler—"

"Are you collecting clippings on me, Alice?" Grace retorted. "Storing them in a hatbox?"

"Does Captain Root know you're pregnant?"

Grace froze and turned to face Alice. They both knew she'd be relieved of her duties if top brass found out. "Please," she whispered.

Those ice-blue eyes didn't soften a bit.

"I can't be...banished...from work, yet." The long, awful months trapped in the house, in the grip of dark melancholy, haunted her.

"You could learn to cook," Alice said coolly.

Does all of Washington, DC, know? "I hate to cook."

"Aren't you worried?"

Grace stiffened. Clearly the grapevine had also buzzed with her miscarriage. "That's a low blow, Alice. The two of us may have developed something of a...a rivalry. But I've always played fair with you."

The other woman paused and cocked her head. "True."

"So...?"

Alice took a final check of her perfect face in the mirror. "You can keep your little secret." She smiled and headed for the door.

Once it had shut again, Grace sprinted for a stall and vomited a second time. It was time to tell Robert. It was time to see a doctor. But she just couldn't, yet. Not until she'd gone to New Orleans and testified for the prosecution in the Conexco trial.

The next morning, the *D.C. Bee* held further mortification for Grace. It was a local rag, but one that everyone read. **Doll of Domestic Intelligence!** announced the headline, which, thank God, was below the fold but still menaced her from the front page.

"My dear," said Robert at the dinner table over Mrs. Delaney's meat loaf and mashed potatoes, "I had a rather unpleasant meeting with my superior officer today. He wished to know why my name and profession are being mentioned in high-profile features about you. And I must ask how *Look* got that sexy photo of you in the white robe?"

"Bobby, I don't know! It's humiliating. I'm not encouraging the journalists, I swear. And I've written countless apology notes to top brass—"

"I was all but forbidden to sleep in the same bedroom as my wife," Robert said. "For security reasons."

"I'm sorry." Grace dragged her hands down her face.

"I knew that behind every successful man there is a strong woman, but you seem to be quite eclipsing me." He smiled.

"Bobby, you must know that I didn't ask for this attention, and I don't want it."

"It's all right. I'm proud of you, Grace." He got up, slipped an arm around her waist, bent her backward and kissed her.

She struggled upright again. "But it's awful! *Doll?* And look what else this article in the *Bee* says. I'd like to smack the journalist."

Beware, bootleggers. Rummies, you'd better run. Because this kitten isn't smitten with your flouting of the law—and she's unraveling your business dealings like so many balls of yarn. Treasury's undercover operative is throwing off her negligee and donning a man's overcoat: to testify in open court...

"Kitten? Negligee?"

Robert chuckled.

"It's not funny, Bobby. They'd never dare write in such terms about a man. It's chauvinist, it's demeaning—"

"It is. I'm sorry, my darling."

"And worst of all, it's couched in a smug, smarmy gossip-column tone that would never be countenanced in a real news article."

"Well. I doubt Captain Root reads it."

"Mrs. Root reads it, and she will prop it under his nose. What am I going to say to him, much less my other colleagues?"

"Laugh it off."

"How can I?"

"Raise your chin, roll your eyes and chuckle."

"It won't be enough. I'll have to write him a groveling memo...*oh!* I feel just sick, I tell you."

"Say, you're looking peaked these days, Grace. Are you all right? Do you need to see a doctor?"

Yes. And yes. But not now. Not yet.

"I'm perfectly fine, Bobby. Don't fuss. I just forgot something." She rushed back upstairs to the toilet and lost her tea and toast as quietly and gracefully as she could under the circumstances. She rinsed her mouth and wished she could rinse her soul for lying to her husband. But she knew very well he'd never let her get on the plane to New Orleans if he knew she was pregnant. And Grace faced another unwelcome truth: neither would she.

A baby—their baby—was far more important than any government trial.

So for now? She'd do her utmost to pretend that no baby yet existed. She might very well have a stomach flu.

Toward the end of the week, Grace received a telephone call from Lieutenant (JG) Cox. "Hallo, my lady codebreaker," he said, his voice crackling over the line.

"How nice to hear from you, Lieutenant," she said.

"Thought you lot would like to know that our radio men intercepted a few transmissions regarding Spanish Marie and her German spy. They've got a couple of boats running cargo to Key West and Mobile and then returning to pick up more in New Orleans. But more importantly, our lovers are personally making a run from Havana to Miami on the *Kid Boots* this coming Monday, where they'll unload and then sail from there to Nassau."

Grace's hand tightened on the receiver and her pulse quickened. "Can you get me exact coordinates and schedules?"

"Check your Telex machine. Should be coming through any moment."

"I'll let the rest of our team here know. Thank you very much, Lieutenant."

"Of course, dar—uh, ma'am. One thing, though: we'd like to be in on the bust."

Grace sucked in a breath. Of course Cox wanted credit—he was no saint. "I suppose that's not unreasonable. But that's not my area. Let me speak to Mr. Irey and Mr. Ness here at Treasury. Then I'll put them in touch."

It was only after Grace hung up that she thought to wonder how, exactly, Cox had broken the codes. Spanish Marie and Otto Schroeder weren't stupid enough to send their transmissions in plain English or Spanish.

But she didn't have much time to puzzle over it. She went to Root with the information to set up the sting operation, wishing that she could somehow be there to witness it. But it was her job to stay in the background, working behind the scenes.

For a brief few moments, she allowed her mind to wander. What must it be like to be a lawman and make a bust in person? Or even to be a woman like Spanish Marie? To work outdoors, rocking and free on the ocean? Feel the wind in her hair, the salt spray on her face and the outlaw in her soul?

"Mrs. Feldman?" Captain Root queried. "Did you register that?"

She blinked. "I'm terribly sorry—my head was in the clouds. Would you mind repeating?"

"I said that Big Jim Clark has been found shot to death in New Orleans."

It took her another moment to remember Clark was the partner of Dan Hogan, the so-called Capone of the Bayous and co-owner of the doomed *I'm Alone*. A business associate of Frenchy Armatou...and, in fact, an associate of the real Capone. "Oh dear."

Root sighed. "They think Hogan's to blame. Making sure Clark can't turn on him and testify against him. As you know, all these characters have something to do with the Conexco case we're building."

Grace nodded.

"Mrs. Feldman, with all the press that's come out—"

"Again, I must apologize, sir. I in no way encourage it."

"Understood. But even so, you've become something of a nation-wide celebrity."

"I refer all reporters to our press office, sir, and have begged the officials there not to release any but the most mundane and uninteresting facts about me."

"Yes, Mrs. Feldman. But unfortunately, your notoriety has brought the attention of some very dangerous people. You need to be careful."

Grace thought of the awful note left in her room at the Warwick.

"Please let me know if you feel uncomfortable or threatened in any way. We'll provide security if you do."

Now was her chance to speak up. But whoever had left the note was only trying to intimidate her. She doubted very much that she was in actual danger, especially not on the busy streets of their nation's capital. She smiled politely. "Thank you very much, Captain. I appreciate it."

On Friday, Grace was called to another VIP meeting in Mellon's office. Secretary Mellon welcomed them, thanked them for coming and then asked for status reports from each.

Rear Admiral Billard spoke for the Coast Guard. "I'm happy to report that we've boarded and seized over a hundred smuggling vessels and impounded their illicit cargoes. We have reached out to both the Mexican and Canadian governments to aid in our efforts, though Conexco remains a major problem. As you're no doubt aware, the smugglers still manage to get around the law by simply docking at free ports like Tahiti or Antwerp and unloading then reloading the same cursed cargo. They then receive a legal, signed landing certificate and thus bypass any tariffs on the liquor.

"Conexco's *L'Aquila*, which was bringing twenty thousand cases from the free port of Antwerp, was seized for us by the Mexican authorities on a registration technicality. They towed it to Ensenada harbor. And do you know what those bootleggers did? Under cover of darkness, they stole back their cargo and dismantled virtually the entire ship, leaving only the hull behind! It's an outrage."

Mellon's luxurious mustache quivered with indignation.

"Sir, if I may step in here?" Captain Root asked, receiving a nod from Billard. "Our patrol boats are intercepting radio messages by the hundreds every month. At least twenty-five per day are generated by Conexco and have been landing on Mrs. Feldman's desk. She's worked tirelessly to decode them, with excellent results. We forward the plaintexts to Mr. Irey and his team—"

"And many of them we, in turn, forward to Mrs. Willebrandt," said Elmer Irey.

Mrs. Willebrandt gave a brief update. "We've made excellent progress on the Bert Morrison/Conexco prosecution in New Orleans, and we have a trial date set. We'll need Mrs. Feldman there as a witness." She glanced at Grace. "I presume you're available?"

"I'll make myself available."

Billard and Root didn't look thrilled, no doubt because if she was traveling and testifying, her daily work on incoming decryptions would suffer. But they stayed silent.

"Say, we do have some good news on our end regarding Conexco,"

Mr. Irey jumped in. He looked at his watch. "In just under two hours, one of the directors, Mr. George Reifel, and his son Mr. Henry Reifel will land in Seattle." He smiled. "We aim to pluck them off the runway to make sure they have a pleasant stay in the city lockup. We've built a criminal case against them."

Mrs. Willebrandt smiled, too. "Indeed we have."

"Then there's the civil complaint," Mr. Wilson said. "We followed all the money trails, and it seems that the Reifels owe the US Treasury somewhere in the neighborhood of seven million dollars," he said, looking pleased.

"Seven million, you say?" Secretary Mellon brightened. "Well, that's excellent news. Quite something. Thank you for your hard work, ladies and gentlemen."

As they filed out of Mellon's office, Grace went back to wondering about Spanish Marie and Otto Schroeder.

Mr. Ness, the prohibition agent, fell into step beside her. As if he'd read her mind, Ness said, "We'll meet up with Mrs. Waite and Mr. Schroeder at around 6:00 p.m. on Monday. Cox's ship will cut them off from an escape by water, and my boys and I will personally greet them at the dock in Coconut Grove."

"Thank you for telling me," Grace said. "I know I don't have to warn you, but do be careful. They'll both be armed."

Ness nodded and patted his sidearm. "No need to worry, Mrs. Feldman. We're prepared. But may I ask as to your interest in this particular case?"

Grace hesitated. Was she violating the Espionage Act of 1917 by telling him? No. The Waberski/Schroeder case had been covered in all the newspapers. "Schroeder was supposed to do life at Leavenworth," she said. She couldn't possibly criticize President Coolidge for pardoning him, not in her present company.

"I'm aware." Ness cocked his head.

"Well. Let's just say that I had a hand in putting him behind bars the first time. Given his present occupation—and the fact that he and Spanish Marie are running rum on the side for gangsters like Capone—clearly, it's where he should stay."

"Mm. Fair enough, I suppose."

"I do so wish I could be there for the takedown," Grace said, before she could stop the words from emerging.

Ness's mouth quirked as he discreetly took in her five-foot, three-inch frame. "Best if we keep you behind the scenes, ma'am."

He was right, of course. And she didn't particularly care about credit—she loathed seeing her name in the papers. But she did adore flying and crossing the country by train. Even the failed chase on *Hogan's Goat* had been exhilarating, whereas lurking in the shadows with her pencil and worksheets didn't feel so glamorous at times.

Be grateful you have a job that feels meaningful, Grace. Be grateful that you're making a difference.

But was she?

We may as well try to empty the Gulf of Mexico with a teaspoon. Mellon's weary words came back to her. Well, the poor man also had the stock market crash to contend with, and several of his friends had jumped from their Wall Street office windows or shot themselves.

On the other end of the financial spectrum, many otherwise normal, average citizens had taken to rumrunning for the simple reason that during this Great Depression, they couldn't find jobs to feed their families. Frankly, Grace felt for them. But they were the minnows, not the whales in her crosshairs.

As for Schroeder? While she still felt relief that a boy his age hadn't been executed, it stuck in her craw that, given a second chance in life, he'd simply expanded his criminal horizons. Who knew what else he was capable of?

As Grace took her leave of Eliot Ness, she couldn't help herself. "Agent Ness, when you see him, will you please give Otto Schroeder my regards?"

Ness gave the briefest of nods, tipped his hat to her and walked away.

CHAPTER TWENTY-NINE

Grace and Robert overheard the news on their brand-new RCA radio.

"Elmer Irey and his T-Men greeted the Messrs. Reifel on the tarmac in Seattle at gunpoint," intoned the announcer. "When the gentlemen demanded to know the meaning of this less-than-warm greeting, Mr. Irey read them their rights. From the airport, the hotel magnates were driven straight to Seattle's main jail, where they were photographed, fingerprinted and booked. Charged with smuggling an astonishing amount of prohibited liquor into the United States through countless ports, and therefore owing seventeen million dollars in taxes, the Reifels' bonds were set at $100,000 apiece..."

Grace knit her brows. "It's an unheard-of sum for bail. But it still seems too low, given what's at stake."

"Well done, my dear," Bobby said. "I wish we could raise a toast." He winked.

"Oh no, my darling. I didn't really have much to do with this case."

Her husband raised an eyebrow. "Meaning there's another case you did have much to do with?"

"Perhaps." Grace loved these evenings when she, at least, was able to discuss her activities with her husband. Robert, on the other hand, had no such freedom any longer. When she asked any questions, even one as vague as, "So what are you working on these days?" he could only respond with, "Oh, this and that."

She understood that he couldn't share the smallest detail; she understood that he'd been tasked with increasingly secret projects. She was proud of him, of course. But she also felt walled off. They'd had such fun in the early days, collaborating. Breaking impossible codes and ciphers together.

"I did have something to do with this one," Grace said, fishing a newspaper article out of her apron pocket. She unfolded it and spread it out on the table.

Smugglers Caught Red-Handed in Miami announced the headline.

> Havana's Rum Queen "Spanish Marie" Waite was arrested today in Coconut Grove, along with one-time German spy Otto Schroeder, aka Pablo Waberski. Mrs. Waite and Mr. Schroeder were personally unloading a cargo of over five thousand cases of liquor off her vessel *Kid Boots* when they were taken into custody by Prohibition Agent Eliot Ness and a team of Treasury agents.
>
> Mrs. Waite is said to have cursed volubly in Spanish and reached for her pistol but was strongly advised not to draw it by the armed agents. The two smugglers were booked into jail where they await a preliminary hearing for a judge to set bail.

"Ha!" Bobby said, looking up from the article to gaze fondly at Grace. "Caught him again, did you?"

She couldn't help lacing her smile with a little triumph. "He shouldn't have been pardoned in the first place."

"Looks a bit older now, if not wiser," her husband mused, eyeing Schroeder's mug shot.

"He's spent quite a bit of time in the sun," Grace said acerbically.

"His lady friend is quite a looker."

"Close your eyes before they're scorched. I have it on excellent authority that she is one 'bad bitch,' Bobby."

"Grace!" Her husband dropped the article, shocked at her language.

"What? I'm simply repeating what I was told."

"By whom?"

"A colorful and somewhat perplexing colleague of mine. The Australian from *Hogan's Goat.*"

"Well, I don't like him speaking to my wife that way. It's quite improper."

"Duly noted. I'll be sure to inform him should we ever again cross paths."

Bobby squinted at her. "Where exactly *did* you cross paths?"

"Let's see…" Grace said wickedly. "I believe…yes, in a hotel in Miami."

"You *believe*—" Words failed him, so he got up and started toward her with mock menace.

She popped up, too, and he chased her around the kitchen table.

"It was a business meeting!" She threw this over her shoulder, laughing, and ran for the stairs.

"I'll give you the business—" Bobby faux growled, in hot pursuit.

"You started this, by ogling that horrid woman in the newspaper!"

"Did I? Well, I intend to finish it, if that's quite all right by you…"

The next morning, Grace took the trolley to the Treasury Building, expecting to find everyone she worked with in a good mood. She found the opposite.

Ambrose, Root's assistant, inclined his head toward Captain Root's office. "You'd better go on in," he said by way of welcome.

"Oh. All right," Grace said, nonplussed since he usually did everything he could to keep her out. She walked down the hallway in the direction of raised voices.

"Who walks away from $200,000 dollars?!" Root exclaimed.

"Folks who have money to burn," Irey said in disgusted tones. "People who rake in so much kale hand over fist that they have tax bills of seventeen million dollars."

Grace's heart sank as she poked her head into the room. *This must mean…*

"Good morning, Mrs. Feldman," Root said. "I'm sorry to say that our Canadian geese have flown the coop."

"Oh no. Oh dear."

Her boss nodded grimly. "Forfeited their bail bonds and scrammed back over the border to Canada, never to return."

"All right, so we can't pursue a criminal case against them personally, but we still have the Bert Morrison criminal trial in New Orleans, and we can certainly still file a civil case against Conexco," Mrs. Willebrandt countered.

Irey nodded. "We can and we will."

Eliot Ness, who'd just entered the room, cleared his throat. "I'm afraid I have some more bad news." He gazed directly at Grace.

No, no, no. Please don't say what I think you're going to say.

But Ness did. "We have the same situation with Spanish Marie and the German spy. They posted bail in Miami, then disappeared. Her radio station in Havana has gone dark. Even her cohorts have somehow vanished."

Grace's spirits sank into her shoes. But nothing could be done, so she took a fat new envelope of coded messages from Ambrose's desk and headed out of the building toward her normal trolley stop. It was hot, even for July—almost as bad as Houston. Heat shimmered up off the sidewalks and bad-tempered clouds had banked to the east, rumbling their displeasure.

Footsteps sounded behind her—male, judging by the way the soles met the concrete sidewalk. As they closed on her, a frisson of alarm had her quickening her pace and turning her head in case of danger.

"Oh, Mr. Ness, it's you."

"Yes. I just wanted to tell you that I did pass on your greetings to Mr. Schroeder. He did not send his compliments."

"I see."

"Mrs. Waite wished to know who the devil—sorry—you were."

"I'm sure you're editing out some even more colorful language, Mr. Ness."

He flushed. "A bit."

"Well. Thank you."

"A word of advice, Mrs. Feldman?"

She nodded.

"You said the same to me: be careful."

Despite telling herself not to be silly, Grace checked behind her before she got on the trolley. She saw no gangsters in zoot suits with machine guns tucked beneath their overcoats. She mostly saw weary white-collar government workers just like herself.

She found a seat in the middle of the car, glad she didn't have to ride outside because of the heat and threat of rain. She couldn't very well pull out a message to puzzle over in public, so she settled for listening to snippets of conversations around her.

"...brought home just the dearest, most precious cocker spaniel, and how could I say no?"

"...worst embassy party ever, darling, *such* a snore. And the canapés were stale."

"...yes, caught in flagrante delicto with the electrician! Of course, he's filing for divorce."

After a while the words all blended together into a buzz of background noise, just as the odors did—wet wool, ripe feet, pipe smoke, auto exhaust, kitchen aromas from local restaurants. Grace settled into the jolting, mechanical rhythm of the trolley.

As they trundled up to the stop nearest the house, she gathered her pocketbook and the parcel of messages. She rose, only to be pushed back down by a heavy hand on her shoulder.

"What—?" Grace turned her head to look. Or tried to.

"Don't, Mrs. Feldman," said a low, bass male voice into her ear. "Don't look. Don't move. And don't scream."

A cold metal object pressed against the back of her neck. All the breath left her body and her own pulse thundered in her ears.

"You've been warned once. But you're a stubborn little lady, aren't you? And a nosy parker. You keep out of our affairs, d'you hear? Or we'll blow your brains right out from under that sweet blue hat."

The metal object receded. The heavy hand lifted from her shoulder and then lodged under her elbow, propelling her upright. "Now, ma'am, you wouldn't want to miss your stop, would you? Go on."

Mouth dry, rigid with fear, Grace moved on stiff legs to the front of the trolley, to the steps down. Her knees had locked, and she wasn't sure she could unlock them. She stood stupidly at the top step, torn between wanting to look back at the unknown man but afraid to risk it.

"Ma'am?" the motorman prompted. "You gettin' off, then?"

"Y-yes." Grace clung to the rail by the door and forced her right leg down to the next step, which meant the left one *had* to bend. Thank goodness it was obedient. She found herself standing in the street like the village idiot while the trolley pulled away. While a few passersby eyed her curiously, she forced herself over to a bench and collapsed upon it, checking to make sure she'd dropped neither pocketbook nor—horrors—the envelope of messages.

The man had likely been on the trolley *before* she boarded. That meant he'd been tailing her. He'd observed her arrive on it to work, and he also knew exactly at which stop she got off. Dear Lord, did he know where she lived?

Her hands shaking, her legs still stiff and trembling, Grace got up from the bench and started unsteadily toward the house. It was time to tell Captain Root. He'd promised security if she felt she needed it.

But what about Robert? What would he say? Would he try to force her to quit her job? Did they need to move?

She let herself into the little house, locked the door behind her and climbed the few stairs from the foyer, holding on to the banister tightly because her legs were still trembling. She dropped her things on the narrow hall table. The mirror above it informed her that her face was deathly pale—not surprising.

She peeled off her sticky gloves, a curse in a DC July, and unpinned her blue hat. She perched it atop the coatrack and stared at it while rubbing at the gooseflesh that broke out along her arms despite the heat.

Tea. She should make some tea.

Grace went through the motions on autopilot, wishing for the first time in years that she had something stronger to pour for herself—but she and Bobby had scrupulously adhered to the law since that first New Year's.

What had the man held to her neck? A gun? Who'd sent him?

How did they know who she was, and what she worked on? Of course: the cursed features and articles. The court testimony she'd provided—and was soon to provide again in the upcoming Conexco case—unless the thugs scared her off.

Grace walked out of the kitchen and stared again at her blue hat, the petals of its silk daffodil drooping a bit, looking as cowed and reluctant as she felt. The gooseflesh on her arms faded, and something hot and angry pulsed through her: outrage.

How dare some thug follow her around, snoop into her life and accost her on the trolley?

Put his hands on her, threaten her, try to terrify her out of doing her job?

How *dare* he? Grace wanted to scream, but it would alarm the neighbors; besides which, the kettle was obliging enough to do it for her.

She made her tea and turned on the oven to heat a cheesy ham and potato dish brought over by one of the neighbor ladies. She heated the iron with particular purpose to fix her hat.

By the time Robert got home, weary and smelling of pipe smoke, she'd made up her mind to come clean with him—well, mostly clean. She was still in denial about her possible pregnancy and was able to stay that way because her monthlies had never been regular.

"Good evening, my darling," he said as he walked through the kitchen door. "May I ask why you're ironing a daffodil?"

"Hello, Bobby. The daffodil was drooping, and if it's going to accompany me then it needs a backbone. How was your day?" She already knew what he'd say. *Just fine.*

"Oh, it was fine. Just fine." He peered at her. "No insult intended, my dear, but daffodils have stems, not spines."

Grace sighed. "All right, then. Its stem needs straightening and its petals need...plumping."

"Far be it from me to argue with a woman on a mission. How was your day?"

"Frustrating, peculiar and frightening." Grace put down the iron, set the freshly fortified daffodil aside and walked over to her husband, wrapping her arms around him and hugging him.

Bobby picked her up, made a beeline for the sofa and sat down on it with her in his lap while she told him about the goon on the trolley. His arms tightened around her, he rocked her and then he dropped a kiss on top of her head.

When she pulled away to look up at him, his hazel eyes were furious, and his jaw had turned to granite. "I don't like this, Grace. I know better than to issue any ultimatums, but I'd prefer that you quit."

"No." She said it baldly, flatly. "That's letting them win."

"I'd rather they win than murder you."

"Captain Root has told me that Treasury will arrange security at the trial."

"And what about here in Washington? Or on the trolley? Here at home?"

She sighed. "I don't know how exactly it will work."

"Well, I do. I will be taking the trolley with you from now on, in the mornings and evenings. I'll pick you up from Treasury headquarters shortly after five each workday."

"But you'll have to go out of your way—"

"I don't care. If you won't terminate your employment, then you'll accept my escort."

She ran a finger along his lips. "Awfully bossy, aren't you?"

"Yes." He bit her finger gently. "Awfully ungrateful, aren't you?"

"I suppose so," she said glumly. "It's just that I hate needing protection. It makes me feel small."

"Well, I'm sorry to inform you that the daffodil over there—no matter how much starch you apply to it—isn't going to get the job done."

"They were probably just trying to scare me, Bobby."

"And they did a good job of it. They've scared me, too, the bastards." He wrinkled his nose. "Darling, what's that smell? Is something burning?"

"Oh no, no, *no*..." Grace scrambled off his lap and ran to the kitchen. She wrenched open the oven door only to have it belch a cloud of black smoke into her face.

Robert appeared in the doorway and the noxious stench billowed toward him. "Say, sweetheart—I have an idea. Shall we go out for dinner?"

CHAPTER THIRTY

In defiance of the thug, Grace traveled to New Orleans for the Conexco trial. The city sprawled in full color from the mouth of the Mississippi River, and Grace was awed by the city's ambiance and living history, its French and Southern charm a genteel glove over the iron fist of its character. It was a place like no other, enlivened by patois and polish, inviting aromas seducing visitors from every corner dive or elegant restaurant. Jazz and swing music wound their way through the streets and had toes tapping involuntarily under café tables. Good-natured bonhomie and hospitality mingled with darker undercurrents of corruption and superstition.

She was there to do her best. And so, to her surprise, were two beefy bodyguards assigned by Treasury to watch over her.

But even with the very large men posted outside her door, Grace slept poorly that first night. The next morning, she bathed and dressed quickly in demure shades of blue. She applied her lipstick, powdered her nose and settled her blue hat—with the now-proud daffodil—upon her head, tearing it off immediately as her stomach lurched and slid greasily. She dashed for the toilet.

"All right, all right. There's no denying it. You're not a flu. You're a baby. And I'm an utter fool to have come here."

Grace righted herself, brushed her teeth, washed her hands and stared into the mirror. She reminded herself that she had two armed federal agents looking out for her.

It was a short ride to the courthouse, and Grace found herself soon enough in the witness box, looking out at the defendants, judge and jury. Amos Walter Wright Woodcock, lead prosecutor on the case, stood next to her. After too many years wasted on little fish, he was at last going after a whale with Consolidated Exporters.

She stated her name and occupation and gave an explanation to the jury of exactly what a cryptanalyst did. The defendants—all twenty-three of them—yawned with condescension, sweat beading on their foreheads. They were not afraid of her. Bert Morrison, Conexco's "land agent," sneered at her.

"Mrs. Feldman," asked Woodcock, "do you have in your possession a message sent at 6:07 p.m. on April 8 of last year? If so, will you please read it aloud?"

Grace located it in her stack of thirty-two messages pertaining to the case and opened her mouth to do as instructed.

Immediately, one of eight—*eight*—defense attorneys leapt to his feet. "Objection, your honor! This *lady* is no expert. She's at best a typist or file clerk. Her testimony is incompetent, irrelevant and immaterial."

"I beg your pardon?" Grace said, before Woodcock could intervene. "I am cryptanalyst-in-charge at the US Coast Guard. I am *fully* competent. My testimony is *relevant* because we captured messages from these"—she gestured toward the defendants—"*gentlemen* via radio, and those messages are *material* because once translated, they clearly related to the smuggling of illegal liquor into the United States."

The defendants suddenly looked as if they had gas.

The jury sat up and paid attention.

Woodcock smothered a smile and looked quizzically at the judge.

"Overruled."

Grace read out the series of coded gibberish in five-letter clumps, followed by its translation: *Out of Old Colonel in pints.*

Another defense attorney erupted out of his seat. "Objection! Your

Honor, this so-called 'translation' is merely a matter of opinion and should therefore be struck from the record."

Grace started to reply, but Woodcock laid a finger across his lips. "Your Honor, a translation is not a matter of opinion. Especially when it's made by an expert in the field."

"Overruled."

Grace translated another coded message into plaintext.

"Objection!" Another defense attorney popped up.

"Is it not plain as daylight that this lady was given her information by some other federal agent? It's not possible to derive her so-called 'plaintext' from such nonsense. Unless she can demonstrate to the court exactly how she does it, I ask that her testimony be excluded and she be excused forthwith from the witness stand."

"Oh, for heaven's sake," Grace said before Woodcock could stop her. "Judge, if there is a blackboard on the premises, I'd be more than happy to educate the defense and prove that I was not handed my information because my pretty little head can't have processed it."

This time it was the judge who smothered a smile. "Bailiff, please locate a blackboard and some chalk."

As the baby slid and swam in her midsection, doing its best to distract her, Grace left the witness box and stepped into the role of teacher to an astonishingly rapt audience. "These clumps of letters, here"—she scratched them onto the board in black and white—"translate into the names of ships owned by the Consolidated Exporters Corporation, also known as Conexco, operated by the defendants." She demonstrated how she'd come to this conclusion. "It's a question of frequency, vowels, consonants...repeated symbols and letters."

"So we now have, instead of the wretched nonsense, the names of the ships: *Concord*, *Corozal*, *Fisher Lassie*, *Rosita*, and *Mavis Barbara*. You see?"

Almost every head in the courtroom couldn't help but nod.

"And here: let's isolate this message to translate." Grace printed out a five-line mess of letters and symbols. She then proceeded to teach the jury how to decrypt the chaos. "And so here we have the plaintext, clear instructions to the smugglers:

SUBSTITUTE FIFTY CANADIAN CLUB BALANCE BLUE GRASS FOR COROZAL STOP REPEAT TUESDAY WIRE CONCORD GO TO LATITUDE 29.50 LONGITUDE 87.44.

Murmurs echoed across the courtroom.

"Your witness," said Woodcock.

The eight defense attorneys conferred before one got to his feet. "Mrs. Feldman. These terms themselves could be code for other...ah... items, could they not? Such as women being transported from Europe."

Grace raised an eyebrow at him. "No, sir. While the Coast Guard is also battling human trafficking as well as narcotics trafficking, these terms are not code for anything but liquor. If you need further proof, ask the gentlemen of Consolidated Exporters directly whether the *Corozal*, a small cutter, has room for fifty women—and whether it has ever once left US waters. May I tell you a little bit about Rum Row and how it works?"

At the close of the day, Grace had thoroughly stymied eight defense attorneys and provided the final nails in their clients' legal coffins. She was excused at last.

She desperately had to use the ladies' room, and her head swam as she tried to keep her pace decorous but the familiar but unwelcome bile rose in her throat. She lost her battle with decorum, ran for the door and burst in—only to have yet another unwelcome choice between two urgent bodily functions.

Grace hurtled into a stall, barely got her garter straps unhooked and then collapsed upon the toilet. Then, without pausing for breath, she opened her pocketbook and vomited into it.

"Okay, baby. Message received. You win."

It was on the way to the airport that it happened. Grace thanked her two burly bodyguards kindly for looking after her, then climbed into a taxi to head for the airport while the driver stowed her suitcase in the trunk.

The musty smell of the cab and the gasoline fumes from the surrounding traffic made her feel ill, and Grace leaned back against the seat, her freshly scrubbed and still-damp pocketbook ready in her lap for another disaster. She closed her eyes for a while.

When she opened them, she noticed that they didn't seem to be heading toward the airport, which was near the south shore of Lake Pontchartrain. They were instead heading north.

"Excuse me?" she said to the driver. "We need to drive south." Was he trying to pad the fare?

"There's a roadblock. Gotta detour, ma'am."

"Perhaps so, but it should take us south, not to Arkansas."

The cabbie just grunted.

"Please turn around at your earliest opportunity," Grace said.

He didn't even acknowledge her.

"Sir?" Unease spiraled through her. "Sir, I'm speaking to you."

"Somebody wanna see you," he said at last.

The unease solidified into fear. Perspiration broke out on Grace's forehead, at the small of her back and under her arms. "I don't wish to see this 'somebody,' you understand? I have a plane to catch."

"Ain't up to me, lady."

"It most certainly is."

"Just followin' orders, ma'am."

"Whose orders?" Sweat soaked her blouse. She'd been almost as frightened when accosted by the goon on the trolley, or when Farquhar had manhandled her into his motorcar. "Listen to me. I am an agent of the United States government. Do you understand?"

No reply. Which meant...which meant that he very likely did understand perfectly well and that he worked for someone very unsavory. Perhaps someone with the name Capone. Grace battled the hysteria rising inside her.

"You cannot kidnap me." *And my baby.* Dear Lord, the baby. This couldn't be happening. Not now.

"Ain't kidnappin' you."

The hysteria became blind panic. What would they do to her? "For the last time, I'm ordering you to take me to the airport!" Grace somehow made her voice hard, like a drill sergeant's.

Open the door and roll out, Grace. Wait quietly for a traffic light. And in the meantime, babble.

"I'm pregnant," she pleaded, losing the drill-sergeant tone. "Please, let me go."

The driver ignored this, too.

"I—I can pay you. I don't have much cash, but I could write you a draft on my account."

Silence.

"Please, sir. Please! My baby..."

He slowed for an upcoming traffic light, and Grace surreptitiously checked to see if there was any traffic in the next lane. She didn't want to roll out only to become roadkill. All clear. Across the street was a diner, a taxidermist of all things and a drugstore.

Grace deliberately dissolved into tears and sobbed again to the driver that she was pregnant. Then, as he sighed and patted his pockets for a handkerchief, she wrenched open the door and threw herself out, landing painfully on her hip. She rolled, scrambled to her feet and ran, quite literally, for her life.

She dodged behind parked cars as the cabbie shouted after her and gave chase, leaving his automobile running in the street. Grace rounded the drugstore—too obvious—ran into the back alley and pounded at the rear exit of the taxidermist.

A man in shirtsleeves and a bloody canvas apron opened the door.

"Please-let-me-in-a-taxi-driver-kidnapped-me-I'm-pregnant-please-help!" Grace blurted. "Hide me. I'm begging you."

He pulled her inside and led her into a workshop bizarre enough that she almost bolted out of it. Claws, glass eyes, stuffings, furs, feathers...

"Under that table," he said.

It was a door laid across two sawhorses and draped with what may have been a bear hide. Grace dropped to her knees and crawled under it, dragging her pocketbook behind her.

Her rescuer pulled two crates over and shoved them after her to conceal her better—and in the nick of time.

Jangling bells at the front of the shop announced an angry, frustrated visitor. "Hello? Say! Anyone in this joint?"

The taxidermist walked out to meet him. "May I help you, sir?"

"I'm lookin' for someone. See a lady—tiny—about yea high? Dark hair, blue dress?"

"No, not that I recall. I don't get many ladies in here, you understand. Though I did have one come in last week, wanted me to stuff her pet dog that had died..."

With a curse, the taxi driver threw open the jangling door again and left to continue his search.

Grace huddled under the table, shaking.

The taxidermist returned and peered at her.

"Th-thank you," she said. "Thank you."

"Well, I'll be danged if I let a pregnant lady get hurt. Or any lady, for that mattah." He handed her a glass of water, which she accepted gratefully.

"C-can I stay under here for a half hour or so?"

"'Course. Want to tell me what this is all about?"

She shook her head.

"Anythin' else I can do for ya?"

Grace looked at her watch. She was going to miss her flight. "I... need to get to the airport?"

He drove her himself. She sent a telegram to Robert and caught the next flight, blaming a traffic jam for missing the original one. And she realized that the cabbie who'd kidnapped her still had her suitcase in the trunk—her suitcase with her name and address neatly printed on its luggage tag.

CHAPTER THIRTY-ONE

"What do you mean, we can't go home?" Robert asked, when he met her after her flight.

She explained, and he grimly drove them to the Willard on Pennsylvania Avenue and booked them a room. He ran her a warm bath and made a series of telephone calls while she was in it. When she came out, wrapped in a hotel bathrobe, he announced that they were moving to a government safe house for a time.

"A safe house? But—"

"No buts."

"We'll need to gather our things."

"Absolutely not. Someone will pack them all up and we'll eventually be reunited with them. For now, we'll purchase what we need."

"With what, Bobby? Money will be tight now—how can we even afford to stay here at the Willard?"

He aimed a puzzled glance at her.

She realized that he didn't know she'd shortly be out of a job. "Honey...I haven't seen a doctor yet to confirm it, but I'm pregnant."

His jaw fell open, and his eyes lit with joy. He sprinted over to her and caressed her face with both hands. Then he looked down toward her midsection. "May I?"

"There's nothing to see yet." But she allowed him to untie the belt of her robe and place his palm on her belly.

"A baby!" he said exultantly.

While this warmed her and reassured her, it also terrified her. What if her body rejected the child, as it had previously? What if it didn't, but she died in childbirth—or worse, was a miserable parent and ruined the child's life? She was clearly undomesticated in most ways. While that could be excused as eccentric in a childless woman, it wouldn't be looked upon kindly in a mother.

"I need a new pocketbook," she said glumly, relating what had happened in the courthouse.

"We'll buy you half a dozen, my darling."

"With what? We're going to lose my income."

"Chin up, sweetheart!" He tugged her into his arms and danced around the room with her.

"I don't want my chin up," she said, pulling out of his arms. "Nor do I want to dance. And yes, I know I'm being ornery. *You* don't have a creature growing inside you that delights in gnawing on your entrails, bloating your belly and making you ill."

"It will all be worth it, love."

"*You* won't be forced out of your job."

"I doubt that Captain Root will lay down any ultimatums, Grace."

"Oh, really? He doesn't need to, Robert. You're not female—you have no idea what expectations are placed on women to be perfect—no hair out of place despite sleepless nights full of wailing and breastfeeding and dirty diapers…if a visitor were to stop by our home, it isn't *you* who'd be blamed for unwashed dishes, unpolished furniture or drifting dust balls. You simply don't understand—"

"Housekeeper," Robert said gently. "Housekeeper, housekeeper, housekeeper, my love."

Grace burst into tears. "We can't afford one," she sobbed. "Captain Root will eliminate my position."

"We'll ask my mother to come for a few weeks," her clueless husband suggested.

"Are you out of your mind? She'd cry more than the baby at the very sight of her shiksa daughter-in-law, at the horrible evidence that we've reproduced…"

"All right, all right—what about your sister Evie? Could she come help for a while?"

"Maybe," Grace conceded.

"Why don't you write to her?"

Why don't you go soak your head and stop being so helpful and countering everything I have to say, whether it's unreasonable or not? Why can't you understand that I want to express my "unnatural" feelings and fears without you solving them in seconds? I want to wallow.

Grace instantly felt ashamed. She had the kindest, most loving husband imaginable, and she was a witch. "All right," she said.

"Evie will come to the rescue," Bobby said, all male reassurance.

Evie has a family of her own. And oh, dear heavens—how does a six-to-eight-pound baby come out of a five-foot, three-inch woman? Grace's hands began to tremble.

Of course she knew how. She just couldn't bear thinking about it. *Oh God. Oh God. Oh God*... And if by some miracle she could produce this child, however was she going to feed it when she couldn't cook?

"I love you madly, my darling."

The poor, long-suffering sweetheart of a man. "I don't deserve you, Bobby."

He reached for her and folded her into his arms, kissed her on the head. "I love you," he repeated.

"Why?"

"Oh, don't be an idiot, Grace," he said fondly.

She might have taken that as an excuse to start a fight, but she didn't have the energy. Babies, apart from making one swell and toss one's cookies into any available vessel, sapped one's energy. "I love you, too, Bobby. Truly. You're the best thing that's ever happened to me."

He was. How could she make him happy, apologize for her surliness?

Grace decided that once they got to this mysterious safe house, she'd conquer her mother-in-law's apple kugel. He deserved a treat.

"Wait a moment," he said slowly, narrowing his eyes upon her. "When exactly did you know you were pregnant?"

Oh dear. So much for not starting a fight. Grace moistened her lips. "Well, I..."

He folded his arms across his chest and waited, his mouth an uncompromising line, his jaw set. "Yes?"

"I wasn't sure."

"When were you not sure?" His eyebrows snapped together. "Were you *not sure* after your trolley adventure? Were you *not sure* before you flew to New Orleans to testify in a trial against thugs like Bert Morrison who work hand in glove with dangerous mobsters? Mobsters like Ralph 'Bottles' Capone and his friendly brother Al?"

Unable to meet his gaze, Grace twisted the ties of the bathrobe and sat down weakly on the bed.

"Were you *not sure*, Grace, when you got kidnapped? Threw yourself *out* of a taxicab and rolled onto the street? Or were you sure at *that* point, when not only *your* life, but also *the life of our unborn child* was in danger?"

She'd never seen Robert so furious.

"I'm sorry," she whispered. "I...I..." She wrapped her arms around herself. "I'm afraid," she said at last, trying to wipe the image of bloody sheets from her mind. "I'm afraid that what happened before will happen again. I'm afraid to be locked up alone all day with nothing to do but worry. I'm afraid to not work. I'm afraid to give birth. And I'm afraid that I'll be a terrible mother if I do."

Her husband exhaled audibly.

When Grace found the courage to look up, she saw, to her relief, that his anger was gone and his eyes held compassion.

"That's a lot of fear," Bobby said, "for such a fearless woman."

Grace still had trouble meeting his eyes. "I never claimed to be fearless."

"Well, you certainly present yourself that way: your perfect posture and your crisp diction and your starched, battle-ready daffodil."

A chuckle escaped her. "Try being five feet, three inches, darling. You'd do everything in your power to seem tall and unflappable, too."

Robert shook his head. Then he scooped her up and lay down on the bed with her in his arms, holding her close. "Rest assured, my dear: in spite of your hidden fears and your small stature, a skyscraper dwells in your soul."

The "safe house" didn't look any safer to Grace than any other house she'd encountered. Its security seemed to lie simply in the fact that its ownership was obfuscated and certainly not in their names. It was a modest Craftsman bungalow with a front porch held up by four brown stone columns linked by white picket railings. Two windows on either side flanked the front door.

It was furnished, pleasant enough, and she could cheer it up with a few flowerpots set on the steps. The first thing Grace added to the décor was a newspaper clipping from the *New Orleans Times/Picayune*, snipped neatly and tacked to the kitchen wall.

MILLION DOLLAR RUM RUNNER TRIAL: ALL 23 DEFENDANTS CONVICTED AFTER LADY CODEBREAKER TESTIFIES.

The conspiracy case brought by the government at a cost of some five hundred thousand dollars is successful, thanks to the testimony of a female codebreaker. Defendants Bert Morrison and other ringleaders operated a syndicate that owned a fleet of rum ships, hundreds of boats and several wireless stations... cargoes of illicit liquor worth millions of dollars were shipped by these bootleggers through New Orleans. All 23 defendants face prison time and hefty fines...

The article made Grace happy, though she would have been even happier if the article had named the owners of the syndicate in question.

No mention of the Reifels was made, nor of the Capones. But she understood that these convictions would be a stepping stone to others.

A couple of weeks after she and Bobby moved into the safe house, their possessions arrived, neatly packed into boxes and unloaded by some friendly fellows from an unmarked truck.

Grace had no idea where the things had been stored or by whom, but she was grateful to have their clothes and books and knickknacks back—though she'd rather they'd have lost the pots and pans.

Those she unpacked dourly, along with her recipe box, which reminded her that she wanted to make her husband his apple kugel.

She found the recipe card the elder Mrs. Feldman had given her and followed the instructions to the letter, measuring ingredients with the care of a chemist.

A pound of noodles—even Grace could boil those. Applesauce. Five eggs. Half a cup of sugar. Two teaspoons of ground cloves. A sprinkle of cinnamon on top.

She'd faced off with the dreaded oven and set it to the correct temperature. She'd greased the pan. She could do this. Grace Smith Feldman could and would conquer the kugel.

Except…it turned out exactly as it had the last time she'd made it.

Bobby, the excited grin of a little boy on his face, spooned a large bite into his mouth, chewed twice and froze as if Medusa herself had turned him into stone.

"Honey?" Grace ventured. She took a cautious bite of the kugel herself, lurched to the kitchen sink and spat it out.

Stoic at the table, her husband managed to swallow his bite.

"But I followed your mother's recipe exactly," wailed Grace. "I did! Where's the card? Where is that cursed recipe card?" She dug it out of a drawer. "Here! Look at it! I did everything she told me to do. Why does it taste this bad?"

Robert read the card carefully. He covered his mouth with his hand. His shoulders began to shake.

"What?"

"It appears," he said diplomatically, "that Mama made a mistake."

"What mistake?"

"I'm not a chef, mind you, but...I've never seen two entire teaspoons of ground cloves added to anything. I believe she must have meant cinnamon."

Grace put her hands on her hips. "And I believe she deliberately gave me a recipe for disaster."

"Surely not, my darling."

"Stop smirking like a gargoyle, Bobby! Your mother did it on purpose. And so much food wasted. All the noodles, the eggs, the applesauce—"

"Perhaps she just wanted to bring her little boy home to see her more often, honey."

"Perhaps she's a—" Grace broke off. Insulting a man's mother never worked out well in the long run. "Never mind. I'll ask Mrs. Liberman for a good apple kugel recipe. I'm going to make you a good kugel if it kills me."

"Don't strain yourself, my dear. It's not good for the baby," Robert said mildly.

She glared at him. "Perhaps we should try the new diner on the corner this evening."

"Perhaps we should."

They feasted on brisket and beans that someone else had cooked. Bobby tactfully ordered cheesecake for dessert even though kugel was on the menu.

Grace noticed this with dark amusement and great affection.

Her pursuit of the domestic arts was failing miserably, but Grace still had a goal before she was forced to retire: pursue justice instead. Why weren't more of the bootlegging cases that she and the Coast Guard codebreaking unit had solved being prosecuted?

She telephoned Mrs. Willebrandt about it. "Well, the courts are backlogged and the prisons are bursting," Mabel said. "But if you're concerned about widespread bribery to officials, you could consult Mr. Hoover about it."

Grace waited as patiently as she could to see the Director of the Bureau of Investigation, none other than J. Edgar Hoover. She didn't particularly want to meet with him. But it was the right thing to do. Hoover was the man to see about why so many of her cases had been sidelined. And perhaps she'd tell him about her kidnapping.

She felt the urge to go to the ladies' room *again*. The baby must be taking joy in sitting directly on her bladder. Mr. Hoover had already kept her waiting for thirty minutes past their appointed time, and, though annoyed, she hesitated to chance missing him altogether if he emerged from his office and found her gone.

He had been elevated from his role as assistant director in 1924 after the firing of his boss William Burns and the downfall of Attorney General Harry M. Daugherty—two of the men deeply tainted by the Teapot Dome scandal during Warren G. Harding's administration. Harding was dead and could tell no tales about the corruption, but AG Daugherty himself had only narrowly escaped prison after a contentious trial.

Grace found it interesting that Hoover, who'd been at Daugherty's side all through the trial, had not been fired along with his boss Burns. But Hoover's reputation remained sterling.

At last, a gentleman emerged from Hoover's inner sanctum—a rather saturnine, oily gentleman who sent a chill up Grace's spine. He gave her a quick once-over and then, to her surprise, stuck out his hand.

"Gaston Means," he said, displaying too many teeth.

"Mrs. Grace Feldman," she said, keeping hers to herself.

"Feldman... any relation to Robert Feldman in Army SIGINT?"

"My husband."

"Interesting. Smart fellow, isn't he?"

"Yes."

At that moment, Hoover's prim secretary, Mrs. Gandy, also emerged from the director's lair. "Mr. Hoover will see you now, Mrs. Feldman."

Well, how kind of him. Grace resisted the urge to check her watch in front of her. She got up and followed her into Hoover's office.

He rose to meet her courteously enough but did not extend his hand. He simply gestured to a visitor's chair set on the opposite side of his looming, carved-oak desk. Grace thanked him and sat, taking in his appearance while trying to gauge how direct she should be.

He was still young, clean-shaven, with the build and demeanor of a bulldog. And he still had the flat, merciless eyes of a shark, his gaze too direct—as if she were prey. Perhaps they were just "cop" eyes. Or perhaps his reputation for chauvinism was well-deserved.

Grace wondered, too late, if she'd made a grave mistake by coming here. But she had a duty to discharge before her pregnancy became so obvious that Captain Root graciously and solicitously suggested that she go home and "rest." It was coming, and she knew it. Bobby was already begging her to resign, treating her like glass and barely allowing her out of bed or off the couch. It was tender, loving, sweet—and infuriating.

"A pleasure to see you again, Mrs. Feldman," Hoover said. "To what do I owe the honor?"

"Likewise. I know you're a very busy man, Mr. Hoover, so I shall try not to take up much of your time."

He didn't deny it, didn't say a word. Just evaluated her with those unnerving eyes.

"As I'm sure you're aware, I'm cryptanalyst-in-charge at the United States Coast Guard."

"Yes. Congratulations." He leaned back in his chair and laced his fingers over his paunch. "I imagine you've learned a great deal from your illustrious husband."

Grace looked down at her lap to disguise her irritation. "As you know, we both studied cryptanalysis under Parker Hitt at Riverbank and then ran—"

"It was your husband who helped you set up the high-frequency receivers and direction finders for the Coast Guard on a fleet of seventy-five-foot cutters, did he not?"

Taken aback that Hoover knew this—*how?*—Grace nodded. "Yes, he did take time away from his duties to spend a couple of weeks on that project."

"And it was only after he did that, that you were able to direct Coast Guard vessels to the exact spots where cargoes were to be dropped."

Grace felt two spots on her cheeks burning. "Regardless, Mr. Hoover, I myself am an experienced codebreaker and have been triangulating—"

"Yes, yes," Hoover said. "I know. 'Key Woman of the T-Men,' and all that. The 'Doll of Domestic Intelligence.'"

Grace clenched her hands upon her new pocketbook. "I am here today because somehow a great number of smuggling cases—for which either myself or other Coast Guard personnel have cracked the communications codes—are somehow not being prosecuted. I can't for the life of me understand why, since we laid out all of the evidence against them."

Hoover's dark eyebrows snapped together, and his ruddy complexion deepened. "Are you implying that the personnel of the Bureau or the personnel of the Department of Justice are not doing their jobs?"

"No, of course not—"

"You do understand, madam, that it takes time to prepare and prosecute a case? That it takes time to get it on a judge's docket?"

"Yes, Mr. Hoover—"

"Do you comprehend that our prisons are bursting because of the Volstead Act? That we are forced to dismiss nine out of ten cases simply because of the backlog in the courts?"

"I—"

"Making the wheels of justice turn isn't as simple as whipping up a batch of cookies or sewing a pair of curtains."

Oh! The words stuck in her craw but she forced them out. "Of course not. It's just that—"

"Are you a lawyer, Mrs. Feldman, in addition to being a Coast Guard

employee and a wife? Are you a doctor of jurisprudence?" His tone
dripped with condescension.

"No—"

"Then might I suggest that you leave matters of the law to men who
are?"

Rather than strangling him, she steeled herself to say what she'd
come to say. "Mr. Hoover, it is truly not my intent to insult either you
or the work of the Department of Justice. Please understand that. But,
after the Teapot Dome scandal—"

Hoover flinched almost imperceptibly.

"—it *is* a concern of mine, having several years of experience decoding the communications of unsavory smuggling sorts, that they tend
to *bribe* their way out of trouble. They pay large amounts of money to
certain people for looking the other way. And I'm afraid that this may
be exactly what is occurring in some of the cases that aren't making
it to trial. Perhaps, Mr. Hoover, it's possible to assign a few agents to
investigate this possibility?"

As she spoke, the director's face suffused from brick red to purple.
He leaned forward and steepled his fingers upon his desk, his soulless
shark eyes smoldering. "Mrs. Feldman, you dare to march into my
office and *accuse this Bureau and the DOJ of being corrupt?*" he bellowed.

"I did no such thing," Grace said, genuinely startled. "The payoffs
are more likely to occur—"

"And then *you*, a housewife with a little hobby instead of children,
tell me how to do my job?"

"I did not, sir." But too late, she realized how he might have taken it
that way. "At least, that was not my intent."

But AG Daugherty, in charge of the DOJ, certainly *had* been corrupt. Grace swallowed. Had Hoover kept his job by looking the other
way while his boss was on the take? *Oh, good Lord, Grace. He must have.
The only other explanation is that the man is a blind idiot—and he's most
certainly not.*

Hoover leaned back again, opened a drawer of his monstrous desk, and retrieved a file folder. "Tell me, Mrs. Feldman. Your husband Robert—was he born in the United States?"

"What?" she asked, dizzied at the sudden change in topic. "No."

"He was in fact born in Russia, was he not?"

"His parents emigrated when he was a tiny baby. Why?"

"Russia, hotbed of Bolsheviks and Communism, Mrs. Feldman. Is your husband a member of the Communist Party?"

"*What?* NO. He is a proud American citizen, a champion of democracy."

"Are you sure of that, Mrs. Feldman?"

"Yes, I'm sure. He works for the United States Army in Signal Intelligence. He fought for this country in the Great War."

"Perfect cover for an informant—or worse, a spy."

Grace's mouth dropped open.

Hoover's black stare never wavered. "Don't you agree?"

"No, I don't, Mr. Hoover."

"Then you're naïve, Mrs. Feldman."

"I'm not—I mean—what I mean to say is that Bobby is no informant, nor is he a spy. But yes, I'd be naïve if I didn't allow that a position like his might be good cover."

"Do you think *I'm* naïve, Mrs. Feldman?"

"Of course not, sir."

"Do you find my questions rude?"

She didn't answer him.

"Or are these quite reasonable suspicions to entertain?"

Again, she didn't answer.

"Is your husband Jewish, Mrs. Feldman?"

This again. "Yes."

"So then you are, too."

"Ah...no."

"You did not convert to your husband's faith when you married him?"

"I did not."

"You were raised Quaker."

How do you know that? "Yes."

"Do you attend a temple with your husband?"

"No."

"Do you attend a local meetinghouse?"

"No."

"Do you attend a church of any kind, Mrs. Feldman?"

"I fail to see how this is any of your concern, Mr. Hoover. I am here for professional reasons only, and the questions you're asking are quite personal."

"I'm asking these personal questions in my professional capacity. I always find that it's best to know those with whom one conducts business, don't you?"

She said nothing.

"Do a little background check, be aware of any red flags." Hoover aimed a tight smile at her, one that she did not return.

"Are you threatening me, Mr. Hoover?" Grace asked quietly.

"Why would I do that, Mrs. Feldman?"

She swallowed. She'd been wrong indeed to come here, to meet with this man, all for the sake of doing what was right. Pursuing justice.

Grace got to her feet and thanked him politely for his time.

Mrs. Gandy appeared as if by magic and escorted her from the room. Hoover's dark gaze burned twin holes through her torso until the door shut behind her.

Grace emerged into the sunlight, quivering with outrage and fear. Had she just put Robert's career at risk? Had she put his very freedom at risk? He was certainly no Communist—the idea was laughable—much less a spy for Russia—but even the barest suggestion that he might be, put to top brass, could create trouble. It could get his top secret clearance revoked.

She was perhaps four months away from giving birth. The loss of her income they could adjust to. But the loss of both their incomes meant disaster. What would they do? Move in with his mother? Move in with her father? Go back to Riverbank and fall upon Farquhar's tender mercies?

Unthinkable.

Grace had never backed down from a challenge in her life. Nor from a powerful man who issued one. But J. Edgar Hoover was clearly not someone she should make an enemy out of—if it wasn't too late.

Hoover hobnobbed with senators, business leaders and Hollywood movie stars. He'd been celebrated in the press for bringing down gangsters like John Dillinger, Baby Face Nelson and Machine Gun Kelly. Hoover was America's bright, shining young beacon of justice.

So why did she feel so distressed and disturbed?

It's simple male chauvinism, Grace. Pull yourself together and realize, yet again, that men don't like to be challenged by women, much less told how to do their jobs.

Grace did her best to put the meeting with Hoover behind her. Instead, she focused on her job. When the Reifel brothers in Canada negotiated a settlement of their seventeen million–dollar tax bill down to a mere $500,000, she was disgusted. So disgusted, in fact, that she brought all thirty bound volumes of messages she'd decoded for the Coast Guard into a secure office, where in every spare moment she huddled with Frank Wilson, Eliot Ness and Elmer Irey to create detailed reports of the Consolidated Exporters Corporation networks and their operations—as well as Capone's.

Though they'd lost Mabel Willebrandt when President Hoover passed her over for attorney general, they still had the full support of Treasury Secretary Mellon. In 1931, their dogged work paid off: A tax adjustment was upheld by the courts, ordering the Reifels to pay $119,885,000—almost $120 million.

And in the same year, the Treasury task force's hard work and tenacious determination paid off when Al Capone himself and his brother

Ralph were convicted of tax evasion and sentenced to eleven years in federal prison.

Grace was euphoric. Despite the difficulties inherent in enforcing the Volstead Act, despite so many of her cases not being prosecuted, despite hostile juries who ruled against the government when they were brought to court—she and her fellow codebreakers had made a real difference.

With Capone in jail, Grace and Robert were able to move out of the government safe house and into their first real home on Military Road.

Grace became a mother for the first time. And again two years later. Both times her sister Evie came to help, and both times Grace marveled at the perfection and sweetness and utter helplessness of her newborn babies.

Though she'd been reluctant to have children, she fell in love with little Isobel and Christopher instantly, wildly, with none of the caution she'd felt about her developing feelings for their father.

And as she fed them, changed them, cared for them, she also realized that these tiny human beings she and Robert had created were the greatest and most difficult riddles she could ever hope to solve. After she'd successfully barnstormed the field of cryptanalysis, it was humbling.

How was she to interpret any given coo or cry or fidget? What flicker of imagination went through Isobel's developing brain when she touched a table leg or became fascinated by a basket? What did Christopher's myopic eyes register when he blinked upward at the mobile hung over his crib?

Far from being retired, Grace felt that she was still, every day, a codebreaker.

Prohibition was repealed shortly before Christopher's birth, and Grace questioned wryly whether much of her work for the last decade-plus had been for nothing. But no: she'd done what was right by enforcing the law, she'd taken down drug smugglers and gangsters, she'd saved her country hundreds of millions of dollars.

They lived the next few years as a relatively normal family, raising babies into toddlers and beyond, while storm clouds blew into Europe.

She and Robert tried—and failed—to absorb the horror of Kristallnacht in 1938, when mobs of Nazi brownshirts all over Germany attacked Jewish businesses and set fire to synagogues, destroying culture and books...killing over ninety innocent citizens with Adolf Hitler's approval.

She began to find Robert awake and sitting on the living room couch in the wee hours of the morning, his head in his hands. He didn't seem to have much of an appetite and left earlier and earlier for work, muttering to himself.

Grace worried, tried to soothe him, tried to be a model wife and mother so that their home would be a comfort and a refuge to her husband. She read *Good Housekeeping* and *Ladies' Home Journal*; she kept fresh flowers on the dining room table.

And then one afternoon, just as Grace had successfully made Mrs. Liberman's kugel and was trying to convince herself that she could ignore the troubling outside world and find bliss in domesticity, a knock came upon the door.

Grace opened it to find James Roosevelt on the other side—Eleanor and President Roosevelt's son.

"Mrs. Feldman?" he asked. "Germany has just invaded Poland. We need your help."

Grace nodded. When James departed, she made a call to an employment agency and promptly hired a housekeeper/nanny. She swore to herself that each evening, she'd make up for her absence during the day. She'd help with homework, give baths, read bedtime stories. Her children needed her...but her country needed her even more.

PART IV

WORLD WAR II

She had the Nazi brain in a jar on her desk, alive and glistening, electrodes running out to her pencil.
            —Jason Fagone, *The Woman Who Smashed Codes*

CHAPTER THIRTY-TWO

Washington, DC, October 1939

Grace was again cryptanalyst-in-charge at the US Coast Guard, under the umbrella of the Treasury Department, working in its annex building near the White House. Though Captain Root had long since moved on, it was wonderful to be useful professionally again, and she successfully recruited and reunited her old team of code gals. Fay, Veronica and Utsidi celebrated with a condensed-milk cake flavored with raisins and marmalade.

Since she had two small children, Grace was again given the flexibility to work from home when necessary. It was a double-edged sword—for after homework, dinner, baths and bedtime stories, she was often up working past midnight.

In violation of the Treaty of Versailles, Hitler had rearmed Germany in the mid-1930s, allied with Italy and Japan against the Soviet Union, sent troops to occupy Austria in 1938 and began annexing Czechoslovakia the same year. But the invasion of Poland on the pretext of being attacked first was even more worrying to all of Europe, and to the United States as well. There was a large German population in South America, after all...raising alarm in the top echelons of the US military at the possibility of bombing runs or an invasion from there.

Coded radio transmissions came flooding in for Grace and her team to decrypt and disperse, indicating unusual activity in Brazil: transmissions from Rio to Berlin and vice versa. She recruited more employees and oversaw their training personally. She supervised and gave orders to men and brushed off any petty resentments they might have—she simply didn't have time for chauvinism and did her best to ignore it when it did occur.

Because of the heightened fears of the US being dragged into what was fast becoming a second world war, Robert almost lived in the vault at SIGINT, doing top secret work for the Army that he couldn't discuss. Grace found her own services in demand from unexpected sources: people at the highest levels of government vied for her cryptanalyst hand. One of those who came wooing was none other than J. Edgar Hoover.

In June 1940, at Hoover's insistence, President Roosevelt signed a directive to expand the FBI's power. It was now an agency with international reach, and Hoover immediately sent several agents of his newly created Special Intelligence Service to South America to put their ears to the ground there.

In the meantime, Americans gathered, tense and nervous, around their radios in the evenings to listen to President Roosevelt's fireside chats and flocked to newsstands by day: Denmark, Norway, Belgium, the Netherlands, Luxembourg and even France had fallen to Hitler and the Nazis, while the Italians under Mussolini wreaked havoc elsewhere in Europe.

Grace's telephone rang one Wednesday morning in mid-1940. She answered it to find the Secretary of the Treasury Henry Morgenthau himself on the line—her boss's boss.

"Mrs. Feldman, how are you?"

She laughed. "Busy, sir. And you?"

"Quite. I'm calling with an unusual request that comes via the president himself. And we've cleared it with Commander Farley."

"Oh?" Farley was her boss now, chief of Coast Guard communications.

"Between you, me and the fence post, Mr. Hoover has sent a number of agents down south. To Brazil, Argentina, Chile and the like—despite many of them not knowing Spanish or, in the case of Brazil, Portuguese. I'm told they blend in about as well as whores in church; pardon the expression."

Grace chuckled. "I've heard it before, Mr. Morgenthau."

"The thing is, Hoover realizes in hindsight that the agents can't gumshoe it down there. He needs to create a cryptanalysis unit so they can listen in over the radio, since the Bureau doesn't have one."

Grace's heart sank. "I see."

"So President Roosevelt suggested you could help. Can you visit Mr. Hoover at the Bureau and give him some direction on how best to set one up?"

Absolutely not. Nor do I wish to. "Certainly," Grace said crisply.

"As soon as possible," Morgenthau emphasized.

"Of course, sir."

"Thank you, Mrs. Feldman. I knew we could count on you."

Grace hung up the phone and aimed a withering stare at it. "Wonderful."

Two days later, she found herself sitting in J. Edgar Hoover's reception area again. The number of citations, awards and framed, fawning articles on the walls had spread like a gilt-and-mahogany rash. Grace was unawed and unimpressed. So the great and powerful Mr. Hoover now needed her, "the housewife with a little hobby," did he?

This time he only kept her waiting for five minutes before Mrs. Gandy came to get her and usher her into his inner sanctum. Here, too, the trophies and autographed pictures of Hoover with VIPs had multiplied.

"Mrs. Feldman," he said, stretching his trap of a mouth into a semblance of a smile. "Nice to see you again."

Grace forced a pleasant smile, then extended her hand to see if he would shake it this time, now that he needed her. He did.

"Please, sit down." He gestured toward the same visitor's chair she'd occupied last time.

"Thank you." Grace sat, crossed her ankles and placed her hands in her lap. "How may I help you, sir?"

"The Bureau needs to establish its own codebreaking unit, as I'm sure has been explained. Your husband is not available, so we are turning to you."

Why, thank you. But Grace kept things light. "Robert has been swallowed whole by the monstrous vault at Army SIGINT. I believe they'll install a cot, a shower and a hot plate for him inside it any day now."

Hoover didn't smile. "I'd like you to get an agent of ours, a Mr. Blackburn, up to speed in cryptology and cryptanalysis. Put him through a rigorous training program, educate him on how to set up a unit like yours. Can you do that?"

"Certainly, sir."

"How quickly?"

"Basic training will take a few weeks of study and testing." *But there's simply no way to give him the years of experience that add an extra edge... nor do I have any idea if the man has any aptitude for codebreaking or the instincts to hire and train the right people to set up your unit.* These were the things Grace didn't say.

"When can you start?"

"Tomorrow, if you'd like."

Satisfaction bloomed on Hoover's face. "I'll have Mrs. Gandy escort you to Mr. Blackburn's office so that you can get acquainted. Thank you for coming in. Do give my regards to Robert. I saw him at the Alibi Club last week, didn't I?"

It was a thinly veiled barb. "Did you?" Grace asked. "Funny—I didn't think they accepted those of his faith."

"Perhaps I'm mistaken. It must have been Harvey's, Mrs. Feldman. At any rate, I wish you a pleasant afternoon and I thank you for taking time away from your busy schedule and your children to aid the Bureau." Another barb to imply she was neglecting her children by working.

"My pleasure, Mr. Hoover," Grace said serenely. *You loathsome toad.*

Agent Blackburn was smart enough to learn the principles of cryptography and cryptanalysis, but he was clearly none too pleased to be trained by a woman. They both had their orders, however, and at least he wasn't openly hostile.

Grace began with a history of cryptography and Parker Hitt's book, then tossed him increasingly complex codes to break, though she was never cruel enough to set the Beale cipher in front of him. He learned fast and she soon pronounced him "graduated" from training.

That was that. He began to establish a codebreaking unit at the FBI.

He repaid her by trying—unsuccessfully—to recruit the male members of her own team. Grace was outraged and lodged a complaint with Hoover, who chuckled and told her that she couldn't blame the man for trying.

In the meantime, the listening stations at the Coast Guard and FCC began recovering thousands of intercepts from clandestine radio transmitters, two in Brazil and one in Chile—messages to and from Berlin and Hamburg. This was ominous, to say the least. The Nazis were up to no good in South America—just as the Germans had been up to no good in Mexico during the Great War, trying to bribe them to turn on the US.

Grace, Veronica, Utsidi and Fay smashed the codes and eked out the plaintexts, working through hundreds per day as they sipped cold coffee at their worktables, chain-smoked and literally pulled out their hair at times.

"Who is SARGO? Who is ALFREDO? Who is LUNA?" Grace muttered. "They're reporting on ships, planes, factories, politics, crops…"

Fay nodded. "All kinds of tactical information about the US."

"Trying to get the lay of the land," Fay agreed.

"MAX and GLENN are two other operatives—but they're in Mexico, communicating with a South African man named Duquesne in New York. A spy within our own borders."

All this activity, reported to her bosses at the Coast Guard and Treasury by Grace, resulted in a directive: the Coast Guard was, from now on, to furnish copies of every decrypt to Signal Intel; Naval Intel; the State Department and, by Hoover's special request, to the FBI Technical Laboratory now run by Blackburn. His fledgling unit was simply unable to handle the enormous traffic they were seeing.

Grace and her team marked each decrypt, "CG Translation, CG Decryption" and "G-2/OP-20-G/SD/SIS Dupe," depending on which agency the copy was being sent to.

Thanks to Grace's codebreaking, Hoover and the Bureau set up surveillance on Duquesne, who met several times per week with a German spy named Sebold in offices on Ninety-Second Street in New York. Sebold then radioed the information to Hamburg from a secret transmitter on Long Island. The Bureau used Sebold as a double agent. The FBI watched, waited and listened in on the meetings.

Grace and most of the country were soon distracted and horrified by news of the London Blitz, as from early September to mid-November the Nazis bombed the British city into rubble while its citizens hid in bunkers and subways, families torn apart as they desperately sent their children anywhere else to keep them safe.

Grace, imagining the terror and agony of the British people under these circumstances, redoubled her codebreaking efforts regarding messages routed between South America and Germany. A similar Blitz could not be allowed to happen in the United States. The very idea chilled her to the bone.

It stunned her that most American citizens went about their business largely unconcerned, apparently thinking that the carnage in Europe didn't have much to do with them.

She was thankful that in a December 1940 fireside chat, President Roosevelt reminded America of the possibility: *"Any South American country, in Nazi hands, would always constitute a jumping off place for German attack on any one of the other republics of this hemisphere."*

For the next six months, both Grace and Robert worked eighteen-hour days, only meeting over the breakfast and dinner table with the children. Bobby's large frame reflected a weight loss of at least twenty pounds, and it couldn't be blamed on her cooking, since the indispensable Mrs. Woolsey, their housekeeper, dished up excellent meals.

His hair grayed, his brow became deeply furrowed; pouches appeared under his eyes, and she often found him wandering the house and muttering to himself in the small hours of the morning, a half-eaten sandwich in his hand. He was clearly trying to solve some massive problem at work. She was worried about him. He gently brushed off her concern.

On July 7, 1941, Grace came home for the evening meal with her briefcase bulging with work to do after she put the children to bed. She brought in the mail, including the Feldmans' subscription to *Newsweek*. **SPY CRACKDOWN!** blared the headline on the cover. She turned to read the article on page fourteen:

> For the past two years, J. Edgar Hoover, chief of the Federal Bureau of Investigation, and his operatives have been just a step behind a far-flung spy ring—shadowing, questioning, probing day after day as they patiently built up a stone wall of evidence. Last weekend, they pounced upon and smashed with one blow what Hoover described as "one of the most active, extensive and vicious groups we have ever had to deal with…"

Hoover, the master of PR, had scored again. And there was not a whisper of any help from her Coast Guard codebreaking unit. No, sharing credit was not Mr. Hoover's style.

Grace smiled sourly at the magazine and took it into the house with the rest of the mail.

She was surprised to see Robert home, romping with Isobel and Christopher on the floor. The sight of him relaxed and happy for once made her heart squeeze.

"Hello, darling," he said, pushing his uncharacteristically mussed hair out of his eyes and getting to his feet. The children clamored for him to get down and be their horsey again. "What've you got there? Anything interesting in the mail today?"

Grace held up the *Newsweek*.

"Well. What a triumph for Mr. Hoover. You know, he came up to my table at Harvey's and filled my glass personally with a bottle of wine he and Mr. Tolson had ordered. Very nice of him."

"Oh. Yes," Grace said, stunned. "Very." Inwardly she shuddered. *The man who insinuated that you were a Bolshevik, a Communist spy, a godless heathen? The man who gloats that you're excluded from WASP clubs and has a file on you?* What game was Hoover playing?

At least she seemed, for the moment, to be back in the Toad's good graces, since she'd trained his man and stayed in the background, unseen and unheard, as a "good" woman should. She'd done most of his work for him in uncovering Duquesne and his network of spies.

"Was the wine good?"

"Very. Expensive. A Château Pétrus. He said it was on the house."

"I should hope so," Grace said. "The taxpayers shouldn't be footing the bill for it."

"He's very much the man about town."

"A national hero." She kept the dryness out of her tone.

"I'm sure he's treated to meals and such 'on the house' quite often."

"I'm sure. Well, my loves, shall we see what *this* house's evening meal is? Anyone hungry?"

"Horsies eat oats and hay," Christopher pointed out.

"Yes, indeed they do."

"So Daddy needs a plate of hay."

Grace's lips twitched. "Yes, well. He's eaten worse."

Over the next few weeks, as the Duquesne trial became a sensation in the news, Grace followed it closely, outraged when FBI agents outed the secret messages—as well as her unit's decrypts and methods for solving them—in open court.

She telephoned Commander Farley. "Sir, it's Grace Feldman."

"Yes?" he growled.

"I'm quite concerned, sir, about the detailed information on our decryption systems and methods that is coming out in court in the Duquesne trial."

"Hell and damnation. I am, too. Begging your pardon for the salty language."

"Is there anything we can do about it?"

"You suggesting that I rap J. Edgar Hoover on the knuckles, Mrs. Feldman?"

"I, ah—"

"Get relieved of my command, demoted back to ensign?"

"Do you really think that likely, sir?"

"That bastard's got secret files on everyone, from waiters to senators. I'm not going to reprimand him—besides which, it's too late. The information is out. Let's hope the papers focus on the danger and glamour of the story and not the mechanics of cryptanalysis."

"I fervently hope so."

"Will that be all, Mrs. Feldman?"

"No. Commander, given the...careless...handling of this very sensitive information, *must* we continue to furnish copies of all decrypts to Mr. Hoover and the FBI?"

A long silence came down the line. Then a sigh. "I'm with you. I'd rather we didn't. But I honestly don't see any way out of it, given Mr. Hoover's great triumph and all the headlines. Not that the Coast Guard got any credit at all in the matter."

"It's not credit I care about. It's protecting national security."

"For which Mr. Hoover is now the official poster boy. So now is not the time to make any attempt to hobble him. I'd have to go to Roosevelt himself. I do appreciate your concerns, though. Good day, Mrs. Feldman."

"Thank you for taking my call, sir." And Grace hung up, temporarily defeated.

CHAPTER THIRTY-THREE

Late 1941

Grace continued her hunt for the identity of the German spies SARGO and LUNA in South America. Her concerns about the security of US intelligence—and the demands on her from the top echelons of the government—didn't make the work any easier. The handsome young James Roosevelt again stopped by to see her.

"Mrs. Feldman," he said, with a warm smile. "How are you? Robert? The children?"

Grace stopped her work and eyed him a little warily. "We're all well, thank you, James. Care to sit down?"

He sat opposite her while she asked after Eleanor, the president and their other children. Then he got straight to the point. "Are you acquainted with Colonel William Donovan?"

She paused. "Bobby knows Wild Bill from the Army. But I haven't had the pleasure of meeting him. Why?"

"Due to the war, my father has asked him to establish the COI, or Office of the Coordinator of Information."

Grace raised her eyebrows. "Sounds very bland."

James flashed a smile. "Intentionally so. We need an agency that essentially does offensive intelligence work—spy stuff, you could call it. We've got to be proactive rather than simply reactive."

"Isn't that Mr. Hoover's domain?" Grace asked carefully.

"Hoover's having kittens over it." James grinned. "He's furious. Views the new unit as trampling on his territory."

Oh dear. And you're about to ask me to—

"The thing is, Donovan has asked for you by name. To help set up a cryptography and cryptanalysis department."

No, no, no . . . Grace suddenly had an inspired idea. "What about Alice Martenz? She'd be perfect for the job."

"You haven't heard? Alice was in a dreadful automobile accident. Unfortunately, she'll be out of commission for some time. Broke both jaws, broke her leg."

Grace covered her mouth with her hand. "That's awful."

"She's still in the hospital."

"I didn't realize. I'll take her some flowers." Poor Alice. She wasn't nice, but she certainly didn't deserve such a fate.

James nodded. "So, back to the matter at hand . . ."

"How does Wild Bill Donovan even know I exist?" Grace asked.

James looked down at his hat, which he'd perched on her desk. "Well. He did request Bobby first."

Of course he did. Just like everyone else. Grace repressed a sigh.

"But you were also recommended by another source within COI."

How curious. "The thing is, I'm rather busy at the moment—"

"Mrs. Feldman," James said, "you've got to be the busiest woman on the planet—besides, perhaps, my mother. But my father suggested you."

In other words, the president *is ordering me to infuriate Mr. Hoover further.*

"I see." Grace straightened her shoulders, which had begun to slump under the very suggestion of this new burden. She folded her hands on her desk and stared at James's hat, too.

"Well, it will have to be cleared with Mr. Morgenthau—"

"Already done."

"And Commander Farley—"

"Not a problem."

Nothing was a problem when one was the president's son.

"Then I'd be happy to . . ." *Drop everything I'm doing in South America, especially hunting SARGO and LUNA.* ". . . assist Colonel Donovan with whatever he needs."

James stood up and retrieved his hat. "Thank you so very much, Mrs. Feldman. As always, it was a pleasure to see you."

"Please give my best to your mother, James."

"Will do."

Alice lay motionless in her white-blanketed hospital bed at a naval convalescence center. Her jaws were wired shut, the entire lower half of her face was bandaged and her leg was in a full plaster cast, suspended from a pulley.

Grace took the vase of yellow daffodils she'd brought and set them with a couple of other flower arrangements and cards from well-wishers. "Alice? I just heard about the accident. I'm so very sorry."

The woman's ice-blue eyes flew open and narrowed on her. They were the opposite of welcoming. The left one seemed to flash *get* and the right one *out*. She actually rolled them, and then flapped her left hand weakly toward the door.

Well. What a welcome. But Grace had a stubborn streak, and she knew that Alice simply wasn't used to other women being nice to her. So she was unpleasant to them first, as a defense mechanism.

"Is there anything Bobby and I can do?" Grace ventured.

Alice had a notebook and a pen next to the bed. She groped for it and scrawled "Pls don't cook."

Really? Grace's mouth worked. "I'll bring you a four-course meal: limp, over-dressed salad; bitter soup; a burnt entrée and an underbaked dessert. With a black rosebud in a vase, a stained napkin and filthy silver. How's that?"

She detected a spark of amusement in the blue eyes. But it faded quickly. Alice turned her head away.

"Magazines? Books?"

Alice rolled her head back toward Grace. She reached for the notebook again. "Here to gloat?" she asked.

"No." Grace eyed her. "That's a horrid thing to say."

Alice shrugged.

"Not everyone is out to get you, so why don't you stop being such a pill? We could try being friends, you know. We have quite a bit in common, and it's all right for us both to be good at our jobs. It doesn't have to be an endless competition as to who's more clever—which neither of us is ever going to win. You do know that, don't you? So I got some press. You got awarded $15,000 by Congress. Are we even?"

Alice closed her eyes and produced a universal and very vulgar hand gesture that told her visitor to do something anatomically impossible.

"Charming," Grace said. She got up. "I'll relieve you of my abhorrent presence, then. I do hope you'll feel better soon."

Alice raised an eyebrow and scribbled another message. "Stop being a better person than I am. It's intolerable."

Grace laughed. She couldn't help it. Alice was beastly . . . but she was funny.

And she received one last directive from the patient. "Go to hell."

"All right, dear. I'll get underway. It's been lovely to see you."

Wild Bill Donovan was criminally handsome, tall and physically imposing, with the craggy face of a soldier, a full head of dark hair even in his fifties, and beguiling Irish blue eyes, which he used to charm when the need arose. Grace was sure the very sight of him annoyed the short, heavyset and neckless Hoover, but that wasn't her problem—at least not yet.

Her problem was that Donovan, after remarking that he hadn't expected her to be so attractive and that Bobby was a lucky man, became demanding, cantankerous and worst of all, even more reckless than Hoover with the rules of secret communication. His men worshipped him—he was utterly fearless on the battlefield—and never turned down a challenge. He was used to being obeyed.

"I'll need you here for three months," he began.

"I can give you three weeks, Colonel."

His dark eyebrows snapped together. "I was informed that you were at my disposal."

"Yes, Colonel. For three weeks. I have an exceptionally demanding job at the Coast Guard."

"What's so urgent at Uncle Sam's Canoe Club?"

She ignored the slur. "But I'm happy to help you establish—"

Donovan interrupted her. "Can you build a system, hire a staff, train them and provide cipher devices in that short a time frame?"

"I can build the system, yes. I can interview prospective candidates and make recommendations for hires, yes. Then I can provide lessons, but most of the work the candidates must do on their own. With the cooperation of the Army and Navy, we should be able to get you devices and customize them to your particular needs. But the most important aspect of your new unit is that each and every employee must adhere to strict security protocols—"

Donovan waved a hand dismissively. "That's what the machines and codes are for."

"Machines can be reproduced with good analysis and guesswork," Grace said. "Codes can and are broken, Colonel. Much of the time because of human carelessness or laziness when it comes to varying them. That's why establishing and following protocols is of utmost importance."

"I don't need a lecture, Mrs. Feldman. What I need is an operational cipher team. Yesterday." He checked his watch. "I'll leave the details to you. And I doubt very much that you'll be going back to your cozy Coast Guard office in three short weeks. But feel free to prove me wrong." Wild Bill winked at her, perhaps in a haphazard effort to take the sting out of his words.

It didn't succeed, and her face must have reflected it.

"Ma'am, forgive me. I'm not used to the petticoat set. I'm used to commanding troops in the heat of battle."

"Of course, Colonel."

"Call me Bill. Now, please excuse me. I have another meeting."

And with that, Wild Bill charged out the door, leaving her seething in his office.

Grace determined that she had precisely twenty-one days to give this cavalier colonel, or a maximum of 504 hours. After that, her focus would return to the spies in South America.

She placed recruitment notices in bulletins and the classified sections of the newspaper immediately. In the evenings after the children's baths and bedtime, she created alphabet strips, grids, worksheets and key concepts for the new COI (or OSS, as it would become). During the day, she interviewed people interested in the new positions, wrote up summaries of their strengths and weaknesses and added her recommendation to hire or not.

In between seeing candidates, she made calls to various contacts she and Bobby had in the armed services—Parker and Genevieve Hitt, Joe Rochefort, Joe Mauborgne—even her boss Commander Farley, James Roosevelt in the Marines, and Cordell Hull at State. She implored them to send over any cipher machines of any type that they could spare.

Fortunately, the name *Feldman* carried some weight in these circles, and her requests were accommodated. Grace assembled ten machines in as many workdays and began to customize them for the COI.

After two full weeks of work on the project, she requested a second meeting with Donovan, who waved her into his office at the appointed time, despite being on a heated phone call with someone.

"Don't snap your cap at me, you fat knucklehead!" shouted Wild Bill into the receiver. "You have no right to bust my chops. Morgenthau himself authorized it, and FDR above him."

From the other end of the line came something indiscernible but furious.

"Because the dame is aces, and her husband is tied up with something so secret that they keep him chained like a dog in the vault at SIGINT."

Another dull roar came from the receiver.

"Don't threaten me, either, you cockeyed pain in the neck. You don't like it, go kiss Roosevelt's lily-white—" Donovan rolled an eyeball in Grace's direction and broke off.

Not that she couldn't easily fill in the blanks.

"Oh, you'll make me sorry?" He sneered at the telephone. "I'll look forward to that. In the meantime, go jump in a lake." Donovan slammed down the receiver, then swiveled his chair in her direction. "Speak of the devil."

Grace raised an eyebrow. "And here I thought I'd hidden my horns and tail so well. Stowed my pitchfork in the supply closet."

Wild Bill's eyes were lit with the flame of a rousing conflict. Now he squinted at her with something like appreciation. "Ha. That bastard Hoover doesn't like me borrowing you. Pardon my French."

"Je suis tres désolé." While the conflict between the two men over her services made her nervous, she was human enough to enjoy listening to the Great and Terrible Hoover be insulted by someone who was refreshingly unafraid of him.

"So. It's only been two weeks, Mrs. Feldman. Why are you here in my office?"

Because SARGO and LUNA are calling to me from Brazil…not to mention their friend ALFREDO.

She handed him a large envelope full of resumes with her notes attached.

"What's this?"

"I've interviewed thirty-seven candidates for your new unit. Of those, I recommend that you hire ten and keep the applications of another five, in case my first choices don't work out for some reason. Other than that, my work here at COI is complete—though I'm happy to send one of my team members to train yours if necessary, once you have them assembled."

Donovan dropped the envelope onto his desk, leaned back in his chair and folded his arms across his substantial chest. Any good humor had disappeared from his eyes. "Mrs. Feldman, it seems to me that you're dumping your unfinished work into my lap and leaving me in the lurch."

Grace could hardly believe her ears. "Colonel—"

"Call me Bill."

I'll do no such thing. "Colonel Donovan, your *lurch* now consists of ten cipher machines culled painstakingly from reluctant sources who did me personal favors by relinquishing them to me. Your *lurch* also boasts a custom-designed coding system and decryption tools. All your *lurch* now requires is for you to personally sign off on a few highly qualified employees prescreened by me."

Grace couldn't help it; she was trembling with rage.

He cocked his head at her and grinned. *Grinned.* "Now don't get sore, sweetheart."

Her head almost blew off.

"I'd just appreciate it if you'd go ahead and finalize those hires for me."

And I'd appreciate being allowed to get back to my work in preventing this country from being invaded by Nazis. I'd appreciate *not being tied up on the telephone doing something your secretary could do.*

"Of course, Colonel," Grace said between gritted teeth. "As long as you trust my judgment."

"I do. You come highly recommended. And if that daisy over at the Bureau is willing to get into a dogfight over you, it says something. You free for lunch?"

"I regret to tell you, sir, that the lady is already claimed for lunch."

Grace whirled to find Lieutenant (JG) Cox in the doorway, grinning. "What are you doing here?"

"Taking you to lunch," he said, before turning to Donovan. "Dogfight with *Hoover*, sir? No wonder they call you Wild Bill."

"This slippery scoundrel Cox," growled Donovan, "now works for me at COI. As a matter of fact, he recommended you to me. How do *you* know him, Mrs. Feldman?"

"It's a long story."

"And we have reservations at the Hay-Adams hotel," Cox said.

Donovan's eyebrows shot up. "Not on what I pay you, you don't."

Cox just amped up his grin. "Shall we, Mrs. Feldman?"

Grace put on her gloves. "I suppose. Colonel, I'll be back in touch shortly."

The Hay-Adams, one of the most elegant hotels in Washington, was directly across Lafayette Square from the White House. The lobby ceilings soared, lit by spectacular chandeliers, but the space retained a welcoming warmth with its rich, dark mahogany doors, walls and trim. Massive sprays of fresh flowers greeted them, as did a maître d' who ushered them to an excellent table in the Lafayette dining room.

Cox had a mysterious gift-wrapped box under his arm, complete with a red velvet bow. He set it down in a spare chair.

"What is it?" Grace asked, once they were seated.

"A present for you."

"Why? And why have you brought me to one of the most expensive lunch venues in the city?"

He pursed his lips provocatively, then flashed her a wicked grin. "There are three possibilities, my lady: seduction—"

Grace's eyebrows shot up.

"—consolation or gratitude. Choose one. Or two, if you like."

"Lieutenant," she said severely, "I'm unavailable; besides which, I'm far too old for you."

"I disagree, and I believe I could persuade you, but I shouldn't like to get my ears boxed in public. So shall we move on to the other choices?"

"I don't understand you," Grace said.

"But you're intrigued."

"How about exasperated?"

The corner of Cox's mouth quirked up in amusement.

"And when did you start working for Wild Bill Donovan and participating in his covert shenanigans?"

"One question at a time, my lady. And shall we order first?"

"Fine." Grace ordered a pear and walnut salad. Cox requested the crispy duck.

Grace smoothed the napkin in her lap. "So why would you feel the need to console me—or express your gratitude?"

"I should like to console you because Spanish Marie and her Hun went on the run. I should like to thank you for the very same reason. They left certain things behind, things that perhaps came into my possession."

Grace narrowed her eyes upon him. "*Things* meaning either money or cases of booze."

"I neither confirm nor deny," he said, blue eyes dancing.

"Things that should, by rights, have been seized by Treasury," she ground out.

"Oh, and many of them were, I assure you."

Grace closed her eyes. When she opened them, she pushed back her chair.

Cox held up a hand. "Hear me out, please. I'm trying to tell you something important. And then there's your gift."

"I'm not sure I can accept it."

"Mrs. Feldman, once again hypothetically speaking, if I did come across a few items in Miami during a certain bust of a certain bootlegging couple, I took them only for safekeeping."

"Safekeeping that also pays for fancy meals?" Grace shook her head.

"Call it a small fee." Cox tried his grin on her again.

"*Incorrigible*," Grace said, as her salad arrived.

"You're too kind." Cox helped himself to the breadbasket.

"Lieutenant, why are we here?"

"Shall I tell you about my first job for Colonel Donovan?"

"Do I have a choice?"

Cox grinned. "It began at a dinner party where both Donovan and a certain admiral were present. The admiral was less than complimentary about the new COI, calling it a 'Tinkertoy Outfit' that spied on spies."

"Donovan prefers 'League of Gentlemen.'"

"Yes. The colonel was insulted and took it as a challenge. So he looks at his watch and says to the admiral, "Tinkertoy Outfit? I'll bet you, sir, that by midnight, we can get hold of your most secret files—and blow up your Navy ammo dump across the river to boot.

"The admiral laughs in his face. So Wild Bill leaves the table to make a phone call to COI. Lickety-split, another fellow and I are on our way to break into the admiral's office at the Navy Building and crack his safe. We nick every last paper, bundle them into a satchel and deliver it to Donovan back at the party. Meanwhile, another couple of COI fellows plant fake dynamite at the ammo dump. Easy peasy."

Grace was riveted.

"We had the pleasure of watching as Donovan walked up to the admiral and handed him a fresh drink—along with the satchel of papers stolen from his personal safe—and told him where he could find the ersatz dynamite. It was only a quarter of eleven, by the by."

Grace couldn't help but laugh…but she was struck by the recklessness of the scheme, the danger and the utter disregard for breaking the law. "So the COI spies on spies," she said.

Cox's eyes twinkled. "Among other things."

"What about German spies who've disappeared without a trace?"

"I thought you'd never ask, my lady. Curious about your man Schroeder, are you?"

Grace nodded.

"He and Spanish Marie fled to South America."

Her heart stuttered. "It so happens that I'm trying to uncover the identities of two spies making trouble for the US down there: SARGO and LUNA. Perhaps you could help."

Lieutenant (JG) Cox smiled. "I thought you'd never ask. You'll take a peek at your gift over coffee, won't you?"

Grace hesitated. But after the waiter had cleared the table and brought the coffee, she allowed Cox to place the box on the table in front of her.

The elaborate scarlet bow on top looked more like a warning than an ornament.

Cox leaned forward over the table. "Lift the lid, but under no circumstances should you remove the contents here in public."

Grace stared at him and pushed the box back toward him. "I don't feel comfortable with this, Lieutenant. Where did this...item...come from?"

"Off a German submarine."

She blinked at him, unable to believe her ears.

Cox laughed.

"*How?*" was all she could manage to say.

"Remember the *Holmwood*, my lady? Disguised as an oil tanker?"

She nodded.

"Well, let's just say that we pulled the same stunt with an Allied submarine. Off we went, in false German naval uniforms, flying a bloodred swastika flag to 'rescue' the crew of a damaged Nazi U-boat."

"You didn't." Grace now knew what was in the box: something precious.

"We did. And in the process, without them even realizing it, we salvaged your prize there. Sent down divers as the U-boat sank."

Grace exhaled audibly. "All right. Why are you giving it to *me*? Why not to—"

"It's been inspected, Mrs. Feldman, by the proper parties. It's actually been duplicated. So I thought that perhaps, given your line of work, you might like to have the original."

She narrowed her eyes upon him.

"No strings attached, my lady. Just a gift from one puddle pirate to another, I swear."

Grace nodded. "Thank you. In that case, I'll pick up this particular check."

Cox looked affronted. "I couldn't possibly allow—"

She snatched the bill, eyed the total, almost fainted and promptly paid it. Robert was going to kill her.

Then she peeked into the box and almost fainted again. Cox had brought her a commercial Enigma machine: the device that the Germans used to encrypt their communications.

Lunch had been worth every cent. Grace splurged on a taxi to get the heavy box back to the office and began analyzing it in her spare time.

On October 31, 1941, a Nazi U-boat blew up an American ship off the coast of Ireland. One hundred men were either incinerated or drowned. Grace tried not to think of that horror as she looked blankly into the grinning, blazing faces of the jack-o'-lanterns Isobel and Christopher had carved with their nanny for Halloween.

She and Robert took the children trick-or-treating that evening as if nothing had occurred, Grace having resurrected her long-unused sewing skills to create Isobel's princess costume and Christopher's pirate one, complete with stuffed parrot for his left shoulder.

Robert had stayed up late with her to create a magnificent, curved cardboard cutlass for his son. He'd painted the blade silver and the handle black.

Grace's concern for her husband was growing. He wasn't sleeping more than three or four hours per night. His hands often trembled. His hair had thinned, he looked gaunt and haggard—he almost didn't need a costume to pass for Edvard Munch's painting *The Scream*, hanging so close by in the National Gallery.

November 1, the next day, President Roosevelt placed the Coast Guard under the aegis of the Navy, instead of Treasury. Grace and her team had been drafted into the military, and her new boss was Secretary of the Navy Frank Knox. As she knew from her previous stint, the Navy didn't welcome women except in the capacity of fetching coffee. So it was with a great deal of reluctance that she, Fay, Utsidi and Veronica prepared to pack up and transfer to the Navy Annex on Nebraska Avenue.

Grace hid her dark mood, though, because Robert came home

whistling one evening. *Whistling*. He was a willing horsey and even a lion, chasing the children around the couch and under the coffee table. He slept through the night, and in by a full hour the next morning. Overnight, he seemed to have lost ten years, and he suddenly had an appetite again. Clearly, he'd had a big breakthrough of some kind at work. She was so relieved for him that tears gathered in her eyes.

Despite the ever-growing fear of war, Thanksgiving was a festive affair, the table groaning with a roast turkey (prepared by the house-keeper, since Grace once tried to stuff the wrong end of the bird) mashed potatoes, gravy, cranberry sauce and candied yams. For dessert there were two pies: apple and pecan.

Grace, relaxed for the first time in months, looked around the table at her family and was truly, achingly grateful for them all: the husband she'd married reluctantly and the children she hadn't been entirely sure she wanted. The poets had it all wrong. This was love: small, chubby faces sticky with butter and smeared with yams, the softening of Robert's eyes when he met her gaze, the flickering candlelight that made their time at the table seem magical.

The children were already excited about Christmas.

"I want a Bubble Wand!" Isobel said.

"I want Tinkertoys!" announced Christopher.

Bobby and Grace took them to get a Douglas fir, which Bobby erected in the living room, emerging from beneath it with an avalanche of needles stuck to his cashmere sweater-vest. They decorated it with strings of popcorn and cranberries, handmade ornaments and a blown glass angel on top.

But on Sunday, December 7, holiday cheer froze when the news of Pearl Harbor reached the United States. Robert's face lost all color and he swayed on his feet. Grace rushed to him, afraid he'd faint, and guided him backward to an armchair. He dropped into it, then covered his face with his hands.

"Is Joe Rochefort all right?" Grace asked urgently. He'd been posted to Pearl.

"They knew," Robert said.

"Joe? And Eddie Layton?" Eddie was Rear Admiral Chester Nimitz's right-hand man.

"No idea."

Grace rushed to the telephone and rang Fay. "Darling, it's me. Is Joe—? Oh, *thank God*. Layton? Thank the good Lord. Yes, yes, I understand—speak to you soon. Bye."

She turned back to her husband.

Rocking back and forth, Robert repeated over and over again, "But they knew. They *knew*."

"What did they know, Daddy?" Isobel asked, trying to climb into his lap. He ignored her, as a statue might. Her face fell.

"They knew," he moaned.

"Where's Pearl Harbor?" Christopher wanted to know.

"Hawaii. Children, please go to your rooms," Grace told them. "Everything's fine."

"What's wrong with Daddy?" Isobel demanded.

"They KNEW." Robert's tone held disbelief, horror, disillusion, agony and a slow-burning fury. "They knew..."

"Nothing's wrong with Daddy, darling girl." Grace stroked her hair. "He's...had a bad day at work."

"Today's Sunday," Isobel pointed out, quite reasonably.

"Yes, well. Sometimes work follows people home."

"Like a dog?" asked Christopher.

"Sort of."

"Can we get a dog?!" Her son was off on a new tangent for Christmas. "Please?"

"I don't know—children, I need you to go to your rooms. Now. Your father and I need to talk."

Isobel and Christopher trailed reluctantly up the stairs.

Liquor now being legal again, Grace poured two fingers of Glenmorangie fourteen-year for both Robert and herself. She handed him one and sat down on the sofa adjacent to his chair. "Bobby."

"Twenty-one ships and two hundred planes destroyed," he murmured. "The *Arizona* and her crew at the bottom of the sea. How...? *How?!*"

He slammed a hand down on the coffee table with such force she feared he'd either cracked it or his own bones. *"God damn it."*

Her husband never swore. Ever.

"Bobby, take a sip. You need it." Grace did. The strong burn of the Scotch wasn't healing, but it was somehow reassuring.

Robert raised his glass and held it to his lips. Then he slammed it, too, onto the coffee table. "No," he said. He got to his feet, went to the hall closet and took out his overcoat and hat. "They *knew*, Grace."

"What did they know?" She may as well have asked a boulder. He couldn't—and wouldn't—tell her. Or anyone else. "Where are you going?"

"To work," he said, as if going to work on a Sunday afternoon were a normal thing to do. "I've got to get to the bottom of this."

CHAPTER THIRTY-FOUR

December 8, 1941

"Yesterday, December 7, 1941, a date which will live in infamy, the United States of America was suddenly and deliberately attacked by naval and air forces of the Empire of Japan..." President Roosevelt stood tall in his leg braces, with his son James by his side, to ask Congress to declare war on Japan. A single hour later, the United States was at war—and three days later, with Germany, too.

Grace and her team stopped packing up, due to the urgent nature of the codebreaking unit's work. It didn't matter where they were, as long as they made lightning-fast progress. It also didn't matter who was in charge—at least Grace told herself so when, as a civilian, she was demoted to plain "cryptanalyst" and a still-wet-behind-the-ears lieutenant commander took over her title after just one course in cryptanalysis. It was a time of ration books, sacrifice and public service, not a time for personal ambition.

For a national security and spy-hunter role, she was prepared. What she was not in any way prepared for was the call from Robert's secretary she received in January 1942.

She was in the middle of demonstrating the basics of the early commercial Enigma machine to her new boss, Commander Jones, when Utsidi interrupted them. "Apologies, Commander, but Grace? There's an urgent call for you."

Grace excused herself and ran to her office, closing the door behind her. She picked up the telephone receiver. "Hello? Mrs. Feldman here."

"M-Mrs. Feldman?" The voice on the other end of the line trembled. "Th-this is Mildred Murtaugh, C-Colonel Feldman's s-secretary?"

Her tone transmitted alarm to every nerve in Grace's body. "Yes, Mildred. What's wrong?"

"Colonel Feldman—I found him slumped over his desk, rocking like a...a baby. H-he was s-sobbing, Mrs. Feldman?"

Grace sat there stupidly, trying to make sense of the words. Pity and horror threatened to overwhelm her. But there was no time to feel. "Who else knows about this, Mildred? *Who knows?*"

"Nobody," Mildred said. "I swear. I got him a glass of water. He eventually collected himself. And then...he asked me to drive him to Walter Reed. He checked himself in and asked that I call you."

Grace sucked in what she hoped was enough oxygen to carry her through the next few hours. "Thank you, Mildred. I don't need to stress to you how highly confidential this is. His reputation would suffer."

"I won't ever say a word to anyone. He's such a good man. Brilliant, he is. But I've been worried about him."

She was right to be. But Grace didn't say the words aloud.

Robert himself knew he needed help if he'd checked himself into Walter Reed hospital.

Grace rushed to northern Washington, DC, to the 116-acre facility. The reception area was in the imposing red-brick colonial main building. It was bright, airy and cheerful, a fountain playing in the sunshine outside. Everything was manicured and orderly, and for the first time since she'd heard the news, Grace's pulse slowed. This was a nice place, the very best, and Bobby would be fine. Just fine.

A nurse in a traditional white dress and stockings, hair pinned neatly under a white cap, looked up from some paperwork and asked if she could help.

Grace produced a wobbly smile. "I'm here to see my husband?" She hated the tremor in her voice. "Colonel Robert Feldman. He checked in perhaps two hours ago."

The nurse consulted a clipboard, running her index finger down a list of names and room numbers. "Oh. Yes. Here he is." Something in her expression and tone changed. The welcoming warmth faded. "In the neuropsychiatric unit." She pronounced *neuropsychiatric* as if it were a filthy word.

But Grace nodded. It sounded scary but made sense.

The nurse hesitated. "I—I'll call an attendant to take you over there. One moment." She turned her back on Grace, picked up a telephone receiver and murmured into it.

A few minutes later, a gargantuan man in a white smock—none too clean—and white slacks came to greet her. "Mrs. Feldman?"

She hadn't seen a man so large since her days at Riverbank with Garrett Farquhar. Grace eyed the dribbles and stains on his smock and swallowed uneasily. "Yes."

"I'll take you to see your husband. Come with me."

Dread built within her as she did her best to keep up with the giant's long strides. She clutched her pocketbook as if it were a life preserver.

She followed him to the back of the building, then down one set of stairs and yet another. Anything bright, airy or cheerful vanished as they made their way through an underground tunnel that reeked of mold, some sort of animal urine—rats?—and disconcertingly of human saliva. It was dark and low. Her guide's head almost touched the ceiling.

Grace felt nauseous and claustrophobic.

At last they reached a set of double doors at the end of the tunnel, secured by a monstrous dead bolt. The attendant produced a ring of keys, then unlocked it, ushered her through the doors, and relocked it.

They'd passed into an industrial, utilitarian space that smelled worse than the tunnel, if that was possible. The stench of urine, feces and vomit fought to bypass an overwhelming scent of strong bleach. Shrieks, moans and sobs reached her ears.

Dear, God. What is this, some sort of medieval prison? Where is Robert?

Her beloved husband, her hero, sat shivering on a metal chair in a large ward with about twenty other men in various states of distress. His hair was askew, his tie undone, his face a greenish white. He rocked back and forth, his arms wrapped around himself.

"Oh, my love," Grace said. "Oh, Robert." She rushed to his side, took him into her arms, and kissed his head.

"Grace?" Tears filled his eyes, then overflowed. "Grace. Oh, my Grace."

She kissed his mouth, his eyes, his cheeks. She didn't care what anyone thought.

"You're here," he whispered. "Thank God."

"Of course I'm here, my darling. Of course I am."

"You shouldn't be," he said, dashing his tears away. Little drops of shame.

"Yes, yes, I should. What happened, my love? Why...why did you come here?"

His eyes clouded. He looked down at his lap. "I was in my office."

"Yes?"

"And lightbulb: no purple...they had no purple."

Stymied, Grace asked, "Do you mean a pencil? A paint color?"

"No purple," Bobby repeated. "And then I must have gone down.

Everything went dark. When I woke up, I was sprawled on the floor in front of my desk."

"Oh, sweetheart. Did you forget to eat? Probably low blood sugar. Are you all right? Did you hit your head?"

"No, Grace. I'm not all right. I couldn't get up. Not for the longest time. I lay there on the floor in my office, like a split log in a grate, and I couldn't move a muscle."

"You felt paralyzed?" Grace couldn't imagine how terrifying it had been.

He nodded. "And then, after trying and trying to move just a finger... or a toe...I sneezed. Dust, you know? Under the desk. Came out to greet me. Say hello."

"All right," Grace said cautiously.

"It was a mighty sneeze," Bobby said. "Almost blew the roof off my office. But after that, I could peel myself off the floor of my office, crawl up into my chair, sit down like a normal human being, fish out my handkerchief and use it. I said, 'Thank you, God.'"

She took a deep breath and looked around her, at the other men trapped here, at their bleak surroundings. Nothing reassured her.

The walls were painted white but were streaked with dirt. The windows were narrow slits set high up—probably so nobody could hurl himself out of one. The floor was a dismal putrid green linoleum. No plants, no art, no books...no telephone or radio for connection to the outside world or hope itself.

Just hard metal chairs like the one in which Robert sat, rocking himself. A few dingy couches along the walls. And men.

A couple of men were unshaven and unkempt, in wrinkled street clothes. Three or four men were shaved—bald—and a little too clean, as if someone had forcibly bathed them. They wore pale blue smocks.

Two men wouldn't, or couldn't, stop sobbing. One man raged in a corner at nothing perceptible, while another observed him as if he were a science experiment and took notes. This particular man wore a doctor's coat and spectacles.

Most disturbing of all were the men who sat with slumped shoulders and utterly vacant eyes, their mouths loose and slack as if trampled by their souls in a desperate rush to escape their bodies. They looked as if God himself had given up and abandoned them in this place.

Grace's skin crawled at the sight of these poor men staring at but not seeing her. Goose pimples broke out along both her arms.

I've entered hell. And I've got to get Bobby out of here.

She marched straight over to the man taking notes and interrupted him without apology. "Hello. I'm Grace Feldman. I've come to take my husband, Robert, home. He doesn't belong here."

The doctor looked up from his leather-bound notebook and inspected her from head to toe. "I'm Dr. Sydney Menzies. And I'm afraid that you don't get to decide that."

"I beg your pardon?"

"Mrs. Feldman, your husband came to Walter Reed in a state of considerable distress, and we are duty bound to make a thorough assessment of his health and well-being."

Grace raised her chin. "There's nothing wrong with Robert. He's exhausted from overwork. Look at him, Doctor." She turned and pointed to her husband. *"He doesn't belong here."*

She turned as well and saw Bobby for the first time through Dr. Menzies's eyes: a distraught, disheveled man rocking himself like a baby, tears streaming down his unshaven cheeks, eyes haunted, hair rumpled, tie crumpled. His left shoelace had come untied, and his right sock had slid down his leg—as if trying to hide itself in his wing tip from this utter humiliation.

The shock made her feel faint. But she said in her firmest tone, "You don't understand, Doctor. That's *not* how he is. *Who* he is."

He peered at her from over the rims of his spectacles. "Ah. And who is he, exactly?"

She stared at him. "He's Colonel Robert Feldman of the Army's Signal Intelligence—"

Alarm bloomed on Dr. Menzies's face. He turned a page in his notebook and scribbled down something.

"—he's brilliant, he's their crack codebreaker, they need him—" *I need him.* "They need him back immediately. He's key to the country's national security, especially during this war..."

Grace, you imbecile. Too late, she realized that she was saying absolutely the wrong thing to Menzies. She was making the case for Walter Reed to keep him away from his work. Locked up.

"You've got to release him to me," she said. "Right away."

Menzies ignored her and made some more notes in his infernal leather book.

She wanted to snatch it out of his hands and destroy it. Rip up the "evidence" she'd just given him to hold Robert here. "Did you hear me?"

"I heard you, Mrs. Feldman." He kept writing.

"Fine. We'll be leaving now." Grace turned on her heel, now clutching her pocketbook like a shield, and marched back to her husband. "Come, my darling. Let's go home."

Relief washed over Robert's face. He got to his feet.

"Oh, sweetheart." Grace put a hand up to his cheek. "Let's tie your shoe."

"Yes, yes. Good idea." He sat back down in the chair and bent to the task.

And a stained white mountain moved between them: the attendant who'd escorted Grace through the tunnel to this particular level of hell. "Mr. Feldman won't be going anywhere."

"It's *Colonel* Feldman," Grace snapped. "And he most certainly is. Now."

The mountain crossed its arms over the drips and dribbles. "My apologies, ma'am."

"I don't want your apologies. I want his freedom."

A stoic silence followed her words. With rising panic, Grace sensed that this was not the first time this argument had occurred in the neuropsychiatric unit at Walter Reed.

Dr. Menzies walked over, all professional patience and calm. "Mrs. Feldman, let's be sensible. Your husband needs a medical evaluation. He came here for that purpose, correct?"

She reluctantly nodded. "But he's fine."

"Look at him, Mrs. Feldman." He echoed her own words. "He's not fine."

"Why don't we include him in the conversation instead of talking about him as if he's not here?" she countered. "Bobby, you want to go home, right?"

He nodded and rose to his feet again. The top of his head came only to the mountain's shoulder.

Grace swallowed. "You're fine, aren't you, my love?"

Robert hesitated. Closed his eyes and squeezed them tightly.

Oh, Jesus, Bobby. Now is not the time to dig deep for honesty. Lie.

Grace's pulse roared in her ears, bellowing at her own sanity. *Lie, damn it! Don't make me leave you in this horror show. Lie. Don't you dare leave me in the middle of a war. Don't you dare not be my rock. You made me fall in love with you... now I can't live without you.*

"You're *fine*," she said in a voice like granite.

But Bobby shook his head.

A devastated Grace walked for miles in a sort of trance before she realized that her feet were blistered and bleeding into her leather pumps. She hailed a cab and went back to the office.

Veronica took one look at her and rushed to get her a glass of water. "*Dios* mio, Grace, what has happened to your—"

"Walking. What's the latest on SARGO and LUNA?"

Veronica opened and then closed her mouth again. "They are tracking Allied ships, reporting their positions to German U-boats."

Grace went cold. "Then we'd best get to work. We have lives to save:

thousands of them." She opened a drawer of her desk and tossed her pocketbook inside.

"There's something else," Utsidi said, also eyeing Grace with concern. "They have a new friend named HUMBERTO."

"Do they? That's very helpful of them. A nice, long name with some less-frequently occurring letters."

"I thought so, too."

"So let's solve for HUMBERTO, shall we? And then we'll have ourselves a nice crib we can use to smash the rest of the code."

The only chink Grace allowed in her armor that afternoon was to slip off her shoes under her desk, soothing her damaged feet against the cool linoleum tiles underneath. She confided in nobody. She refused to contemplate how Robert was being treated in that...seventh bowel of hell. She did mentally pack a bag for him, meticulously placing in it a freshly pressed suit, three starched dress shirts, three ties, a week's worth of undershorts and undershirts, his Brylcreem, his shaving necessities and his toothbrush. Belatedly, she added toothpaste.

And she solved successfully for HUMBERTO, blistered, in stocking feet and half mad with worry.

At the end of the workday, she made her way home and let herself quietly in through the back door. She eased up the stairs, ran some cool bathwater in the tub, washed and dried her abused feet, then applied Band-Aids where necessary. She didn't want the housekeeper or children to see her like this.

How was she going to face them? What would she say? How was she to get through the rest of the evening or sleep tonight?

Grace changed into a housedress, sat on the toilet with the lid down and stared at her own feet, which, unsurprisingly, did not provide answers to those questions. She found grim amusement in the odd fact that Band-Aids had been invented due to a woman's misadventures in the kitchen.

Downstairs, Christopher's childish voice announced, "But I don't want to go to bed with no supper!"

I do. I want to crawl under the eiderdown and never come back out.

The housekeeper said something to remonstrate with her little boy, probably telling him to behave himself if he didn't want to face the consequences.

I don't want to face the consequences, either. The fallout from the years of grinding, stressful overwork. The Army had requisitioned and then used up Robert's brain. It was a smoking tangle of rubber. Would top brass now kick it to the curb like trash?

I won't allow it. Grace got up and hobbled out of the bathroom to find her slippers. *I simply won't allow it.*

She greeted and kissed the children, exchanged a few pleasantries with the housekeeper and then shocked the woman out of her own shoes by gathering every vegetable she could find in the house. Grace systematically and viciously murdered two onions, three carrots, a few stalks of celery and some potatoes. "What can I cook with these?"

"M-ma'am?" Mrs. Woolsey was perplexed. "You... don't cook."

"As of this evening, I do." Robert was not going to eat institutional slop in that Bedlam. She was going to battle for his brain, and the first thing it needed was nutrients. Home-cooked meals. "What can I make with these vegetables?"

"A stew. Or a soup. First, I'd— Can I help you remove the peels from the potatoes, ma'am?"

Grace looked at the pale, slaughtered little chunks. "Do we really need to?"

"It's best, ma'am," Mrs. Woolsey said diplomatically.

"Very well."

And so Grace, fiercely and awkwardly, made her first beef stew.

Mrs. Woolsey seemed to sense that she was in some kind of emotional distress, but didn't pry. The children were another matter.

"Where's Daddy?"

"He's... gone on a trip."

"For work?"

"Yes." *One could say so.*

"When will he be back?"

"I'm...ah...not quite sure, my darlings. But he *will* be back."

Robert was not staying in that godforsaken place.

Grace peered at the recipe card that Mrs. Woolsey had produced. Like any recipe, it was comprised of a list of ingredients, portions thereof and instructions for how to use them.

It's a code. I simply have to examine it, learn its secrets and follow where it leads: to a casserole, or a fricassee or a pie. Why have I never seen it that way before?

Grace slept hardly at all. She threw off the eiderdown that she'd wanted to take refuge under. There *was* no refuge. Not for the victims of the bombing strafes in Europe, and not from this mess. Was Robert sleeping? Or lying wide awake like her?

She hadn't decoded her *own husband* properly. She'd somehow missed the red flags that warned of his imminent collapse. What kind of wife was she?

And what had he meant when he'd babbled about the color purple? *No purple...they had no purple.*

An unwelcome flash of intuition had her flying out of bed, running to the toilet to retch, much as she'd had to while pregnant with Isobel in the courtroom years ago.

Red, green, blue...purple.

Every intelligence unit had labored to solve the red, green and blue versions of the horrifyingly complicated military version of the Enigma coding machine. She herself had worked on it, even before Cox's gift of the simpler commercial one. There was no purple version of Enigma. But...

Robert had repeated over and over again that "they knew." It had to mean that her husband and his team had somehow solved the Japanese equivalent of the Enigma: code-named Purple.

No Purple...they had no Purple.

His collapse.

The pieces of the puzzle all locked into place in Grace's mind. She retched, then retched again.

Robert's distressed babble gave her information that she desperately wanted to unlearn. He could only mean that somehow Army SIGINT had *discovered* the coming attack on Pearl Harbor—but the island itself hadn't had the correct machine to receive warning.

No wonder poor Bobby had collapsed. He could never unlearn this information, either. And it had literally driven him insane.

Grace rinsed her mouth, brushed her teeth and felt nausea swirling through her stomach all over again. She refused to give in to it. She walked to the window, clutching her own arms, and stared out at the darkness. She shivered.

Her husband had gone mad. He was locked in a mental ward. Held hostage by a single man, a doctor.

She'd gone to war against far more intimidating men and won. She'd win this time, too. Failure was not an option—or his life, and hers, too, would collapse around their ears. The stigma of mental illness was too great. Nobody could know why he was in the hospital. Not a soul.

If it got out, his career, his reputation, his identity... the very essence of Robert would be ruined. Grace looked up at the sky, searching for the reassuring light of even one star. But they were all obscured by clouds.

I won't allow my husband to stay in that place. I swear by all that is holy, I will win the battle for his mind. I'll get it back. And bring him home.

Washington, DC, 1958

"What's wrong with Daddy?" Isobel asked. She'd come home for a visit after getting her master's at the London School of Economics. Grace's tomboy with dark pigtails had grown into a poised, self-possessed, beautiful young lady. She was a Radcliffe graduate, too.

Robert was still in his monogrammed pajamas, sprawled in a lawn chair under an elm in the backyard. He was staring at nothing, though there was a book open on his chest. This wouldn't have been so odd in itself, but he was also getting showered by the sprinkler and didn't seem to notice.

"Oh dear," Grace said.

Krypto, lying on the floor by the door, rested his nose on his front paws and whined.

"What's wrong with him, Mom?"

"For heaven's sake. Nothing's wrong with him, Iz. He's just puzzling over something, as usual."

"Mom." Isobel put her hands on Grace's shoulders and forced eye contact with her. Same hazel eyes she'd had as a baby, though they'd been rounder then, her features soft, her mouth a tiny, gurgling rosebud. She'd been much easier to distract or outright fool back then.

"*Mom*," Isobel said again. "What's wrong with him? That's not normal. You know it."

Grace squirmed. "Your father has never been *normal*. He's a genius. A thinker. An extraordinarily gifted—"

"*Stop it*," Isobel said, in a hard, no-nonsense tone.

Grace pulled away from her daughter's grasp and walked to the kitchen sink, where she stared out the window again at the inappropriately cheerful cherry blossoms. "He's upset, Iz. Federal agents came to raid the library. They took almost fifty of our books."

"Why?"

"Because some idiot bureaucrat has decided that we can't retain custody of them for reasons of national security."

"That's—" Isobel struggled for the right words. "Insulting. Ridiculous. He practically *created* the NSA."

"Exactly. So that's why he's upset."

"Well, we can't let him just sit out there and get soaked."

"What do you propose I do about it, Isobel?" Grace's voice rose, despite her best efforts to remain calm. "I could barely get him out of bed this morning. I left him briefly in front of a plate of waffles to turn on the sprinklers and check the mail. When I returned, he'd dragged the lawn chair there and sat in it with his book."

"But—" Isobel threw up her hands.

"But what? Did I try to get him to come in? Yes. Did I explain to him that he was getting wet? Yes. Did I even try to tug him out of the lawn chair? Yes. What else can I do?"

"It's *weird*," Isobel said. "Something isn't right with him. He should see a doctor. A psychiatrist."

"Sweetheart, sit down." How could Grace explain to her that as long as Robert was visible in a lawn chair under a sprinkler, she at least knew he was safe and not suicidal today?

"I don't want to sit down—I want to go get Daddy out from under the sprinkler! And take him to see a doctor. If you cared about him at all, you'd have already taken him."

If I cared about him at all?! For the first time in her life, Grace's palms itched with the urge to slap her daughter's face. "Sit. Down. Isobel. Now."

Isobel blinked. She sat down at the kitchen table.

Grace sat opposite her. "Do you remember Daddy being gone for about three months when you were nine years old?"

Iz shrugged, then nodded. "He traveled a lot, though."

"This wasn't for travel. It was right after Pearl Harbor. He had a breakdown, Isobel, due to exhaustion, overwork and shock. He kept wandering around with tears in his eyes, repeating over and over again, 'But they knew.'"

"Knew what?"

"He never explained. He never will. But he was so distraught that he checked himself in to Walter Reed's neuropsychiatric unit. He stayed there for three months before they discharged him. I went to visit him there every day, and it was terrifying."

Isobel, for once, didn't interrupt.

"There were men in straitjackets, men shouting at walls, men drooling in corners because they'd gotten violent and been medicated. And there was your father, like an oversize frightened rabbit in the middle of it all. I've never, before or since, seen your father display fear of any-thing." *That's a lie, Grace. He was even more terrified of the electroshock therapy. But Isobel doesn't need to know about that.*

"So in the midst of this...this...chaos, Bobby was supposed to tell the psychiatrist what was troubling him, which he could not and would not do because the nature of his work was so secret. So he was diagnosed—if one can call it that—with anxiety, if you please. One doctor thought his shaking hands might even be a sign of Parkinson's disease. They came up with answers that they could write on a discharge form and then they sent him home. They were of no help at all."

"But Mom, that was in 1941. There have been medical advances since then, surely?"

"Would you like them to perform a lobotomy on your father?"

"What? *No...*"

"Give him drugs that will utterly incapacitate him?"

"Of course not."

"And then there's his career and his reputation to consider. Do you think I advertised that Bobby had checked in to Walter Reed because of a breakdown?"

Isobel shook her head.

"No. I had to keep that even more secret than any code we ever broke or created. Yet someone," *J. Edgar Hoover, that despicable toad,* "has somehow delved into his medical records, since that was the excuse used by the agents to steal books from our library."

As Isobel processed all of this, Grace rose and went to the coffeepot. She poured a cup and offered it to her daughter. Then she poured one for herself and sipped at it absently, noting that her own hands were trembling.

"Mom, I know you want to protect his good name and his legacy, but—"

"And his job, Isobel. His *job.*"

"—surely his health is more important."

Isobel jumped—and Krypto barked—at the crash of Grace's coffee cup into the wall. It shattered into fragments, leaving a dark, ominous stain on the wall. A stain that spread and dripped.

"What is wrong with you, Mom?!"

Grace aimed a bitter smile at her. "I love that man out there, your father, with every fiber of my being. We've given everything within reason to the United States government—and I'm proud of that. So is Robert. But I won't let the faceless bureaucrats steal or destroy his brain, his identity or his very life."

"What are you talking about?"

"He's a proud man, your father. And justly so. He's beaten poverty, prejudice, discrimination and snobbery in his decades of dedicated service to this country. He's—" *Suicidal.*

Grace simply couldn't say it aloud to their daughter. She was still her mother; it was still her job to protect her from the grimmer realities she herself battled daily. Instead, she said, "We'd lose the house."

Isobel stared at her. "You're worried about losing the house."

Grace ignored the judgment in her tone. She bent to pick up the shards of her coffee mug and began to clean up the mess.

"Well, I'm more worried about Daddy." Isobel marched to the back door, slamming it behind her. She stalked to the faucet, turned off the sprinkler, and wound up the hose.

Robert didn't seem to notice that his "rain" had stopped. He just lay there on the lawn chair in his soaked pajamas with his ruined book still open on his chest.

Isobel took his hand and tried to pull him to his feet. He didn't budge, though he smiled at her. Isobel's mouth moved as she reasoned with him to the best of her ability. Robert smiled again but shook his head. Then, utterly ignoring her, he plucked the wet book from his chest and held it up, to all appearances reading it upside down.

Grace dumped the splinters of her mug into the trash. *Welcome to five minutes of my life, darling girl.*

CHAPTER THIRTY-FIVE

Washington, DC, 1942

There was a war on. Grace could not forget that, even if she was also fighting a private battle to bring her husband back from the dark forces that were holding him hostage at Walter Reed. She could not abandon her job, because according to her decryptions, Hitler had launched Operation Drumbeat. This was a systematic and diabolical continued attack on Allied ships up and down the Atlantic coast. German U-boats were tracking, targeting and sinking US and British vessels carrying supplies—and men. Despite her team's—and the Navy's—best efforts to frantically decode and warn the Allies to take evasive action, the lives of five thousand men had been torpedoed. A million tons of munitions and other supplies sank to the bottom of the ocean with them.

Grace spent several hours with Robert daily, rubbing his shoulders, updating him on the children's antics, reading to him, doing crossword and jigsaw puzzles and coaxing him to return to reality. But she made up the time at work. She frantically analyzed and decoded the transcripts of radio transmissions by 5:00 a.m., and she worked until 11:00 p.m. Outwardly, she was gracious and calm. Inwardly, she feared she might be heading for her own nervous breakdown if she couldn't get Bobby home soon.

She tossed, turned and thrashed in their bed at night, longing for his presence, his warmth beside her, his arms around her. And she prayed. Then she got up the next morning and did it all over again.

In early March, Robert was still "in custody," as Grace inwardly referred to it, though she outwardly told concerned friends, family and colleagues that though he'd been very ill, he was recovering. She was deliberately vague, and if anyone pushed for details, she intimated that it had something to do with heart trouble.

It's not a lie, not really. He is heartsick over what happened at Pearl Harbor. He's ill because they came so very close to preventing it...

One morning, she was working in her office at the Annex when Utsidi and Veronica came running in, waving an intercepted message, undecrypted. "Grace! F-21 needs our help."

F-21 was the unit under the Combat Intelligence Division in charge of tracking German U-boats in the Atlantic.

The three of them got to work on decrypting the message.

"Oh dear. Oh, good Lord. The Nazis are tracking troopship HMS *Queen Mary*," Grace said.

She read the plaintext aloud: On board Queen Mary: 7K to 8K troops, tanks, disassembled planes. Came from Dutch Indies via South America.

"We've got to alert F-21 right away." Grace all but ran to the room where the unit was housed.

"U-boats are chasing the *Queen Mary*," she told the stunned men.

"You're sure?"

Grace nodded. "We're listening in to a spy network in Brazil, and the QM is off the coast of Brazil right now. This is urgent: Hitler's offered a reward to the captain who sinks her: the Knight's Cross of the Iron Cross with Oak Leaves and a million Reichsmarks," she said, disgusted. "That's close to $250,000! I suppose one can't blame them for being in hot pursuit. But let's make sure, shall we, that they all miss payday."

"Can the QM turn around and dock somewhere in Brazil?" one of the men asked.

"Negative," said another. "She'll be a sitting duck."

A discussion among the men erupted around Grace.

"Can we get escort carriers launched in time from Recife?"

"No way."

"And if we try, the Nazis will have confirmation that we've broken their Hydra code."

"For eight thousand men, it's worth it," Grace broke in.

They looked at her, the codebreaker, in surprise. Then the discussion resumed.

"How fast can the *Queen Mary* go?"

"Top speed is twenty-eight and a half knots."

"Right. It takes around ten minutes for a U-boat to line up in order to fire—"

"Radio the captain immediately. Tell him he's got to take evasive action. Tell him to change tack every seven miles, all right? Zigzag. It's the only way to outmaneuver the bastards until they run out of fuel."

Grace held her breath as the senior officer of F-21 sent an urgent coded message to the *Queen Mary* via a SIGABA, the US's version of an Enigma machine. She strongly suspected that her husband had had a hand in creating it, but of course, she couldn't ask him.

She had to return to her own office, but asked Unit F-21 to keep her apprised of the situation. Utsidi, Veronica, Fay and Grace sent up a prayer for the ship's safety.

They learned later that the *Queen Mary* was able to make a series of evasive maneuvers and arrived in port safely. Secretary Knox sent over a bottle of champagne, with a cryptic note that read, "God Save the Queen."

Fay, Veronica and Utsidi all clamored to open it, but Grace demurred. Robert was still at Walter Reed. The U-boats were still menacing other Allied ships. "I think it's bad luck," she said, frowning at the fistful of other odd decrypts she held.

In the meantime, her Coast Guard decrypt unit had other troubles developing in Brazil, as well as in Chile.

The same listening station that had alerted them to the *Queen Mary* situation picked up alarming news:

CANDACE, BRUNO, SELIG raided, Rio de Janeiro.
QUENTIN, ZAFTIG, ALGERNON in police custody Sau Paulo.

HAROLD, NIEMAN arrested Santiago; DORN, JAMAL arrested
Valparaiso...
What is happening? Please advise!

And so on.

The German spies they'd been tracking in South America were sending panicked messages to each other about police crackdowns. Why? Who was leading these? And how had South American law enforcement learned of the spy networks?

Grace had a sinking feeling in the pit of her stomach. Copies of the Coast Guard unit's decrypts were still being furnished to Army, Navy, State and the FBI. Army, Navy and State knew better than to compromise the stream of useful information that gave them a window—even a red-carpet entrance—into the Nazi brain: what the plans were for defeating the Allies, how those plans operated, what attacks were imminent and the details of time and place.

But the FBI? With the neophyte at the helm of its tiny cryptanalysis unit? Led by J. Edgar Hoover with his insatiable need for power, press, publicity?

The Toad was up to something. Something that could jeopardize national security.

Before she could decide in whom to confide—if anyone—Grace got a telephone call that changed her world and brought her to the brink of weeping on the job.

"Mrs. Feldman? It's Doctor Menzies at Walter Reed."

Oh, dear God. Robert. "Yes? He's all right? Please tell me he's safe? What's happened?"

"He's fine. Nothing's happened. I'm ringing you to inform you that I've finished my evaluation of your husband."

"And?" Her heart almost hurled itself out of her chest.

"He's suffering from extreme anxiety and exhaustion, but he's healing. I believe he's ready to be released."

Grace almost fainted with relief. She couldn't even speak.

"Mrs. Feldman? Are you there?"

"Yes. Yes, I'm here."

"He can go home, and he can go back to work gradually, as long as he's not overloaded. I'm prescribing some sleeping pills—Amytal— because it's imperative that he gets rest and that he's not exposed to prolonged stress."

You clearly still do not comprehend the nature of his job. Lives depend on how quickly we intercept and break coded messages.

But of course, Grace didn't say this aloud. "I understand. So...? May I come and get him?"

"Yes, Mrs. Feldman. Late this afternoon, he should be ready."

Grace's whole body began to shake uncontrollably. Robert was coming home. His mind was back. She'd won.

She couldn't help a single, dry sob.

"I beg your pardon? Did you say something, Mrs. Feldman?"

"Something caught in my throat. Thank you, Doctor. I'll be there to collect him at 5:00 p.m."

Grace placed the receiver in its cradle and stared at it until it blurred. In the past two months, she'd singlehandedly saved the lives of approximately ten thousand men. But the only life that truly, deeply mattered to her was Robert's. Was that selfish? Probably.

And she'd saved him not through cryptanalysis, but through her voice, her touch, her affection, her attention—her love.

She got unsteadily to her feet, plucked the bottle of champagne off the corner of her desk, then went out to find the rest of her team. "On second thought, ladies and gents, let's take a ten-minute break to celebrate. Our achievements today have been nothing short of remarkable, and it's important that we acknowledge that."

CHAPTER THIRTY-SIX

Robert came home lucid, but a shadow of his former self. The children made him drawings and clamored for his attention, but their "horsey" had left the stables. Grace found herself unable to let go of him in bed at night. She and Mrs. Woolsey went into competition in the kitchen, where every evening was a new experiment for Grace: layer cakes with whipped cream and fruit toppings, chocolate tortes, chocolate-chip cookies. She liked baking the most, to her surprise.

Mrs. Woolsey didn't, so eventually they settled into a routine: the housekeeper made lunches and dinners, and Grace made desserts.

After a week resting in bed, Robert went back to work and was soon consumed by it again. He worked feverishly, worrying Grace. But though she couldn't discuss it with him, she knew he was seeking some sort of redemption for the bottleneck in crucial intelligence at Pearl Harbor. She had to keep her educated guesses, her unwelcome insight, to herself.

Back at the Navy Annex, there were even more alarming developments to watch in the South American Nazi spy networks. Several radio transmitters were seized and went dark, limiting the amount of information available to Grace and her team. Police in Brazil rounded up ninety German spies. SARGO, LUNA and ALFREDO issued warnings and went dark—but not before handing Grace the evidence of J. Edgar Hoover's misdirected machinations.

She stared in disbelief at one of her decrypts from SARGO himself:

American FBI confronting Brazilian officials in Fortaleza, Manaus, Curitiba, Salvador, Belo Horizonte. Have copies of our own communiques...CEASE ALL TRANSMISSIONS. CEASE ALL OPERATIONS.

Utsidi, glancing at Grace's face, asked, "Are you all right?"

Too furious to answer, Grace slowly shook her head. She handed her the message without a word, and paced back and forth in order to think.

It was no use going to Commander Jones—she knew it instinctively. She'd already asked for help with Hoover once from Farley, who'd refused. The only man she knew who outranked *him* was Treasury Secretary Morgenthau, the very same person who'd directed her—at the behest of President Roosevelt—to aid the FBI in setting up its own cryptanalysis unit. She could hardly go to Frank Knox. There was no man who would intercede on her behalf. Which left her with no alternative but to wage her own battle.

Grace knew she should follow Genevieve Hitt's advice from long ago: *Be smart, but be quiet about it . . . Always be a lady. Don't challenge a man directly . . . Come at them sideways instead, with a pretty smile.*

In this case, she simply couldn't do it. J. Edgar Hoover had ruined—destroyed—all her unit's progress on the spy networks. Thousands upon thousands of hours, wasted. The Nazis now knew that their code had been cracked and would change it immediately.

Grace sat, seething, in Hoover's now opulent reception area, where fine European antiques had sprouted upon the premises. Chinese porcelain planters, bronze statues and original oil paintings announced that he'd become a man of stature, wealth and taste.

She didn't care that her visit was ill-advised. She was several miles beyond furious.

She'd waited twenty minutes past her appointment time when Mrs. Gandy came to escort her in. "Mr. Hoover," she said as the door had barely shut behind her, "your agents in South America are out of control."

Hoover, who'd begun to get to his feet as she came in, dropped back into his chair and scowled at her. "*What* did you say to me?" He did not offer her a seat.

"You heard me. Do you not understand that there's a war on, that it's crucial for us to know what the enemy is doing, and now *all of Brazil has gone dark* because your agents actually showed *hundreds* of my unit's decrypted messages to government officials there?"

"How dare you question my agency's activities?"

"I am enraged, Mr. Hoover. Your agents have alerted the enemy that we were successfully monitoring them, which gave us an edge to save thousands of Allied lives! Your agents singlehandedly ruined our surveillance and codebreaking operation."

"My agents," Hoover retorted, "rounded up and destroyed a hotbed of spies that were plotting against this country. I will not apologize for that, and especially not to an emotionally overwrought woman with delusions of self-importance. I will be telephoning Frank Knox at the Navy about this, you may be sure."

"Do what you think best."

"I always do, Mrs. Feldman. And I certainly don't answer to you."

"Mr. Hoover, the problem is that you *didn't* round up all the spies. You let a crucial few escape—and those spies warned Berlin that their codes had been broken and needed to be changed. You've set us back *months*, and many more Allied soldiers and sailors will die because of this. I—and my unit—will have to start over from scratch—and the encrypted messages will be even more difficult to break now because of heightened security."

"Are you quite done with your hysterical outburst, Mrs. Feldman?"

"I'm not in the least hysterical, Mr. Hoover. I'm stating facts and lodging a complaint."

"You don't have the rank to lodge a complaint with me."

"Excuse me?"

"A mere cryptanalyst in the Coast Guard." Hoover's voice dripped scorn.

"A *mere cryptanalyst* whom you chose to train your own man."

Hoover ignored this. "I can't believe Commander Jones allowed you to come."

"I didn't ask his permission."

"That was a mistake, Mrs. Feldman."

Probably. I don't care.

"I'll make sure you're officially reprimanded."

She stared at him. "Have you not heard one word I've said? We must work in coordination, not in opposition, to each other. 'We' meaning Army, Navy, State and FBI. This cannot happen again."

"Do you consider yourself good at your job, Mrs. Feldman?"

"Of course." She said it without a trace of modesty.

"Then I suggest that you go and do it. If you're such a brilliant lady codebreaker, then 'starting from scratch,' as you say, shouldn't present such a difficulty."

Bastard. She squinted at him, willing the word not to fly out of her mouth.

"You have some nerve, to question my authority and doubt the actions of my agents. Some nerve, indeed."

If he was waiting for an apology, he was disappointed. She offered none.

"How's your husband, Mrs. Feldman?" Hoover asked silkily. "I heard a rumor that he's been ill."

Grace froze. "He's quite recovered. Back at work. Thank you for asking." Hoover couldn't access Army personnel medical records, could he? Surely even he couldn't do that.

"Give him my best, won't you?"

She managed a stiff nod.

"And now Mrs. Gandy will show you out. Good day, Mrs. Feldman."

His secretary appeared as if conjured, wearing a wooden expression along with her pearls. And that was that.

Exactly three weeks later, Robert threw open the front door after arriving home from work. He slammed it behind him, threw his coat and hat on the couch and stormed upstairs.

This was unlike him. Her husband was always calm and was neat to a fault, hanging up his coat each day and storing his hat on the top shelf of the hallway closet.

"Bobby?" she called after him. She got no response. Grace climbed the stairs after shooing off the children, who hadn't given up on their "horsey" yet. "Sweetheart?"

She entered their bedroom as he threw one of his shoes at the wall.

"I've been honorably discharged from the Army," he said bitterly, throwing the other shoe after it. They landed splayed and wrong-footed, upside down.

"What?"

"By reason of physical disqualification."

"But there's nothing wrong with you. Walter Reed cleared you for active duty."

"Well, someone at the top appears to doubt that I'm fit for service, Grace."

A seed of dread sprouted in her gut. "Someone? But…your medical records are private. Aren't they?" Could Hoover have sent an agent to break in to the relevant file cabinet? Had she so offended his ego that he'd play this dirty?

Utterly paranoid, Grace. Hoover has far more important things to do.

"I should have known better than to go to the hospital. What was I thinking?"

"You were past thinking. You…you needed help, Bobby. You got it. There's no shame in that. None at all."

He scoffed. "Of course there's shame in it. Needing help for one's head is highly suspect, and you know it. If word's gotten out, I'm finished."

"If word's gotten out, it's illegal. Therefore, nobody can corroborate it. Which means it's unsubstantiated rumor—which means, Bobby, that all you have to do is be your brilliant self and convince everyone that it's just gossip and speculation."

"But it's not."

"Nobody has to know that."

"You're asking me to lie."

Grace took a deep breath. "I'm asking you to omit."

Her husband was silent for a few moments. Then he nodded and stood up. "I'm going to sue," he said. "For reinstatement. I'll fight this. They have no right, after all these years of dedicated service."

Grace stilled. Could he sue? She supposed so...as long as J. Edgar Hoover wasn't breaking into files and stirring up trouble. But it appeared that he was. The timing of Robert's discharge couldn't be coincidental.

A cold rage bloomed deep within her. Hoover had to be behind this. He'd decided to get even with her by going after her husband: ending his career in the military, depriving him of his rank, whispering about his mental stability, and God alone knew what else.

J. Edgar Hoover was now one of the most powerful men in the United States. In order to fight him, Grace was going to need the help of someone equally—if not more—powerful.

Eleanor Roosevelt was just as unassuming and friendly in her role as First Lady as she'd been when Grace initially met her, when FDR had been assistant secretary of the Navy. She still had a bracing, almost manic energy.

"Why, Grace, dear! How lovely to see you. Myrna took your coat and hat?"

Grace nodded.

"I feel quite dreadful that I only have ten minutes, but I've got a speech to give at the League of Women Voters, followed by a luncheon, followed by three meetings—and must write my column, of course. In addition to leaving Franklin several things to look over..."

She was an admirable woman. And it occurred to Grace that she, like Nellie Farquhar, held power in an unconventional marriage. Nellie was no doormat, as Grace's mother had been. Nellie led her own life independently with her steers, her garden, her potbellied pig. And Eleanor was no doormat either: not only an activist for many causes, but essentially Franklin's business partner.

"Please don't apologize, Mrs. Roo—"

"Eleanor, dear," the first lady said firmly. "How long have we known each other?"

"Thank you for even taking a few minutes to see me."

"Do sit down. Tea?"

Grace shook her head but seated herself on a green damask sofa, and Eleanor sat opposite, giving her a wide, warm smile. "What can I help you with?"

"This is in the utmost confidence, you understand..."

"Absolutely."

Grace summed up the situation with Hoover.

"That awful man. I've had my own run-ins with him. He had *me* under surveillance, can you imagine?! *Me*. Tried to tell Franklin I was having an affair with a young man in his twenties! He even had a trumped-up *recording* of our supposedly 'intimate' moments."

Grace gasped.

Eleanor's friendly blue eyes had gone icy-cold gray, and her warm smile had become a rictus. "He had the temerity, the *vulgarity, the sheer indecency* to play this tape for Franklin!"

Grace put a hand over her mouth.

"Franklin knew it was ridiculous. Threatened to fire him on the spot and ordered the disgusting creature out of the Oval before he personally throttled him."

Grace sat, speechless.

"The only way to fight such a horror of a man is to do so on his own level." Eleanor rose, went to an elegant Chippendale writing desk and produced a business card, which she briskly handed over to Grace. "There you are. Contact him and get him started."

Grace looked down at the card. *Gaston Means*, it said. *Private Investigator.*

"By the way, he's almost as dreadful as Hoover. An oily, sycophantic con man. A relic of the Harding days, when Daugherty was AG. But if there's dirt to be had, he'll find it—or manufacture it. And there's no love lost between him and J. Edgar, though the FBI does use him for some things."

Grace remembered meeting him. He'd come out of Hoover's office on her first visit. She looked at the card again, uncomfortable. "Hire a PI? It feels...immoral."

"Is what's happening to your husband *moral*?" Eleanor asked, her eyes steely.

Grace eyed her unhappily.

"My dear, you're not dealing with someone who even *has* a moral compass," the First Lady said. "Sad, especially given his stature as America's Top Cop, but true. So I shouldn't have any compunction about it, if I were you."

Grace sucked in a deep breath, then released it slowly. "I can't really afford to hire—"

"Nonsense," said Eleanor. "It's on the house, so to speak." And she winked.

On the White House? "Oh no, ma'am—I couldn't possibly accept—"

"Grace, dear. Your integrity does you credit. But I myself have a vested interest in the collection of this information. Failing in his previous salacious accusations, Mr. Hoover is now whispering that I have an improper relationship with a dear *female* friend. He's a menace. So if you'd rather, *I'll* call Mr. Means. And you're not to worry about the bill, because I'll benefit as well." Mrs. Roosevelt checked her watch and got to her feet. "Now, I do wish we could have a nice, long, relaxed chat, dear. But it's not possible today." She twitched the card out of Grace's fingers. "I'll call that weasel Means this very day, between one of my blasted—excuse me—meetings. All right?"

Grace took her cue and got to her feet as well. "Thank you, Eleanor. I'm not quite sure how I feel about all of this, but..."

"That's all right. You don't *have* to know how you feel. And you don't have to use any information Means digs up, either. But you'll have the ability to do so, should you need it." The First Lady squeezed Grace's hands and gave her a peck on the cheek. "Have a lovely day, dear. So nice to see you. And by the way, I'll see if there's anything Franklin can do about getting Robert reinstated. Ridiculous after his many years of service. An outrage."

Grace's coat and hat were briskly returned to her by Eleanor's social secretary, and she was politely escorted from the White House.

Well. It's nice to have friends in high places.

She was troubled, though. She'd just crossed a line that she'd never imagined she'd cross. She didn't find it particularly immoral to crack codes and ciphers to spy on criminals. They were criminals, after all. But hiring a PI to "dig up dirt" on someone in law enforcement? Her conscience wrestled with it.

Not to mention that it was dangerous.

J. Edgar Hoover was the *head of the FBI.*

And if he's trying to ruin Eleanor Roosevelt, what will he do to me, if this gets out? Not to mention Robert?

CHAPTER THIRTY-SEVEN

Robert was still going to work each day at SIGINT headquarters—albeit as a civilian. He was sleepless, angry and depressed at his discharge. His hands often shook. He disappeared into trances.

The Navy eggheads had taken over a girls' school on Nebraska Avenue anchored by a five-story building—the Navy Annex—and Grace's Coast Guard unit would soon be joining them there. She did not look forward to encountering Alice Martenz again, but it couldn't be helped.

Personal rivalries didn't matter. Grace and her team had a giant mess to clean up after Hoover's blunder in Brazil. They now numbered about twenty, which seemed an impossibly small group of people to crack thousands of coded enemy transmissions on several different continents.

"We're starting over, ladies and gents." Grace stood at the front of the room, great maps studded with pushpins and stretched with string spread on the wall behind her. "As of this morning, we're monitoring eighteen circuits in eight different countries—and not only stations in South America. We're now listening in West Africa, Portugal, Spain, France, Morocco, Iran and Crimea. And new ones are springing up all the time.

"The Germans have changed all the codes. They've stepped them up. We're no longer dealing with book cipher codes or single transposition codes. We're looking at something vastly more complicated: running key systems, double-transposition systems and polyalphabetic substitutions with columnar transpositions...and a more advanced Enigma machine, especially on the mysterious Circuit 3-N.

"When you break the code on any given circuit, go in and solve all messages in that code. Some will be more useful than others—but specific *dates* or *times* in seemingly innocuous items like birth announcements or love notes—pay attention to those in case they're code for an attack. Flag questions—especially questions about munitions and supplies. Those are important, because those indicate gaps in the enemy's knowledge. Gaps that can be exploited by Allied counterintelligence. Got it?"

There were nods and murmurs, groans and yawns before the team settled into work and the dominant noises became the scratch of pencils on worksheets, the creaks of chairs, muted coughs and sneezes, the clacking of heels or the occasional grind of a pencil sharpener.

Pipe and cigarette smoke fogged the air at the long worktables; sandwich crumbs littered surfaces and fell between the keys of typewriters.

Grace herself worked on Circuit 3-N, the most impossible one, some hideous iteration of an Enigma. It wasn't one of the simple commercial versions that Cox had presented her with. This one was a bear.

She went at it systematically, though, seeking the patterns that would eventually reveal themselves and give her a small opening. Utsidi and the girls wanted to help—but they needed Grace's insight, first.

"Put on a pot of coffee," she told them. "Actually, this may take two." When they reconvened, she tried to explain.

"Look, an Enigma machine is essentially a more complex, better encrypted version of Heburn's gadget twenty years ago. It cranks out polyalphabetic ciphers. Like Heburn's, the box contains three or more rotating alphabet wheels—but these are connected to electrical wires. There's a typewriter keyboard on the outside, the keys arranged in normal order. Above the keyboard is a "lamp board" of the same twenty-six letters in the same order. When the sender presses a key, a different letter illuminates on the lamp board—the cipher letter, lit by a small bulb. The receiver of the message, operating his own Enigma with the same settings, decrypts the message one letter at a time. Are you with me?"

"Uh…"

"Each press of a key completes an electrical circuit," Grace continued, "and the machine's first rotor steps one letter forward. At the end of its alphabet, the next rotor begins to step through its own alphabet, and then the third."

"So it's sort of like a car odometer logging miles?" Fay asked.

"Exactly!" Grace took a moment to be proud of her. "Our problem is that Enigma generates almost *seventeen thousand* nonrepeating cipher alphabets before its wheels return to their original starting positions."

"Dios mio." Veronica threw up her hands. "How es possible—"

"Hear me out. It sounds hopeless. But in any given day, if we intercept, say, sixty or so messages typed with the same starting position, then we can solve them in depth. We take each batch of messages and line them up on top of each other, looking down the columns for similarities and patterns. Clear as mud?"

"Clear as all of Middle-earth," muttered Fay. "Actually…all right. It makes sense."

"In theory, anyway," Utsidi said.

"And if we run into trouble, we can apply Bobby's index of coincidence—his statistical frequency analysis."

Despite their doubts, the team got to work. They solved the plaintexts, which were in German, and Grace decided to go a step further: she'd use their alphabets to figure out the Enigma's wiring. And she'd use that knowledge of the machine's wiring to deduce new keys when the codes were changed.

She drew diagrams as various pairs of letters repeated vertically on the page and inadvertently disclosed information about the spacing between pairs of wiring contacts on the Enigma's rotors. With the help of her gals, she solved the wiring for all three wheels of this new monster Enigma without ever seeing it.

"It's a G model," she informed Commander Jones.

"You're sure?"

"Yes. You can send the diagrams over to Army SIGINT for corroboration, but I'm confident that it's a medium-security model made for the Abwehr. And it's transmitting to the Nazis out of Buenos Aires, among other cities in South America. Where, by the way, our old friends SARGO and LUNA are operating, the spies who escaped the FBI bust in Brazil and Chile."

Jones leaned back in his chair and shook his sandy head. "Mrs. Feldman, I must tell you that you're the most extraordinary woman I've ever met."

Grace blinked. "It was a team effort."

"Sure it was. Well, I can't wait to cable Bletchley Park in Britain that my team at the US Coast Guard has solved Enigma."

"I doubt they'll appreciate that," she said dryly.

"They certainly won't." He chuckled.

"Commander, I do have a request."

"Yes?"

Grace didn't hesitate. "I have no issue with sharing our decrypts with Army, Navy, State or the British. But—"

"No need to worry, Mrs. Feldman," said Jones. "We're freezing him out."

"Hoover?"

"Yes. He's a liability and a publicity hound. Don't worry. This time, Mr. Hoover will *not* be taking credit for our work."

"What if he finds out he's being excluded? And he will, eventually."

Jones looked at her quite seriously. "You do realize that I can't take the fall for it."

Grace stared right back. "It was a...rogue employee."

"Yes. I'm sorry."

She nodded. "I understand."

She understood too well. Jones wasn't a bad sort, but he was a careerist, unwilling to earn the enmity of Hoover. So Grace herself would be thrown under the bus without hesitation. But it couldn't be helped. Hoover could not be allowed to expose—yet again—to the Nazis that she and her unit were reading their communications.

Once Grace and her team had cracked open Circuit 3-N, they were able to detect SARGO and LUNA at work again in Argentina.

Grace took her core unit with her to brief Commander Jones.

"SARGO is the spy," Grace said with certainty. "LUNA is some sort of radio whiz. They're expanding the network at breakneck speed."

Fay handed him a decrypt. "They're asking specific questions about munitions again. They want to know what Henry Ford is manufacturing in Iron Mountain. They want to know about a new antiaircraft gun made by Fisher in Detroit. The caliber and material of US armor bombs. Details on development of rocket weapons..."

"Con respeto, these questions are nothing new," Veronica said. "Of more concern is that the Nazis are forming a shadow army in Argentina—with the help of the new regime."

"And worse," Fay put in gravely, "the end game is to overthrow the governments of Brazil, Paraguay, Bolivia and Chile—to make *all of South America* fascist."

Jones nodded soberly. "And then, of course, the Nazis will be perfectly poised to bomb—or flat out invade—the United States."

Grace was still trying to absorb the awful ramifications of a Nazi invasion of the US from South America—or Nazi bombs strafing American cities—when she got word that Mildred Murtaugh, Robert's secretary, had mysteriously arrived and refused to leave until Grace made time for her. Mildred's presence kindled panic in Grace. It had to be about Bobby.

"Ms. Murtaugh?" She composed herself and greeted the wisp of a woman.

Mildred peered left and right to make sure nobody else heard her. "It's your husband. It's as though he's gone from his body," she whispered to Grace. "No one's inside. Certainly not Colonel Feldman." She twisted the strap of her pocketbook nervously. "I tried calling, but the line was busy, so I—I just decided to come and find you. I didn't want to tell anyone else...so I just closed and locked his door. Said he wasn't to be interrupted. I hope I did the right thing?"

"Yes, of course you did, Mildred. And please, don't share this with anyone."

"Of course not."

"He's been under tremendous strain."

"That he has, ma'am."

As they stood in Grace's small private office, the telephone jangled. She ignored it.

"All right." She plucked her gloves and pocketbook from her lower desk drawer, her coat and hat from the rack that stood behind the door. "We'll go to Arlington Hall and...and...fix things." Not that she had any idea how.

Once they arrived at Arlington Hall, Grace greeted a few WACs, WAVES and codebreakers she knew. Then Mildred discreetly unlocked the door and they entered Robert's office.

He sat in his chair, hands folded on the desk in front of him, staring at something neither of them could see.

"Bobby, dear? Bobby?" Grace touched his shoulder but got no response. "Sweetheart, it's me, Grace. Can you hear me?"

Nothing.

"Robert," she said, louder. "Snap out of this."

He sat like a statue, unnerving her.

Mildred looked half confused, half scared.

"Have you ever seen him like this before?" Grace asked.

She shook her head.

"Is he working on a problem in his head?"

"I...I don't know."

Grace tried to reach him for a good fifteen minutes or so, even shaking him by the shoulders, snapping her fingers in front of his face, lightly slapping him on the cheek. Nothing worked.

What had happened last time? He'd been sprawled on the floor of this same office, unable to move, until...he sneezed. *Dust bunny.*

Grace searched the corners and under the desk. If she could make him sneeze, maybe everything would be all right. She collected all the dust she could find while Mildred clearly wondered if she was as lunatic as Robert. Then she held it in her palm, put her hand in front of Robert's nose, and blew the dust at him.

He sneezed.

Then he blinked, looking at her and Mildred. "What...?"

"Sweetheart, you've been...catatonic. Mildred came to get me."

Robert's hands began to shake uncontrollably.

"I need help, Grace," he whispered.

There was no doubt. But how to get him out of the office without anyone suspecting why?

"I know, my darling." Grace thought fast. Then she turned to Mildred. "He's having a 'heart attack,' you understand?"

Mildred nodded.

"No, I'm not," her husband said.

"Bobby. Pay attention to me. We are going to get you help, dear. But we have to get you that help without anyone in the office knowing that you need it. We must protect your professional reputation at all costs. So Mildred is going to call an ambulance. I'll stay with you. She'll go meet it outside and explain to the medics what's really going on."

Robert hesitated, then nodded. "Not Walter Reed. I can't go back there."

"No, my darling. Over my dead body. We'll take you to George Washington University Hospital. Mildred, make the call? Thank you. And bless you for being such a discreet soul."

Mildred picked up the phone.

Shortly afterward, two medics brought in a stretcher, and behind Robert's closed door, helped him onto it, then wheeled him out and down to the waiting ambulance. Grace followed, reassuring his colleagues that he'd be all right, thanking them for their concern. Then she hurried to join him for the ride to the hospital.

She held his hand during a bout of his silent weeping, squeezing it reassuringly. And she battled her own terror that he was falling back into the dark abyss of extreme melancholia—caused, no doubt, by the discharge. He was no longer a lieutenant colonel; he'd lost half of his identity. And the unbearable strain of his job continued, nobody noticing or caring how he felt as a human being.

They got him into a hospital bed, where her big, strapping, elegant husband lay like a wilted lettuce leaf. It broke her heart. *Damn Hoover to hell. Please, Franklin, get him reinstated somehow.*

"Grace," he croaked.

"Yes?" she bent closer to him so she could hear. Nobody else was in the room.

"Another...attack...coming...Pacific. Trying to find out when... and where."

She was horrified. "*Shhh.* You can't tell me things like that."

Robert closed his eyes. "Joe Rochefort's at Station HYPO in Hawaii trying to pinpoint it...Redman believes Station CAST in the Philippines. I need to help Joe. But I—"

She shushed him again. "Bobby, be quiet!"

"I'm *useless*." The tears came again, his shame pouring down his cheeks. "And afraid. The things the Nazis are doing to Jews—my people, Grace! My *people*. Hitler must be stopped. Sent to hell where he belongs. And—" His voice broke. "We *cannot* have another Pearl Harbor."

If anything demonstrated his desperate need for help, for relief from his demons, it was this indiscretion about a coming attack. He shared a table, a bed and children with Grace, had for years, but the fun they used to have working together was gone, ever since they'd both signed numerous confidentiality agreements with the government. They had an unspoken pact that they never talked about their work. *Never*. Despite the fact that nobody else believed it.

"Not another word, Robert Feldman," Grace said fiercely. "This is not who you are. You're *not* weak and *you do not talk about your work*. Not even to your own wife. *Ever*."

Bobby leaked more tears of shame, tears that tore out her heart, but he nodded.

They both subsided as a nurse bustled into the room to take Bobby's vitals. She was followed minutes later by a doctor.

"Hello, there. I'm Dr. Finnegan." He was tall, balding, with serious gray eyes behind steel spectacles. He seemed kind and thoughtful as he reviewed Robert's chart. "Tell me what led up to this incident, Mr. Feldman."

"He can't," Grace said baldly.

"Hmm..." Dr. Finnigan consulted the chart in his hand. "You spent time at Walter Reed. Diagnosis: 'an anxiety reaction' caused by 'prolonged overwork on a top secret project,' I see here." The doctor tapped his pen on his clipboard.

Robert nodded, then turned to face the wall.

"Has your work gotten any less—"

"No," Grace answered for Bobby. "And it won't. There's a war on."

Her husband said to the wall, "I need help, Doc. I need it *yesterday*. This can't happen to me. It especially can't happen on the job."

Dr. Finnegan eyed the back of Robert's neck, noting his hunched shoulders, his tense fetal position, the agony of his shame. "There's an experimental treatment," he said slowly. "It's called electroconvulsive therapy. We'd administer several courses of it per day, between three and five, depending on your response. And the courses would go on for a week or two. It's...rather unpleasant."

Bile rose in Grace's throat. "What...that is to say, how..."

Finnegan turned to her. "How does it work? Well, electric currents are introduced to the brain in order to mimic a seizure." Doctor Finnegan went into a lengthy explanation that did nothing to reassure Grace.

"What are the risks, Doc?"

"Who cares, Grace?" Bobby said to the wall. "Anything is better than this. *Anything*."

"Well, Mrs. Feldman." Finnegan looked down at the floor. "I must say the procedure is not easy for the patient. He'll be prone, strapped down, with a padded tongue depressor in his mouth. He'll experience repeated electrical shocks and seizures. But the hope is that the procedure will 'jolt' him—please excuse my choice of verb—back into normal function."

"And the side effects? The risks?" Grace probed, trying to swallow a lump in her throat the size of Bobby's hospital bed.

"Headache. Jaw ache. Nausea. Shakiness. Muscle stiffness. Anxiety, confusion, disorientation and fear. Possible temporary memory loss along with hallucinations. And intense fatigue."

Grace stared at him, horrified.

Bobby displayed no reaction at all. "Do it," he ordered.

"Sweetheart, I think we should discuss this—"

Her husband utterly ignored her. "DO. IT."

Grace, her own body trembling, went to him and touched his

shoulder, whether to reassure him or herself, she didn't know. "But my darling—"

He shrugged off her touch. "I'm as scared as you are, Grace. I am petrified. But I'm even more fearful of the alternative, which is *this*. Living half dead. Half a man. Never knowing when I'm going to check out, just when I'm most desperately needed. Requiring my wife to come and extract me like a decayed tooth from my own goddamned office!"

"That's not how it—"

"It sure as hell is. So. I love you. But this isn't your decision. It's mine."

Grace blinked back sudden tears while the doctor, his expression sympathetic, scribbled something on Robert's chart.

"Just don't leave me," her husband begged. "Don't go. Promise?"

Grace rushed to reassure him. "Of *course* I won't leave you. How could you think I would?"

"Assuming you pass various tests, we have a window this afternoon," Doctor Finnegan said quietly. "Due to a—well, never mind the reason. If you'd care to begin today. Otherwise we'll have to wait until—"

"Yes. Today," Bobby said. "I cannot live like this."

CHAPTER THIRTY-EIGHT

Grace only saw it briefly: an innocuous wooden box containing a black machine that vaguely resembled a radio. A black cord snaked from it, attached to two yoked devices that reminded Grace of old-fashioned telephone mouthpieces. These would be placed on either side of Bobby's head, to deliver the electrical shocks to his brain.

The very idea of it made her knees tremble. She had to clutch the doorframe to ensure she wouldn't faint. The brilliant Robert Feldman, the man whom she secretly knew had cracked the unbreakable Japanese Purple code—about to have his remarkable, genius-level brain electrocuted.

Most terrifying of all was Bobby's complete lack of emotional affect as he was strapped down. He lay like a wax figure, displaying no feelings at all.

Grace's mouth dried of saliva.

"Mrs. Feldman?" Dr. Finnegan said gently. "I'm afraid we'll need you to leave the room for the procedure."

But I promised Bobby I wouldn't leave him alone. She had to stay.

She tried to unstick her tongue from the roof of her mouth but failed. She simply looked at the doctor mutely. Shook her head.

"Mrs. Feldman. I know this is extremely difficult for you. But you cannot stay."

On cue, a nurse took her free hand and pried the fingers of her other hand off the doorjamb. "Come, dear. I'll escort you to the waiting room."

Shameful, shameful, *shameful* that a part of Grace felt relief. She wouldn't have to witness this atrocity. Bobby didn't seem to notice her being ejected, breaking her promise not to leave him. Thank God for that.

She moved on rubbery legs alongside the nurse, unconsciously leaning on her arm. When she realized what she was doing, she jerked her hand away. *You don't lean on anyone, Grace Feldman. Don't you dare start now.*

She was deposited like a human parcel into a chair in a drab room, enlivened only by a wan, discolored silk flower arrangement. The delicate threads of several leaves were coming unraveled, rather like Grace herself.

She wanted to shriek, wail, tear her hair, smash the dusty porcelain vase containing the flowers. *Anxiety, confusion, disorientation and fear. Possible temporary memory loss along with hallucinations...*

What if Bobby didn't recognize her? Remember her? What if he saw her as some demon, come to steal his soul? Worse, how would she ever explain this to the children?

What if something went wrong? What if the side effects were permanent? What if the electric shocks were too great for her husband's system? What if they triggered a real heart attack? *What if... what if... what if...*

She was going mad.

She didn't even see, much less register, that a different nurse now stood in front of her.

"Ma'am? Mrs. Feldman? Ma'am?"

The woman and her white uniform swam into focus. "Yes? Excuse me. I was... distracted."

"You have an urgent telephone call."

Grace blinked at her. "That's impossible."

"No, ma'am. It was routed from the switchboard at the Navy Annex to the switchboard here. If you'll come with me..."

Who would disturb her at the hospital when her husband was ostensibly having a heart attack?

Grace followed the woman into an office and accepted the proffered telephone receiver. "Grace Feldman."

"Grace! Thank God..." It was Utsidi. "You have to come to the office right away."

"Utsidi, I can't—"

"You *must*. It's Joe at Station HYPO in Hawaii—you've got to call him on a secure line. *Now*."

"But—" Grace recalled Bobby's ramblings from the hospital bed. Another attack. Oh, dear God. "I'm on my way."

She turned to the nurse. "I would never ask this under ordinary circumstances. But this is a matter of national security. Do you have an ambulance on hand that can rush me to the Navy Annex on Nebraska Avenue?"

The woman opened and closed her mouth like a guppy.

Grace dug into her pocketbook and flashed her old special agent badge. "It's no joke. Please."

Within three minutes, she was careening through the streets of Washington in the emergency vehicle, sirens blaring. The driver rushed her right to the door of the Navy Annex, Grace thanked him profusely and she ran inside to a secure telephone.

"Operator, connect me to Joe Rochefort at HYPO, please. It's urgent. I'm returning his call."

Joe didn't waste time on greetings. "Grace. Couldn't reach Robert. This is emergency priority. Ongoing debate regarding a Japanese attack on AF."

"AF?"

"Just listen, Grace. AF is Midway. We all finally agree on that. What's been in question is the date of the attack. I don't have time to explain, but you've got to find Redman and King in person and tell them it's not mid-June. It's the *third* of June. Only three days from now. I have confirmation."

"As in *Commander* Redman? As in *Admiral-of-the-entire-Navy* King?"

"Yes. Grace, this is no joke. Nimitz can't act without their authorization."

"B-but Joe, why can't you call them directly? They won't listen to some civilian Coast Guard cryptanalyst!"

"Redman won't take my call. The top brass are locked in some meeting. Layton is locked up with Nimitz and I can't get through to them, either. Grace, we have less than seventy-two hours to prepare. Battleships and destroyers don't turn on a dime. The *Yorktown* is badly damaged and Nimitz will need her, too. *Stop asking questions and GO.*" Rochefort cut the line.

Shaking, Grace slammed down the receiver and erupted from the room. She sprinted for Admiral King's office and almost knocked down his secretary. "I have to see him. It's an emergency."

"Ma'am, he's in a high-level meeting with Commander Redman and others. I'm unable to interrupt."

"And I'm telling you that this is a matter of national security! Get me in there."

"Your name, ma'am?"

"We don't have time for my name—" Grace rushed past the shocked secretary, grasped the knob and tried to fling open the door to the admiral's office. It was locked.

"You are utterly out of line, Madam!" uttered the secretary. "And they're not in there."

Think, Grace, think.

Alice. Alice had an office in this place somewhere. Alice could help. She was a legend in the Navy. She'd helped *train* Joe Rochefort—*and* Nimitz's top intel officer, Edwin Layton.

"Where's Miss Martenz's office?"

"I'm not at lib—"

"Damn it! This is an emergency, I tell you." Grace grabbed her phone and dialed the operator, ignoring her squawks. "Operator. Connect me to Alice Martenz, please. Hurry."

"Hello?" Her voice was still sultry after all these years. Even after having both jaws broken.

"Alice. Grace Feldman. URGENT. Where is your office, or better yet, meet me outside Admiral King's. It's a flat-out emergency. I need your help."

"All right." Alice cut the connection.

Within moments, she appeared outside the office.

Grace sucked in a breath, shocked at her appearance even a couple of years after the accident. The once-beautiful Alice limped with a cane, and the lower half of her face—both jaws—were severely distorted.

"Don't say a word," Alice hissed, squinting at her, "except for why you're here."

Grace nodded. "Privacy first."

Alice led her into a small conference room and shut the door. "Talk."

Grace explained.

"Good God."

"Do you know where they're meeting? Redman and King and the others?"

"I have a very good suspicion. Large secure conference room, one floor down."

"Can we get in?"

Alice shrugged. "All we can do is try. There really isn't any time to waste. Rochefort's eccentric, but he's brilliant."

She led the way, Grace pushing away the long-ago memories of the sensual woman in a silver gown, undulating like a cobra in a basket on New Year's Eve.

As expected, the conference room doors were closed. And locked.

Grace didn't overthink it. She just rapped smartly on the door.

This was ignored.

"Stand back," Alice ordered. Grace could tell she despised having to do so, but Alice leaned heavily on Grace's shoulder, drew back her cane and walloped the door with it, again and again.

A naval officer threw it open and snarled, "What is the meaning of this?"

"An emergency." Alice poked him in the chest with her cane and drove him backward while Grace supported her.

The long, polished oak conference table was surrounded by uniformed officers: frowning, outright scowling, blustering and, in general, furious.

"We need the room, gentlemen. Alone with Admiral King and Commander Redman," Grace said politely. Too late, she identified her own boss, Commander Jones.

King surged to his feet so fast that he almost tossed all the salad on his uniform. "How dare you? Who the hell are you?"

"Admiral, Commander, this is Mrs. Robert Feldman, cryptanalyst, US Coast Guard," Alice and Jones said simultaneously.

"We have an extremely urgent message from Station HYPO in Hawaii."

"Why isn't HYPO communicating with us directly?" Admiral King snapped.

"I don't know, sir." Grace avoided looking at Redman.

"Clear the room. At once!" King gestured toward the doors, and a mass exodus followed.

Grace explained what Rochefort had told her, and why—because her husband was indisposed, Joe had entrusted the message to her—while Redman's expression and complexion turned to brick.

"I am very sorry to intrude upon your meeting," she finished. "If there had been any other way to reach you, I would have employed it."

Admiral King drilled her with his gaze, then turned it upon Alice. "You vouch for this woman?"

"Without reservation," she said calmly. "It's not for just anyone that I weaponize my cane."

The admiral's lips gave a barely perceptible twitch. "Fine. My best wishes for the speedy recovery of your husband, Mrs. Feldman."

"Thank you."

"All right. That will be all. Dismissed, ladies."

Once they were on the other side of the door, Grace touched Alice's shoulder. "Thank you."

Alice eyed her fingers as though they were a tarantula. "I thought I told you to go to hell. And you said you were getting underway, if I recall?"

Grace's mouth quirked. "Yes, well. It seems to be a long journey. Care to join me? I'd be glad of some company."

While top secret preparations—ones that Grace wasn't privy to—presumably unfolded in the Pacific thanks to Joe Rochefort's tireless codebreaking and relentless character, Grace was worried sick about Robert at George Washington University Hospital. How many times had they electrocuted him? How was he reacting? How terrified was he? Was he asking for her, devastated when she didn't come to his side?

Grace took a taxi, not an ambulance, back to the hospital. She made her way to Robert's room and peeked in. He was fast asleep, but not peacefully. He twitched and writhed. His brow was damp with sweat, his eyes jittered under his closed lids, his complexion was greenish gray.

Her hands and knees trembling, Grace went in and sat next to him on the bed with its sterile white sheets and blanket. She twined her fingers with his, but he didn't seem to notice she was there. She bent forward, smoothed his hair then kissed him on the lips. "I love you beyond reason, my darling. My brilliant, brave soldier."

It was one thing to combat an enemy through cryptanalysis. It was yet another to fight fascist soldiers, as Robert had, in person. But the most monstrous, blood-chilling, debilitating war possible was to face the enemy in one's own brain. A hostile force dealing blow after blow to one's equanimity, one's reason, one's self-possession, one's self-esteem. To one's very soul.

Robert had been battling darkness and depression and denial all alone, unprepared, undrilled, unarmed. There were no fellow soldiers standing shoulder to shoulder with him. There were no foxholes or trenches in which to take cover. There was no helmet to protect his head during this war. He was exposed, vulnerable, without even a map to guide him.

There wasn't a word in the English language that could express how much Grace ached for him, or how helpless she felt in the face of this nebulous enemy.

She didn't know how much time had passed when Dr. Finnegan found her, cheek against Bobby's chest, rising and falling with every troubled breath he took.

"Mrs. Feldman."

She raised her head. "How...how is he? How did he respond? How many times...?"

"He's doing fine," the doctor said.

Don't patronize me. "He's clearly not fine," Grace said evenly, "or he wouldn't be here."

"He's responding well to the treatment. We administered it five times."

"And the side effects?"

The doctor sighed. "He tried to lash out. When we removed the tongue depressor, he began to shout. He was hallucinating. Thought we were SS officers sent by the Huns. We were forced to give him a sedative afterward. Odd, since usually patients are exhausted."

Grace compressed her lips. "How many more times must you do this to him?"

"As I mentioned before, it will take several courses over several days."

She opened her mouth to ask another question, but a nurse came bustling in.

"Mrs. Feldman? You have another urgent call from the Navy Annex."

For the love of God, cannot anyone leave me in peace? Cannot anyone have a shred of empathy that my husband is gravely ill? No of course not. There's a war on.

"Thank you, Doctor," Grace said dully. And followed the nurse out of the room.

It was Fay. "Grace, I'm sorry. But—there's action in the Pacific. You're needed here. We all are. We may be sleeping at the Annex for a couple of days."

CHAPTER THIRTY-NINE

Japanese Admiral Yamamoto wanted payback after all sixteen B-25 Mitchell bombers launched from the USS *Hornet* caused fifty casualties and the loss of a hundred or so homes. He was determined to show the US just who was boss by commandeering Midway and utterly destroying American forces in the central Pacific. But he was unaware that cryptanalysts like Joe Rochefort, Edwin Layton, Alice Martenz, Grace's team and—on better days—Robert Feldman with his team were reading every communication of the Japanese that they could get their hands on.

A combination of Army, Navy and Marine aircraft arrived at Midway to ambush the would-be ambushers, while the carriers *Hornet* and *Enterprise* joined the *Yorktown* (heavily damaged at the Battle of the Coral Sea, but somehow patched up in time) to back them up.

Grace, Veronica, Utsidi and Fay wore their pencils down to stubs, going through several every couple of hours. At one point, Grace found herself smoking two cigarettes at the same time, and she accidentally doused the one in the right corner of her mouth with a gulp of coffee.

She wasn't the only one. The codebreakers' quarters were so full of toxic tension and smoke that it smelled as if it were on fire, which it was—with urgency, with fear, with dread. They couldn't possibly be losing the Battle of Midway...could they?

But the Japanese continued to bomb and strafe the island's airstrips and any buildings or infrastructures in sight.

Nimitz sent out a swarm of Douglas TBD Devastator torpedo planes next, flying low and slow. Every single one got annihilated—either by antiaircraft guns or Zeros.

Grace found herself chewing an unlit cigarette and mumbling prayers, as tears streamed down Fay's face and Utsidi dropped her face into her hands. Veronica silently rocked back and forth.

Then came pilot Dickie Best and his boys in their Dauntless dive bombers. Bomb after bomb after bomb targeted—and miraculously, *found*—the decks of three Japanese imperial carriers, blowing them and the refueled enemy aircraft sitting aboard to hell. They burst into flames.

There was one last remaining Japanese carrier...and somehow Dickie and his boys sank it, too—though the US was unable to save the *Yorktown*. That grand old girl, likely patched with Popsicle sticks and chewing gum, gave up the ghost after being hit broadside with a couple of enemy torpedoes.

Yamamoto retreated, stunned that he'd walked into such a trap, devastated at the loss of hundreds of his best pilots and planes. The last coded intercept that Grace and her unit decrypted was his grave communication to Prime Minister Tojo Hideki: that Midway had been a resounding defeat for the Imperial Japanese Navy.

A hoarse cheer went up all over their offices, which rose to a crescendo as the cryptanalysts screamed with joy and jumped on top of their desks. Somehow, champagne materialized through the fog of smoke and exhilaration. Corks popped, bubbly filled dirty coffee cups and got slugged back, song broke out—and more cheers. "To Midway! To Joe Rochefort! To Ed Layton! To Nimitz! To Dickie Best!"

It was seventy-two hours before Grace was allowed to leave the Navy Annex, exhausted but overjoyed after monitoring the triumph at Midway. She couldn't wait for the news to break; for Bobby's face to light up. It was the battle that redeemed the codebreaking community after the debacle of Pearl Harbor.

She arrived back at George Washington University Hospital, walking on legs that carried her like strands of cooked spaghetti. She'd finally had a shower after going without for two days and sleeping in snatches on a couch in her office. She had two Crayola-colored get-well cards from the children and a big slice of pineapple upside-down cake tucked into her pocketbook. She hummed with impatience to see Robert, prayed that he was sleeping now without drugs, that he had some color back in his face ... and that he wasn't hallucinating, or worse.

She pulled up short outside of his room when she heard the strains of a Russian lullaby, sung in a voice quavering with age and emotion. *No ... it can't be.*

Robert's mother, clad all in black, sat like a vulture by his bedside, crooning to her firstborn. He smiled at her as she stroked his cheek and patted his forehead with a cool, damp cloth. "There, there, my boy. Mamoshka's here for you, even if your selfish wife can't be bothered, hmm?"

Grace quivered with outrage. "Mrs. Feldman," she managed to say. "What a...lovely...surprise. So kind of you to visit."

Robert's mother barely restrained herself from spitting at her. "You leave him alone in this place? During this ordeal? This barbaric course of treatment? Because you have, what, *better things to do?!?*"

Grace swayed on her feet. *You know nothing.*

Worse than her mother-in-law's words, though, was Bobby's expression when he turned to look at Grace: blank, hard, unforgiving. No tender, loving, musical smile. And even more unbearable: he turned his face away from her and gazed out the window, instead. Not even a hello.

Grace felt it like a blow and almost staggered. "I was here, my love. But I got called away. To work."

"'To work,' she says. To *work*." Robert's mother repeated the word like a curse. "What more honorable job is there for woman than care of husband and children? But you—you have *housekeeper* for that. Because you're not content with blessings God showers upon you. You seek glory by doing *man's* job in world where you do not belong. You mortify my son—you mock what he provides for you and your children. Not enough for Your Highness. Shame on you! *Shame*."

"Mama," Robert finally said, in a rusty voice not his own, "enough."

But the elder Mrs. Feldman wasn't done. "The nurses, they tell me he ask for you, but could they reach you? No. So they call me. His mother."

Deep breath. You will never be able to explain, Grace. "I'm glad you were able to be here for Robert. I'm sure you've been of great comfort to him. Now, would it be possible for the two of us to have some privacy?"

Her mother-in-law laughed. "He want no privacy with you. He not want even to see you. You leave him in his most terrible time of need. Now get out."

Grace felt the blood draining from her face and corresponding lightheadedness. She wobbled on her already fatigue-weak and trembling knees. "That's not true."

She waited for corroboration of those last words from her husband. Waited for him to turn his head and stretch out his hand toward hers. It didn't come. He kept his face turned toward the wall.

"Bobby?" she whispered. "My darling?"

"Take yourself off, shiksa," Mrs. Feldman spat. "I beg him to unmarry you. I warn him. But only now has my boy seen the light."

Grace stood there for a last moment, swaying again on her feet. Willing Robert to realize her absence could only have been due to a desperate emergency. For him to say something, anything, in her defense. But he didn't.

And she couldn't speak of Midway or the South American spy ring, not even to him—and certainly not in front of his mother. Grace had to pretend that, like everyone else, she'd heard it on the radio or read it in the newspapers.

For the first time in her life, Grace spun and ran. Ran away from her disbelief, her shock, her hurt, and her sudden fear that due to circumstances beyond her control, her marriage was over.

She ran back to the only place where she felt safe, valued, integral: to work. She picked up a stack of decrypts to work on, began a worksheet to decipher them. But the letters swam in front of her eyes, distorted, blurry and senseless. Numb, Grace put her head down on her desk.

It was Utsidi who noticed first, followed by Fay, who called for Veronica. They helped Grace to her feet and walked her into her private office, depositing her on the couch. They slipped off her shoes and put a blanket around her shoulders.

"Tea? Will one of you make tea?" Fay asked. "Let me talk to her."

Once the door had closed behind them, Grace said dully, "Robert's in the hospital."

Fay took her hand. "I know, dear. His heart."

"It's not his heart. I had to leave him—and he was all alone—during electroconvulsive therapy."

Fay sucked in a shocked breath.

Grace looked at her. "What would you choose in such a situation? Your husband or your country?"

"Oh, dear Lord, Grace. That's an impossible question. An impossible choice."

"And yet it's a choice I had to make. I swore an oath to him when I married him. But I swore an oath to the United States, too, Fay."

Her friend squeezed her hand.

"I didn't mean to leave him for so long," Grace said simply.

"He must know that, surely?"

Grace shrugged. "His mother is there by his bedside, now. Poisoning him against me."

"Robert loves you," Fay said.

"He feels I betrayed and abandoned him."

"So explain to him."

"I can't. You know that." Grace clutched the blanket around her shoulders and bowed her head.

"You're a cryptologist, Grace. Perhaps you can't spell it out in plaintext—but surely you can speak to him in code?"

Grace's head came up, and she let go of the blanket so that she could lean forward and hug Fay. "Yes. I can. You brilliant girl. Thank you."

"Why don't you sleep for a couple of hours, Grace? It will do you good."

"I don't think..." But by the time the words were out of her mouth, she'd lost consciousness.

Grace pulled herself together, went to see Robert at the hospital the next day and offered the elder Mrs. Feldman the guest room, though getting the words out of her mouth felt as if she were hoisting the massive rusty anchor of *Hogan's Goat* up her throat, then tossing it to the tiles at the old crone's feet.

"I sleep here," her mother-in-law said. "In chair."

"Yes," Grace said. "I see that. But it must be quite uncomfortable. And you must wish to bathe, Mrs. Feldman? Change your clothes?"

But the woman simply pointed to a small bag in the corner. "Everything I need is there. And there." She pointed at her son.

Grace looked over at Robert.

He still refused to meet her gaze. Dark circles pooled under his eyes, he retained a greenish pallor, and he seemed to have lost several pounds in only three days.

"Would you care to go and get yourself some breakfast, Mrs. Feldman?" Grace asked.

"Nyet. No. You try to get rid of me."

Can you blame me? You're always such a ray of sunshine.

Unable to dislodge her, Grace kept Fay's advice in mind and produced a copy of the *Washington Post* from under her arm. News of the Battle of Midway screamed from the headlines. She sidestepped the old crow and laid it on Robert's chest. "My darling. Listen to me. *I had to go get a cup of Joe.*"

His brow furrowed. He picked it up and scanned it.

"Do you understand, Bobby?" *Joe. As in Rochefort. Do you remember your indiscretion with me? Please remember . . . don't ever, ever do it again. But please remember.*

Her husband's face lightened. His eyes, so dull when she'd come in, brightened. And when he looked up from the article, he met her gaze with the ghost of a smile on his lips.

"They pulled victory out of the jaws of defeat, Bobby. Can you believe it?"

"This is marvelous," he said, his voice still sounding rusty. "Simply marvelous."

"What?" demanded his mother.

He showed her the paper, while Grace excused herself to go and speak to Dr. Finnegan.

She found him coming down the hallway toward Robert's room.

"Why, Mrs. Feldman!" he said, eyeing her disapprovingly. "We haven't seen you in a few days." His unspoken words hung in the air between them: *bad wife.*

"I—I had an emergency with one of my children," Grace told him. *My how the lies roll so easily off my tongue these days.* "I was dreadfully afraid it was polio." *Another whopper.*

But how else to explain her absence from her husband's bedside? A "normal" wife wouldn't have abandoned him. Her mother-in-law's words echoed in her ears, though she tried to shoo them away.

"Oh dear." Finnegan displayed instant empathy, for which she felt guilty. "I do hope your...?"

"Son," she supplied.

"...has quite recovered."

"Yes, thank you so much. It was a dreadful scare, though." *Not a total lie. I have been afraid. Of so many, many things.*

With a start, Grace realized the doctor's lips were moving, and she hadn't heard a word.

"...so although your husband is responding well to the treatments, his memory is indeed impaired, and he's often disoriented. No hallucinations today. No violence. He's been gentle as a lamb since his mother arrived."

Wonderful. "How many more courses of treatment will he need, Doctor?"

"If all continues to go well, we should be able to release him at the end of next week. He'll be much more himself after a few days. He'll need lots of quiet and rest, mind you—otherwise he runs the risk of a relapse."

Quiet and rest. The opposite of Robert's daily—and nightly—routine. Grace swallowed. "And what, exactly, are the chances of a relapse?"

Dr. Finnegan sighed. "Every patient is different, Mrs. Feldman. If he takes care of himself, then his prognosis is quite good..."

But it's my job to take care of him. And I've been lousy at it. Perhaps I'm one of the best codebreakers in the US, but I'm one of the worst wives—possibly the worst.

"However, if he returns to a high-stress, exhausting environment, then I cannot guarantee..."

Doctor, there's a war on. A war against my husband's heritage, his ancestry, his religion, his people. Do you really think he's going to lie by some poolside in Palm Springs while Hitler merrily pursues his Final Solution?

"I see," said Grace. "Well, then. Everything should be perfectly fine." She produced a smile from God only knew where—possibly it had been stuck to the bottom of her shoe, like a wad of discarded chewing gum. She stretched it into place on her lips, while Finnegan looked at her quite strangely, as if he'd witnessed the whole imaginary process.

"Everything will be *fine*," she repeated. "Thank you for the update."

They were able to bring Robert home the next Saturday. He was in good spirits, thanking Dr. Finnegan with a hearty handshake, thanking and kissing the nurses on the cheek like a kindly uncle. "I feel like a new man," he declared, tossing his hat in the air and catching it again.

If only he were as warm to Grace.

He was unfailingly polite to her—but not loving. He caressed his mother's wrinkled old cheek, but not his wife's. He insisted on driving home, to Grace's distress, because of course a man couldn't be seen being driven by a woman.

Please God he doesn't have some sort of seizure on the way home. But she said nothing, though tense and ready to wrench the wheel out of his grasp if need be, because more than quiet or rest or vitamins, Robert needed his pride back.

The children were ecstatic to see him and wanted to climb him like a jungle gym. Grace had to remind Isobel and Christopher that Daddy had been ill. Meanwhile, her mother-in-law and Mrs. Woolsey, the housekeeper, faced off and barely refrained from spitting at each other.

Funny that Grace thought of Mrs. W as an angel, while Robert's mother clearly thought she was, if not the devil, his close subordinate—so that lazy Grace herself could hobnob with other men in an office and get up to no good.

Dinner was strained, with Mrs. Feldman poorly disguising her distaste for Mrs. Woolsey's carefully prepared dishes, and the two almost came to blows when Robert's mother invaded the kitchen to inspect the larder and icebox.

But even more strained was the atmosphere between Grace and Robert when they went upstairs to bed. He changed into pajamas in the bathroom with the door closed. She quickly disrobed and put on her nightgown while he brushed his teeth.

And presently, they found themselves lying side by side in silence, without touching, as though a wall stretched down the center of their bed.

"Bobby," she whispered. "I love you."

"You left," he said simply. "I came back from being electrocuted, Grace. It was unspeakable. I told myself I could bear it as long as the first thing I saw afterward was your beautiful face. But you weren't there. Nor for the next treatment. Nor the next."

Tears welled in Grace's eyes and spilled down her cheeks. "Bobby, I had no choice. I was called to the Navy Annex—"

"You *promised* me, Grace. *Promised*."

It unnerved her that there was no anger in his voice, only betrayal. Sadness. Disappointment. Once again, she'd been a disappointment as a wife. When he had needed her the most.

Bobby turned away from her and twitched the blankets up over his shoulders.

The tears spilled over and ran down Grace's cheeks. She stretched out a hand to touch him, reach him somehow, bridge the yawning, terrible gap between them.

There'd been a time that he would have sensed the movement, sensed her intent. There'd been a time when they never slept turned away from each other...only turned inward, or in each other's arms.

She ached at the memories, at the loss, at the lack of their old teamwork, which had somehow led to compartmentalization of their lives...and now this utter breakdown in understanding and communication between them.

Grace let her hand drop and rolled over to stare blindly at the opposite wall. It seemed eons before she fell into an unhappy, restless, wounded sleep.

CHAPTER FORTY

Grace was awake, staring in misery at Robert's broad back, when the telephone jangled from the study downstairs. An icy sliver of moon sliced through the bedroom curtains to illuminate the clock: it was 3:15 a.m. It could only be bad news or an emergency summons for her husband, who was in no condition to go into the office.

Grace flew out of bed and took the stairs at breakneck speed, trying to silence the ringing before it woke the entire household. "Hello?" She kept her voice low as she spoke into the receiver.

"Grace?"

"Utsidi—what's wrong?"

"I'm very sorry, but you're needed here at the Navy Annex."

"You realize what time it is?"

"Yes. Please come at once. It's urgent."

Grace hung up and sprinted back up the stairs, stealthily retrieving some clothes and shoes. Robert didn't move a muscle—she suspected he'd taken a Seconal before bed. She shimmied into her underthings, quickly fastened her stockings to the accursed girdle, dropped a slip over her head and then finally put on her dress. Holding her shoes, she crept back down only to behold her mother-in-law, hands on her ample hips, awaiting her at the door.

"Oh! Good morning, Mrs. Feldman." Grace slipped on her shoes as if it were perfectly normal to leave the house at 3:30 a.m. She tied a scarf over her hair and snatched her gloves and pocketbook off the hall table.

"Where you go?" asked the old lady. "You meet lover?"

Grace almost laughed. "Mrs. Feldman, I'm so far beyond tired that I wouldn't have the energy to run off with Cary Grant himself. There's an emergency at the office."

"Emergency," Mrs. F scoffed. "Someone need coffee?"

"That's exactly it." Grace nodded and produced a vapid smile. "Now, I'm terribly sorry, but I must go. I do hope you're able to go back to sleep."

Her mother-in-law was blocking the front door. She didn't move one inch.

"Mrs. Feldman." Grace set her jaw and pulled on her gloves. "Please step aside."

Her mother-in-law folded her arms over her chest and simply glared at her.

Grace felt her blood pressure rising. "Look, I don't have time for this."

No reaction.

Grace had two choices: she could either physically drag the woman out of the way, or she could traipse through the house to the back door and walk all the way around, losing more time.

"Fine," she said, settling on a third option. She walked to one of the large windows on either side of the front parlor that provided a cross-breeze during the summer. She threw up the sash, unlocked it, raised the glass and knocked out the screen. Then, as gracefully as possible, she climbed out, dragging her pocketbook and coat behind her. She ran for the car, leaving Robert's mother gaping behind her.

When Grace got to the Navy Annex, Utsidi, Fay and Veronica were all there, looking bleary-eyed but also frantic.

"It's South America," Utsidi said, her face pale.

"Argentina." Veronica had chewed off almost all of her red lipstick; only smears and blotches remained.

"SARGO and LUNA?" Grace asked.

"Yes, but worse." Fay had twisted up her mass of red curls and speared it through with two pencils to secure it. "They're messaging about a major arms deal between Argentina and Berlin—already underway."

"What kind of arms deal?"

"We're still trying to figure that out. But the 'shadow army' seems now in danger of becoming a real army, and one that fully supports the Nazis. If they were to make their way up from Argentina, through Paraguay and up to northern Brazil, get to a sympathetic pocket of Mexico…"

Utsidi closed her eyes.

Veronica caught her lower lip in her teeth, eviscerating more lipstick. "Mexico has sided with the Allies. But there is still much anger at the United States, bad feelings from the past. Es possible that someone, how you say, look the other way."

"What's the range for the average bomber?" Grace asked.

Fay thought for a moment. "Around seventeen hundred miles, I think."

"How far is it from the middle of Mexico…to, say, Miami?"

Veronica consulted their map of Latin America on the wall. "Less than seven hundred miles by flight."

"They could also go by land or sea, of course," Utsidi said.

Grace ditched her coat and gloves. "If the Nazis succeed in their plan to take over not only Argentina, but Chile, Brazil, Bolivia and Paraguay, they have the potential to build an *enormous* military force that would control almost the entire continent. Just because Hoover rounded up a few spies in Brazil doesn't mean there aren't thousands of others willing to take their places."

Thirty-six more messages had piled up, which meant that they had a long night—and day—ahead of them. Grace rolled up her sleeves with the rest of them, reverse engineering the Enigma-generated codes in the interceptions.

They drank coffee, they drank tea, they smoked small mountains of cigarettes. They paced back and forth or went to the ladies' room to splash cold water on their faces when they were in danger of falling forward face down onto their desks.

Grace stared at clumps of letters until her eyes crossed, finally settling on the words *der Abgesandte*. Envoy or emissary. "They're sending an emissary from Buenos Aires to Berlin in two days' time."

"The ship is *Cabo de Hornos*," Veronica said. "It will dock in Trinidad before continuing across the Atlantic."

"Trinidad," repeated Grace, thoughtfully.

"A British port," Fay pointed out.

Utsidi nodded. "Allied. Friendly."

Other members of the unit began to show up for work—it was almost 8:00 a.m.—registering surprise when they saw Grace and her gals already there.

"Are you thinking what I'm thinking?" Grace asked them.

Fay grinned, a bit ferociously. "Well, this emissary will surely know who SARGO and LUNA are."

Though Grace had a pretty good idea who they were herself, she needed confirmation.

Veronica picked up a nail file and brandished it like a weapon. "And if the British pick him up, they can...how you say...interrogar—interrogate him."

"While we Americans can claim we had nothing to do with it." Utsidi smiled.

Grace met her gaze. "Hoover and the FBI are not—and cannot—be involved. Commander Jones agreed. The fact that we're able to decrypt the new German Enigma codes *must* remain a secret."

Excitement hummed between them until Fay's face fell. "There's only one problem, ladies. Mr. Envoy from Buenos Aires will have diplomatic immunity."

Grace extracted another cigarette from the current community pack and lit it, drawing in a lungful of blessed nicotine. It was a food group these days. She exhaled thoughtfully. "I think I know a couple of gentlemen who can get around that issue—but we'll need to brief Commander Jones."

Jones was gobsmacked. "Argentina's professed to be a US ally!"

"But is it really? According to SARGO and LUNA, Argentina and

Berlin are working together to negotiate a major arms deal," Grace reiterated. "And they consider the USA their greatest mutual enemy. They're sending an emissary, Herr Osmar Hellmuth, from Buenos Aires to Berlin to finalize the details. His ship, the *Cabo de Hornos*, will dock in Trinidad en route. If I may say so, this man is our only hope of disrupting this South American plot *without* Berlin knowing that we've yet again cracked their codes."

Commander Jones clasped his hands on top of his desk. "Agreed. We'll need to work closely on this with the British, since Trinidad is their territory." He eyed them all. "I'll need a copy of every decrypt you have regarding these matters."

"Of course." Grace handed over several fat file folders. "More come in each hour."

"Get them to me as soon as you solve them."

"Commander? I'd like to ensure that the US doesn't get shut out of the operation. What would you say to bringing in Donovan and the OSS?"

Lieutenant (JG) Wimberly Cox was positively delighted to be of service, as was Wild Bill Donovan. "Wish I could go myself," he said to Grace regretfully. He looked at Cox. "Let's pull Chubby Stratton into this one. He can get word to the boys at Trinidad."

"Who is Chubby Stratton?" Grace asked.

"British counterintelligence. Astronomer by training. Brilliant."

Cox scrubbed a hand over his auburn head. "Chubby's a must for strategy and communications with the Brits. But I don't suppose I could go myself to Trinidad to join the fun? Hitch a flight heading that way?"

Donovan drummed his fingers on his desk. "I'm not your babysitter, Lieutenant. I don't need to keep tabs on exactly where you are. But if anything goes awry—"

"Understood, Colonel. You'll disavow all knowledge of the situation."

"One last thing." Donovan side-eyed Grace. "Cover your ears, little lady."

She cast her eyes heavenwards instead, which didn't stop Donovan.

"Cox, I know the flight is over six hours from Miami. But you will arrive *sober*. You will *not* knock up any local girls. And while I couldn't care less if this Nazi envoy pisses himself or cries for his mama, you will not actually harm him. Got it?"

The lieutenant saluted. "Yes sir."

"At ease."

"Spoilsport," Cox murmured.

"What did you say?" Donovan bellowed.

Cox bit back a smile. "Nothing, sir. Nothing at all."

"Get the hell out of my office—oh, sorry, Mrs. Feldman—didn't mean you."

But Grace chuckled. "You probably did, Colonel. That's all right." She headed for the door. "Keep me in the loop, sir, would you?"

Herr Osmar Hellmuth had a very unpleasant voyage. Courtesy of Grace's unit, Chubby Stratton and Kangaroo Cox, who was indeed there to supervise, Hellmuth was yanked off his ship in the middle of the night when it docked in the British colony of Trinidad.

He stood on the dock in his pajamas, dressing gown and slippers, hair askew, waving his identity papers. He squawked loudly about his diplomatic privilege. He demanded a phone call to his embassy.

Cox regaled the unit with the tale upon his return. "So I say to the lousy so-and-so, I say, 'Oy, mate! Shall I use those papers of yours to light the barbecue or shall I use them to wipe my arse?' *Whah, whah, wha...* The ruddy earbash natters on and on, switching from German to Spanish and back again—until one of the Brits roars at him to shut his yap.

"And I say, 'We'll be the ones posing the questions. So you're an arms dealer, are you?' 'Oh no,' says he, he's got no idea what we mean. And then repeats over and over, 'Diplomatische Immunität! Immunidad diplomática!' At which point—I'll have you know that *I* was joking when I threatened it—but at which point, one of the Brits nicks Herr

Hellmuth's papers, pulls down his trousers and *literally* wipes his arse with them." Cox chortled.

Grace winced. Veronica burst out laughing.

"I then call out Herr Helmuth as the despicable spy he is, and we escort him—luggage, pajamas and all—to a nearby British vessel. Once he starts to realize just the kind of danger he's in, he sings like a star soprano. Yes, he's meeting a couple of chaps in Berlin. Yes, he's authorized to negotiate a bit. No, it wasn't just a few caches of rifles he was after...it was ammo, 88 mm cannons, bombers—even Panzer tanks.

"We still don't have an ID on LUNA, but SARGO, madam, is the code name for one SS Hauptsturmführer Wolfgang Roth. Interesting background, by the by."

Cox walked over to her desk and slapped down a copy of a passport photo.

Grace's hunch was correct. She was once again gazing at a picture of Otto Schroeder.

"Looks as though he survived Spanish Marie," Cox said ruefully.

CHAPTER FORTY-ONE

The story of the Hellmuth affair hit the newspapers on November 4, 1943, with the British getting credit for busting up the spy ring and the plot. Grace celebrated quietly with her unit—keeping secret their triumph over the German Enigma was worth all the champagne in France to her.

The US sent warships to mass in the estuary between Argentina and Allied-friendly Uruguay, while both the Americans and the British dispatched diplomats to Buenos Aires to confront President Pedro Pablo Ramírez and the Argentine government about being in bed with German spies.

Realizing at this point that the war wasn't going well for the Axis powers, the Argentines collapsed under the pressure. To Berlin's shock, Argentina abruptly severed all relations with Germany and Japan, even as the Nazis kept urgently radioing their spies trying to find answers.

Grace and her gals were no saints—they took pleasure in monitoring the increasing agitation of Berlin that their backup plan in South America was misfiring.

But, while they didn't give a fig about claiming credit, J. Edgar Hoover was furious that he'd been blindsided by the entire situation. Not being "read in" by the British was insult enough, but being excluded by the Army, Navy/Coast Guard, State and especially his nemesis, the OSS, enraged him. Hoover demanded an explanation. It was only a matter of time before her own telephone rang. He wanted someone's head.

The only head Grace wanted was Otto Schroeder/Wolfgang Roth's. Though if she were honest with herself, perhaps she wanted her mother-in-law's, as well. She stayed. And stayed. And stayed.

And while Grace doggedly kept tabs on Schroeder/Roth during her every moment at the office, the elder Mrs. Feldman dripped poison into her son's ears.

Grace had no proof of it, of course. But she could sense the tension in the atmosphere as soon as she walked through the door, see how much Robert enjoyed his mother's cooking and feel the growing chill between the two of them.

Robert was still not himself. His hands trembled, he wandered the house at night muttering, he seemed lost. So under the circumstances, she could hardly ask his mother to leave—besides which, to do so would be utterly disrespectful.

Christopher and Isobel adored their grandmother since she spoiled them shamelessly. They ran to greet Grace at the door, of course, but she began to feel superfluous in her own home—and helpless to do anything about it. She tried to talk to her husband, but he brushed her off, saying there was nothing to talk about. They were at an impasse.

Grace didn't need excuses to stay longer at the office. Schroeder/ Roth was up to something...on his own. The Argentine government had obligingly rounded up all the other German spies, but Roth and the still-unidentified LUNA had somehow escaped.

Coast Guard listening posts picked up illicit transmissions from northern Brazil to Venezuela, from Venezuela to Nicaragua, and then from Nicaragua to Nassau. SARGO and LUNA were on the move... and every step of their journey brought them closer to the southern tip of the United States. But what was their objective?

It certainly wasn't friendly. They weren't coming to vacation in the sun and drink mai tais on Miami Beach. SARGO was not only a spy, but also a smuggler and a saboteur.

It was Utsidi who decrypted the name of a British ship shortly to depart Nassau: the HMS *Bahamas*. It was Fay who cracked the word *everglades* and Veronica who then guessed *port*.

Slowly, the team put together the pieces of the puzzle...and Grace's telephone rang ominously. "Don't answer that," she said.

"What if it's important?" Fay asked, quite reasonably.

Grace massaged her temples. "It will ring again."

They turned back to the messages.

"They're boarding a ship that's docking at Port Everglades. But why? Where are they intending to go from there—and to do what?" Grace and the unit racked their brains.

Her telephone rang again. "Will someone take a message for me?" she pleaded.

Utsidi answered. "Oh, hello, Mrs. Gandy." She listened for a moment, glancing at Grace. "My deepest apologies, but Mrs. Feldman is not available. Yes, I understand. I'll have her return Mr. Hoover's call at her earliest possible convenience."

They returned to work, and Grace did not return Hoover's call.

Two hours later, the cursed telephone rang again. This time, Veronica answered on Grace's behalf. "Sí, Mrs. Gandy. Cómo está? Mrs.

Feldman? Sí, she has just now returned." Veronica covered the receiver with her hand. "He knows somehow that you are here."

Grace eyed her telephone as if it were a viper and massaged her temples again, while entirely inappropriate laughter rose within her. It was probably hysteria, but she didn't have time to analyze it. How much could one woman take?

She straightened her spine, took a deep breath and reminded herself that she would *not* be intimidated.

She picked up the receiver. "Good afternoon, Mr. Hoover. How kind of you to call."

"Why didn't I have copies of those decrypted messages, Mrs. Feldman?" he barked.

"I beg your pardon—which messages?"

"Don't be coy. You know damned well I'm talking about the Hellmuth affair."

"Oh dear. Was the Bureau out of the loop on that? I didn't realize." *Liar, liar, pants on fire.*

At the long worktable outside her office, Fay smirked. Utsidi bit down a smile. Veronica winked and applied more red lipstick.

Something like a snarl came down the line.

"Mr. Hoover, you know I don't have the rank to make such decisions. They're entirely out of my hands."

"If not you, then who cut the Bureau out of the communications loop? I'm not going to ask you again."

"Any such decisions are above my pay grade. Perhaps it was Commander Jones, or even Secretary Knox himself?" *Not an outright lie, Grace. A redirect.*

"Knox knows nothing about it. Jones says he was working on a different project. The only one left is you, Mrs. Feldman."

"I don't know what to tell you, Mr. Hoover."

"I won't forget this," Hoover hissed. "Now, put me through to Jones, this instant."

"Oh dear. I'm terribly sorry, sir." *But I'm not a telephone and coffee girl.* "I can't—I'm not at the switchboard."

"Then have Jones call me!" he thundered. "Right away."

"Of course. Have a lovely afternoon, Mr. Hoover."

Grace replaced the receiver and stared at it.

Behind her, the gals burst into applause. Shocked, she turned to find them all grinning at her, and it buoyed her spirits.

"Grace under pressure," Fay said. "It's a beautiful thing to see."

Grace went back late that night to the chilly, awkward atmosphere of her home and found the house dark—everyone had gone to bed. She went to check on Isobel and Christopher, who were both sleeping like lambs. She smoothed Isobel's hair back from her forehead and kissed her. She tugged Christopher's blanket up higher to keep him warm, then kissed him, too.

The door to the bedroom she shared with Robert was locked. *Locked.*

Grace stood there and stared stupidly at it. She tried the knob again, just to make sure. Her palm, sweaty and shaky with hurt and pent-up emotion, slipped off the smooth, rounded metal. She mechanically wiped her hands on her skirt and descended the stairs to the kitchen again. No supper had been left for her, so she unearthed an apple and some crackers. She went into the study, which doubled as their library, sat down on the couch and stared blankly from the apple in her hand to the rows and rows of books on codebreaking that had brought her and Robert together so many years ago.

Cracking open the mysteries of cryptanalysis had brought them such joy and freedom from the mundane, had allowed her to live a life out of the ordinary—her dream. And now they each worked in separate silos of secrecy.

What was the old saying? *Be careful what you wish for. You just might get it.*

Grace fell asleep on the chapped, cracking leather sofa in the study and woke to a nightmare in which the books had all crashed down on top of her, pinning her down, smothering her. She couldn't move, couldn't breathe, couldn't think for the tonnage of knowledge that was suffocating her.

Her heart tried to gallop out of her chest, her throat seized and only allowed in a trickle of air, her eyes rolled wildly in her head—until she made out in the darkness that the books still stood sentry on their shelves, impassively eyeing the silly human being whose imagination had run amok. Nothing was crushing her but her own fears and worries.

She was sweaty and trembling. She ordered herself to calm down, to breathe properly, to massage her chest until this strange, unwelcome panic passed.

And as she did so, the word *perry* popped into her brain. A five-letter clump that had resisted her wiles today, stubbornly refusing to give up its identity. Perry?

What did it mean?

The books weren't going to tell her. She needed to brainstorm with a person. Grace thought longingly of Robert, lying upstairs behind a locked door. Perry...he'd have some thought or insight as to what it signified. He'd once been her puzzle partner, her friend, her lover. How had this wall sprung up between them?

It was four in the morning, but there was no possibility of Grace going back to sleep. She crept upstairs to the bathroom, found a washcloth and refreshed herself as best she could. She patted her hair into place, then, since she couldn't access her bedroom, fished a totally inappropriate-for-the-season dress out of a spare closet and changed into it. And off she went to work, leaving her personal troubles at home.

"Does the word Perry mean anything to you ladies?" Grace asked her core team.

"Nada," said Veronica, looking grave. "But we just decrypted the word *zunden*."

"German for *detonate*," Fay translated for Utsidi.

"Oh, good Lord." Grace's pulse kicked up. She glanced at her watch. "When does the HMS *Bahamas* arrive in port?"

Utsidi pinched the bridge of her nose. "Tomorrow morning. The clock is ticking."

"Perry has no possible meaning, other than the name of a person. But is it a given name? Or a surname?"

"Could it be a high-ranking officer?"

"I suppose so."

"Let's take a look at the messages again to see if we can glean any further information. If we can't, we still need to pass this up the chain to Jones because of the implications and the urgency."

"Can't they just pluck them off the ship when it arrives at Port Everglades?"

"It's not that easy—we don't know what name or nationality Roth is traveling under. We don't know who LUNA is at all." Though Grace had her suspicions. LUNA, the "radio wizard." LUNA, out of all of the spies' code names, sounded female. LUNA was clearly not afraid of adventure and was probably one bad bitch.

She went into her private office and picked up the telephone, almost dialing Robert at home. Robert, with his Army Intel background, could probably help identify "Perry." But she couldn't discuss her work with him—and especially not over a home line that was not secure. Not that he'd even want to hear her voice, anyhow. She still couldn't bend her mind around the fact that he'd locked the bedroom door.

Grace thought of Donovan and Cox—who easily had the skills and wherewithal to snatch two people off a boat. Especially if Cox shared her hunch that LUNA was stunning and six feet tall, with black hair and blue eyes.

But she had to go up the proper chain of command, which meant paying Commander Jones a visit.

"This isn't an OSS matter," Jones said unequivocally. "This falls squarely under the umbrella of the Navy, and if these people are smuggling contraband into the United States, it's fair to argue that it's a Coast Guard matter. We get to make this collar."

Ah, her boss the careerist. Grace supposed she couldn't blame him. She told him of her suspicion that LUNA was none other than Spanish Marie, and why she'd stand out in a crowd.

Jones agreed with her. "With Farley's permission, I'll get a few men together and go personally to meet the HMS *Bahamas*."

"Sir, the ship is British," she reminded him.

"Blast. So it is." He sighed. "I'll have to loop in Chubby Stratton and his boys."

Grace had a dark thought. "What about the FBI? If Roth is planning to harm someone, then it's arguable that—"

Jones assumed a grim expression. "Hoover's furious over the Hellmuth affair—"

"Yes," she said wryly. "I know."

He avoided her gaze. "But let's keep a lid on this, too. This is *our* operation, not his."

Grace nodded. It was perfectly fine by her. "Sir, one last question: Do you know of an officer of some importance in Florida by the name of Perry?"

"Army? Navy? Coast Guard?"

She shrugged.

Jones shook his head. "Can't say as I do."

Still stymied, she went back to her team and together they decrypted the rest of the messages. SARGO and LUNA would disembark the HMS *Bahamas* and travel northwest. They would ostensibly stay in a motel overnight, but they'd be doing reconnaissance on "Perry." The following night they would strike.

Who was Perry? All Grace knew was that he was somewhere northwest of Port Everglades.

She dreaded going home and stayed at the office as late as she could. But she was finally driven out by the need to go to the deli to get herself something for dinner, since even if Mrs. Woolsey was setting something aside, her mother-in-law was doing away with it. She couldn't live on crackers and apples every night.

She got there only ten minutes before closing time, and the clerk behind the counter shot her an impatient look. "I just need a sandwich," she called. "Won't take up any time at all."

She ordered turkey and tomato and then looked without appetite, but with visual pleasure, at the delicacies in the cake case. There were éclairs and pies, cookies and tarts.

A familiar figure appeared in the reflection of the glass. "Grace?" it asked.

She turned to find her former neighbor Dot Brawley standing there. "Dot! How are you? It's been so long…"

"Oh, fine, fine. And you?" Dot's face looked drawn and pale.

They chitchatted about this and that.

The clerk handed over an entire prepared family-sized meal to Dot, who looked mortified that Grace was a witness—why, when she knew how undomestic her former neighbor was, Grace couldn't imagine. She took her sandwich with thanks, and the two of them walked outside.

"Dot, can I call you a taxi? You look peaked."

"Oh! No, thank you. I—well, to tell you the truth, I've just been so worried, even though the war seems to be turning in our direction at last. Our son Kenny is in the AAF learning to be a pilot, you see, and for some reason they've got him in a special training program with *naval* aviators at North Perry Airport down in south Florida. Which means he's going out miles over the water, and it scares me to death…"

Grace stared at Dot, frozen with sandwich in hand. All she heard were the words "North Perry Airport." The rest were an incomprehensible buzz for a few moments. Perry was not a person, not an officer. Perry was an airfield. Full of pilots and trainees and planes. Perry was a *target*. What was wrong with her? Why hadn't she pursued that possibility? She was an idiot.

"I'm so sorry," she said, after too long. "I'm sure they'll keep Kenny safe. Especially as a trainee. He surely won't be in any danger."

But that was an outright lie, especially if Grace didn't somehow stop SARGO and LUNA from blowing North Perry Airport to smithereens. And it was a lie to a woman who'd been nothing but kind to her.

Dot nodded miserably. "I keep telling myself that. But the fear—it's just paralyzing. I have the hardest time doing the smallest of things." She held up her deli meal. "Even cooking. When he gets home, Walter wants to know what I've done all day...and I don't even know. I...lose time somehow."

Grace wanted nothing more than to sprint home and into action. But she forced herself to stay and talk a few moments longer. "Dot, I do understand how worried you must be, but it's going to be okay. Really. Kenny's in excellent hands, flying the safest and most technically advanced aircraft that the US makes."

Dot nodded and wiped at her eyes.

Grace wrapped her arms around her, patted her back and kissed her cheek.

"Aw, you're sweet, Grace." Dot sniffed woefully. "Say, you still doing that translation stuff?"

"I am, and...well, the workload's gotten to be something else. I'm afraid I've got to get back to it."

Dot eyed the small paper bag with the sandwich in it. "Is that your dinner?"

Grace nodded.

"What does your husband eat?"

"Oh. Well." Grace felt beyond awkward. "We have a...housekeeper...now."

"My, my! A housekeeper." Dot eyed her as if she'd just sprouted a tiara.

"Yes, for the time being, at least. So terribly busy at—"

"Work." Dot nodded. "Well, thanks for the pep talk, dear. See you around."

CHAPTER FORTY-TWO

Grace drove home like a B-52 out of hell, peeled into the driveway and barely remembered to turn off the ignition before she flew into the house. She had to alert Commander Jones immediately, and failing him, then Captain Farley.

The children bounced down the stairs and into her arms. She hugged and kissed them. "So sorry, my darlings, but Mommy has an emergency." She dashed into the study and snatched up the telephone.

Jones was gone for the day, but Grace asked the operator to connect her to his home telephone. The line rang and rang before a woman answered, clearly in an agitated state. "J-Jones residence. Mrs. Jones speaking."

Grace explained that it was urgent that she speak with her boss.

"I'm sorry, Mrs. Feldman," the woman said in a choked voice. "The commander has been shot in Port Everglades. He's en route to a hospital in Fort Lauderdale—" She broke away on a sob.

"Dear Lord," Grace managed, through her own shock. *"Shot?"*

"While trying to m-make an arrest. I-I'm waiting for a t-taxi to t-take me t-to the airport," Mrs. Jones added.

"I'm so terribly sorry. Will he be all right?"

"N-not sure."

"Mrs. Jones, this will seem callous in the extreme, and I do apologize— but do you know if the people he attempted to arrest got away? It's urgent, or I wouldn't ask."

"Y-yes. They f-fled."

Grace's heart sank. "All right. Mrs. Jones, my heart goes out to you and yours. I'll be praying for your husband."

"Th-thank you." The commander's wife hung up.

Grace frantically asked to be connected to Captain Farley, but he could not be reached. Nobody who outranked *him* was going to take a call late in the evening from some agitated lady codebreaker.

Grace hung up the phone in frustration and thought for a moment. If she couldn't reach Coast Guard or Navy brass, perhaps she could alert someone with the Army Air Forces. Dot's son Kenny was AAF, not Navy—participating in a joint training session at North Perry. General Hap Arnold was commander of the Army Air Forces; General George C. Marshall commanded the Army. And Robert knew them both.

Grace dashed out of the study. "Robert? Robert, my darling, I need you!" she called up the stairs.

No answer.

Rob-*bert!*"

The elder Mrs. Feldman emerged from the kitchen, wiping her hands on her apron. "He is resting. He sleep now."

"Well, I need him." Grace dodged around her and hurtled up the stairs. "Robert, I must speak to you. It's important!" She tried the handle of their bedroom door. It was locked again. This time, she banged on it.

"Go away," he said from inside. "I'm tired."

"Robert, open the door at once. This is urgent! It's bigger than us. Open. The. Door."

The bedsprings squeaked, his feet hit the floor with two thumps and at last he unlocked and opened the door. "What is it?"

She almost wept with relief at the sight of him, even though he didn't look exactly welcoming. His hair was still neatly parted, his pajamas had knife-edge creases in them (no doubt thanks to her tirelessly toiling mother-in-law) and his expression looked...store-bought. As if it weren't his own, but something plucked off a shelf and fixed into place.

"I've got to come in," she said.

"Why?"

Grace wanted to punch him, if only to see his face change back to her husband's, and not this stranger's. "It's about work."

"We don't talk about work."

"Damn it, Robert," she ground out. "This is an utter emergency. Stand aside, let me in, and give me your help."

Once inside, she didn't know where to sit. These days, the bed seemed to be his, and his alone. So she sat in an armchair in the corner. "Lock the door."

He complied. "What's all this about?"

She told him the bare minimum as Robert paced back and forth.

"Good God," her husband said.

"Indeed. Can you possibly ring Hap Arnold or George Marshall?"

"Not from our home telephone, I can't. We need a secure line. We'll go to my office."

"Are you—are you well enough?" Grace asked cautiously.

"Don't be ridiculous." Bobby was already stripping down and jumping into suit trousers.

That stung, but she ignored it.

"Not that you seem to give a damn."

"I beg your pardon?" Grace asked icily.

He buttoned his shirt, stuffed the tails into his waistband, chose a tie. He threw it around his neck and fumbled with it. His hands still shook badly. His face betrayed fury at his own traitorous motor skills.

"Let me." Angry and wounded though she was, Grace couldn't stand to see him this way, mortified by his own human frailty.

Bobby locked eyes with her, still gripping the tie as best he could.

She glared right back, her mouth trembling. She peeled his fingers off the tie one by one, until he at last let his hands drop by his sides.

Tears stung her eyes at this tiniest fraction of progress between them. She blinked them back, refusing to give in to them, and worked her husband's tie into a Windsor knot.

She could feel his warm, minty breath on her forehead, see the razor burn on the skin of his neck above the collar and the motion of his Adam's apple when he swallowed to combat her proximity.

If she allowed herself to look up, she'd see the hard, square contours of his chin and the mouth that had always played a melody that only she could hear. If she raised her gaze even further, she'd meet his eyes… which once had been so full of love for her.

Grace couldn't. What if his gaze was simply dismissive and painfully courteous again? She wouldn't be able to bear it.

She slid the knot upward so that it was snug under his collar. She straightened it. And then she turned away. "Let's go."

Robert drove like a demon to Arlington Hall, his hands clenched on the wheel. Grace was glad to see that they weren't shaking. The tension in the car was high, but it was because of a shared sense of crisis, and not because of the iceberg that had hit their marriage.

They all but ran to his private office, where Bobby asked the operator to connect him via a secure line to General George Marshall. "It's imperative that I speak to the General at once," he said.

They waited anxiously until a click came over the line. "Feldman? What the—?"

"Sir, my apologies for the late hour and for troubling you at home."

"I assume you have good reason, Colonel."

"I do. This is a bit awkward, but as you know, my wife is a cryptanalyst, too. It's crucial that she speak with you."

"Your wife?" General Marshall repeated.

"Yes, sir. With your permission, I'll put her on the line and leave the room."

"You don't need to leave your own office, Colonel."

"It's sensitive to national security—"

"Just put Mrs. Feldman on the line."

Robert handed the receiver to Grace, and she found herself speaking personally to the chief of staff of the entire US Army. Wonders would never cease.

She offered him a succinct explanation for their call. "Sir, there is an active threat to North Perry Airport in the next twenty-four hours."

"Good Lord," said General Marshall.

"The saboteur is a German spy named Wolfgang Roth traveling under a fake passport."

Marshall whistled. "Roth. The ringleader of the South American spy ring?"

"Yes, sir. As you know, he escaped capture in Argentina. He's now entered the United States with a female companion via Port Everglades and shot a Coast Guard officer in the process. I believe he's seeking to do maximum damage to what he views as a softer target than an active AAF or naval base—because North Perry is a training center, he'll be betting it's not as well guarded."

"I'll alert the necessary folks, Mrs. Feldman."

"Sir, he's dangerous and slippery. He operated as a smuggler between Florida, Havana and the Bahamas, so he knows the terrain exceptionally well."

"Duly noted. Thank you, ma'am."

"Thank you for taking the call. I wouldn't trouble you ordinarily, but the Coast Guard officer who was shot is my boss, and I couldn't reach his immediate superior—"

"Understood. You and your husband are quite a pair. Good night, Mrs. Feldman."

Grace replaced the receiver and exhaled. Her own hands were trembling now. Robert withdrew a cigarette from a pack in his desk drawer, offered her one, and lit it for her. She drew on it, and they stared at each other in silence.

They'd just helped avert a national security crisis. Surely, they could navigate their marital crisis?

Robert remained silent, but she discerned something different in his expression. It wasn't so frozen and polite. What was it? Certainly not tenderness... but perhaps respect.

It was all over the newspapers. **SPY AND SABOTEUR ARRESTED IN FLORIDA!** blared the *Washington Post*.

Thanks to masterful counterintelligence by the United States, a Nazi plot to blow up an airbase near south Florida's Everglades has been stymied, and the perpetrator arrested. When the suspect crept onto the base in the dead of night, US troops were already in position, awaiting him. The enemy combatant covertly cut through a chain-link fence at the airfield. He was in the process of hauling two trunks of explosives onto the premises when floodlights at the field were activated, illuminating him. He reportedly fired a weapon when he was rushed by military personnel but was easily overcome and taken into custody. Sources say the culprit had detailed diagrams of the base on his person, as well as several passports, one of which identified him as SS Hauptsturmführer Wolfgang Roth...

"Do you see that, girls?" Grace said, with a smile. "We're 'masterful.'"

The second two papers arrived at the Navy Annex with none other than Commander Jones himself, looking pale with his left arm bandaged to the shoulder and in a sling.

The *Miami Herald* screamed, **DISASTER AVERTED: PILOT TRAINING BASE SAVED**.

PLOT TO BLOW UP AIR BASE FOILED! shouted the *Sun Sentinel*.

Everyone in the unit stood and clapped at the sight of Jones, and his pale skin flushed.

"Thank God you're alive," Grace said. "Roth *shot* you?"

Jones shrugged. "Things didn't go as planned."

"But we got him in the end." Not for the first time, Grace wished she could have seen the results of her team's work in person. She kept her lips sealed about her alert to General Marshall.

"We did." He shot her a half puzzled, half suspicious glance that told her he had no idea exactly how the capture had developed, since he'd been on a stretcher and then in a hospital bed at the time. But his wife would have told him Grace's question when she'd telephoned. *Did they get away?*

She kept her face blank. "We took him alive? Roth is in custody?"

Jones nodded. "Had two trunks' worth of grenades and dynamite with him. He planned to take out not only the planes at the base, but also the entire barracks full of sleeping pilots and trainees."

Grace thought of the "kid" she'd testified against so long ago at Fort Sam Houston. Thought about her guilt at sealing his fate. How did she feel about him now? Did he deserve execution?

To Americans, of course. To Germans, he was no doubt a hero.

"What about LUNA?" Grace asked. "Spanish Marie?"

A peculiar expression crossed Jones's face before he could suppress it. "She escaped."

"Did she?" Grace was torn between disappointment and admiration for Spanish Marie. Had she swum away through the Everglades, braving its toothy wildlife and mosquitoes the size of airplanes?

Jones turned to go toward his private office. "Thank you for the warm welcome back."

"We're just glad you're safe." Grace exchanged glances with Veronica, Fay and Utsidi. "He's not telling the full story," she said, under her breath.

"No, he isn't," Fay agreed.

Veronica pursed her lips. "Hijole. I will ask around..."

Grace's telephone shrilled, and she winced. Was it Hoover again? He was no doubt enraged at being cut out of this collar, too. But she truly wasn't to blame. She'd gone to her boss, and she'd followed orders. Mostly. Ahem.

It rang twice more before she forced herself to answer it, already preparing to eat a large serving of raw crow—beak, feathers, feet and all. "Hello?"

"G'day, my lady!" Kangaroo's voice boomed into her ear.

She slumped in relief. "And good morning to you."

"I hear that one of your sheilas—the one wears a lot of lippie—is making inquiries into what happened down in Port Everglades."

"Lieutenant, you're so wired in that it's really rather frightening." It was. Grace almost wondered if she should hunt for a Donovan-placed bug in her office.

Cox laughed. "Just doing my job. Anyhow—you won't hear this from your man Jones."

"And why is that?"

"Jones isn't a bad sort, but he's a straight arrow. Boy Scouts shouldn't mess with professionals," Cox said cheerfully. "He made a right dog's breakfast of it down south."

"Oh dear. What happened?"

"He hitches a ride down on a sky gator—"

"A what?"

"Aeroplane. So he takes one other puddle pirate with him, *one*, and they arrive at the dock, where they await Herr Roth and the Bad Bitch—begging your pardon."

"It's fine."

"They spot Spanish Marie, who spots them at the same time, mind you. She strolls down the gangway cool as you please, swinging her assets. And Jones's mate, he steps forward to arrest her. Quick as a snake, she elbows *him* in the throat, then pulls a pistol on Jones and wings him. Both drop, astonished, while Roth gets a head start running and Marie—well, she disappears, too."

"Good Lord," said Grace.

"Thought you'd enjoy the tale. As I said, you won't hear it from Jones. Bloke's not going to advertise the fact that he was shot by a woman, is he?"

"No, probably not." Grace recalled his peculiar expression when she'd asked about LUNA.

"All right then, darling—"

"*Cox,*" she said sharply.

"—er, ma'am." He paused. "Can't blame a fellow for trying."

Grace sighed. "*Incorrigible.*"

"Persistent," he said. "Until next time… cheers, love." And the line went dead.

CHAPTER FORTY-THREE

Grace actually got home at a decent hour that evening. Under normal circumstances, she'd be in a decent mood, too, given her behind-the-scenes triumph at work—but nothing in her house was normal at the moment except for the children, the little blessings in her life.

She stared at the front door, noting a few dings and scratches that needed attention. She fantasized briefly about flinging it open and announcing to her family that she and her team had foiled a plot to invade and/or bomb the United States from South America. And saved a great lot of pilots' lives. And caught a dangerous über spy.

She'd march in, toss down her things and announce to her mother-in-law, "I, Grace Feldman, shiksa, am a war hero!"

Her mouth twisted. It wasn't going to happen.

The family was still at the table when she walked through the door, and they all stopped midbite to stare at her, since this had become unusual of late.

"Mommy! Mommy!" screamed Isobel and Christopher, erupting from their chairs to greet her.

"Hello, darlings. How was your day?"

They chattered at her while her mother-in-law glared at her as though she were something a dog had deposited on the rug, and her husband resumed eating after murmuring, "Hello, dear."

Mrs. Woolsey seemed to have gone home for the day.

The *Washington Post* lay folded on the coffee table in front of the sofa. Grace glanced at it casually as she walked into the kitchen to get herself a plate of food, a napkin and some silverware.

The adults ate mostly in silence, responding only to the children's questions and tales about their school days. After dessert, Robert's mother got up from the table and began clearing dishes.

Grace looked at Robert, who looked out the window. She lit a cigarette and took a long drag on it. She was sick of the brick wall between them. To hell with it. She was going to tear it down, even if all it got her was bloody hands and broken fingernails.

She'd cracked the fearsome Enigma machine, she'd alerted a fleet admiral to the danger at Midway, she'd warned a four-star general of a saboteur. She could, and would, speak to her own husband. Now. Without her mother-in-law listening in.

"Bobby? We need to clear the air."

He looked at the smoke spiraling up from her cigarette and lifted an ironic eyebrow.

"Will you please ask your mother to take the children to the park to play for half an hour?"

He hesitated, then got up and went into the kitchen. He made the request, got pushback and politely insisted.

They waited while the elder Mrs. Feldman did what he asked, shooting venom at Grace while they bundled into coats.

Grace serenely ignored her. "I'll finish up the dishes. Thank you for the delicious meal."

After the door had slammed shut behind her mother-in-law and the children, Grace dove in without further ado.

"Robert. It's long past time we talked about this, and I need you to *hear* me."

"I'm all ears."

"I did not abandon you in your time of need."

He crossed his arms over his chest, which made her despair a bit, but she plunged on.

"I *didn't*. And you need to know that. First of all, they wouldn't let me stay in the room during the treatments. Second, I was called away on a true emergency. An emergency that lasted three full days—because we had to break, read and transmit messages in real time—or as close as we could get to it."

"Go on."

Well! Look at that: *two entire words* out of her husband's mouth. What progress. But Grace refused to be discouraged. "My darling. Think back to when I took you to George Washington. Do you remember the conversation we had when we first got to the hospital room?"

"What conversation? What does it have to do with anything?" There was bitterness in his tone, but bitterness was better than total withdrawal.

Still, Grace wanted to scream. She, too, was sworn not to speak about her work. Even after the fact. She remembered what she'd said to him: *Not another word, Robert Feldman... This is not who you are. You're not weak and you do not talk about your work. Not even to your own wife. Ever.*

She took a deep breath. "About the...uncertainty...in the Pacific? You mentioned it."

"I'd never do such a thing. I don't discuss my work with anyone, not even you. And you know it." Outright anger in his tone, now.

"Bobby. You weren't yourself—"

"Don't you dare lie to me!" Robert rose to his feet and glared at her, fuming. "It's the outside of enough."

Grace felt her own frustration flaring into anger. "I'm. Not. Lying."

"The hell you're not!"

He was shouting. *At her.* Never, in all the years they'd been together, had Robert raised his voice to her. His ego must be roaring at the idea that the great Robert Feldman had been indiscreet. She had no use for his ego at the moment.

Without conscious thought, she snatched the glass of water at her right and tossed it into his face.

He sputtered in shock.

"Now you listen to me, Robert Feldman. LISTEN. You're right: it's not in your character to be indiscreet. But you were in the middle of a nervous breakdown, and you spoke to me of something forbidden. I shut you up, and no damage is done. But you did mention that Joe Rochefort needed your help."

Her husband mopped at his face with his sleeves.

"And he couldn't reach you. So he reached me. That is why I had to leave, Bobby. It was an utter emergency. Nothing less would have torn me from your side. Do you hear me?"

He sat for a moment in sopping wet silence. Then he nodded. "I remember what you told me when you brought me the newspaper. You—you had to get a cup of Joe."

"Yes. And that cup ran over. For three days, during the Battle of Midway."

"I'm sorry," he muttered.

She'd torn a hole in the wall, but she herself was still enraged. "Why is it, Bobby, that when *your* work has called you away from my side during times of crisis, I'm always supposed to understand? Oh, that's all right, dear—I can drive myself to the hospital and get through a miscarriage alone because you're away. Oh yes, darling, it's perfectly *fine* for me to give birth to your child without your presence, support or encouragement—because you're in another state on a top secret project."

"Grace—"

"But when it's *my* job that leaves *you* alone to deal with something awful, you feel entitled to be horrid to me and allow your mother to insult and degrade me!"

Bobby tried to speak again, but she was incapable of stopping the torrent of words flooding out of her mouth.

"Do you know that your mamoshka had the *nerve* to ask me if I was sneaking out to meet a *lover*?"

He sucked in a shocked breath. "She didn't."

"She did! *And* she blocked the door. I had to *climb out a window*, Bobby! To get to my job in another emergency situation."

He looked down at the floor. "My mother can be...difficult."

"Is that what you call it? She makes me feel unwelcome in my own home!"

He had nothing to say to that.

"Did she urge you to divorce me?"

"Do I have to answer that?"

"*Yes!* Yes, you do."

He reluctantly nodded.

"Even after all these years and two children." But Grace wasn't surprised.

Robert dragged his hands down his face. "I'm so very sorry, love. I should have known that you would never intentionally leave me alone there."

"Yes, you should have! When you were at Walter Reed, I was there every day with you for hours."

"I know. I suppose I—well, the doctor said that sometimes spouses simply cannot cope with electroshock therapy and its aftermath—"

"Robert Feldman, after all these years, are you really under the impression that there's anything—anything at all—that I cannot cope with?"

He raised his head and looked her in the eyes. "No."

The word hung in the air between them.

"It's *me* who couldn't cope," he said almost inaudibly. "I was desperate for help, desperate enough to try the treatment. But I was, quite simply, terrified. That it would either fry my brain and leave me a husk of a man, or that it wouldn't help at all."

The words broke her heart.

"But you went through with it," Grace said softly. "That, Bobby, is true courage."

"Let me finish, please. Men aren't supposed to be fearful. We're raised to deny or ignore fear. And perhaps, Grace, mine got all twisted and manifested as anger that you weren't by my side. For that, I am truly sorry. I love you..." His voice broke. "I love you," Bobby repeated, "and I respect you, and—" He stepped forward and took both of her hands. "I cannot live without you."

Grace went limp with sheer relief. He still loved her. He wasn't going to leave or divorce her. "I'm sorry, too," she whispered. "Sorry for leaving you alone."

He kissed her and then snugged her against his chest, tucking her head under his chin.

"You're wet!" she protested feebly.

"And whose fault is that, my love?"

"Certainly not mine," Grace said shamelessly, feeling his heartbeat, strong and sure, against her cheek. *Oh, thank God. Everything is going to be all right between us.*

Robert's mother was disappointed at this outcome, to say the least. She stayed on for the longest week of Grace's life. In all fairness, she *was* wonderful with the children and they loved her dearly. Grace at last came up with an inspired plan: she made the old bat's apple kugel, correctly, and served it for dessert with a wink and a smile.

The elder Mrs. Feldman prodded it suspiciously with her spoon as the rest of the family scarfed it down with delight and Grace looked on fondly.

At last her mother-in-law took a bite, outrage blooming on her face as she, too, found it good. She finished it and stomped up the stairs to the guest room while Grace inwardly cackled.

Mrs. Feldman bought a train ticket and left the very next day.

Washington, DC, 1958

Grace opened the door to find a uniformed FBI agent on the other side. He was young, green as a salad, his hat in his hand.

"Mrs. Robert Feldman?" he asked, eyeing a growling Krypto.

"Yes." To the dog, she said, "Hush."

"Is your husband home?"

Grace sighed. "He's indisposed." *Meaning I haven't been able to get him up yet. Sisyphus is weary, and this morning the boulder is immoveable.*

"I'm sorry to hear that, but I need to ask him a few questions, ma'am."

"Is there anything I can help you with instead?"

"Well." The agent shifted his weight. "Ah. Were you present on the day two federal agents came to take custody of certain books in your husband's library?"

"*Our* library," she corrected. "And yes, I was."

"Did you witness your husband threaten to shoot one of the agents if he were to touch certain books?"

Oh, Dear Lord. Grace froze for a moment, praying that the NSA man, Thompson, had listened to her plea. She didn't know. It was time to gamble. She mustered a chuckle. "Don't be silly. Robert never said anything of the kind."

"That would be a Class C or D felony, ma'am. Punishable by a large fine or up to ten years in prison."

"Yes, yes, I'm sure it would be. Dreadful to threaten a federal employee who's only trying to do his job. But it didn't happen," Grace lied.

"Your husband didn't extract a revolver from a drawer and place it on the corner of his desk as he watched the agents go about their task?"

"Gracious, no. Robert doesn't even own a gun anymore." Not a lie, because she'd found more bullets and tossed them, along with his service revolver, into the Potomac.

The young agent checked his notes and frowned.

"You must be chilled to the bone, dear. Would you like a hot cup of coffee? A slice of pie?"

"Well..." He looked sorely tempted.

"Do come in. *Pie and coffee* isn't a Class C or D felony, now is it? And I'll see if my husband can come down for a quick chat. How would that be?" Grace held open the door.

The agent accepted her invitation.

Grace settled him on the sofa in the living room, started a pot of coffee and shut Krypto into the kitchen. She excused herself momentarily. Then she sprinted up the back stairs.

"Bobby? *Bobby.* I need you to get up, right now. Get up, put on your bathrobe and slippers. And listen to me."

He didn't move.

"Up!" Grace ordered. "Up, right now. And then, you genius man, you're going to pretend to be dumb as a stump and twice as useless. Do you understand?"

"No."

She pulled him out of the bed and forcibly dressed him in his robe. She shoved his slippers onto his feet. "There's an FBI agent downstairs, Robert. You need to deny that you ever did what he's saying you did. You never threatened to shoot that NSA agent—"

"The books," Bobby remembered.

"Yes. When they came for the books. *You did not do that*, understand? Otherwise this man can arrest you. You could spend years in prison."

"You . . . want me to lie."

"Yes, Robert. For the first time in your beyond-honorable life—I want you to lie like a *rug*."

"That's not right, Grace. You—we—always do the right thing."

"Not this time, my darling. Got it? We're going to do the wrong thing for the right reason. You've spent over forty years in service to the government, and you aren't going to prison for losing your temper with a couple of imbeciles. *Lie*. Do not even think about telling the truth. I will not let J. Edgar Hoover—or the paranoia of the NSA—ruin our lives."

"Hoover?"

"Never mind. Lie, Bobby, or I'll go back to making apple kugel with two teaspoons of ground cloves."

That got his attention. He shuddered. "Grace, you wouldn't."

"I would! Now, do you trust me?"

Tears filled his eyes. "One hundred percent."

"Then lie for the first time in your life. And do it well."

She brought her husband down the stairs to meet the agent and settled him on the other end of the couch. Bobby's posture was hunched—gone was the proud military bearing of his younger days. His hair was still mussed, and there were sheet marks on his face. He looked the part of a confused older man, which suited their purposes exactly. "How may I help you, Officer?"

The young FBI agent repeated the questions he'd asked of her while Grace brought them both coffee and thick slices of apple pie.

"Heavens," Robert exclaimed. "Why would I say such a thing?"

"Because you were upset, Colonel. They were taking away your books."

"I'll admit that I wasn't pleased. But threaten anyone with violence? Absolutely not."

"Your wife says you don't even own a gun."

That was news to Robert. He paused.

Grace prayed.

He met her gaze and took his cue. "My wife is a woman of total integrity. Why would you doubt her word? I did once own a gun—I served in the Army and was deployed to Chaumont during the first war. It was kept in my desk drawer. But I no longer have it."

"What did you do with it, Colonel?"

Grace broke in. "He threw it in the Potomac after Japan surrendered."

This earned her a baleful glance from Robert.

She gave him a tiny shrug in return.

"Why would the FBI agent say that you threatened to shoot the NSA agent, then, sir?"

"I have no idea. Grace, why would he say that?"

She took a sip of her own coffee. "Perhaps he embroidered the tale with a little extra drama to make his job seem more glamorous? To make a routine visit seem dangerous."

The young man wrote that down. "The agent says emphatically that he witnessed the threat, though. To the NSA fellow."

"Very curious. Why not ask *him*?"

"We did. The NSA man doesn't recall any type of threat being made."

"How...interesting."

"I thought so." The young officer aimed a level gaze at her.

Green, but not stupid, then.

He set down his pie plate on the coffee table. "That was absolutely delicious, Mrs. Feldman. Best pie I've ever eaten."

"Why, thank you." Grace smiled blandly. "My mother-in-law's recipe."

Bobby choked, then coughed into his napkin.

"Any further questions, Officer?" Grace asked.

"Evidently not." He stood up and retrieved his hat. "Thank you for your cooperation and hospitality, Colonel and Mrs. Feldman."

"Of course, of course." She walked him to the door. "Don't catch cold, dear."

"Grace, darling," Robert said when the officer had gone. "Why did you see fit to throw my service revolver into the Potomac?"

She swallowed before turning to him with a lovely smile. "Leaves such a mess, Bobby. Traumatizing for me to find. And with no housekeeper any longer, I'd be scrubbing for days."

"I see. When did you do it?"

"Well, darling, it was around the same time that I found the coil of rope in the back seat of the Studebaker."

He nodded. "That disappeared, too."

"A dreadful way to go. It elongates the neck, you know, before one strangles to death. The face swells and turns a mottled plum color, the tongue protrudes... very undignified."

"And the absence of rat poison in the garage?"

"Do you *want* to die rolling in an oil stain, in paroxysms of pain?"

"Grace, my sleeping pills are missing as well."

"They never did anything for your insomnia anyhow."

They sat in silence for a few moments.

"Grace, can you understand that I'm furious with you?"

"Bobby, can you understand how furious I am with *you*? By the way, the garage is full of furniture, so you can't pull a car into it."

"And you bought me an electric shaver. Thoughtful of you."

"Yes, wasn't it?"

"I could always jump off a bridge, you know."

Grace put her hands up to her throbbing temples. "Stop. Please, please, please just *stop*. Don't even think about it."

"But I do, you know," he said gently. "I'm sorry. But I do."

Silence stretched between them. Grace wanted to fill it by shouting at him, by shaking him, by denying that he faced a chasm of darkness, hopelessness and despair at any given hour of the day or night. By questioning the reasonableness of that...

But depression didn't answer to reason. She'd learned that much, at least. It was a toxic fog rolling into harbor in the brain, a sticky, murky humidity coating and clinging to everything in its path, smothering joy, light, love or any creative impulse.

And shrieking at melancholy did not disperse it. It simply swallowed the rage into the gloom, where it festered.

Grace jumped to her feet. "We need a project, sweetheart. A big one."

Robert sighed. "You're probably right. But we've already reexamined the so-called Bacon ciphers and proven, once and for all, that they're nonsense. What next?"

"Do you really wish to leave our library—incomplete as it now is—to the government, after they've raided our home? Do you want the National Archives to house everything? Or shall we find a private museum, perhaps the one being planned for George Marshall, so that they're not able to tamper with the rest? Either way, the collection will have to be indexed and cross-indexed."

"Yes, very true."

"So let's discuss how to go about it..."

"Grace?"

"Yes?"

"I know exactly what you're doing, you know." He gave her a heartbreaking smile, and along with exhaustion, disappointment and cynicism, she could still see traces in it of music and youthful optimism, wit and playfulness, love and light.

She ruffled the wisps of his hair. "So do I."

"Do you think you can win this war, too, my tiny general?" He peered at her, seeking reassurance only she, after a lifetime of love, could give him.

"I know I can."

"Against my will?"

"What kind of question is that?"

"An unfair one," he admitted.

"Yes, it is unfair. Robert. It's not only my country at stake. You're my entire world. So hell, yes, I will win this war."

He nodded in resignation. "You're a frighteningly competent woman, my darling."

She kissed him on the lips. "Yes, Robert. You're quite right. I am."

CHAPTER FORTY-FOUR

Washington, DC, 1944

Robert's rank in the Army was mysteriously reinstated—though he never received an explanation for why he'd been discharged in the first place.

Grace received a wryly delivered, apologetic, official reprimand from Commander Jones for "inadvertently" leaving the FBI out of the loop on South American decrypts. She assured him equally wryly and unapologetically that it would never happen again.

The Toad himself found a way to claim credit for the Hellmuth operation and, indeed, the entire Invisible War, as it became known— the undercover war to defend the United States from an invasion from South America.

Confronted by the far more powerful US government, and seeing that Germany was losing to the Allies, the Argentinian government folded like a cheap suit. But how could they save face? J. Edgar Hoover, Johnny-on-the-spot, came to the "rescue."

Working hand in glove with an embarrassed Argentina, Hoover and the Bureau crafted a juicy, lurid spy story about Wolfgang Roth, SS Hauptsturmführer and mastermind of plots and coups. Roth had created clandestine networks all over South America for the Nazis... but only the Argentine police had been "clever enough" to uncover his activities. In conjunction with the United States and the FBI, they arrested Roth—and forty of his collaborators.

It was Fay and Veronica who, looking disgusted, brought in the latest edition of the *American Magazine* to the Coast Guard unit. Veronica dropped it wordlessly on Grace's desk.

HOW THE NAZI SPY INVASION WAS SMASHED!
One of the great undercover victories of the war—the defeat of a vast Axis plan to penetrate South America—is revealed here for the first time by the Director of the FBI...

She scanned farther to find that the Bureau, apparently without any aid at all, had disrupted seven thousand Axis operations, caught 250 spies and seized twenty-nine radio stations.

Grace snorted.

"I'm going to be sick," Fay said. "The Bureau didn't monitor the radio networks. It didn't intercept any messages. It didn't decrypt them. It sure didn't break any Enigma machines."

Grace sighed. "Army, Navy, State and the British know the truth. *We* know the truth."

"But he's taking credit for our work—"

"Listen, girls. There's a war on. It means group effort. Credit isn't important during times like these. The only thing of significance is beating the enemy and not bowing to fascists and murderers." But as she spoke these "good leader" words, Grace burned with anger. How dare the man? How did he look into the mirror each morning?

Worse was Frank Capra's film *The Battle of the United States*, which starred Hoover in fifteen minutes of blatant propaganda as "he" triumphed in South America. It was shown to US troops overseas. "I'll make popcorn," Grace said wryly to the unit. Under the appearance of serenity, she was once again seething. But what could she do?

There was simply no time to dwell on these things. Each day, Grace stuffed her anger, her ego and any personal ambition into her lower desk drawer, along with her gloves and pocketbook.

Grace and her core team were summoned one morning to Commander Jones's office.

He ushered them in, told them to have a seat, then picked up his telephone handset. "Mamie, would you send in Colonel Donovan and Mr. Stratton? Thank you."

"Chubby" Stratton, that ebullient, quintessentially English chap from British counterintelligence, and his boys had cooked up an audacious plan, shared with Wild Bill Donovan and the OSS, that the codebreakers were never to speak of to anyone. Ever. They'd been handpicked to monitor its results.

"Hallo, lovelies!" Chubby, an astronomer by training, looked like Santa Claus minus the red suit and reindeer. He was hard to take seriously, which was one of the reasons he was so effective at his job. Nobody suspected that the jolly prankster who told off-color anecdotes at cocktail parties was, in fact, a diabolical genius.

Stratton proceeded to brief them in Jones's office about Operation Bodyguard.

Grace, Fay, Utsidi and Veronica all listened, astonished, as he gave them the details, his eyes dancing.

"Well? What do you think?"

"You must be joking," Grace said faintly.

"It's no joke," Commander Jones told her.

"It's beyond the realm of insanity."

"Yes!" Chubby agreed. "That's why it will work."

The women eyed him dubiously.

"Who would even conceive of taking a deception to such lengths? The Germans will never suspect a thing—simply because it's so preposterous."

Grace shook her head. *You're a lunatic. But a highly creative one.*

"It'll work. You'll see it play out in real time."

Let the man have his fantasies . . .

"And when it does, ladies, you'll owe me a very good bottle of Scotch."

Dubiously, they all got to work, encrypting messages full of disinformation for the Germans to intercept—which they did with their customary efficiency.

"We have some good news," Utsidi told Grace early one morning, eyes sparkling. "The Nazis are falling for the Operation Bodyguard ruse."

Grace smiled for the first time in days. *"Are* they? What's the chatter?"

"They've swallowed reports of the fictitious Fourth Army in Scotland hook, line and sinker." Fay grinned. "In reaction, Berlin is sending thousands of troops to Scandinavia."

"They also believe in Patton's greatly exaggerated First US Army Group in southeast England. The Germans have been fooled by the dummy planes and landing craft and are preparing to resist them at Pas-de-Calais."

Grace's smile got wider.

"And by the bogus radio transmissions we've sent about troops and munitions movements." Utsidi laughed. "How did they come up with this stuff?"

"Who knows? But credit goes to Stratton and the boys in British counterintelligence," Grace said, admiration creeping into her voice. "What audacious, devious, brilliant minds."

"I'll say."

"I truly thought the man was mad," Grace murmured in wondering tones. "Inflatable dummy Sherman tanks? Rollers to simulate track marks?"

"German aerial reconnaissance has also been taken in by those," Utsidi added.

"Better yet," Fay put in, "they've spotted the fake General Montgomery in Algiers, so they surmise that he's scouting out the Mediterranean for an attack there."

Grace began to laugh and took her seat at the table. "Anything else?"

"Yes: Axis radar has been fooled by the aluminum strips dropped by Allied planes. They anticipate a large fleet approaching Calais. Normandy hasn't entered their minds at all."

"But the pièce de résistance?" Fay announced, "The dummy paratroopers wired for sounds of explosives and gunfire—and the special ops guys dropped in with *phonographs* to broadcast the voices of soldiers and the noises of combat."

Veronica nodded. "They're falling for it *todo*—all. If this war were not such a serious business, it would be comical."

Grace shook her head. "We owe Chubby and the boys that bottle of single malt for doubting them."

"Verdad!" Veronica said. "It will be, how you say, a pleasure."

"But remember, ladies: not a word to anyone. What do we do here in the Navy Annex?"

"Answer the telephone."

"File and make coffee."

"Boring translation work."

"Stenography."

"Our nails."

Grace nodded. "The very idea of you ever seeing anything top secret is ridiculous. You don't chat to friends, boyfriends, mothers or dogs."

"Hey," Fay protested. "My dog is very discreet."

Grace frowned at her. "You don't have a dog."

"Exactly."

On June 6, 1944, the Allies landed at Normandy, despite casualties of 29,000 and over a hundred thousand wounded or missing. The Germans were simply unprepared for the invasion, and thanks to further counterintelligence operations, they continued to be.

In the first quarter of 1945, Allied bombs rained down on Germany by the thousands, lighting entire cities on fire, ripping holes in buildings, reducing them to blackened rubble.

The radio intercepts poured in, and the exhausted codebreakers solved them with record speed, translated and dispersed copies of them, then turned to the next pile.

German troops had gone into full retreat after the Battle of the Bulge—wonderful news, until word came that the Americans had lost twenty thousand men. And word of the horrific, inhumane death marches from Auschwitz-Birkenau and other camps came down, stories so horrible that nobody wanted to believe them. Ravensbrück. Bergen-Belsen. Dachau.

The Soviet army closed in on Germany from the east as the Allies pushed toward it from the west. The second world war was at last coming to a close.

Grace had gone home for supper with Robert and the children after a long day in the office at the Navy Annex. Mrs. Woolsey set a meal of lamb, roasted potatoes and spring peas on the table, and Christopher proudly displayed his prowess with a knife—a recently acquired skill.

Robert had tuned the radio to a classical music station, and Rachmaninoff played in the background while Isobel asked a series of unanswerable questions.

"Why do the Nazis hate Jews?"

Grace sighed. "Partly because they need a scapegoat for their economic problems."

"What's a scapegoat?" Isobel chewed her lip.

"Someone to blame," Robert said.

"Chew your food, not your lip," Grace put in.

"Why do some people want to kill other people?"

"Usually out of fear and hatred."

"What's a master race?"

"A complete illusion," Robert, the former geneticist, said acidly. "Dreamed up by eugenicists."

"What's a eugenicist?"

"Oh dear," said Grace. "Someone who thinks that we can breed better people."

"Can we?"

Her husband reached for his wine. "No."

"Then why do they think we can?"

"Because," he said, slugging some down, "they're deluded."

"What's that mean?"

"Eat your supper."

"What's a shiksa?" Christopher wanted to know.

"Your mother," Robert said, chuckling.

"Bobby!" But Grace's mouth worked. "Where did you hear that term, sweetheart?"

"Grandma said it on the telephone to her friend."

"Isn't that nice?" Grace reached for her own wine. "Eat your peas."

"But I don't like—"

Suddenly the music stopped. *"We interrupt our regular programming to bring you this announcement. President Franklin Delano Roosevelt died this afternoon, April twelfth, at his retreat in Warm Springs, Georgia."*

Grace dropped her fork with a clatter and put a hand over her mouth.

"He's only sixty-three," Robert said in disbelief.

"Cause of death is a cerebral brain hemorrhage..."

"No, no, no— Oh *no*. Poor Eleanor."

"*Vice President Harry Truman has been sworn in by Chief Justice Harlan Stone as the nation mourns…*"

"The president is dead?" Isobel whispered.

"We've just lost one of the finest men this country's ever known," Robert told her gravely.

Despite her very real grief, Grace had an unwelcome realization. *We've also lost the one man who could protect us from J. Edgar Hoover.*

Five hundred thousand people turned out to watch the somber procession of the late president's coffin from Union Station to the East Room of the White House. Grace and Robert squeezed in among the hundreds of mourners there, where Franklin Delano Roosevelt lay in state with an honor guard.

A black-veiled, grief-stricken Eleanor and the children stood in an endless receiving line, thanking those who'd come to pay their respects. Thousands more people milled outside.

"We're so very sorry for your loss." Grace squeezed Eleanor's black-gloved hands. Her eyes lacked their usual energetic sparkle, her cheeks sagged and it looked as though it physically hurt her to smile. "He was a truly extraordinary man. A great man."

"Thank you, dear. His health had been failing…but we certainly didn't see this coming."

"Of course not…" Grace longed to give the First Lady a hug, but protocol forbade it.

She moved on to give her condolences to James and his siblings.

"Grace, dear?" Eleanor said.

She turned.

"I'll put something in the mail to you before we leave for Hyde Park."

Grace gave her a questioning glance.

"The report, dear. You should have it."

"Oh my goodness. Please don't trouble yourself at a time like this—"

"No trouble. Thank you for coming. It's very kind of you both."

As Grace and Robert somberly left the White House for the last time, he asked, "Report?"

"Oh, it's nothing, Bobby. Some statistics on the League of Women Voters," Grace improvised. *My, haven't you gotten good at dissembling.*

"What an odd thing for Eleanor to think of under these circumstances."

"Yes, isn't it? But she's so efficient—almost to a fault."

True to her word, Eleanor mailed the report. It arrived two days later, marked *Personal* and sealed in an official White House envelope that clearly held more than a couple of pages.

Grace eyed it uneasily, as though its contents were toxic. Quite possibly, they were. It was not only immoral, but also quite dangerous for her to possess the information, whatever it was.

She picked it up gingerly. *You don't have to open it. You don't have to read it. And you don't have to actually use what's inside.*

She wrestled with her conscience.

Finally, Grace took the unopened envelope upstairs and taped it to the underside of the bottom shelf in the linen closet. It wasn't something she wanted to put in the safe that she and Robert both had access to.

Then she went back downstairs and busied herself in the kitchen, where a wife was supposed to be—not digging for dirt on one of the most powerful men in government.

Two weeks later, on April 30, Adolf Hitler committed suicide in a Berlin bunker, and on May 7, General Alfred Jodl surrendered unconditionally to General Dwight Eisenhower. The war in Europe was over, though the battle in the Pacific raged on until September, after the bombing of Hiroshima and Nagasaki.

When the news broke that MacArthur had accepted Japan's surrender aboard the USS *Missouri* in Tokyo Bay, Bobby and Grace embraced fiercely and wordlessly, their tears mingling.

"Why are you crying, Mommy? Daddy?" Isobel asked.

Christopher seemed perplexed, too. "Isn't the war being over a good thing?"

"Yes. It is." Grace ushered them all to the dining room table, where they sat down. "But sweetheart, tens of millions of people have died. Because of the ego, insanity and hatred of one man who should never have risen to power in the first place."

"Everyone is hugging and kissing and throwing parties...dancing in the streets," Isobel said. "Why aren't you?"

Perhaps because it doesn't seem quite real, yet?

Grace and Robert exchanged glances. Both of them were haggard with exhaustion. Robert still had tremors in both hands; his hair had thinned and grayed even more; his smile wobbled any time it did make a rare appearance.

She'd seen herself in the mirror, too: under her eyes were bags she could pack and take on vacation—if she could remember what the term meant. Her skin was sallow from too many pots of coffee drunk far too late at night in a woolly haze of cigarette smoke. Her clothes hung loosely on her frame, searching aimlessly for the ten pounds she'd somehow lost and that would never find her again.

"We're too tired to dance at the moment, my dears," Grace murmured. "Sorry to disappoint you."

"Perhaps next week," Robert said. "It's been a—it's been a long war."

"A very long war," Grace agreed.

They celebrated by sleeping for almost forty-eight hours straight while Mrs. Woolsey took the children for the weekend.

Washington, DC, 1958

This is the last time I will ever set foot in this office. Grace made the promise to herself as she sat once again in the reception area that led to J. Edgar Hoover's lair in FBI headquarters. The walls groaned under the collective weight of all the plaques, framed press clippings and photos of him with celebrities.

Since her last visit, he'd added shelves of leather-bound Harvard classics and rare first editions that, given their pristine condition and uncracked spines, she suspected he'd never read.

An ornate gilt frame boasted a vintage map of Europe, though to her knowledge he'd never traveled there. And a large globe of the world stood turned to South America, which set her teeth on edge.

She cooled her heels for forty-five minutes before Mrs. Gandy ushered her into the inner sanctum.

"Mrs. Feldman," Hoover said with a cold, fake bonhomie. "To what do I owe the pleasure?"

She sat without being invited to do so, stripped off her gloves and didn't waste time pretending. "Call off your attack dog."

He smirked. "Why would I do that? Your husband did threaten to shoot a federal agent."

She opened her mouth to deny it.

"Don't bother, Mrs. Feldman. We both know you're lying to protect Robert. And under a little pressure, the NSA man will come around and forget his regrettable deafness. How *is* good old Robert, by the way? Did that electroshock therapy help him?"

Grace's blood chilled. She shut her mouth with a snap.

"It's bound to come out in a high-profile trial, you know. Unfortunate, but what can you do?" Hoover lifted his shoulders to his ears and spread his hands.

"There won't be a trial," she said through gritted teeth.

"Oh, Mrs. Feldman. Don't tell yourself fairy tales. There will most definitely be a trial." Hoover's smile didn't reach his shark eyes. He leaned back in his chair and clasped his hands over his substantial girth.

You no-neck bastard. She stood up again and dropped her pocketbook into the visitor's chair. Then she leaned forward and placed her palms flat on his desk. "Mr. Hoover," she said evenly. "Call off your FBI attack dog and don't even think about prosecuting my husband."

He adopted an amused expression. "Or? I feel sure that there's an *or* coming."

"Or I will call *you* out publicly for taking credit for winning the so-called Invisible War in South America. Your public image will be ruined, Mr. Hoover, and the entire country will know you for the villain and the fraud that you are."

He actually laughed. "You can't. You swore an oath of secrecy. Remember the Espionage Act?"

"And you swore an oath to uphold and protect the Constitution."

"You'll go to prison, you know."

"There are some things worth going to prison for, Mr. Hoover. Not many, perhaps. But protecting my husband is one of them."

He sneered at her, unfazed. "You don't have the nerve."

Grace drilled her gaze into his. "Try me."

"You also have no evidence."

"Don't I? May I remind you, sir: every single copy of every single translated message my unit sent to you was marked Coast Guard decrypt? And a good number of them also have my initials on them."

He smiled broadly. "Taken care of upon receipt. We created our own."

Grace took a moment to marvel at his shamelessness.

"You must have missed the word *copy*, Mr. Hoover. Do I need to explain to you what that means? That there is also an original. Which you don't have."

His mouth tightened as he changed tacks. "You're blackmailing me, Mrs. Feldman."

She aimed a frigid smile at him. "I prefer the word *persuading*."

"It's a crime, by the way. Punishable by—"

"You'll be *ruined*," she said simply. "All that flagrant propaganda you put out...the articles, the Capra films—"

Hoover lost his cool. "You are blackmailing the director of the FBI, lady!"

"Persuading," she said gently.

"Who in the *hell* do you think you are?!" Ah, her favorite question, yet again.

"I'm a loving and devoted wife, Mr. Hoover."

"You're a first-class bitch, Mrs. Feldman."

She smiled. "So much better than being a second-class one."

Hoover stood up himself and leaned in until his face was inches from hers. "Lady: Do. Not. Fuck. With. Me." His breath was hot, humid and foul with coffee and stale plaque.

She didn't back up a centimeter. "I wouldn't dream of it, Mr. Hoover."

They locked eyes until, with a growl, he sat down again. His chair creaked in protest. "You'll regret this."

Grace nodded. *I already do. You've changed me, and not for the better. I used to have a moral compass. I always did the right thing. I was proud of that...*

The Quaker-raised girl still locked deep inside the hardened, cynical, warworn woman she'd become was appalled at her own actions. But she'd always hated a bully. And this man was a thoroughly dishonest, hypocritical, sanctimonious bully.

"Yes," she said. "I'll regret it—but not for the reasons you think."

Hoover eyed her, baffled. Then he changed tacks again. "Is your daughter still dating Communists?"

Isobel had once had a brief flirtation with a boy who'd read Lenin. The scope of Hoover's invasion of her family's privacy was miles beyond disturbing. But why was she surprised? She recalled Captain Farley's words: *That bastard's got secret files on everyone, from waiters to senators.*

"My daughter," Grace corrected him, "is dating a Navy man. And don't even think about throwing her—or any other member of my family—to the wolves. I promise you that *you'll* regret it if you do."

Hoover eyed her stonily.

"Perhaps I should make clear, Mr. Hoover, that two can play at this game. You are not the only person capable of hiring an investigator to poke around in other people's affairs. You're not the only one who can put together a secret file on someone."

"Go on," Hoover said in ominous tones.

"For example, would you care to tell me about your father Dickerson, Mr. Hoover? Would you say he was in his right mind for the several years before he died?"

Hoover went utterly still. She wasn't even sure he was breathing.

Grace pressed her advantage.

"Who pays for those annual vacations that you and Mr. Tolson take to California and Florida? Has anyone ever audited the slush fund that you help yourself to so freely? And is the public aware that taxpayer dollars funded additions to your private home? What about your chauffeured car? And have you been *entirely* honest with the IRS?"

Hoover's face turned a mottled purple; his nostrils flared and his flat shark eyes were incandescent with rage. *"How dare you?!"*

"How dare *you*, Mr. Hoover?" She said it flatly. "And all while burnishing your image as America's Top Cop, defender of truth, justice and the American way."

"I will *end* you, lady. You have no idea who you're dealing with."

"I wouldn't advise murder," Grace said coolly. "My lawyer has copies of every decrypt and all the information from my private investigator. He has instructions to release it to the newspapers should anything happen to me."

Hoover's mouth worked. "Get the hell out of my office!" he roared.

"Gladly, Mr. Hoover. Do we understand each other fully?"

"Get *out*! Out! *Get the hell out!*" Spittle flew from Hoover's thin lips along with the words. He trembled with fury.

She was half afraid that he'd lunge and try to strangle her. It was time to leave.

Grace put on her gloves, then retrieved her pocketbook and slipped the strap over her arm. "Oh dear, Mr. Hoover," she said, as she started for the door. "My PI found an empty digitalis bottle in your garbage pail. Do be careful not to give yourself a health incident."

He threw his telephone at the wall, followed by a stapler and then a blown glass paperweight. Mrs. Gandy came running but stopped outside his office, clearly alarmed.

"What on earth—?"

Grace aimed a serene smile at her. As she slipped out, she could still hear animal-like snorts and pants of temper coming from Hoover's lair.

Knowledge is power.

CHAPTER FORTY-FIVE

Washington, DC, 1958

Grace had far more appreciation now for the rioting cherry blossoms outside her kitchen window. As the sun set, bathing them in golden light, she spread a luxurious amount of fresh raspberry jam over two sections of a chocolate layer cake. She dolloped whipped cream onto two other sections and coaxed it all the way to the edges. Then she began the careful process of stacking the layers.

Dusk allowed her faint, ghostly reflection to appear in the window, and once the cake was assembled, she met her own clear-eyed gaze without flinching. Her hair had silvered. Crow's feet radiated from the outside corners of her eyes; grooves now bracketed a generous, firm mouth.

She didn't look like a woman who'd prevailed against a domineering father and gone to college, or one brave enough to face social ostracism by marrying outside of her faith.

She didn't look like someone who'd stood up to sexual harassment and bullying . . . or learned the dark arts of codebreaking on the fly—and then taught them to a never-ending series of male chauvinist military officers.

Who would suspect that this frail, feminine figure had busted bootleggers, or testified in court at great personal risk against mobsters and racketeers? Clawed back hundreds of millions of dollars from them for the US Treasury?

How could a woman such as herself have braved the horrors of a psychiatric ward for months on end and fought a male medical authority for custody of her husband?

She looked a far cry from someone who'd broken the German Enigma machine, monitored enemy radio networks, aided in an audacious counterintelligence plot and saved the United States from a fascist invasion via South America.

And who would believe that the little woman reflected in the window had lost her mind and her morals, gone toe to toe with the fearsome J. Edgar Hoover—and won?

Don't get smug, Grace Feldman. It's all fantastical.

She checked her watch as she melted chocolate in a double boiler. Just coming up on six o'clock. The guests would be here for their fortieth wedding anniversary party in an hour or so.

She made ganache, spread it smooth and shining over the cake and dotted it with raspberries in a careful sequence.

IBQQZ
BOOJWFSTBSZ!

Christopher, arriving early, pushed through the swinging kitchen door to say hello. He was now as tall as his father.

"My darling boy," Grace said, as she folded him into a hug.

"Hi, Mom." He pulled out of her arms and glanced at the cake. "Simple shift cipher. Happy Anniversary!"

"Very good. But you and Isobel *did* used to write letters home from camp using it."

"I'd have expected something more complicated from you," he teased.

"Not all of the guests are codebreakers," she reminded him. "Just most of them."

"Can I lick the icing bowl?"

"Aren't you a little old for that, honey?"

"No one's ever too old to lick an icing bowl."

"True."

Isobel came through the door next. "Daddy is snoring with his feet on the pillow and his head at the opposite end of the bed."

"Sometimes he does that," Grace said. "But we'd best wake him up and get him dressed so that he doesn't come down to the party in his pajamas."

"The cake looks nice, Mom."

"Slide it into the icebox for me?"

Isobel nodded.

Grace took off her apron and went upstairs. "Bobby?" she called to her upside-down husband. "My darling, it's time to get up for the party."

He stirred and opened his eyes. "Why are my feet on the pillow?"

"I don't have the faintest idea. Why did you put them there?"

Robert puzzled over it. "To send more blood to my head?"

"Sounds perfectly reasonable to me." Grace sat down next to him. "Come on, get up. People will be here soon."

"I don't *want* to get up."

"You sound exactly like Christopher did as a little boy."

"A lot of fuss and bother..."

"Yes. People are making a fuss over us, so you're going to bother to get up. It's rude not to."

"People. What people? I don't want to see any. I'd rather drive to the river and fill my pockets with stones."

"Not on our anniversary, Robert," Grace said.

"Tomorrow, then."

"I'll think of an excellent reason not to do it tomorrow, either."

"You always do." He shot her a look of annoyance. "It's quite frustrating, really."

"I know." She patted his cheek.

Bobby grumbled and rumbled and muttered and puttered. But she cajoled him into shaving, brushing his teeth and combing his hair. She got him into a dark suit, crisp white shirt and silk tie; helped him into his socks and tied his shoelaces.

"Very handsome, dear. You still clean up nicely."

"Thank you." He eyed himself in the bedroom mirror, satisfied.

"You *almost* resemble the gentleman who fathered the NSA." Grace lifted an eyebrow.

"You don't look at all shabby yourself, my darling."

"I suppose I'll do." She patted her hair into place, then lifted a bottle of Shalimar from her dressing table and dabbed some behind each ear.

Once she'd set it down, he slipped his arms around her and held her tightly. "I'd marry you all over again, Grace. You're my reason for living."

Tears filled her eyes, and a lump rose in her throat as she hugged him back. "And I you, Bobby."

He pulled away, looked down at her and tipped up her chin for a kiss. "You do realize that *I'm* not the one who's mentally ill, don't you?"

She breathed in the familiar scents of him: soap, aftershave, starch, man and love.

"It's *you*, sweetheart," he said. "My lovely lunatic. Nobody else would live, day after day, under these circumstances."

Grace took his arm and led him downstairs.

A disgruntled Krypto had been put in the guest room—but with a monster bone to keep him busy. Mrs. Woolsey and the children had let in the guests, and everyone milled about with drinks and canapés in hand.

To Grace's shock, Alice Martenz had sent a stunning flower arrangement, which Mrs. Woolsey put on top of the baby grand piano.

Countless Coast Guard, Army, Navy and NSA people came to celebrate with them. Parker and Genevieve Hitt had flown in from San Antonio, Joe Rochefort and Fay had flown all the way from Hawaii, where they'd retired. Veronica brought her new husband. Utsidi came with Daniel.

Wild Bill Donovan stopped by with his wife, and Kangaroo Cox arrived with his outsize personality, his compromised integrity and a gorgeous woman on each arm. He grinned cheerfully. "Couldn't for the life of me choose between 'em," he said. "Will you help, darlin'?"

"It's still *ma'am* to you, Mr. Kangaroo," Grace said. "And absolutely not!" She turned to the ladies. "He's trouble. Dance with him this evening; by all means, be charmed by him. And then *run*."

They both laughed.

"You wound me, my lady," Cox protested.

Grace wagged a finger at him and turned to her other guests.

It was a great honor that General George C. Marshall and his wife accepted the invitation.

And an even greater one when Eleanor Roosevelt and her son James stopped by for a few minutes, secret service agents trailing them.

And Nellie! Though Farquhar had passed on. Nellie, now quite an old lady, arrived in style, wearing a hailstorm of pearls and one of her custom-made hats: this one was designed to look like a wedding cake, complete with a ceramic bride and groom standing on top. Her gift to the Feldmans: a large trunk full of her late husband's books on cryptanalysis. Robert almost wept with gratitude.

All the guests talked and laughed late into the night. They toasted Bobby and Grace by candlelight. They scarfed down Mrs. Woolsey's delicious hors d'oeuvres. They cut and enjoyed the cake. And everyone who could played the piano and sang and danced to Glenn Miller tunes, Rosemary Clooney and Eddie Fisher numbers, Johnnie Ray and Doris Day.

Despite himself, Robert had gone pink with pleasure and wine.

Grace gazed at him fondly. *You beautiful, brilliant, passionate, kind, impossible man. You cajoled me into loving you, and there's no turning back now—even if the US government devoured you and only spat back out half of you. Even if I must come up with a reason for you to live, each and every day, for the rest of our time on earth.*

You're an Enigma, my darling... but I've solved your wiring.

ACKNOWLEDGMENTS

Thanks to my tireless and deft editor, Leah Hultenschmidt, for introducing me to Elizebeth Smith Friedman in the first place. I can only hope I've done her justice.

A huge thanks as well to enthusiastic font of knowledge Melissa Davis, director of Library and Archives at the George C. Marshall Foundation library in Lexington, Virginia, which houses the Friedmans' papers. Melissa is a treasure, and it was a privilege to visit and see Elizebeth's materials in person.

Thanks to Wanda Ottwell for suggestions on, and insight into, the first raggedy draft.

Thanks to Donna Scott for being a fabulous and eagle-eyed beta reader.

Thank you to Lila Selle and Daniela Medina for an eye-catching, intriguing cover.

Thanks to copy editor Alayna Johnson for catching some true bloopers! And to Mari C. Okuda, senior production editor.

Thanks to my agent, the always kind, helpful and tolerant Evan Marshall.

Thanks to readers everywhere—we authors wouldn't exist without you.

Last but not least, thank you to everyone else at the helm and behind the scenes of Forever and Grand Central Publishing for championing, editing, packaging and selling my books. If not for you, they wouldn't see the light of day.

While I was writing the draft of this book, both my husband's father and my own passed peacefully, within a month of each other.

Thank you, Dad, for your love, encouragement and the particular brand of humor that you passed along to your often disrespectful children.

Thank you, Young Royce, for being the best father-in-law ever. Thank you for my husband. And thank you for your service to this country.

May you both rest in peace.

YOUR BOOK CLUB RESOURCE

READING GROUP GUIDE

READER DISCUSSION QUESTIONS

1. Grace Feldman is a "working mother" long before her time. Could you relate to any of the career situations in which she found herself? Would you have handled them the same way? If not, how would you have reacted? If you work outside the home, do you ever feel torn between the demands of job and family?

2. Do you associate the words "code," "codebreaking" or "cryptanalysis" with mathematics? If so, did reading *Lady Codebreaker* change your mind? Were you able to relate to the basic methods Grace and Robert used to crack codes? Do you think you'd enjoy it or find it frustrating?

3. When Grace marries Robert, she is honest about not being in love with him at the time. How did you feel about that? What did you think about the evolution of their relationship?

4. How do you think it would affect your own marriage or relationship if you were unable to speak to your spouse/significant other about anything you did on the job?

5. What do you think of Prohibition in hindsight? Was it a good idea to ban the sale and distribution of alcohol in the United States? Was the Volstead Act an example of government overreach into citizens' personal lives?

6. During World War II, codebreakers lived in an unbearable pressure cooker as they tried to protect the United States and save thousands of lives. To conceal breakthroughs from the enemy, difficult choices had to be made.

In part four of *Lady Codebreaker*, Grace is furious at J. Edgar Hoover for preemptively rounding up dozens of spies in South America, because the Germans then knew the Allies had decrypted their communications. The cryptanalysts' job then became even harder since the Nazis reacted by changing all their codes. If it were your call, what would you have done? Round up the spies, or let them keep operating so you could keep tabs on them?

7. Robert eventually "cracks" under the pressure of his job, which he's unable to discuss even with his wife. He also struggles with depression, which the Feldmans go to great lengths to keep a secret because of the stigma surrounding mental illness at the time. Has depression affected you or anyone you know? Do you think that there is still a stigma attached to seeking help for it?

8. At the beginning of the novel, Grace feels that her own integrity is something of a curse. What did you think about the evolution of her moral character? Do you approve of the choices she makes later in the story? How would you have handled a similar threat by someone as powerful as J. Edgar Hoover to your own family or loved one? Do the means justify the end?

FACT VS. FICTION IN
LADY CODEBREAKER

By K.D. Alden

Lady Codebreaker is based on the life of true heroine Elizebeth Smith Friedman.

The plot of a novel can be an enigma of its own, and it makes curious and unreasonable demands of an author. This book spans four decades, two world wars, hundreds of thousands of hours of mind-numbing code-breaking work and stacks upon stacks of research books—so wresting a plot out of it for readers was particularly challenging. At times, it was like alligator wrestling, and the gator seemed to be winning.

But I'm a stubborn sort, so a plot there *is*—with apologies to historians for what I call Fictional Fudging (switching more than a few dates around) to songwriters for enjoying their music a year or two early and to journalists for inventing a couple of nonexistent publications (for example, there was never a *D.C. Bee*.) Apologies to Elizebeth Smith Friedman herself for taking some minor liberties with her character.

If you're curious about where fact meets fiction in *Lady Codebreaker*, read on.

The owner of Riverbank did virtually kidnap Elizebeth Smith from the Newberry Library, and he did roar at her, but he did not actually pick her up by the armpits. He did sexually harass her, but the incident in the Hell Chair is fictional.

The zebras, the monkeys and the bears at Riverbank are fact—but the potbellied pig is fiction. The furniture at the Villa hanging from chains? Bizarre, but factual.

The "collecting virgins" fruit fly story is real—it just happened to be my father-in-law who employed the line with my mother-in-law the night they met. They were married for sixty-one years.

William and Elizebeth Smith Friedman were married in 1917, not 1918.

Nelle Fabyan (aka Nellie Farquhar) and Elizebeth were not great friends, but I wondered what kind of woman could tolerate George Fabyan (aka Garrett Farquhar) and so the fictional friendship was born.

The character of Alice Martenz is inspired by Agnes Meyer Driscoll, who was indeed a brilliant codebreaker and the Navy's secret weapon, though to my knowledge her personality was not disagreeable. I embellished it because of the very real rivalry between Agnes and Elizebeth, which was aggravated by the fact that William Friedman did "bust" Ed Heburn's "unbustable" coding machine.

Friedman's mother was indeed horrified by his marriage and never got over it. Because of it, she treated her son (as one of his brothers later said) as if he "had murdered someone."

Yes, Elizebeth and William were trained on the fly to become two of the US government's first codebreakers during WWI. Yes, they ran the unit at Riverbank, taught countless other officers and were later employed by the Army—Elizebeth then by the Navy and Coast Guard.

Codebreaking isn't visually exciting. Forgive me, but I had to get the characters in this novel out from behind their desks and into action. So...

Elizebeth never spent any time on board *Hogan's Goat*, though the potato war incident is real, as is the tale about the sailors pouring all the booze into the drinking water supply of a ship. Thank you, Harold Waters, for these hilarious and factual tales from *Smugglers of Spirits: Prohibition and the Coast Guard Patrol*—I simply couldn't resist using them.

Though Elizebeth's life was in very real danger from gangsters during Prohibition, the kidnapping incident in section three never happened, nor did she ever move into a government safe house.

With respect to Elizebeth's womb: to my knowledge no miscarriage occurred, and the children were born much earlier than they were in this story.

Elizebeth was not, in reality, a bad cook.

It wasn't actually Elizebeth who solved the Waberski code (my apologies to Captain John Manly, who did) but the angelic face of this particular spy caught my imagination, and it ran amok from there. Lothar Witzke (aka Otto Schroeder in the novel) was a real German spy operating under the alias of Pablo Waberski in Mexico, but he and Siegfried Becker, a real spy operating in South America (aka Wolfgang Roth in the novel), were not the same person—I threw them into a blender for plot purposes.

My apologies extend as well to Colonel Alfred Wainwright Bloor of the 142nd Infantry Regiment, who overheard a couple of Choctaw enlisted men speaking their language and was inspired to ask them to become the first Native American Code Talkers at the front—in World War I, long before the more famous Navajo Code Talkers were also of invaluable assistance in World War II. In this novel, I credited the idea to Utsidi Nashoba, a Choctaw woman in Grace's unit.

Spanish Marie Waite was a real, colorful and ruthless woman, who did indeed expand her late husband's smuggling business after he was shot by the Coast Guard during Prohibition. But to my knowledge, she never got involved with a German spy or had anything to do with Nazis.

Spanish Marie Brewery in Miami is named after Mrs. Waite, as is Bad Bitch Spanish Marie rum.

Commander Jones was indeed Elizebeth Friedman's real boss, but he was never shot by Spanish Marie.

Elizebeth did not have an all-female codebreaking unit, as depicted in this novel. She actually worked with a number of talented and intelligent men. Sorry, guys!

William Friedman's depression was all too real, especially after he broke the Japanese Purple code. He did spend time in Walter Reed's neuropsychiatric unit, but it was before, not after, Pearl Harbor.

William did undergo electroshock therapy, among other treatments, but it was after the war. The stigma of receiving psychiatric care in those days was genuine, and the Friedmans hid William's illness from almost everyone. He was indeed suicidal, and Elizebeth was forced to contend with that.

Joe Rochefort did break the decrypts about when the Midway attack would occur, and there was heated debate between HYPO and command in Washington, but he did not ask William or Elizebeth for help in persuading Redman and King.

Joe's wife, Alma Fay Rochefort, was not confined to a wheelchair, nor was she a codebreaker or a redhead. (The original character with polio was named Sophie, but then she and Joe began to fall in love… and Joe's real-life wife was named Alma Fay.)

SARGO and LUNA were real code names for real Nazi spies. SARGO was unmasked as Siegfried Becker (aka Wolfgang Roth in the novel). LUNA was actually a different spy, not Spanish Marie.

Though J. Edgar Hoover did take credit for much of Elizebeth's work, she never confronted him as this novel depicts. She also never hired Gaston Means (a real PI) to gather information on Hoover, nor did she blackmail him—or have reason to do so. Hoover, though absolutely guilty of the "dirt" dug up on him in this novel, managed to hide it until after his death. He was not behind the raid on the Friedmans' library—which did happen. It was the NSA that became uncomfortable with the knowledge amassed within the Friedman home.

Finally, Elizebeth and her codebreaking unit did not (to my knowledge) have any part in the unfolding of Operation Bodyguard, which enabled the Allies to land at Normandy—but the ruses involved were so brilliant and fascinating that I couldn't resist including them in the book as the story approached the end of World War II.

Researching and writing this book has been an honor and a privilege. Though I've done my best to understand and explain rudimentary cryptanalysis, corroborate facts and catch mistakes, some may still be lurking in the text. Any errors that do still exist in *Lady Codebreaker* are my own.

PARTIAL LIST OF RESOURCES

Jason Fagone, *The Woman Who Smashed Codes*

G. Stuart Smith, *A Life in Code*

Amy Butler Greenfield, *The Woman All Spies Fear*

Liza Mundy, *Code Girls*

Betsy Rohaly Smoot, *Parker Hitt: The Father of American Cryptology*

Ronald Clark, *The Man Who Broke Purple*

Herbert O. Yardley, *The American Black Chamber*

John Lisle, *The Dirty Tricks Department*

Sarah Elisabeth Sawyer, *Anumpa Warrior*

Richard Hack, *The Secret Life of J. Edgar Hoover*

David Kahn, *The Codebreakers*

Simon Singh, *The Code Book: The Secrets Behind Codebreaking*

John F. Dooley, *Codes, Ciphers and Spies: Tales of Military Intelligence in World War I*

Harold Waters, *Smugglers of Spirits: Prohibition and the Coast Guard Patrol*

Parker Hitt, *Manual for the Solution of Military Ciphers*

Lt. Eric S. Ensign, USCG, *Intelligence in the Rum War at Sea, 1920–1933*

William F. and Elizabeth S. Friedman, *The Shakespearean Ciphers Examined*

Ben Macintyre, *Operation Mincemeat*

Douglas Waller, *Wild Bill Donovan: The Spymaster Who Created the OSS and Modern American Espionage*

AUTHOR'S NOTE

This is the most difficult but also the most rewarding book I've ever had the privilege to write. I was in awe of Elizebeth Smith Friedman, but codes, ciphers and cryptanalysis scared the hell out of me. I was always the kid savoring a juicy novel behind my algebra book, to the despair of the retired air force colonel who tried to teach me that subject.

When my first research book (David Kahn's intimidating five-inch-thick tome *The Codebreakers*) arrived on my doorstep, I literally ran screaming from it—though it turned out to be very readable and a great resource.

On innumerable occasions, I said to my husband, family members, friends and dogs, "I don't know how to write this book."

At one point I looked at Elizebeth Smith Friedman's iconic photo and begged for help.

In a moment of synchronicity that I can't explain, I then opened Jason Fagone's absolutely brilliant *The Woman Who Smashed Codes* to a passage in which Elizebeth herself explains that codes are everywhere and aren't necessarily intimidating; that a child's report card is a code: an A stands for excellent and an F for the opposite.

I looked at her photo again. Her expression seemed encouraging—even challenging.

I reflected that she, like me, had very little math training. Yet she'd become one of the world's foremost cryptanalysts. So I said to myself: *Stop being a chickensh*t.*

Yep, the glamorous life of an author is full of directives like this.

I began to read about codes and ciphers and cryptanalysis. I read until my eyes crossed and my brain hurt, but I'd mastered the (most basic) basics of how it all worked.

The next hurdle, however, was to convey those basics on the page in an entertaining way for a reader. Codebreaking is, for the most part, a painstaking, slow, dull, monotonous, frustrating process. Who'd want to "see it" unfold? How could I make it more interesting than watching grass grow? Fortunately, I had Parker Hitt, a real-life US Army colonel, available to me. And he decided to toss in Adam, Eve and the serpent, to my everlasting gratitude.

I then struggled for months to find the *heart* of this novel, which did not lie in numbers or letters or symbols. I returned over and over to the first line in Jason Fagone's book: "This is a love story."

Huh. Why did I find these words so intimidating? In another life, I'd written no fewer than twenty-five love stories—all with happy endings.

But this one was different. Was there a handsome suitor? Check. Was there a villain? Check. A fake engagement? Sure, why not. Was there a reluctant bride? You bet.

But Elizebeth and William got married young and stayed married for decades. There was no way to get around that. The "romantic tension" that every good romance novel needs had already been resolved.

Or had it?

I returned to the subject of William's recurring and severe depression and then marched away from it, telling myself with no sense of irony that I was nuts. Who wanted to read about a Davey Downer whose most pressing personal goal was to off himself? That was even worse than watching someone with a pencil try to break a code for hours!

"I don't know how to write this book," I said again, to anyone who would listen. My dogs yawned. My husband lifted an eyebrow and returned to his video game. My father asked, "Now, is this the novel about *Roe v. Wade*?" (He was referring to *A Mother's Promise*.)

"No, Dad," I said. "I will never write about *Roe v. Wade*. I wrote about *Buck v. Bell*."

"Well, isn't that pretty much the same thing?"

Sigh.

So there I was, juggling all the elements of a breakout novel: nerds with pencils and depression who never leave their desks for forty or so years. Who wouldn't rush to the nearest bookstore to buy this story?

And then I looked again at Elizebeth's portrait, which now seemed amused at my expense.

I wanted to meet her, which of course wasn't possible—because she was dead.

So resurrect me.

Wait…did she say that? No, of course not. But we authors like to embellish, exaggerate and embroider the truth just as much as we like writing fiction.

Stop being a chickensh*t.

This I repeated into the mirror until I mustered the courage to creak open my laptop and type *Chapter One.* And those two words annoyed me until I began the book, which at that point had only two-thirds of a plot, because we'd decided to extend the time frame through WWII instead of ending with Elizebeth's work during Prohibition and a dramatic attempted murder.

I wrote and worried and researched and wrote…and still, the plot dangled like a burglar, stuck in a window with his pants down, for far longer than I'd like to admit—and my dogs have been sworn to secrecy.

During the writing process, I also forgot most of what I'd read in the dozens of research books I'd consulted and had to go back to them repeatedly.

Suffice it to say: if I've forgotten to thank someone, credit someone, acknowledge a stray research book or apologize for swapping yet another historical event with one that preceded it, please forgive me.

K.D. Alden, September 2022

ABOUT THE AUTHOR

K.D. Alden is the pseudonym of an award-winning author who has written more than twenty-five novels in various genres. *Lady Codebreaker* is her second historical novel.

K.D. is a graduate of Smith College, grew up in Austin, Texas, and resides in south Florida with her husband, two rescue greyhounds and a menagerie of wildlife that parades past their back porch.